THE REALMS OF ELSWYTH

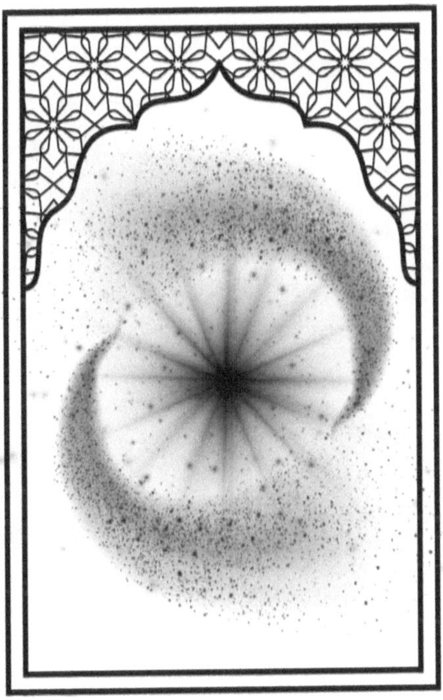

SERIES OMNIBUS

WILLOW ASTERIA

The Realms of Elswyth

Series Omnibus

Willow Asteria

Realms of Elswyth

In the land of Elswyth, six portals exist that lead to the fae realms.

Orilon. Irolyth. Alari. Aeros. Khaldon. Tarak.

ELSWYTH
THE HUMAN REALM
VARIA
ZAMORA
N
W E
S
MAGLA
CALDOR
PENDRIL
Town
Capital
Portal

The Guardian of Tarak

A Realms of Elswyth Standalone

Willow Asteria

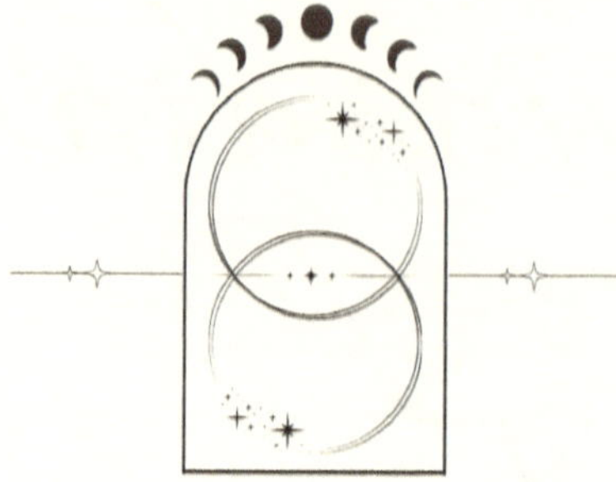

Eternal. Always watching. Never doing.

These are the traits I must carry. For a millennium each day has been the same. It is my duty and honor to do so, as I was chosen by The Mother all those years ago.

Stepping out of my cottage, my bare feet sunk into the warm sand. For miles, there was endless ocean. When I was young, I found myself wondering what was beyond the horizon. I even made a boat and sailed out into the sea. Only to find that beyond the horizon, was my tiny island. There was no way I could go that wouldn't return me home.

The sun warmed my face and I took a deep breath. Birds flew overhead and their song filled my ears. Looking to the left, I saw two young children playing on the water's edge. Offering them a small smile, I waved to them. They faced me and bowed their heads.

"Good morning, Lady Davina," the two of them said in unison.

"Good morning. Please continue playing. Thank you for bringing a smile to this old woman's face."

They looked up at me in confusion. "You're not old!" One of them shouted.

"You are so young and beautiful!" The other added.

I chuckled. They were right, I did look young and beautiful. As if I wasn't a day over twenty. White hair flowed down to my waist, bright blue eyes, and skin so fair that you never would have known I lived on a tropical island, was my eternal form. As long as the gates stood, so would I. I would outlive these children, and theirs, just as I have their ancestors.

"Thank you, children. Now I must be off to complete my duties."

They bowed to me again, then continued playing. Turning away from them, I walked along the shore. The sand began to transform from beautiful white to black as the void. At the end of the beach was a natural staircase that led up to the mouth of the volcano, which we named Tarak. Only I was allowed to climb the steps and take in the knowledge that the volcano held.

To anyone else, traveling the one hundred thousand steps would be quite the task. For me, it is no problem. The farther I travel, the smaller the village gets. The fae here were chosen by The Mother to live in peace. Many Years ago, the leader of these people gained the favor of The Mother, her name was Senna. When she ascended to the beyond, she took her place at The Mother's side. Oh, how I miss my mother, even though it's been so long I could still remember the sweet sound of her voice and the warmth of her embrace. I wonder if she ever looks down from the heavens and if I made her proud.

Once at the top, I peered down into the hollow volcano, inside carved into the rock were six portals, all currently filled in by stone. Descending the stairs, I made my way to the volcano's floor. In the center was a pedestal with a silver dagger. Taking it in my hand, I stared into my reflection for a moment before I sliced my hand and allowed the blood to drip onto the pedestal. Quickly, it was absorbed by the black stone, and the portals filled with a black mist.

Stepping to the first portal, I chanted in the ancient language. The mist began to clear, and I could see into Orilon. For centuries, my heart wept as I watched the once beautiful land transform into ruin. The colorful forest once filled with magical creatures was now filled with monsters called the vox. They were once the people of Orilon, but they were cursed. The King only had one year left to save his people, or he too would be doomed by the curse that destroyed his kingdom. The fae King sat in a small room, shirtless. Shadows clung to his large black wings with golden speckles, and his long white hair was draped past his shoulders. He had a book in his hands and seemed unbothered by the world. I was shocked to see a small golden-haired human sitting across from him, looking very flustered. I wondered if she was the key to saving Orilon from ruin. Before I could learn more, the mist turned black once again.

Moving to the second portal, I chanted once again, and the mist cleared. The Kingdom of Irolyth was taken by a tyrannical King several years ago. He went by a new motto, 'join the flame, or be swallowed by it'. It would not be long before the redwood forest was consumed by fire if he had his way. The true heir to the throne fled to save herself. It appears she is back, with a tall and handsome shadow trailing behind her. The look on his face said that he would not fail in helping her reclaim what was rightfully hers. I saw the magic thread that connected them. A bargain had been struck and needed to be seen through to free them from their bond. The auburn-haired princess looked so different than she did when she fled, life had hardened her. I wondered where she was all those years that she was gone. Hopefully, the royal flames had not been snuffed out. Again, the mist turned black and blocked me from seeing more.

Repeating the process, I opened the third portal. The Queen of Alari panicked as her daughter had been missing for days. She ordered her guards to search the entire realm to find her. They swam off as fast as their tails could take them. The mermaid princess secretly visited the human realm for the past year. Her mother tried to warn her of the dangers that lurked beyond the portal, for the oceans of Elswyth held a dark secret the Queen was not ready to face. But young curious girls never listen, especially when they spend their days locked away, not able to explore their true potential. I wonder if he found her. Mother save Elswyth if he did.

The fourth portal is one I often dreaded peering into. Aeros was a group of floating islands. Long ago it was on land until a calamity hit that made the King raise the capital high above the clouds. Lucky for them, these fae already had wings, beautiful white feathered wings that I was envious of. On the smallest of the islands, was a portal that led to the human realm. Often, a poor human had the misfortune of passing through the portal and meeting their end before they could see the beautiful cloudscape. As my view came into focus, I was shocked to see a human with the current King, his white tattoos glowed against his dark skin as he taught her how to use magic. The fae of Aeros practiced gravitational magic, but the seed of power inside her was something else. Something that I had not seen in hundreds of years, long before the calamity struck. I was not able to get anything more before the view vanished.

As always, the fifth portal is still blocked by stone. The realm of Khaldon was built inside of a mountain range, the stone of the mountains protected it from my magical sight. The Mother told me not to worry about them, for the fae of Khaldon and I have something in common, we are trapped. I took pity on them. My prison was a paradise, and I was blessed with feeling the sun's rays on my flesh. They were trapped under cold stone, cursed to never see the light of day. The only other thing I knew about them was that the fae of Khaldon were shifters, and they were vicious and brutal. If that was true, part of me was glad I could not see into their realm.

The final portal only gave me a look into a body of water. Fish swam as if they were above wherever this portal led to. It was not like the others. In the other realms, I could peek in and view any part of the world. The portal to Elswyth was the only one that was finite. Could it be because the magic in the human world was limited? It was also the only one I was able to pass through. I found that out many years ago when I misstepped and tumbled into the portal. It was then I realized, I was at the bottom of a lake, with a far swim upward. I quickly returned to my realm, soaking wet. This was my one escape, but I was sure it would kill me if I tried.

Going back to the pedestal, I knelt. My prayers were sent up to The Mother, informing her of the happenings in the realms. It was silent for a moment, then a warm breeze hit my back.

"Thank you, child." The Mother's voice came from above. I looked up and saw a rainbow formed in the sky above me. Two white birds flew overhead.

I stood and offered a smile. I left the volcano and descended the stairs back to the beach below. An orange glow cast over the island as the sun set across the sea. The beach was now filled with the villagers. Baby turtles rushed toward the ocean to begin their journey. Every year, we had a festival to send off the turtles after they hatched to their new life. Music filled the air and the scent of roasted pork caused my stomach to growl. The two children from earlier rushed over to me, each taking a hand.

"Lady Davina! Please come and dance with us!" Before I could answer, the two of them pulled me into the crowd and to the water's edge with the dancers.

The three of us danced together for some time. Their laughter filled me with joy.

"I hope you do not mind if I cut in," a deep strong voice said from behind me.

The children stopped dancing and bowed to the man. I turned to see the village chief. The colors of the sunset reflected off his golden skin. He was shirtless, leaving his dark tattoos on display. His dark and curly hair was pulled up and into a loose knot behind his head. I stepped toward him and gently tucked a loose piece behind his ear. The children ran off to join some others just down the seashore.

The chief planted a kiss on my lips. "I missed you today," he purred as he pulled away.

"As I you." I stole another quick kiss. Was I really trapped on this island, if I had my mate by my side for all eternity? "But, duty calls."

Bastian was the strongest warrior in our tribe long before the fae realms split. When The Mother gave me my duties, she gave some to my mate as well. Keep Tarak happy, and lead the people to prosperity, that was The Mother's demands of him. That he did. No one here suffered. We all worked together to get what we needed. The land provided everything we could want. Looking around, I knew our people were safe and at peace.

I was proud to be the Guardian of Tarak.

THE CURSE OF ORILON

A REALMS OF ELSWYTH STANDALONE

WILLOW ASTERIA

Content Warning

Please be advised that this book may not be suitable for all audiences.

This book contains sexual content, kidnapping, shadow bondage, death, attempted sexual assault, graphic violence, and other topics some readers may not find suitable.

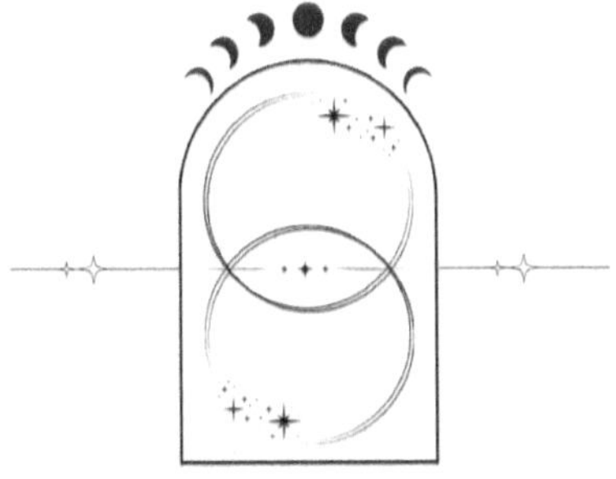

One

Days like today were my favorite. The apothecary wasn't too busy, but there was enough business to keep the day flowing smoothly. My aunt trusted me to run the shop alone while she made the deliveries to some of the more sickly and elderly clients.

As the only apothecary in the secluded town of Pendril, we were normally quite busy. However, for the past hour or so I didn't have a single customer. Using up my free time, I took inventory and made elixirs to keep our shelves full. With the change of the seasons, our tincture to soothe sore throats was running low. I was crushing some mint leaves when I heard the bell above the door chime, signaling someone was coming in.

"Good afternoon!" I said in a cheery voice before I looked up and saw who it was. "How can I help you today, Caden?" I said through clenched teeth. He was the last person I wanted to see today, especially alone.

He smirked as he adjusted the sleeve on his bright red shirt and approached the counter. Brushing back his light brown hair, he flashed a predatory grin as he leaned forward and rested his elbows on the glass countertop.

"You can help me by finally agreeing to be my wife," he said plainly.

I took a step back from the counter and crossed my arms angrily. Rolling my eyes at him, I replied with a huff. "As I have told you for years, I will never marry you."

Caden had been asking me to be his since we were teens. Now we were twenty-six, I was hoping he would move on, but unfortunately, that was not the case. He was not a very nice man. It was well known he would lie, cheat, and steal to get whatever he wanted. I had no interest in being his wife.

Anger contorted his face. "Amara, please be reasonable. You are almost thirty years old. Your timer is ticking."

I let out a chuckle under my breath. "Caden, we are the same age. If my timer is ticking, so is yours. Stop wasting your time on someone who hates you."

Caden's expression darkened. He stared at me for a moment with violence in his eyes. Before I could do anything else, he jumped over the counter and slammed me into the wooden wall in an instant. The shelf next to me rattled, and several of the jars crashed to the floor. His hand was wrapped around my throat to cut off my breath. I tried to push him away, but he grabbed my hands with his free one and held them above my head. He leaned in, towering over me, with a scowl on his face. His body was pressed against mine, pinning me fully to the wall.

"Amara, we live in a secluded town. There is no one else for you."

"Fuck you," I spat in his face.

He shook his head in shock and staggered back in surprise before anger flashed back to his face. "Oh, you little bitch. You will pay for that!"

The doorbell chimed, and my head snapped to the door. My aunt was walking in with a paper bag in hand. Caden quickly changed his demeanor as she cleared her throat.

"Hello, Caden. You know we do not allow customers behind the counter," she said in a firm tone. "I just saw your father at the market. He said he was looking for you. You better get home." Her eyes narrowed as she stepped closer to us.

"Yes, ma'am. I hope you have a lovely evening," he said with a warm smile before rushing to the exit.

I watched as he left, and the glass door shut. My hands trembled as I could still feel his fingers wrapped around my throat.

Glenda sat the bag on the counter and rushed over to me. "Oh, sweetie! Are you alright?"

I swallowed hard and nodded. "Yes, I am alright." My heart felt as if it was about to burst out of my chest. "Just a bit shaken, is all."

"Caden is a waste of air," Glenda said with a snarl. She walked over to the door, locked it, and flipped the open sign to 'closed'. "Next time he comes into the shop, make sure you have the dagger ready." She eyed the section of the counter where we had the mentioned dagger hidden. Luckily, we had never had to use it, and I hoped we never would need to.

In response, I nodded. To be honest, I was not sure I would have the strength to use it.

Glenda grabbed the bag and made her way up the stairs. The second floor of our shop was our two-bedroom home. I followed her upstairs and into the kitchen as she emptied the bag's contents onto the kitchen table and put them away.

"Other than your unfortunate run-in with that boy, I hope your day was ok. While I was out, I learned of two more fae attacks. A young couple snuck into the woods last night and were found dead this morning. Those poor dears, they were so young. Just last week, the Latoi family did not lock up on the new moon, and they did not survive the attack."

I couldn't help but shudder. The fae were horrid creatures that only came out at night and were the stuff of nightmares. Their skin was like snow and they had jagged teeth, long sharp claws, and large bat-like wings.

Every new moon they seemed to be the most violent and bloodthirsty. I heard of so many lives lost to the fae at this point, I was numb to it. We all were.

Deep in the forest that surrounded the town, there was a stone archway filled with purple mist. It was there long before the first settlers of Elswyth came to this mountain valley. This was where the fae came from, and was the only place in the entire country where any sort of magical beasts resided. We tried to build a wall around it, but every time we did, it would be destroyed within a few days. No one knew what was on the other side of the portal because any who passed through never returned.

It was a strict rule that no one was allowed in the forest at night, and many villagers gave themselves a curfew of dusk.

"I will pray to The Mother that they will find peace in the beyond," I said softly.

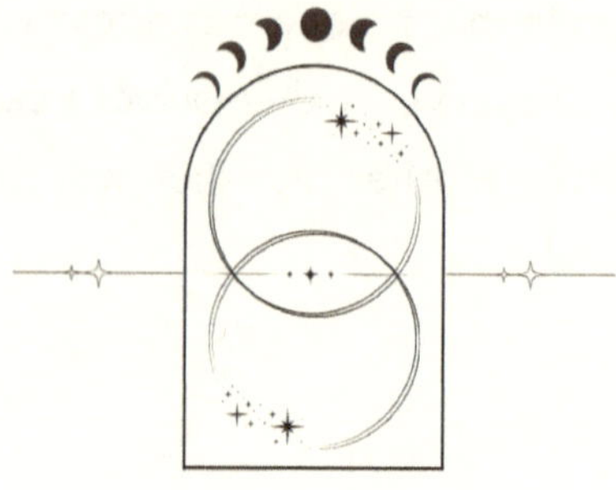

Two

One of my favorite things to do in this small town was meeting with my best friend every Wednesday night at Drago's, the local tavern, to discuss our latest reads we had gotten from the merchant that traveled through a few weeks ago. Jade and I were huge bookworms and had been since we were kids. We would constantly get into trouble in school for reading instead of paying attention to class.

Every week, we would sit in the same booth and watch as the bar filled with people. There were not many places for the locals to hang out in Pendril, so this tavern was always packed. It didn't hurt that they had amazing food and drinks. Jade and I shared a plate of nachos while we sipped on our drinks. If she had a good day, she would have a frozen cocktail with pineapple, coconuts, and strawberries. If it was a bad day, she had cinnamon whiskey, straight. Today was a good day.

I always drank the same thing, and the bartender, Sam, always had it ready for me as I was walking through the door. Sipping on my peach vodka cocktail, I listened as Jade went into detail about the morally grey hottie she was reading about in her dark romance. He was tall, dark, handsome, and very well-endowed. I had to grin because this week I read a vampire romance about a girl who was fated to be killed by her vampire mate. The man in that book was also very dark and handsome. I loved reading about men who were assholes, but I hated them in real life.

"Do you ever think you will leave this small town and travel across the mountains to find love?" Jade asked. Pendril was in a mountain valley, which is why it was so cut off from the rest of the country of Elswyth. Everyone who was born here lived in this town and would die here. We had very few visitors, the last ones being a family from Magla, who were traveling merchants.

Jade married her high school sweetheart, Jack, the Mayor's son, the day she turned eighteen. The two of them have been in love since grade school. I loved seeing my best friend happy.

In a town so small, pretty much all eligible candidates were taken by the age of twenty. I think the only man who was my age who wasn't married was Caden, and I would rather die a dusty old spinster than marry him.

"My duty is here," I sighed. "I will continue to learn the trade and take over as the town herbalist once Glenda retires." Of course, I would have loved to travel, but there was nothing I loved more than herbalism. It was the only thing that made me feel close to my mother.

My mother and Glenda were twins and were taught herbalism through their mother. For generations, the trade was passed down from woman to woman in my family. A part of me was sad, thinking it would end with me. Hopefully, I would get lucky, and a man from across the mountains would come and be the answer to my prayers. I wanted love, but I feared it would not be in the cards for me.

My parents were killed by the fae during a full moon attack when I was just a baby. Unfortunately, our home was set ablaze, and everything was lost. That fateful night, I was with my aunt and spared from the flame's wrath.

"You will be the greatest herbalist this town has ever seen," Jade smiled.

"Thank you!" I offered her a huge smile in return.

We went back to eating our nachos and talking about the books we wanted to read next. I dipped my cheese-covered chip into some sour cream as the tavern door opened. A group of men walked in, and the room filled with their loud and annoying voices. Already drunk, they stumbled and headed right to the bar.

"Seven shots of tequila." Caden's voice rang through my head, causing my body to tense.

Jade's head turned to me and raised an eyebrow. I started to tap my fingers against the table. My vision started to twist and turn as a pit grew in my stomach. Seeing Caden again so soon was not something I wanted to do. Especially with him drunk, who knows how he would react when he saw me.

"Amara, are you ok?" Jade's concerned voice snapped me back to the present.

I turned to her and gave her a nod, swallowing hard. "A headache just randomly popped up. I think I should probably head home."

"Oh, alright. I'm sorry you don't feel well. That hit you pretty fast." Worry filled her voice. "Do you want me to walk you home?"

"No, it's alright. It's not a long walk." My eyes never left Caden. I needed to know exactly where he was at all times. Luckily for me, he was too busy doing another round of shots, he hadn't looked this way.

She stared at me a moment before letting out a sigh and nodding. "Okay. Stay safe. It is almost dark."

I got up from the table and gave her my final goodbye with a hug. Making my way through the crowd, I tried to slip out of the tavern without Caden noticing me.

Once I was outside, I let out a breath of relief that he hadn't seen me. At this time of night, the town was already empty. So many people had already settled into their homes. The street lamps had already been lit for the night and filled the streets with an orange glow. I quickened my pace not wanting to be outside longer than I had to be. Even though it was not a new moon, that did not mean I was safe from the fae. Tonight, I also had another type of predator I needed to be even more afraid of.

The sooner I was home, the better.

Hearing the sound of heavy footsteps behind me, I quickly turned to see Caden and his friends. My eyes went wide as he stepped ahead of his group, and a devilish smirk took over his face.

"Hello, doll. It is time for your punishment, unless you have come to your senses and agreed to be mine," Caden purred.

"I will never be yours," I snarled at him.

"Then I can't protect you from what's going to happen next."

The men behind him fell into a full sprint, and my heart pounded in my chest as I turned and ran to make my escape. I turned down an alley, hoping to lose them in the maze between the townhomes. Blood pulsed in my ears the more I ran.

They screamed and called after me. Their voices filled my head with all the vile things they were going to do to me. As I kept up the breakneck pace, my breath got heavy, my vision tunneled, and a stitch grew in my side. I felt myself losing momentum. I was in no shape to be running through the streets of Pendril. Despite every attempt to keep my speed up, a strong hand grabbed my hair and yanked.

I fell backward and into the arms of one of Caden's friends, Amos. He wrapped his arms around me and held me in place. Screaming to be released, I squirmed and kicked. It wasn't long before Caden walked forward and stood in front of me. Seemingly unbothered from the run, he gently picked up one of my blonde ringlets.

"Oh, doll. You're definitely going to get what you deserve."

Just as he went to grab for my shirt the air filled with an ear-piercing screech. My heart skipped a beat, and my ears felt as if they were bleeding from the sound. Everyone's heads snapped in the direction of the scream.

Twenty feet away stood three fae.

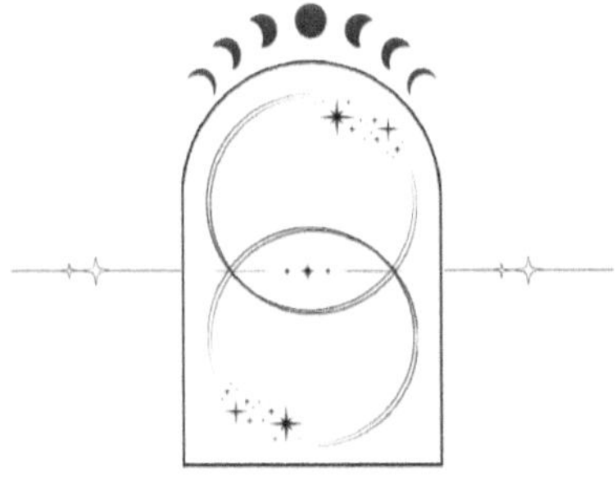

Three

Amos dropped me and ran off. Quickly, I scrambled to get back onto my feet. The fae rushed us, and their battle cries filled my ears. Their long claws tore through one of Caden's friends. His blood-curdling screams echoed off the brick homes as he was ripped to shreds. I watched in horror as the fae bit into his neck and ripped out his heart with its claws.

Bile rose in my throat. Never had I seen the fae in person, nor had I experienced such violence. My body quivered as I stood there frozen. A fourth fae joined the attack and pounced on Caden as he tried to escape. He fell onto his back, as the fae flared his bat-like wings and tore into his chest, feasting on Caden's flesh. More fae came into view, and their blood-red eyes locked onto us.

In my mind, I screamed at myself to run. It was what I needed to free myself from my paralyzing fear. I turned and ran as fast as I could as I caught my second wind. Sprinting through town, I screamed for the town guard, and almost immediately two came rushing toward me.

I finally stopped running, and I placed my hands on my knees as I tried to catch my breath. Finally, I forced the word out of my throat.

"Fae."

Falling to my knees, the contents of my stomach spilled onto the ground. I watched as their feet left my vision, and I heard the town's alarm begin to sound. One of the guards stepped back in front of me and helped me to my feet.

"Rush home and secure your doors," he said to me as more guards flooded the streets.

I nodded and collected myself. Quickly, I made my way back home. Chaos filled the streets as the guards sped past me and the screeches of the fae filled the air. I slammed the door of the apothecary shut behind me and locked it.

"Oh, Amara!" Glenda's terrified voice called from behind me. I turned and saw her standing on the stairs, in her pink wool robe, worry all over her face and tears welled in her eyes. "I am so glad you are alright! I heard the sirens and thought the worst!" She pulled me into a hug and held me close.

"I... I am ok..." I whimpered, still reeling from everything that had happened since I left the tavern. "I saw them... up close." I steadied my breath.

"Let's get down to the basement. It is safest there." Glenda grabbed my arm and guided me to the basement door. She opened it and ushered me in first, allowing me to descend the cement stairs as she locked and barricaded the door. Lighting a lantern, the small space illuminated. Wooden boxes were stacked against the wall, keeping the room neat. Opening the chest that stored our supplies for lock-ins, I grabbed our sleeping bags and set them up on the floor.

All we had to do was wait for the sun to rise and this nightmare would end.

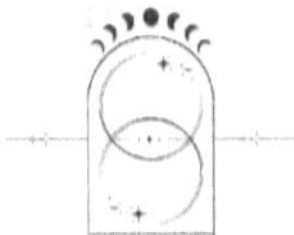

Unfortunately, by the time the alarm sounded, it was too late. Many people did not have enough time to secure their homes before the fae overwhelmed the town.

The next day was pure chaos. This attack was one of the worst the village had ever seen. Never had the fae gone that deep into town. The fae I encountered were not the only ones to invade. Other groups also came from the east and west. Over thirty fae in total attacked.

Glenda and I spent all morning making salves and elixirs to help heal the injured. The two of us had a system where I would gather and muddle ingredients and she would combine them into the proper potions. As we made them, the village healers and our regular customers took them just as quickly.

We were so busy throughout the day we did not have much time to talk about anything other than work. In the afternoon, when it finally slowed, Glenda finally spoke.

"It was not a new moon last night. It is so strange that so many fae attacked."

"Makes me worry about the new moon that is right around the corner. If it was this bad last night, how much worse could it get?"

"Indeed, a cause for concern." Glenda turned and went to grab the jar of vitella flower pollen, an important ingredient used in healing salves. She opened the jar and sighed. "We only have enough for two more batches." Glenda took out a scoop of pollen, added it to her mortar, and mixed it in with the other ingredients.

The vitella flower was a rare plant only found deep within the forest. It was very difficult to harvest. If done incorrectly, you would damage the plant, and it would not produce seeds for the next year or re-bloom. I had been practicing for years to get it right. The last time I harvested, I did not damage a single flower.

"I will go and collect more in the morning," I said to her with a smile.

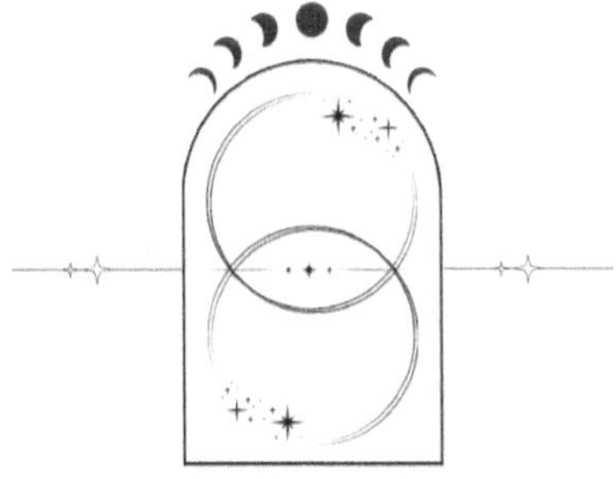

Four

I packed a small backpack full of harvesting equipment, water, and snacks the next morning and set out into the forest just after dawn. Throwing on my black cloak to fight off the autumn chill, I secured a dagger on the harness built into my cloak. The forest around Pendril was thick and filled with pines and firs, and the air smelled of fresh rain.

I traveled and searched for hours without any luck. My usual spots were bare, leaving me to go on a wild goose chase. The sun peeked through the canopy and illuminated the forest with a soft golden glow. The deeper in the forest I went, the more nervous I got. I did not want to get too close to the portal, but unable to find any vitella, I found myself heading in that direction.

After another hour of searching, I finally found a single flower placed in the center of a ring of mushrooms. Never had I seen anything like them. They were black-capped with a white stem. And a black, ink-like substance dripped from the gills. I would need to come another day to study these. There was no time to spare on side tasks today.

Stepping into the ring, I knelt before the plant and sat my backpack on the ground next to me. I pulled out my harvesting equipment and got to work. Luckily, there was a break in the canopy and it cast light down directly where I needed it to be so I could get a good look at the plant in the light. Using my tweezers, I opened the petals gently before sticking in my brush to pet the stoma delicately to release the pollen and trap it within the bristles.

The sound of a branch snapping caused my head to shoot up. Standing just on the other side of the mushrooms stood the most beautiful and terrifying man I had ever seen. Ice-blue eyes stared down at me with disdain. His hands were in the pockets of his black pants. My eyes went wide as my gaze rose to his wings. They were black as the void with golden flecks throughout that looked like the starry night sky.

"You are a long way from home, sunshine." His voice was like a smooth melody.

I hated how much I loved his voice. Everything around me darkened as if the sun focused all its rays on the very spot where I knelt. "Not too far. I spend much time in these woods." I pulled away from the plant with trembling hands, but I couldn't stand. My body wouldn't allow it.

The man chuckled as he pulled one of his hands out of his pocket and pushed back his long, white hair. Two thin braids with golden hoops framed his face. I could not stop staring at the black crescent moon, with the points facing up, tattooed on his forehead. Never had I seen anyone with such strange markings.

He knelt, so we met eye to eye. "Not enough to know you should never step into a fae circle, lest you be trapped."

His cold tone sent a shiver down my spine.

Fae circle? Was this man a fae? He did not look anything like the monsters I had grown so accustomed to seeing. What did he mean by trapped? Was I stuck here? I quickly reached for my dagger and pointed it at him as I finally stood, the paralyzing hold that was on me was now mysteriously gone.

"Stay back!" Slowly, I backed away. Something hard hit my back and my body tensed. Nothing should be there as before it was just air. I turned to see that I was now at the inner edge of the mushroom circle and a dark wall was now behind me, stopping my exit. It was as if the shadows transformed into this barrier. The dagger shook in my hand.

"I am not afraid of a tiny blade that you call a weapon," he chuckled as he stood and took a step into the circle. "All of you humans are the same. You come into the forest and take and take." Rage filled his voice.

Everything in me screamed for me to throw the dagger into his ice-blue eyes and run. My body betrayed me again and would not allow me to move a single muscle. He continued to step closer toward me. Pausing just before the flower, he looked down at it. His face softened and his gaze lifted back to me.

"Please," my voice shook. "Let me go."

As he took the final step to close the gap between us, I flung the dagger at him. All hope escaped me as he glided out of the way as if it was no issue. A deep laugh escaped his throat as he reached forward and grabbed my wrist, pulling me to him. I squirmed and tried to pull away, but his grip tightened, and his gaze dropped to my wrist, eyes widening in shock. Pulling my wrist up to his face, his gaze locked onto the eight-point star-shaped birthmark on my wrist. I attempted again to yank away.

"Let me go! Why are you doing this? Who are you?" I cried out.

He pulled me to him once again, wrapping his other arm around my waist, and held me against him.

In a faint whisper, he said, "The man who's going to marry you."

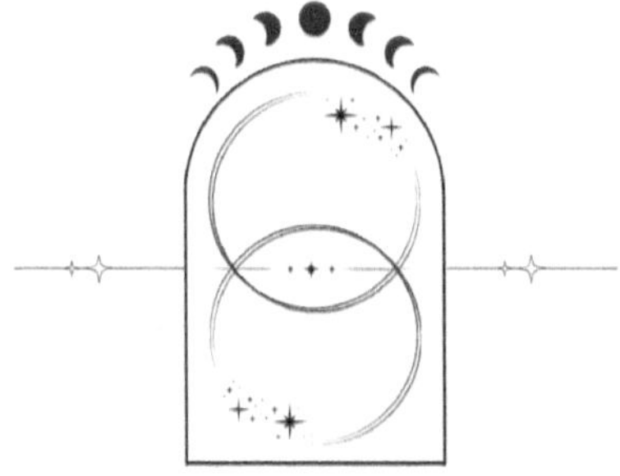

Five

I looked up at him and blinked hard. For a moment, I could not even articulate how I felt about his statement. Never did I expect anyone other than Caden to demand marriage from me. With him gone, I hoped I would be free. He held me closer, and the scent of bergamot and pepper filled my nose.

"I absolutely will not marry you! Release me at once," I demanded.

"Oh, you absolutely will, sunshine. Whether we like it or not." With a flap of his wings, we took to the sky.

Panic rose in me once again, and I now clung to him. My body trembled as I looked down at the world below us grow smaller and smaller.

"Please do not drop me!" I pleaded with him.

"I would never drop a woman as beautiful as you," he purred.

A faint purple mist filled the trees, and it snapped in my head exactly where we were going.

"No! No! Please not through the portal!" I screamed. "Please take me home!"

"I am." His voice was calm and collected.

Shadows filled my vision, and my eyes grew heavy. I found myself yawning, unable to fight back the sudden exhaustion I let sleep take me.

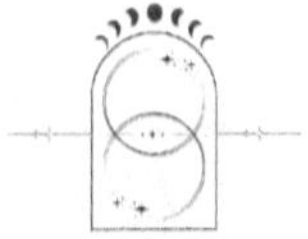

I couldn't open my eyes. Taking a deep breath, the warm scent of vanilla sugar encased me. Was everything that just happened a dream? The bed in which I laid felt much more comfortable than my own. I finally forced them open and shot up, the blankets piled around my waist. A new place surrounded me. The room was large and the bed was centered against the back wall. The walls were stone and bare.

Panic welled in my chest. To add to it, I realized I was now in a small black silk nightgown. Where were my clothes? Who put this on me?

On the left wall was a large window, and in desperation to know more about where I was, I jumped out of bed and rushed over to it. Looking down, I realized I was in a tower of a very large castle that sat on a plateau, surrounded by a few mountains. Beyond the mountains was a large forest. The castle was made of dark stone, but green moss and ivy had taken over many of the outer walls.

This forest was like nothing I had ever seen. The treetops were varying shades of blue, purple, and green. In the distance, I could see that undeniable shimmering purple mist of the portal as it clung to the treetops. Even if I could escape here, would I be able to traverse this forest to get to the portal? My heart broke as I realized how far away I was from the only thing that could return me home.

I turned toward the door and rushed over to it. Twisting and yanking the handle, I quickly learned the door was locked, and I was trapped. I banged on the solid oak door, pounding harder and harder with each knock, but it did not budge. I screamed for help. For anyone to release me.

To free me from my prison.

Hours passed, and my throat grew sore. I gave up. Turning back to the bed, I flung myself into the soft feather pillow, sobbing and screaming into it.

After what felt like many more hours, I heard the door open from behind me. I shot up and saw a young woman walking in with a cup of tea. She quickly shut the door behind her.

Her wings also looked nothing like the fae from back home, or like the wings of my kidnapper. They were light orange with a white border. Her alabaster skin was covered in freckles.

"Good morning!" Her voice was so cheerful. "My name is Poppy, and I will be your lady's maid during your stay. I made you some licorice and honey tea for your throat." She walked over to the side table and sat down the cup. Her fiery red braid fell to her front as she bent over. She looked back at me and gave me a warm smile.

"Are... you fae?" I finally spoke.

"Since the day I was born," she giggled. Her voice was light and bubbly. She sat down on the bed next to me.

"You don't look like a horrid monster. Where are your fangs? Your claws? Your eyes are bright amber, not blood red." I raised an eyebrow at her.

"I am not a vox! How dare you!" A look of anger took over her face. "I will let that one slide since you are from the human realm." Just as quickly as the anger came, it went. Her face was back into a soft smile.

Offending her was the last thing I wanted to do. Though she was fae and I did not trust her, Poppy seemed kind. "Vox?"

"Yes. The vox are fae who were cursed into turning into those horrid creatures. Bless their souls. No need to worry, here in the castle you are safe." Poppy stood back up and took a step toward the door.

"The vox are all we know back home. I never encountered an uncursed fae before the man in the woods."

"Welcome to Orilon," she giggled, "one of the fae realms. You can expand your knowledge of the fae tonight."

"Tonight?" I raised an eyebrow. Also, did she just say *one of the fae realms*? How many realms were there, and did others also have monsters like the vox?

"Oh yes. You are going to have dinner with the king." She clapped her hands together excitingly.

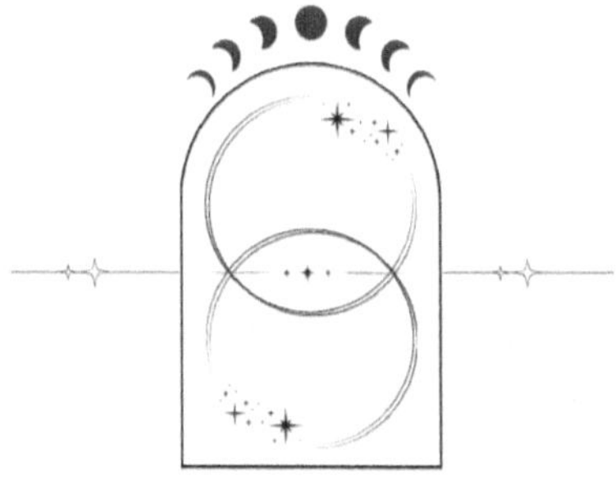

Six

For the first time in my life, I found myself being pampered. Back home, we could not afford luxuries like these. I hated I could easily find myself getting used to this. Poppy prepared me a warm bath, using a variety of exotic soaps. Once washed, she did my hair and make-up and dressed me in one of the most beautiful gowns I had ever seen. It was a dark blue satin fabric with a silver shimmer running throughout it. Once I was ready, she took me over to the full-length mirror with a golden frame.

My eyes welled with tears as I had never seen myself look so beautiful in my entire life. My fair skin was radiant from the cosmetics Poppy applied. My bright green eyes were accented by a golden shimmer on my eyelids. My shoulder-length curly blonde hair was pulled back on both sides with golden clips.

"Come along. We do not want to be late," she said as she opened the door and waved for me to follow her. We walked through the halls of the dark stone castle. The floor was lined with a black rug with golden trim. Focusing hard, I studied every turn, every direction. I would take my time and plan out my escape.

Not once did I see any form of exit as we traveled the twisting hallways. Most of the doors were kept shut, leaving only my imagination to fill in the blanks. Finding my way out was going to be harder than I thought.

Once we reached the dining room, Poppy guided me to the end of the long table that was set for two, a place setting on each end.

"The king should be here shortly. Please sit," she said as she motioned to the chair.

"Are you not staying?" I questioned as I took my seat.

"Oh, no." She walked back toward the exit. "I have other things I must attend to. Enjoy dinner." With that, she left the dining room, leaving me alone.

Looking around, I once again took in as many details as I could about the space. There were two exits on the east and west walls. The far wall had a fireplace centered with a large black tapestry above it. Gold sparkled through it, matching the wings of the man who took me. Some of the gold spots appeared slightly larger than the rest and formed a geometric pattern.

I stood and walked over to it, examining it. When I looked over to the doorway I came through, I noticed there were no guards that I could see. Thinking back on it, I did not see any-one while Poppy was guiding me through the halls. How easy would it be for me to leave and escape? The better question was, how far would I make it dressed the way I was in an unknown forest?

Annoyance built in me as I continued to await the king's arrival. I decided I would stand by no longer. I had to take the chance and make my escape. I turned toward the door and took a step as a familiar dark and smooth voice came from behind me.

"Sorry for keeping you waiting. I had business to attend to."

I turned and saw the man who had kidnapped me. He wore a black suit with golden trim and buttons. His wings were neatly tucked behind him.

"Very rude of you to kidnap someone and then make them wait for you," I snarled.

He motioned for me to return to my seat, and I did. I understood the role I had to play for now. If I could get him to trust me, and think I would follow his commands, perhaps he would offer me some freedom. It would be then I would escape.

"I do not keep time based on humans," he growled. "I have more important things to worry about." He took his seat at the far end of the table. Leaning back in his chair, his facial expression cold, he lifted his right arm and snapped twice.

Servants filled the room and brought wine and food. I stared down at the broth-based soup and took in the scent of the herbs from the meatballs, spinach, and pasta that floated in it. It looked delicious and my stomach growled. But no matter how hungry I was, I would not eat this food. I was afraid it was enchanted or laced with some sort of poison. This was the same reason I avoided the tea Poppy had given me.

"No, thank you. I won't be eating."

"Yes, you will. I will force you if I need to. I can't have you die on me before I am done with you." He looked at me with contempt through his thick eyebrows as he sipped his wine. His ice-blue eyes pierced my soul with their intensity.

"Done with me?" My chest tightened as I fought against my rage and rising panic.

"Yes. As I told you before, you and I will wed. Then the curse will be broken, and then I can return you to the human realm." He set down his glass and leaned forward. "Take a bite now, or I will force-feed you," he snarled. Leaning forward, he watched me intensely.

I picked up the spoon and scooped up a meatball from the soup and ate it. It was so tender and juicy. Struggling to keep my composure, I nearly melted from how good it tasted. It was so amazing, I nearly had forgotten where I was and who was in my company.

I snapped back into the conversation. "I don't know what makes you think I could help you lift a curse among the fae."

"You're the chosen one. I have waited centuries for you." He shrugged his shoulders as if this was just an everyday occurrence for him.

"The chosen one?" Sitting down the spoon, I leaned back in my chair. My gaze fixed on the king.

"A story for another day." He waved his hand, dismissing me. "I hate humans, so this is not a walk in the park for me, either. We *will* be wed, and I *will* save my people." He snapped his fingers once again and the main course was served, only to me. "Enjoy your dinner. I will tell you when I have everything ready for our wedding." With that, he stood and vanished into shadows.

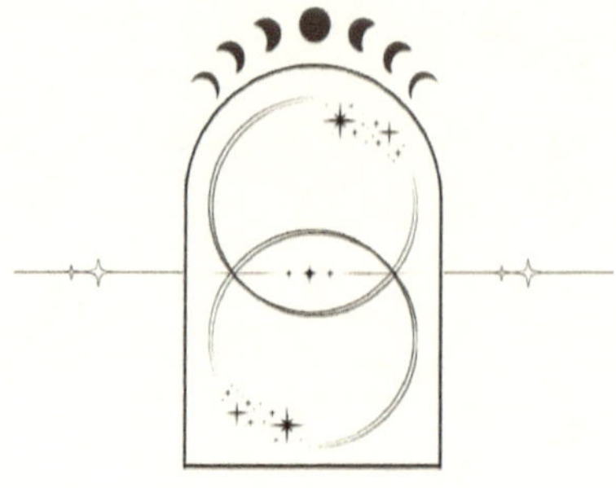

Seven

For the next two weeks, I stayed locked in my room. Poppy only allowed me to leave for dinner. She visited for only about an hour or so a day. When I woke up in the morning, breakfast was already sitting on the table by the window. She would stop by to deliver lunch and new books around noon. In the evening, she would take me to the dining room, disappear during dinner, then return me to my room. She refused to tell me anything about the king, the castle, or Orilon. According to her, the king would tell me everything I needed to know.

The king had not shown his face since our first dinner.

I hated being here, but being locked away and kept on a tight leash, I did not have any more of an idea of how I was going to escape. What type of psychopath kidnaps someone, tells them they are going to marry them, and then ignores them for two weeks?

Luckily for me, Poppy brought me tons of books to read, and with nothing else to do, I found myself reading one to two books a day. She also brought me a million articles of clothing. Never had I seen so many different fabrics, colors, and patterns in my entire life. She said the clothes I was wearing when I arrived did not fit my station here at the castle.

As the days went on, I found myself getting extremely lonely. It was getting harder and harder to get out of bed. My head was filled with thoughts of Pendril. Every night I found myself sobbing myself to sleep thinking of my aunt and Jade. I missed them so much. Did they think I was dead? After this much time, were they still looking for me, or did they think I was another victim of the 'fae'?

This morning, the sun shone through the window just right, covering the room in an iridescent rainbow. I sat up and stretched my arms above my head. Walking over to the table, I picked up the perfectly sweet coffee and took a sip. The scent of maple and butter filled my nose from the waffle that had been left for me for breakfast. I sat down and ate it, staring out the window, my gaze focused on the portal.

Once I was done eating, I made my way to the adjoining bathroom and took a shower. Lavender-scented steam filled the room. Once clean, I stepped out of the shower and dried off. As I ran the towel through my hair, a firm knock sounded at the bedroom door. I nearly jumped at the sound of it. I stayed in the bathroom, ignoring the knocking.

"It is me," he called out through the door. "May I come in?"

I wrapped the towel around me and walked over to the door. "No."

"Please," he growled.

"Fine," I sighed.

The door opened, and the king stepped inside. His gaze fell to me, and he choked on his breath. He quickly straightened his back and looked up at the ceiling. Clearing his throat, he finally spoke.

"Poppy told me it is bad to keep you trapped in here and you like to read. Please allow me to escort you to the library." He cleared his throat once again. "I will wait outside. Be ready in five minutes." With his final word, he turned on his heels, walked out, and shut the door behind him.

I giggled to myself. The thought of him being flustered brought me joy. I finished drying off and put on a simple blue dress. Excitement filled me. I could not deny I could not wait to get out of this room, even if it was with the man who kidnapped me.

I opened the door and stepped out. The king leaned against the wall with his arms crossed. All evidence of him being bothered was now gone.

"You look lovely, for a human," he said coldly. He kicked off the wall and took a step to close the gap between us. The citrus-spiced scent filled my nose as he lifted my chin so our gaze met.

"When you say it that way, it is not a compliment." My heart pounded in my chest.

He smirked down at me and then pulled away. The king walked down the hall and waved for me to follow him. "Come along, sunshine."

The nickname started to grow on me. It was one of the few things of light in this castle of darkness. My kidnapper and I walked the halls in silence for some time. His white hair floated behind him as he walked. Shadows clung at his fingertips. I watched as he squeezed his hand into a tight fist. The white of his knuckles showed through the shadows.

I had been so caught up in watching the king I stopped paying attention to the castle. I had absolutely no idea where we were. This section of the castle had some of the most beautiful paintings of the forest. I had never seen such gorgeous oil paintings. If I was not trapped here, I could see myself falling in love with the beauty of Orilon.

"What is your name?" He questioned, snapping my attention back to him.

"Why would I tell you my name? You have not told me yours."

A deep chuckle escaped his throat. "That is fair. My name is Ezra. Ezra Kincaid, the last King of Orilon." He continued walking, but never once did he look back at me as we spoke.

"The last?" I asked as I continued behind him.

"I am the last of my family's line. With the curse, there are not many fae left." He spoke in a distant tone. "The other realms have abandoned us. You, sunshine, are my last hope to save my kingdom."

"That is a lot to put on someone. How are you sure it is me? You don't even know my name!" The questions forced their way out of my throat.

Ezra turned toward me and stopped. I froze in my spot, my heart pounded as he slowly took a step toward me and said nothing as he closed the distance between us. I stepped back and felt something hard hit my back. I turned my head and saw a wall of shadow formed behind me, just as it had in the mushroom ring. I turned my head back toward Ezra, who was now directly in front of me. He lifted his arms and pressed his palms onto the shadow wall, trapping me between the wall and him.

Swallowing hard, I refused to break his gaze. A shiver ran down my spine as his power radiated from him. I did not want to be this man's enemy.

"What is your name, sunshine?" He snarled. His blue eyes pierced my soul. His tiny braids hung in between us.

"A............... Amara."

"Amara what?" His gaze and tone did not falter

"Amara Smythe."

He smirked and pushed off the wall. The wall behind me vanished, and I stumbled back, but he reached out and caught me by my wrist to steady me. Once I was stable, he turned and continued to walk away. I stood there frozen. My heart pounded in my chest, and I could still feel the electrified air around me.

"Don't fall behind, Amara," Ezra called out to me. His voice pulled me out of my own head. My name on his tongue was intoxicating.

I rushed to catch up to him, and we entered a massive library. There were two levels with floor-to-ceiling bookshelves. In the center of the room sat several tables, with rows of shelves surrounding them. There was not a single empty shelf. There had to be more books in here than I could read in my entire life. My jaw dropped as I stepped past Ezra to get a better look at the library. Never in my life had I seen so many books. Ezra came around to my front.

"Poppy told me the type of books you like. They can be found over in section X. I will allow you to make your selection in private." He pointed over to the section of the library he mentioned. Heat rose to my cheeks, and that playful smirk returned to his angled face. "No need to blush. I understand now that we met you will think of me as you read them."

"Absolutely not!" Though he was handsome and charming, I would never think of him in that manner.

"Just keep telling yourself that, sunshine," he said as he winked.

I gave him a vulgar gesture, and he let out a deep chuckle.

"You seem to ask Poppy a lot about me," I said with a raised eyebrow as I studied his face.

"Of course." He sat down at one of the tables. "I told her to learn all she could about you so I did not have to waste my time doing so."

I rolled my eyes. Just like that, all the charm he had was thrown out the window. "You're an ass." Turning away from him, I made my way over to the section he told me about. Every romance author I ever heard of and more lined the shelves. With no idea where to start, I slid over the ladder, climbed it, and took the first book on the top shelf.

"You are free to come to the library whenever you please, but only the library. Call for Poppy and she will escort you. If you go anywhere but the library, you will be punished." His voice was right in my ear, but as I spun and looked around for him, he was nowhere near me. I got down off the ladder and walked back to the table he was sitting at.

Ezra was gone.

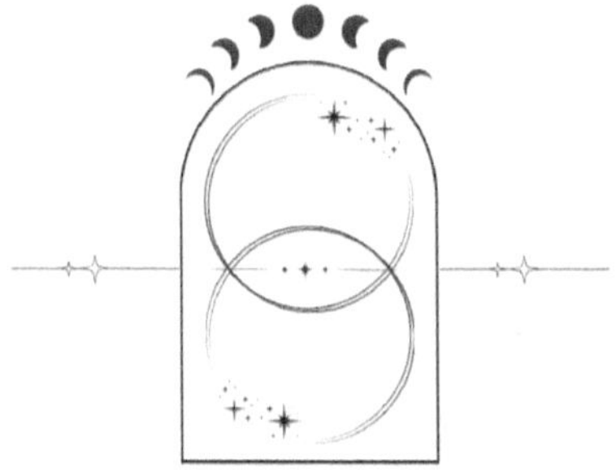

Eight

Over the next few days, I found myself spending every waking moment in the library. I discovered a tiny reading nook on the back wall with a window that overlooked the forest. The window seat had so many cushions I ended up removing some of them to make room for myself and my stack of books. There were more books than I could read in a lifetime. Spoiled for choice, I read them in the order they were arranged on the shelf. Gathering a small stack, I made my way to the reading nook.

Deep into my novel, I heard sounds of rustling papers and footsteps from deep within the library. I sat straight up and looked around. The noise stopped. "Poppy?" I called out. "Ezra?" I followed up when there was no response.

Maybe it was just my paranoia building that caused me to hear the noise. I brushed it off and went to read my book once again. It had just gotten to a very smutty scene that caused my core to melt when another noise pulled me out of the book once again. I shut my book and sat it down on the bench as I stood.

I tiptoed, following the sound of the rustling. Peering around a corner, I saw an older man stocking the shelves. His short silver hair matched the metallic gleam of his wings, and they both stood out against his dark complexion. He turned and his brown eyes met mine. He jumped, reaching for his chest.

"My Lady!" He gasped. "I am so sorry to disturb you! I will be done and gone in just a moment."

"No, it's ok! You don't need to go!" I exclaimed. "I just did not know anyone was here. The noise startled me."

"I am always here. I was ordered not to disturb you. The king did not want you to be afraid."

I raised an eyebrow at him. "Afraid? Of what?" Now that I thought about it, the only staff I had seen was Poppy and the servants at dinner. "Are there others who work in the castle?"

"Yes. He said you were afraid of the fae. There are a few of us left here in the castle. Unfortunately, many of the fae have been turned into the vox." He continued to stock the shelves with the books on his small metal cart. "My name is Gil. I am the royal archivist. It is a pleasure to meet you."

"It is nice to meet you as well." I offered a soft smile. "I feel bad you have had to work around me the past few days."

"It is no worry," he said with a shrug. "It truly is no issue. Please let me know if you need anything."

"Could you tell me how to leave the castle and go home?" I asked in a sarcastic tone. I knew it was a hopeless question.

"No," he let out a deep belly laugh. "The king would have my head. I understand he is hard to deal with. He has not been the same since he lost his family to the curse. Please know he has a good heart."

I leaned against the bookshelf and gnawed on my lip for a moment before speaking. "He lost his family?"

"Oh, yes. The royal family of Orilon all turned into vox about twenty years ago. Well, all except King Ezra, who was Prince Ezra at the time." Gil stopped stocking the books and sighed. "They had killed most of the castle staff before Ezra was able to cut them down." He choked on those last few words, and his eyes misted. "It was one of Orilon's darkest days."

"That sounds horrid," I whispered. Thinking about my own parents and how they, too, were claimed by the vox, I could not imagine what it would be like to have to hunt them down and stop them from killing more of the town of Pendril.

It seemed like the king and I had more in common than I thought. The vox had taken from us both.

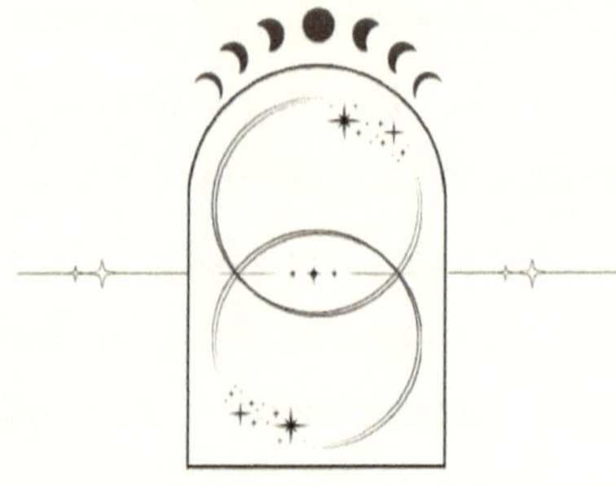

Nine

The next day, I sat at the table near the window in my room, sipping a cup of coffee. The mug pressed to my cheeks, and my eyes closed as I took in the sound of the rain. I had yet to make my way to the library for the day. It was one of those dark and dreary days that made you want to stay curled up in bed.

My eyes opened to a soft knock on the door. After calling out to see who it was, the door opened, and Poppy entered. She had a huge grin on her face.

"Good afternoon, Poppy." I smiled.

"Good morning! I hope you have had enough coffee this morning!" She motioned to the mug that was still pressed to my face. I nodded in response. "You are going to be full of energy for tonight! Wonderful!"

I narrowed my eyes at her warily. "Is something special happening tonight?"

"King Ezra requests you have dinner with him. He has things to discuss!"

"Good, because so do I."

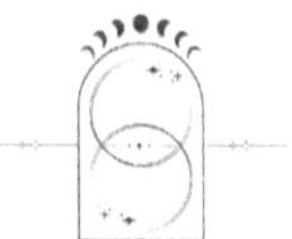

When we arrived at the dining room, Ezra was standing just past the entrance. He wore a black button-up shirt with the top few buttons loose and the sleeves rolled up just before his elbows. He was more casual than I had ever seen him.

"Good evening, Amara. It is time for us to discuss our wedding. Please sit, and I will have dinner served to us shortly." He gently took my arm and led me away from Poppy and to my seat. He even pulled my chair out for me. I looked at him with narrowed eyes as I sat, and he pushed in my chair. He made his way over to his seat, his white hair flowing behind him. Once sat, he snapped his fingers, and servants came out and served wine with a cheese soufflé. I watched as he sipped from his glass, his ice-blue eyes glued to me.

"Why did you tell your staff to hide from me?"

He stared at me through his brow and lowered his glass. "Gil told me the two of you met." He leaned forward. "I knew the fae made you uncomfortable. The situation is not ideal. I am just trying to make it easier for you."

"That is very kind," I said as I took a bite of the soufflé.

"Contrary to popular opinion, sunshine, I am a kind king."

I rolled my eyes and chuckled. "Sure, you are."

Ezra finally took a bite of his food and smirked at me. Shadows danced around him as if they begged for his attention. He sat down the fork and swallowed his bite, leaning back in his chair once again. "Our wedding will be held in two weeks. Poppy will get everything coordinated for you."

I hated the idea of marrying him, but at this point, escape seemed impossible. "And once we are wed, you will return me to my family?"

"Yes. I will take you back to the human realm." He took another sip of his wine. "For the next two weeks, each day you and I will spend one hour together, and we will have dinner together every night."

My eyes went wide. My heart pounded in my chest. I didn't want to be around him more than I had to be. A pit formed in my stomach. Ezra was terrifying to be around. His cold gaze stared down at me. I could sense his power and it threatened to devour me. I could not lie. I was also excited to spend more time with the King of Orilon.

"Why? I thought you did not want to be around me and you had better things to do." I raised an eyebrow.

"Oh, I do. I hate being around you," he said rolling his eyes. "There are many things I need to be doing and I would rather be doing." He leaned forward and rested his elbow on the table. Holding his head in his hand, he rubbed his temple with his thumb. "However, we need to convince the priestess we are in love."

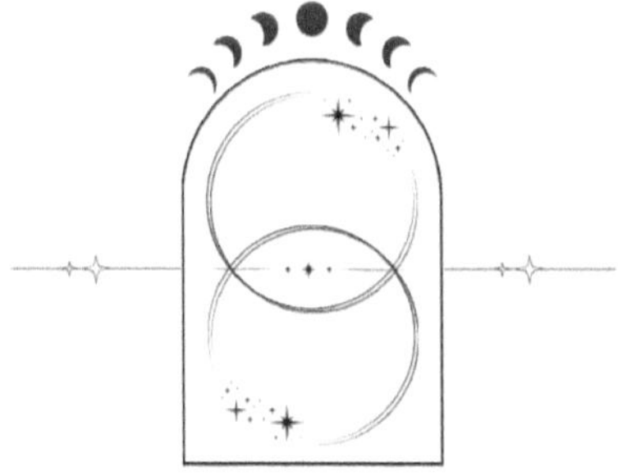

Ten

The next morning, Poppy barged into my room, and the sun hit her face just right, illuminating her golden eyes. She had a white sundress draped over her arm.

"Good morning!" She squealed. "The king requests your presence. He wants to give you a tour through the royal gardens."

"There are gardens?" I perked up, a large grin forming on my face.

"Oh, yes. I think you will love them."

I knew I would. As an herbalist, plants were one of my favorite interests. It was one of the hobbies my aunt and I shared. Thinking about all of the plants I kept back home in my room, I knew Glenda would take care of them until I returned. "Sounds wonderful."

"Great! Let's get you ready." She dressed me in the white sundress and pulled my hair back with a white ribbon. "You look wonderful!"

Poppy guided me to the greenhouse entrance, which was a large set of frosted glass doors. Ezra leaned against the opposite wall. His gaze was on the ceiling. He toyed with the golden hoops that were woven within the braids that framed his face. Once we got closer, he looked over at me and smiled.

"Thank you, Poppy!" He pushed off the wall and stepped over to us. "Are you ready, sunshine?" He looked down at me with a genuine smile.

Poppy gave me a little wave, then ran off.

"I am so excited! I love plants!" I giggled, not able to hide my enthusiasm.

"I could tell. I was shocked at how well you harvested vitella. Most cannot harvest it without damaging the plant. Only someone who truly cares for plants would be able to do that."

"My aunt taught me. I come from a long line of herbalists." Again, I felt my heart crack just a little as I spoke of home. I prayed to The Mother she was doing alright.

"Fascinating," he said as he opened the door to the gardens. Humidity hit me as we entered the large glass dome. I was awestruck by how many tropical plants there were. The gardens were filled with leaves and floral blooms in all shades of green, purple, pink, red, and orange.

As we walked the stone pathways, Ezra pointed out some of the rarer plants as well as some that were exclusive to Orilon. As he talked, I saw a blue glow emanating from one of the plants. It was absolutely enthralling. Ezra continued to walk, and while

I heard the deep hum of his voice, I could not understand the words. I needed a closer look at the blue glow of the flower. I needed to be near it. A large blue flower bud was in the center of the glow.

The flower opened and revealed large sharp teeth. Vines shot from the ground and wrapped around my body. I wanted to squirm and fight, but my body would not allow me to move. The vines lifted me into the air and brought me closer to the flower.

Shadows darted from behind me and enveloped the plant. Before my eyes, the life was drained from the plant and the vines dropped me. Before I could compose myself, strong arms lifted me, and the bergamot and pepper scent filled my nose. Calm washed over me, and I leaned into him.

"Ezra," a soft whimper escaped my lips.

"Are you alright? I am so sorry, sunshine." His voice was filled with worry, his breathing was heavy, and I could feel his heart pounding in his chest as he held me close.

I looked up at him. "You're sorry?" He sat me down on my feet.

"Yes! There are not many gardeners left, they used to keep the plants in line. I thought all the carnivorous plants were removed ages ago. I should have been more careful. That one is known to lure humans in with their light. Once a human sees it, they are put in a trance and cannot escape. Did the vines hurt you?"

I shook my head in response. My entire body quivered in fear. Ezra took my hands in his to hold them steady. "What were those shadows?"

"I have shadow magic. I can control and manipulate the shadows around me. I can also use those shadows to drain life from anything. Do you want to return to your room? I would understand if so."

Somehow the thought of returning to my room felt like a worse choice even after being attacked by a plant. "No, I want to continue. Just keep me close," I said softly.

"Always." He wrapped his arm around me and continued the tour of the gardens.

Just last night he told me he hated me. I couldn't help but wonder if that was the truth. He was being so tender with me now. I saw the terror in his eyes after I had been attacked. That was not the look you gave to someone if you hated them.

He walked me over to a side door. "There are no other carnivorous plants in here. You will be safe." He opened the glass door and ushered me inside. This greenhouse was filled with a wide variety of orchids, all in bloom. They were truly divine. I took a step into the room and looked around at the flowers.

"Wow, they are all so beautiful," I said. I heard Ezra mumble something from behind me, and I turned to face him. "What was that?"

"Nothing." He brushed his hand through his hair to keep it out of his face as he looked away from me. "What do you want for dinner tonight? I realized I have always chosen. I don't even know what you like to eat."

"I like everything." I shrugged as I looked at a cattleya orchid with its bright orange flowers. "Everything we have eaten has been so delicious!"

"Perfect," he smirked. "I love surprising you, sunshine."

I was confused by his kindness, but maybe part of his strategy of convincing the priestess was just faking it constantly so that our love looked real when the time came. Still, I needed to be cautious and mind whatever games he was playing.

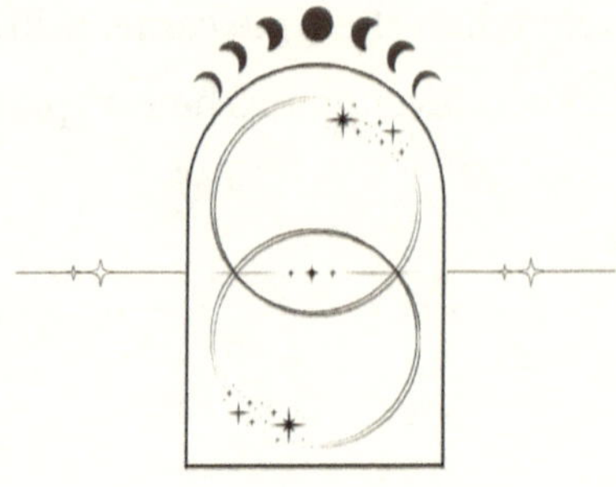

Eleven

Music filled the air, and it was light and romantic, and a calm washed over me as Poppy guided me to the dining room. It was as if all my worries washed away, I wasn't sure what caused this change in my mood. She had dressed me in a black satin dress with golden accessories. Long chain earrings dangled from my ears that matched the necklace that hung down my neck.

A shadow figure stood in the corner of the room, playing the violin, and I was mesmerized by the bow gliding across the strings.

"Have a good dinner," Poppy giggled as she left me alone in the dining room.

Waving goodbye, I let out a huff of air. Of course, Ezra was not yet here. Part of me was excited to see him, but I should not allow those feelings to exist.

The shadow figure lowered the violin and turned to me. "Please sit. I will be there in just a moment." Ezra's voice projected from the figure. I jumped from the shock of it, then took my seat, my eyes never left the figure. It played once again.

After a few moments, Ezra walked out with a bottle of wine in one hand and two glasses in the other. "Good evening. I'm sorry I am late." He sat the two glasses on the table next to me and popped the cork. "This is a sweet white from my family's vineyard." He filled both glasses, took his, and headed to his seat.

He sipped his wine and his free hand sat on the table, with his nails tapping against it.

I took a sip of mine as well and let the sweet, effervescent taste wash over my tongue. "I wanted to thank you for saving me." I had not been able to get the attack out of my mind all day. Nor could I forget the softness he showed me after the attack.

"As long as you are a guest in my castle, I will strike down anything that tries to harm you." Fire burned in his ice-blue eyes, and my core melted.

He lifted his hand and snapped his fingers. Like every other time, the fae servants brought out dinner. They placed a plate in front of me, and a savory scent hit my nose. The most beautiful beef wellington sat on top of mashed potatoes with a side of roasted carrots.

"Would you like gravy, my lady?" The servant asked as he presented a silver gravy boat.

"Yes, please," I said with a smile.

He poured the gravy on top of the meat, and I watched as it pooled, and then dripped down the side. My mouth salivated, and I could not wait to devour it. Taking my fork and knife, I cut into the wellington, taking the medium rare meat into my mouth, which almost immediately melted. I could taste the savory umami of the mushroom duxelles as it hit my tongue.

Ezra leaned forward. He had not even touched his food. I sat down my fork and stared back at him. Swallowing hard, I leaned back into my seat.

"Why are you looking at me like that?"

"Do you like it?" He questioned, his focus flicked down to my plate before returning to my face.

"Yes, it is very good." I raised my eyebrow. "You have never asked that before. What did you do to it?"

He leaned back in his seat, and his shoulders relaxed. "I made it," he said in a soft tone.

"What?" My jaw dropped and my eyes widened.

"I prepared it," he said again, this time a little louder. "You told me to surprise you, so I cooked tonight's meal."

"This is absolutely delicious! I did not expect a king to know how to cook." I picked up my fork and knife and continued eating.

"My younger sister taught me." He finally picked up his fork and started to eat. "She wanted to be a chef, not a princess." He let out a soft chuckle, and he looked off in the distance. The sad expression on his face told me everything I needed to know. We stayed silent for a little while as we ate.

"I am sorry about your family," I finally broke the silence. "Gil told me what happened."

Ezra's gaze snapped toward me, and fire returned to his eyes. His lips pressed into a straight line. We stayed there for a moment, gazes locked before his face softened and returned to sadness. "Just another thing the curse has taken from me." He shrugged and continued eating.

"You never told me why the fae were cursed."

Ezra clenched his jaw and twirled the fork in between his fingers. "Long ago, a human girl crossed into Orilon and met my grandfather. She told my grandfather life across the portal was terrible and she never wanted to return. He provided her refuge within the castle and they fell in love. When her sister came looking for her, she begged my grandfather to keep her safe." He stabbed the fork into the dark wood of the table. "My grandfather lied to her, saying her sister died. That the wilds of Orilon claimed her. In a fit of rage, she cursed the fae to turn into horrible beasts. Turns out, she was no mere human, but a sorceress. Over the years, more and more fae turned into these creatures."

I could feel my heart break as he spoke. I thought the fae to all be horrid creatures, but the monsters I feared were created by a human. All along, it was the fae who wanted to keep a human safe.

"She added only one way to escape the curse. The fae king would bear a strange mark," he continued. "He would have five hundred years to find a human with the same mark and fall in love. My grandfather was the first to turn into the vox as soon as the curse was placed. He had no hope of finding the human with his mark. Even if he did, it wouldn't matter. He loved my grandmother more than anything in this universe."

His grandmother was human. The man who I feared, who hated humans, and ruled over the fae, was part human.

"My father never gained his mark. I had nearly given up before I found you. This was my final year to find someone with *my* mark."

He slowly unbuttoned his shirt and revealed an eight-point star birthmark under his collarbone.

It matched the one on my wrist perfectly.

"So, when you saw mine..." I said softly.

"Yes," he nodded. "I am so terribly sorry to pull you into this mess. You now understand time is truly of the essence."

"I understand." I took another bite and looked away.

"Let's talk about something lighter, shall we?" He gave me a soft smile that didn't reach his eyes. "How about some dessert?"

"Sounds lovely," I smiled back at him.

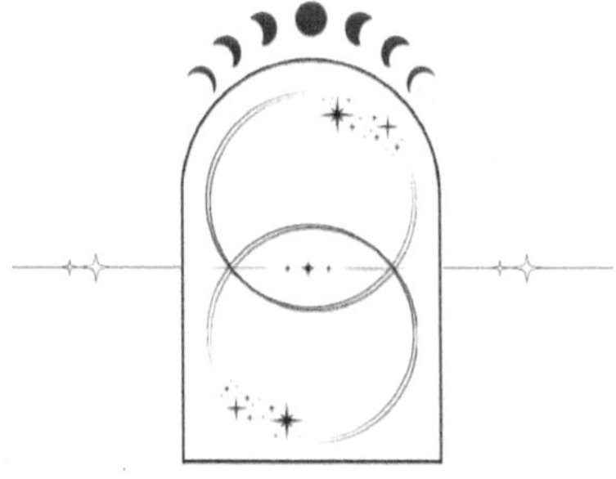

Twelve

I was so excited when Poppy told me Ezra planned to show me more of the gardens today. He wrapped his arm around me and held me close as we made our way through the main section, his shadows surrounded us to keep us safe from any plants that wished me to be their next meal. A door in the back of the garden led to yet another greenhouse. Rows of garden boxes with perfectly organized herbs filled the space. Around the perimeter were beds filled with pink roses.

"I thought this may be your favorite part of the gardens," Ezra said with a smile.

I stepped away from him and took a closer look at the garden box in front of us. It had some of the rarest herbs I had ever seen. Glenda would have absolutely freaked out if she saw them. I could already hear her now listing off all the elixirs she could make with these.

"This is wonderful," I said softly.

"What are you thinking about? Your eyes are looking elsewhere."

"Just thinking of my aunt. I miss her so much."

"I am sorry, sunshine. You will see her again soon. I promise you that."

I let out a sigh in response and turned away from his gaze. It was then I noticed the garden box filled with what looked to be vitella but was in multiple colors. My eyes went wide and a huge smile crossed my face. Back home, the vitella had green blooms. Here the blooms were blue, red, and purple. I walked over to the box to examine them more closely.

"Aren't they wonderful?" Ezra asked from behind me.

"I have never seen vitella in these colors. This is vitella, isn't it?"

"It is." Ezra walked over to my side. "Here in Orilon is where the vitella originated. Only the green variety made it across the portal and into the human realm. The others are not able to survive in the human world. I suppose they hate the mundane soil. Each color has slightly different properties. The green can help speed healing, but the red can elongate your life. The purple is actually a poisonous variety that steals the life from those who ingest it for the giver to take."

"That is fascinating!" I exclaimed.

"Any time you want to come here, please let Poppy know. I will happily escort you through the main garden to keep you safe."

"Thank you, Ezra."

"You're welcome, sunshine."

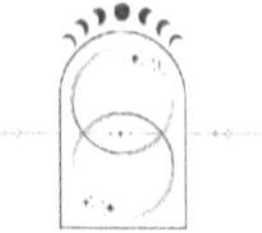

The next three days were filled with Ezra and I spending time with each other in the library and the gardens. Each evening, Ezra would prepare dinner for us to eat together. I hated to admit it, but the fae king was not so terrible to be around. Gods, if only I could tell Glenda and Jade of the man I met 'across the mountains'.

We sat after dinner, enjoying our lemon cream pie and talking about the books we read today in the library. Ezra also enjoyed the same books I did, which I found quite hilarious.

"Tomorrow I will not be able to join you in the gardens or the library. I have business to attend to." He took another bite of his pie.

"Business?" I tried to hide the disappointment on my face. After spending so much time with him, I truly enjoyed his company.

He let out a deep sigh. "Yes, unfortunately as king, I can't spend every day lounging around with you. Even if that is more enjoyable than what I need to get done."

I chuckled. "Oh? Did you just admit that you enjoy spending time with a human?"

"I would never admit such a thing," he said with a smirk.

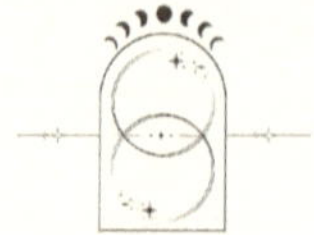

I spent all of the next day in the library, nestled in my reading nook. Staring out the window, I watched the rain hit the glass. Water droplets trailed down the glass, putting me in a relaxed state. The book I was reading could not hold my interest, I kept putting it down to watch more of the rain. The library had been very quiet, and I had not seen Gil all day. I wondered what he was up to today.

I really enjoyed speaking with Gil. He always had great book recommendations. They were always outside of my normal genre, but each of them ended up being amazing reads. I sat down the book I was reading and went to find him, hoping he would have a suggestion for me.

I wandered through the full library and was not able to find Gil. I looked over toward the door. Walking over to it, I peeked my head out and looked both ways, finding the hall empty. I decided to leave the library and explore. Wandering through the maze of hallways and staircases, I quickly found myself in a part of the castle I did not recognize.

I had gotten myself lost. I had no idea how to get back to the library. Most of the doors were shut and locked. Only one door had been opened and the room beyond it was empty.

I found a black wooden door with a golden doorknob at the end of a long hallway. The other doors had been natural wood. I twisted the handle, and beyond the door was a downward staircase made of dark stone. Closing the door behind me, I made my way down the stairs quietly. The sconces on the walls were covered in dust and cobwebs. Paintings were either crooked on the wall or had fallen completely. Stagnate must filled the air. At the bottom of the stairs, I found another maze of hallways.

I continued to walk down the halls, and the sound of my footsteps echoed. After a little while of traveling through the labyrinth of hallways, I realized I was lost. My heart pounded in my chest. Panic was creeping in as I had no idea how I was going to get back to my room or the library from here. A familiar and terrifying screech sounded off from behind me. I turned and my heart dropped as I saw a vox. It was hunched over, claws dragging on the floor, with its blood-red eyes locked on me. I slowly took a step back, wanting as much distance between the two of us as possible.

It let out another scream, and its wings flared open as it sprinted toward me. I spun and took off running for my life. The monster made loud clicking noises as if it were communicating. Never had I heard those sounds come from the vox. More screeches and clicking filled the halls, but I was too afraid to look behind me. Tears ran down my face. This would be my end. No one had been in this section of the castle in years. This is where I would die, and no one would find my body. That is if the vox left a body to be found. Tears fell down my face and blurred my vision as I frantically searched for an escape.

I turned a corner and quickly regretted it. At the end of the hall sat a dead end, where a black suit of armor, which held a spear, faced me. I rushed to it and tried to yank away the spear, but it was stuck in place. Turning my head, I saw three vox now standing at the end of the hall. Baring their fangs, they progressed down the hall, slowly.

I was trapped.

I screamed and sobbed, still trying to free the spear. Shadows filled the space in between me and the vox, and Ezra emerged from them, his wings flared. This was the first time I saw them on full display. They were truly magnificent. The black of his wings were devoid of all light, causing the gold within them to shine. He flapped them hard and shadows rushed forward, forcing the vox to stagger back. The shadows enveloped them, and more of their screeches echoed off the walls. The shadows recoiled, and the vox fell to the floor. Their bodies shriveled, as if life was sucked out of them and their once red eyes were now a dull grey.

Ezra turned toward me, tucking his wings behind his back. Rage contorted his face. "I told you not to roam the castle!" His voice was filled with anger and boomed off the walls, causing me to cower. I finally looked into his eyes, and they were solid black. "*This* is why. You could have been killed!"

"I... I'm sorry," I whimpered.

Ezra grabbed me by the arm and yanked me toward him, squeezing so hard that I let out a yelp. "You would have been more than sorry if you had gotten hurt," he snarled. In a sudden motion, he lifted me and threw me over his shoulder. I did not fight him. The grasp he had lessened slightly, but he still held firm. I turned my head so I could look forward to see what Ezra was doing. He twisted the head of the suit of armor and the side wall slid open, revealing a secret passage.

I opened my mouth to speak, but as the first sound escaped my lips, Ezra cut me off. "Don't. I do not want to hear what you have to say." His voice was cold and distant.

We walked through the secret tunnel in silence. Tears still flowed down my face as we made our way. The torches on the wall illuminated as we reached them, and extinguished as we passed. After a while, Ezra pulled on one of the torches and the wall opened.

He sat me down and guided me into a small room with a desk, a library cart, and books. A shut door was on the far wall. The door to the secret tunnel shut behind us. Ezra looked down at me. The look of anger was gone, but the new expression was now much worse.

Disappointment.

"This," he pointed to the door at the far end of the room, "opens to the library. You will return to your room and Poppy will bring you dinner." He turned away and walked to the door, twisting the knob. The door did not budge. He pulled harder, his muscles flexed.

"Stop messing around. Let us out."

"The door is stuck," he said plainly as he stepped away from it.

"Then let's go back through the secret tunnel and find another exit!" All I wanted to do was to crawl into bed. After what just happened, I wanted a safe quiet place to hide.

"It does not work that way," he sighed. "The door doesn't open from this side. Unfortunately, I used up a lot of my magic fighting the vox. My reserves are not as large as they used to be. Just another effect of the curse." He sat down on the floor and leaned his back against the wall. "We are stuck here until Gil comes back and finds us. This is his office, so he has to come here at some point."

"Some point?"

He nods. "Either until he finds us or my magic replenishes. Get comfortable, sunshine, we could be here for a while."

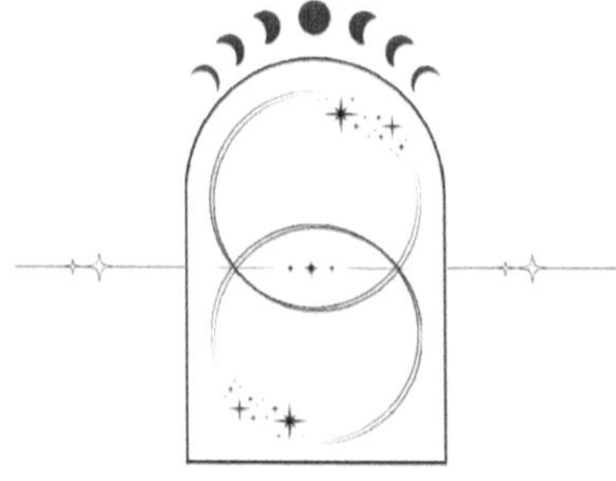

Thirteen

We sat in silence for an hour. Ezra grabbed a book off of Gil's desk and had been reading it for a while now. It was impossible to tell how much time had passed. I grabbed a book as well, but I could not focus on it. I was still shaken from the attack, and from the way Ezra reacted when he found me. I was thankful to him for saving me, but he showed me why he was the fae king. His power was beyond my comprehension. I will never forget the anger in his eyes.

Heat built in the room, and I felt sweat bead on my hairline and drip down my face. Ezra seemed totally unaffected by the heat, and I could not help but stare at him as he flipped through the pages of the book. After a while, he closed the book and sat it by his side. He didn't even look at me or say a word before removing his shirt, in one swift movement. Sweat glistened on his chest, and I blushed hard before looking away.

"Is that really necessary?" I looked back at him, trying not to stare at his muscles.

"It is hot." He finally looked toward me. "Your wandering gaze is not my problem." He sneered and then smirked. "You could remove your shirt and make it even." A deep chuckle escaped his throat, and he offered me a wink.

"You are such a pervert! I will absolutely *not* be doing that." I rolled my eyes, then focused my attention back to my book. Frustration built within me, as I hated I was attracted to him.

There was silence for a long moment before he answered. "Can you blame me? I am trapped with a beautiful woman."

"You think I am beautiful?" Heat filled my cheeks as I looked back up at him.

"I have told you many times. I am now ending this conversation." His gaze returned to his book. "I am still mad at you."

"I said I was sorry!" I huffed. Sitting my book in my lap, I crossed my arms.

"Amara." His tone lowered and softened, causing my heart to skip a beat. "If you had gotten hurt..." His voice trailed off as he closed the book and sat it down again. Pushing off the wall, he slowly crawled to me. His ice-blue eyes never looked away from mine. When his face was just a few inches from mine, he stopped. His two braids hung in the space between us. "I don't know what I would have done."

My body tensed as he got closer. Every part of me screamed for me to close the gap between us. I took in a deep breath of the electrified air and bit my bottom lip, trying to force those thoughts away. "Because if I died, we couldn't break the curse?"

"Well, yes." He smirked. "Though there are other reasons."

"Other reasons?" My voice shook as I spoke. My mind raced at all the possibilities. I thought his kindness all had to do with him needing me to break the curse. Could he have gained feelings beyond that?

He leaned in just a little more, and my heart pounded harder. I swore my chest was about to explode. Just before our lips touched, he quickly pulled back. In a blink, he was back against the wall, reading his book again.

The door swung open, and Gil looked down at us and let out a laugh. I looked up at him in shock. Ezra didn't even look up from the book. "There you two are! We have been looking for you everywhere."

Quickly, I jumped up. Ezra, still shirtless, slowly stood with an air of grace, flicked his hair back behind his shoulder, and walked out. As he passed Gil, he stopped and looked down at him. "Will you take Amara to her room? I must return to my duties."

"Yes, Your Majesty," he said with a nod.

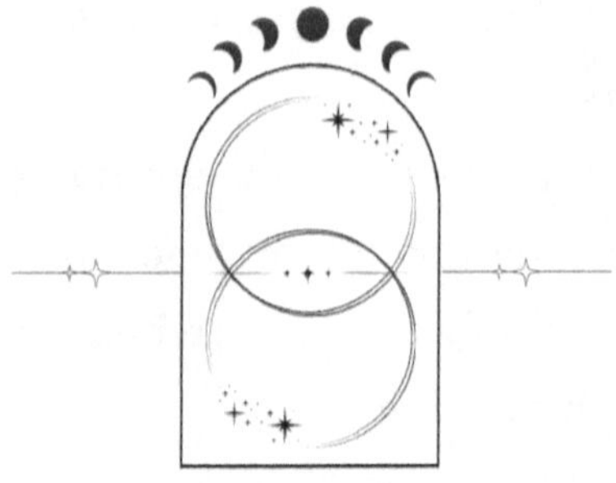

Fourteen

After being returned to my room, Poppy brought up a dinner of roasted lamb. Once she put my meal on the table and offered me a greeting, she left. I sat at the table by the window overlooking the forest, pushing around the peas that sat on my plate.

I found myself totally overwhelmed by what happened. Why had I been so drawn to leave the library? I knew better than to do that. Normally, I was so cautious. How did Ezra find me in that final moment? How did the fates weave this tale, and how would they continue to?

My body heated at the thought of Ezra, shirtless. I hated I loved the way he looked. When he was so close, I craved his touch and wished he had closed the gap between our lips.

What I hated even more was Gil interrupting us.

Thoughts continued to race through my mind. Did Ezra truly feel that way? Did he have feelings for me, or was it just the heat of the moment fueled by the romance he was reading?

My dinner had gone cold while I was busy running through all the thoughts trapped in my head. I pushed it away, folded my arms down on the desk, laid my head down, and stared out at the soft purple glow in the distance. A firm knock pulled me out of my daydream, and I sat straight up.

"Who is it?" I called out.

"It is I." His deep, smooth voice was like music to my ears.

I jumped from my seat, calling for him to come in. The door swung open, and Ezra stepped in. He looked down at me, took a deep breath, and shut the door behind him. We stayed locked in each other's gazes for a silent moment.

My heart pounded in my chest, and I twiddled with my thumbs as I anxiously awaited for him to speak.

"I apologize for how I reacted earlier. I was so angry with you. You disobeyed the rules and endangered yourself." He took a step closer to me. "I should not have spoken to you the way I did. I understand you think the rules are to keep you trapped. I promise on the heart of my kingdom they are in place to keep you safe." He spoke in a firm, yet gentle tone.

"I am sorry for wandering off. It will never happen again," I whimpered, looking down and away from him.

"Very good. Good night, Amara."

My head snapped up. "Wait!"

Ezra had been reaching for the door, but quickly turned toward me, hope gleaming in his eyes. "Yes?"

"You never answered my question."

"What question?" A smirk formed on his lips.

"What were the other reasons?"

Ezra closed the gap between us. My heart pounded and heat rose to my cheeks as he gently lifted my chin, his thumb gently brushing my bottom lip. "If something had happened to you," desire burned in his eyes, "I couldn't do this." He softly pressed his lips to mine. His arm wrapped around my waist to hold me close, and his spicy citrus scent filled my nose.

I was glad he did because, without his support, I would have fallen to the floor when my knees buckled as I got on my tippy toes to press into the kiss.

After a moment, he pulled his lips away. A hollowness took over the space where the heat of his touch had been.

"Sunshine, your kisses taste like sweet nectar from the gods. Will you allow me another taste?"

I slammed my lips back into his as my response. The passion grew between us as I wrapped my arms around his neck as we kissed. His tongue slipped into my mouth and danced with mine as he held me closer. Heat flooded me, and I released a curse as he released me and pulled away. His shadows flared around him.

"Good night, sunshine. I will see you tomorrow." With that final word, he stepped back and vanished into his shadows.

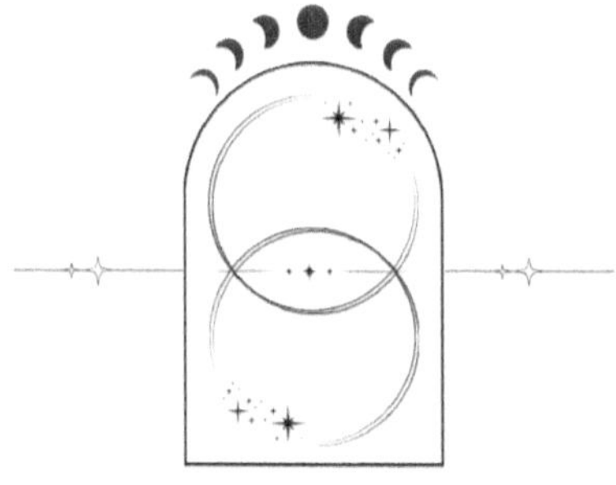

Fifteen

"Amara." Poppy's voice jolted me awake. I felt her hand on my shoulder, gently shaking me.

"I'm up," I yawned. "I'm up." I sat up and stretched my arms above my head. Looking out the window, I saw the moon still hung in the sky among a sea of stars. I looked over to Poppy, confused. "What time is it?"

"Early. Get up. I have to get you ready. The king requests your immediate company!"

My eyes widened in shock. "Why now? Can't it wait a few hours until dawn?"

"No! Now, get up!" She let out a huff, as did I.

I got out of bed and allowed Poppy to get me ready. She styled my blonde bob into soft curls and placed me in a light purple knee-length dress. Once I was ready, we quickly made our way to the library. Ezra was already waiting.

"Good morning, Amara," he said with a smile. His voice was way too chipper for this hour. "Since you are so set on exploring, you and I will be taking a little trip today. We must make haste, as we are already late. Come along." Ezra quickly turned on his heels and walked away. Waving goodbye to Poppy, I followed him.

"Are you going to tell me where we are going?" I quickened my pace to keep up with his stride.

"No," he chuckled. Turning toward the wall, he twisted the sconce and the wall slipped open to reveal a hidden path. He ushered me into the secret passage, following close behind. Once we were both in, he closed the entrance. For a while, we walked side by side in a hall with no windows. It took me a while to realize this was not a man-made hallway, but a tunnel carved out of solid stone. I begged him for any information on where we were going, but he refused to give in.

Finally, sunlight could be seen in the distance. As my eyes adjusted to the warm glow, it revealed we now stood on a mountainside cliff. The sun had just risen over the peaks. On the ground sat a red blanket with a basket sitting atop it.

"I thought you would enjoy some fresh air," he said with a smile as warm as the sun.

I walked closer to the edge of the cliff, and my jaw dropped as I took in the view. Nestled in a small gap below ran a creek. White stags with rainbow iridescent antlers drank. I had never seen such a beautiful creature in my entire life. I turned back to Ezra, who was standing next to the basket.

"I baked fruit and cheese danishes. I did not know what kind of fruit you liked, so I made a few different kinds." He sat down next to the basket and laid out its contents.

I sat next to him, looking over the options, and decided on the lemon. I took a bite, and the bright flavor filled my mouth. The pastry was so flakey and light, and the sugar crystals that were baked on top gave it a nice crunch.

"This is divine," I said as I took another bite. "Thank you!"

"You are so welcome." He grabbed an apple danish and took a bite. Once he swallowed, he spoke again. "Since we are now so close to the wedding, I wanted to check on you. How are you feeling?"

I took another bite, thinking about that for a moment. "Honestly, I am alright. I am still very worried about my aunt. She must be worried sick about me, at this point she may presume me to be dead."

"I took care of that," he said plainly.

"What do you mean?" I lowered my pastry.

"I visited her the day I took you and glamoured her memories. She thinks you are delivering herbs to the capital."

"How did you know who she was to do that?" I raised my eyebrow. A pit grew in my stomach.

"I followed your scent."

"My scent? What do I smell like?"

"Honey and lavender," he said without a single thought. "A scent that is sweet and calming. A scent of love and kindness. A scent of sunshine and home."

Heat rose to my cheeks. I stared into Ezra's eyes, truly mesmerized, and too stunned to speak. He offered me a smile that did not reach those gorgeous ice-blue eyes.

"Amara?" He questioned softly, snapping me out of my own head.

"How do you feel about the wedding? Are you excited to send me back to the human realm?"

This was it. This was my moment to get the answers I needed. Did he truly care for me, or was I just a new shiny toy to pass his time?

He turned his head to look over the cliff and released a deep, slow breath. "I can't wait to not have a little human sneaking around my castle and taking up my time."

My heart shattered.

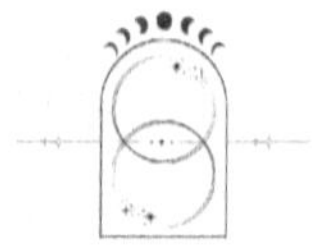

That afternoon, I found myself back in the library. I chose the book Ezra was reading while we were trapped in the office, squirming in my seat as the romance heated up. I heard light footsteps from behind one of the shelves.

"Hello?"

"It's me!" I heard Poppy's cheerful voice.

I shut the book and sat it on my lap. "I am back in the reading nook!" I called out to her.

Her footsteps quickened, and shortly she was by my side and sitting next to me.

"Did you enjoy your breakfast while you watched the sunrise?" She gently bumped me with her shoulder.

"It was lovely. I was happy to get some fresh air." I shrugged. My heart still ached from the rejection I received from Ezra. Part of me hoped he truly cared for me. What a silly little human I was to think that.

"And you agreed to stay with us, right?" Her voice rose in pitch, and she quickly clapped her hands.

My gaze snapped to her and raised my eyebrow. "What did you say?"

"Didn't Ezra ask for you to stay with us after the wedding?" Her excited expression dropped, and concern took over.

"No, he said he could not wait for me to return to the human realm."

Anger took over Poppy's face. "He is such a coward!" She jumped up, grabbed my wrist, and pulled me to follow her. Yanked from my seat, I stumbled before I caught up to her pace.

"Where are we going?"

"To speak with the king!"

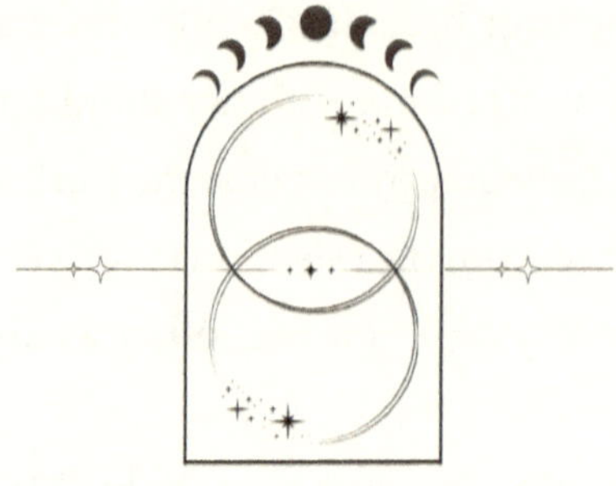

Sixteen

Poppy dragged me through the halls, pulling me into sections of the castle I had never seen. My heart pounded in my chest. I worried about what lurked within the shadows, but then I remembered shadows were his domain.

"Poppy! Stop it! I am not allowed to be in this part of the castle."

She ignored my pleas and continued charging ahead, pulling me behind her. Finally, she released my wrist as she stopped in front of a large black wooden door with golden accents. Poppy yanked the door open and barged in.

Ezra stood in the center of the room in front of his bed with a towel wrapped around his waist. His damp hair fell loose over his shoulders. A look of terror crossed his face. "Excuse me, ladies?"

"Why did you not ask her to stay?" Poppy blurted out, stomping her feet and crossing her arms.

Embarrassment took over Ezra's face. "Poppy," he sighed, "it is complicated. She has a family to return to."

"You didn't even ask her! She may have said yes!" She grabbed a vase that was on a nearby table and threw it at him. He easily stepped away from it, causing it to shatter against the wall behind him.

"Enough!" His voice boomed. "Poppy, leave us."

"Gladly!" She turned and stormed off. Winking at me as she left. The door slammed behind me, causing me to flinch.

Ezra turned toward me, a softness in his eyes. "I apologize for her behavior."

"Were you going to ask me to stay after the wedding?" My voice quivered as I spoke.

"Never mind that." He threw his hands in the air and turned away.

"No! Do not try to change the subject. Answer me!" I demanded.

He turned back toward me, dropping his shoulders in defeat. "Yes, but I understand you would not want to stay here with me."

I stared at him for some time, taking in a deep breath as I collected my thoughts. "I could not leave my aunt behind permanently. Would I be able to visit her? And my best friend?"

His eyes lit up, and a smile crossed his face. "With an escort, yes. As my wife, you would be Queen of Orilon. It would be dangerous for you to travel alone."

"How often?" I raised my eyebrow, stepping closer to him.

"As often as you wish. You are not a prisoner, Amara. You never were." He inhaled sharply, tightening his jaw. Silence hung in the air for a moment. "Will you stay with me? Please, be my true wife. Not just to break the curse, but until the world ends and we are nothing but stardust."

I smirked. "I shall think about it."

"Oh, sunshine, it would be an honor." He smirked back at me.

"Oh, I am sure it would be."

"Just as it is an honor for you to gaze upon me in a towel. Do not think I have not noticed your staring."

Heat rushed to my cheeks. "We are speaking! Where do you want me to look? The ground?"

He closed the gap between us and wrapped his arms around my waist, pressing my body to his. I felt something firm press into my stomach that caused my core to ache with need. "Oh, sunshine, you weren't looking at my face. Ask nicely, and I will show you what you want to see," he teased.

"I... I do not know what you are talking about," I stumbled over my words. I felt as if I could melt in his arms.

A devilish grin spread across his face. "Let me show you." His shadows slivered up from behind me and wrapped around my body. Ezra released me and stepped back. His shadows pulled me to the bed, forced me to sit on the edge, and then held my face, making me look forward.

"Ezra," I breathed.

He dropped his towel, revealing his full length to me. Air caught in my throat from the sight of it. Good gods, I had never seen anything so magnificent.

"If you ask nicely, I will allow you to touch it." His shadows wrapped around me tighter and rubbed against my thighs and breasts.

A soft moan escaped my lips. "Who said I wanted to?" What a lie. I wanted nothing more than for him to tear off my clothes and take me. I could not look away from his fist that slowly pumped his fully erect cock.

Ezra leaned down so we met eye to eye. "I can see it in your eyes, sunshine." He bit his bottom lip, and fire burned in those ice-blue eyes. At this close proximity, his scent drove me wild, nearly distracting me as the shadows slithered up my skirt and teased the fabric between my legs.

I squirmed as shadows played against my most sensitive parts. "Ezra," I moaned.

He cut me off before I could say anything. "The only thing that should come out of your pretty little mouth is 'yes, sir' and moans. Do you understand?"

"Yes, sir." My body tensed as I spoke the words and let Ezra command me.

"Good girl. Now spread your legs and let my shadows explore that beautiful body of yours." His tongue slowly dragged over his top lip as he straightened his back and continued to fist himself, quickening the pace.

I obliged, spreading my legs and leaning back. The shadows pulled off my clothes, exposing me to the King of Orilon. The man I once hated. The man I once feared... before I knew his soul.

My core melted as his shadows wrapped around my bare breasts, squeezing them, and flicking my nipples. Another of his shadow tendrils found its way back between my thighs and gently lapped at my delicate skin. It then slowly slipped inside me, causing me to arch my back.

"Please," I begged.

The shadow pumped faster inside of me. Ezra arched a brow, and the tendril pulled out of my aching pussy. "I didn't remember telling you that was one of the things you could say." The shadow whipped against my clit, causing me to release a yelp. Pressure and heat built within my core as the tendril slapped against me once again. "Please what?" His voice was deep and sensual. It alone could cause me to come undone.

"I need more," I pleaded.

"I will tell you what you need. Now not another word."

"Yes, sir." I bit my bottom lip, as I submitted to the king.

The shadow forced its way back inside me, opening me up. The ones around my breasts flicked harder. My attention could not pull away from Ezra's cock. The sight of him was everything. I found myself so close to the edge as pleasure built inside me.

"Don't you dare cum until I tell you to," he snarled.

"Yes, sir." I held it in, allowing the ecstasy of it to take over my body. I couldn't allow myself release. Not until he gave me permission, which only added to the thrill.

"You are such a good girl for me. Use your words. Tell me what you want."

"I need your cock inside me. I need to cum. Please," I moaned. My body was so close to exploding. The shadows recoiled, leaving me feeling empty.

"Get on your knees. Open your mouth," he demanded.

Again, I obliged, quickly getting onto the floor. My knees rested on the black and gold rug as I stuck out my tongue for him. He stepped closer and smirked down at me as he rested his tip on my tongue. I slowly licked and teased it. My hand gently massaged his balls as I dragged my tongue from base to tip.

Ezra let out a groan, ran his fingers through my hair, and gripped it to hold me in place. Taking his tip into my mouth, I gently sucked, swirling my tongue against his sensitive head. Looking up at him, I carefully watched his expression. Ezra tilted his head back in pleasure as he bucked into my mouth.

His shadows found their way in between my legs once again and quickly thrust into my dripping slit. I moaned against him as I took him deeper down my throat.

In opposite rhythms, Ezra's cock and shadow thrust in and out of me, and I quickly found myself at the edge of pleasure once again. His pace quickened as he hit the back of my throat, and my saliva dripped down his balls.

He pushed forward, holding himself deep down my throat, and my nose pressed against his bare skin. I could barely hold in my pleasure. It would not be much longer before I lost control and disobeyed him.

"Cum for me, sunshine," he groaned.

My eyes rolled back in my head as, for the first time in my life, I experienced true bliss. I let out a moan around him, causing him to twitch in the back of my throat. My entire body quivered, and I craved more of him. I bobbed my mouth from base to tip as our eyes stayed locked on each other.

His shadow left me once again, leaving a puddle dripping out of me. He then slowly pulled himself from my mouth, reached down, and pulled me to my feet. Spinning me around, he grabbed me by my hair and pushed me down on the bed, my legs hanging off.

"You thought my shadow felt good?" He leaned down and whispered in my ear. "Just wait until you feel the real thing." In a swift motion, Ezra plunged his cock into me. The shadows were nothing compared to the real thing. He showed me no mercy as he made me his. He pulled on my hair, causing my back to arch.

I gripped the sheets and screamed in pleasure, begging him not to stop.

He was right. This was nothing like I had ever felt. The immense pleasure sent me over the edge once again, without permission. I clenched around him as I found my release.

Ezra let out a growl. "Fuck, you're going to pay for that," he groaned, as he pulled my hair tighter. "Tell me what you just did."

"I came," I squealed.

"For who?" He thrust in hard.

"You!"

"Only for me?" He pulled out almost all the way.

"Only for you!"

He pounded into me harder. I ached as he thrusted, and I screamed his name.

"That's right, Amara. You are mine." Heat filled me as he spilled into me. He did not slow his pace but instead pushed his release deeper. I moaned and begged for him not to stop. He continued to fuck me until I found my release once again.

Only then did he finally pull out of me and spin me around. A hunger still filled his eyes as I looked up at him, breathless.

"Are you ready for round two?" A predatory grin crossed his face.

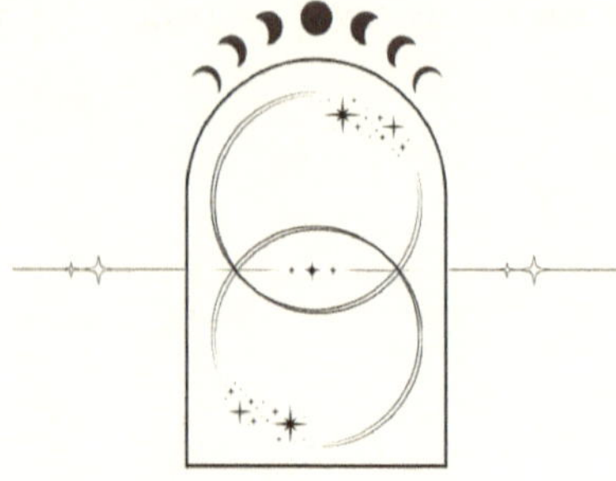

Seventeen

The soft sound of birdsong awoke me from the best sleep I had ever had. Sitting up, I gave a small yawn, stretching out in front of me. I spent the entire night in Ezra's bed, though we did not fall asleep until the moon was past its peak. Last night was more perfect than I could ever imagine. Never did I expect my first time to be like that. Before I met Ezra, I did not think there would be a first time for me.

I was always so content being alone. Living my life as the town herbalist, and taking one of my friends' children under my wing to continue the craft. Once my eyes locked on Ezra, everything changed, even if I hated to admit it. He was every-thing in a man I had been looking for.

Jade would be so happy I found a man across the mountains who brought me this much joy and pleasure.

I looked over and saw the glass door to the balcony open. The sun was shining directly on Ezra, just another sign from the heavens that he and I were meant as one. His dark black robe was wrapped around him as he sipped his mug of coffee.

Slipping out of bed, still nude, I slipped on the ivory silk robe that had been laid out for me and tied it shut. The plush rug was so soft against my bare feet as I exited the room and joined Ezra on the balcony. Nipping at my nose, the cool morning air blew against my face.

"Good morning, sunshine," Ezra said before I could speak. "Would you like a cup of coffee?"

"Good morning. Yes, please! That sounds delightful." Sitting in the chair across the table from him, I watched as he poured my cup. A small tray sat on the glass table with cream and cubes of sugar. Once he handed me my mug, I added more sugar and cream than was good for one person.

"I am glad I asked for it," Ezra chuckled. "I drink my coffee black."

"That is a terrible way to live!" I smiled as I took my sip. The hot sweetness rushed down my throat and warmed my core.

"I quite enjoy the strong and bitter taste."

Sitting back in my seat, I pressed my mug against my cheek, and shut my eyes.

"You look truly beautiful," Ezra said softly.

"Thank you." I smiled. Even though the events that led me to be here with him were not ideal, I could not be happier with the way everything was turning out.

There was another moment of silence before Ezra spoke again. "Was it ok? Did I hurt you?"

My eyes jolted open, and I turned toward him. "It was amazing!"

"Good, good." His gaze fell to his mug. "I did not want to disappoint."

"Disappoint?"

"I am a disappointment to my entire kingdom. I would not be surprised if I was a disappointment to you, too."

I leaned over and placed my hand atop his that held the handle of his mug. His gaze lifted to meet mine. "You are not a disappointment. You will save your kingdom. I promise you that."

"Thank you, Amara," he choked on his words. Ezra cleared his throat and straightened his back. "I will be away for a few days. Final preparations need to be made for the wedding. The seamstress is coming to meet with you today to design your dress. Have her create whatever your heart desires. Poppy will take you to meet with her."

"How are you going to give me the best night of my life and then leave me?"

"It will just make you crave me more." Ezra stood and walked over to me, leaning down and kissing my forehead gently. "I will be back soon. I will make up for all the pleasure lost as soon as I return."

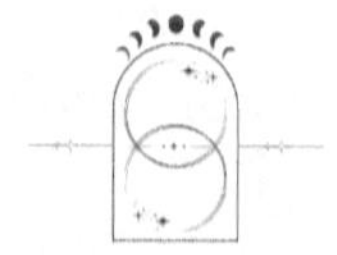

That afternoon, Poppy took me into a new section of the castle. She led me into a room with a small circular stage in the center of the room. The stage was about one foot high and solid black stone. Next to it, there were racks and racks of different fabrics, corsets, and embellishments. A large window was on the far wall, filling the room with natural light.

"Good afternoon." A short woman with long and straight dark hair approached me. She wore a beautiful purple dress. Around her waist was a belt that dangled all sorts of tools of a seamstress. Her teal eyes were filled with joy as she took my hand. "What a joyous time!"

"Yes, I am very excited! I have never had a custom dress made!" I gleamed as the seamstress helped me step onto the stage.

Poppy walked over to the racks and looked at the different lace fabrics. "Wow, I don't know how you are going to pick!"

"Yes, you're getting married to the king. You must look your best. What kind of idea of a dress are you looking for?"

"I would love a big, beautiful ballroom-style dress. I want to look and feel like a princess!" To be honest, I had never thought about the type of dress I would wear, since I never believed this was going to happen to me. But now it was happening, I wanted to go all out for the big day. I had seen many weddings back home, and the ballroom-style dresses were always my favorite.

The seamstress slowly circled me, her eyes scanning me. "That could work. But, remember dear. You are no princess. You will be a queen. Let me help you down so you can change into a slip, and we can get to work."

She assisted me down and took me over to a changing screen. Slipping out of my olive-green dress, I put on the ivory slip. I got back onto the stage and the seamstress pulled out different corsets and fabrics. Before I finalized, we went through twelve corsets and way too many lace patterns. I decided on a tulle with flowers embroidered throughout it.

Poppy gave her opinions on everything, she wanted me to have exactly what I wanted. The seamstress was so kind and helpful. She really helped me envision the dress, and I could not wait to see the final product.

"I have never met the king. What is he like?" The seamstress asked as she sketched out the final design.

"He is very kind." I offered her a small grin.

"That is good to hear!" She smiled and continued her sketches.

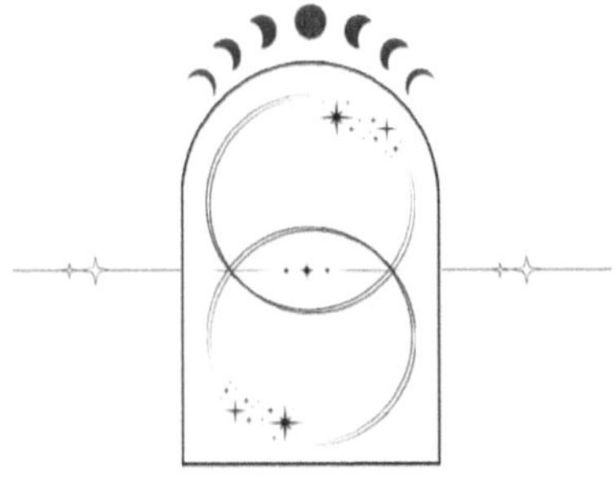

Eighteen

Days passed quickly as Poppy and I were busy finalizing things for the wedding. Every day was filled with meetings with the seamstress for fittings, picking floral arrangements, selecting a cake, and finalizing a dinner menu. I was surprised to hear this would be a large event. With very little fae left, I expected it just to be the priestess, Ezra, and myself.

Ezra told me the other realms turned their backs on Orilon when he first showed me the library. Now, with the wedding, they would all show up. Was it in support, or to see if Orilon was for the taking if the last king fell victim to the curse?

I was very interested in learning about the other fae realms. My whole life I had been told there was only one portal, but now I knew there were five more were hidden throughout Elswyth. Poppy did not know much about the other realms, but Gil had several books on the subject and was happy to hand them over.

Aeros sounded very interesting. It was a group of floating islands, high in the sky. Even though the fae of this realm were winged, little was known about the world below the islands. Legend claimed that the floating islands were once a part of the land below, but when calamity hit, the King of Aeros raised the capital city and surrounding lands to save them from disaster.

I found myself daydreaming about the realms as the seamstress finalized the dress. Only a few more tiny alterations to the straps needed to be made.

"I cannot believe how gorgeous this dress is!" Poppy squealed in delight.

My gaze snapped over to the mirror. She was right. The dress was perfect. The bodice had a sweetheart neckline and beautiful beading, making it sparkle. The bottom of the dress was a full skirt with beautiful floral lace. My eyes teared up from happiness. This was everything I imagined and more.

"You made this so quickly!" I looked over at the seamstress and smiled.

"I am the best seamstress of all the realms. This is what I do," she said nonchalantly as she organized her pins.

"I really do love it!" I did a little twirl, watching myself in the mirror.

"Thank you!" Her gaze raised to meet mine. "Are you nervous about marrying the king? Was this an arranged marriage? You seem like such an odd pair."

"It is a complicated situation..." My voice trailed off.

"Oh?" she pried as she knelt to pin the hem just a little higher.

"Well... the marriage was not exactly my first choice, but I am glad to have met him. I can't wait to see what unfolds." I gave

Poppy a nervous glance. She sat just a few feet from the small stage on a stool, her eyes locked on the seamstress.

"You seem a bit apprehensive." The seamstress looked up at me with an inquisitive look. She stood and walked over to a small cart, and looked through a tiny box she brought with her.

It felt odd she was asking so many questions. I knew a lot of nosey women in my life. Growing up in a small village, I was way too familiar with women collecting all sorts of gossip.

"I was at first, but not so much anymore."

"How interesting." The seamstress walked back over to me and continued to work on my dress.

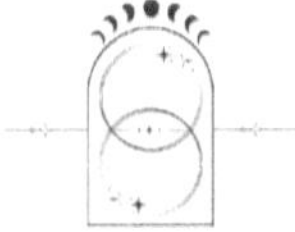

After the fitting wrapped up, I finally was able to get a moment of relaxation. Once again, I found myself in the library, curled up in my nook with a romance novel, shutting out the world around me. Just as I was fully enthralled by the book, shadows filled my peripheral vision.

"Did you miss me?" I heard his deep, velvet voice purr in my ear. A shiver sent down my spine as his shadows found their way under my dress once again.

As I closed the book, I quickly sat up. Ezra stood a few feet away, leaning against a bookshelf with his arms crossed and a predatory grin on his face.

Gods, how I missed those angular features. The moon on his third eye looked darker than it ever had as if it was the void itself. The shadows found their way under the thin fabric that was my only protection from them and teased the small bundle of nerves.

"Ezra, stop that! What if someone comes in here?" I let out a moan as the shadow slowly pushed its way inside me. Gods, it felt amazing, but it only made me crave the feeling of his cock.

Ezra walked over, stopping right before me. "Then they will see their king pleasuring his queen. I made you a promise before I left, and I plan to keep it." A low growl escaped his lips. The shadow's pace quickened, and my wetness grew. "Get on your knees."

I quickly did as I was told. Ezra released himself from his pants and gave it two strokes. A small bead of liquid pooled at the tip. Without hesitation, I slowly dragged my tongue against it to lick it away.

"Such an eager one you are," he purred.

"I won't lie. I missed your cock."

He knelt before me so that our eyes met. "And I missed that pretty little cunt of yours. Will you give me the honor of getting on your hands and knees, lifting your dress, and show me how you get fucked by my shadow?"

I spun around and did as I was told. I lifted my dress, and his hands gently removed my panties, leaving them around my knees. The shadow pounded into me harder. I let out a squeal as I found my pleasure.

"Oh, you are such a bad girl. You didn't ask permission." His shadow slowly pulled out of me.

"No, please don't stop!" I begged.

"Don't stop, what?" He spoke in a playful tone.

"Don't stop fucking me, please!"

It was silent for just a moment, then he thrust himself deep into me. His hands tightly gripped my hips, pulling me back onto his cock. My eyes rolled into the back of my head as I fully came undone around him. Gods, I loved how he made me feel.

Releasing my hips, one of his hands found its way in between my shoulder blades, pushing me down to the floor, pinning me in place as he fucked me. I screamed his name, begging for him never to stop.

He let out a groan as he pressed in firmly and held it. His cock twitched as he released himself inside me. I throbbed against him, craving all of him.

"I never expected to find such pleasure in my human queen," he groaned as he pulled out of me. In a blink, he was in front of me, sitting in the reading nook, his cock still erect. He slowly raised his hand, palm up, and called to me with two fingers. I crawled to him, kneeling in between his legs.

Without a word, I slowly dragged my tongue from base to tip. My gaze locked on his ice-blue eyes. He let out a groan and tilted his head back as I swirled around the tip. Ezra's hand found its way to my hair and laced his fingers through my golden curls, keeping me in place.

I wrapped my lips around his head and gently sucked as my hand lifted and stroked his length.

"Oh, fuck," he groaned, as he pushed my head down and forced me to take more of him into my mouth. He continued to push until I felt him hit the back of my throat, causing me to gag. He then pulled me back up by my hair, until my lips sat at the tip before forcing me down again. "Play with your pretty cunt while I fuck your throat," he demanded.

I found myself lifting my skirt and sliding my hand in between my thighs as I gagged and drooled on him. My fingers delicately teased the soaked entrance. Drool dripped down Ezra's balls as he continued to pound my throat.

Slipping my fingers inside, I quickly forced them in and out of me. Gods, I craved his cock inside my pussy once again. I knew I would never experience such pleasure by my own hand. Ezra held my head down and he released in the back of my throat. He did not pull away until I swallowed every last drop.

"Ezra," I moaned as I looked up at him.

"Amara, you are so perfect. I am so glad you have come into my life. Here, let me help you up." He put himself away and assisted me up off the floor. "Let's get you cleaned up, and then have a nice dinner on the balcony. How does that sound?"

"Amazing," I said with a smile.

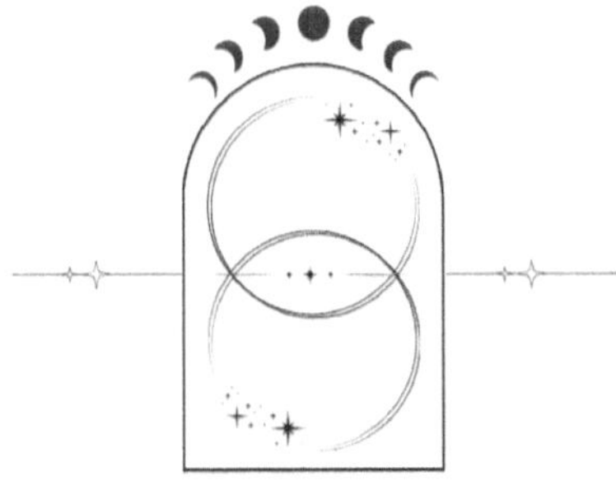

Nineteen

The day of the wedding came faster than I expected. I did not get a single moment of sleep the night before. It seemed so wrong to be wed without my aunt and Jade by my side. I was not ready for my new home to be filled with fae I did not know.

Before the guests arrived, I stayed in my room, hiding away. I accidentally ran into one of the first to arrive in the library yesterday morning. He was a tall, slender, older man, with cruelty in his eyes. I quickly ran away from him before he could speak.

Poppy told me he was the new King of Irolyth, just crowned a year ago. He had accused his brother of treason and had the entire royal family executed. The Princess had gone missing during the siege on the castle. Still to this day, she has not been found.

Poppy said it had been a very messy affair, and she was worried for one of her sisters who had moved there decades ago to live in The Glade, a religious sanctuary. She had not heard from her in years.

The next morning, Poppy had awoken me very early and took me to the suite where I was to prepare for the wedding. So many people filled the halls, and all eyes were on me as we passed them. They never spoke a word to me, nor I to them. I could not help but wonder why they were all in the halls, instead of in their rooms or the dining hall for breakfast.

Anxiety crept in. My skin crawled, and I vigorously scratched at my arms. This was all becoming too real, too fast.

Poppy quickly spun to me and swatted at my hand. Quickly, she pulled us into an empty room and shut the door behind us. "Stop that! Do not dare damage that beautiful skin of yours on your big day! Most of these fae are from other kingdoms. You will not see them after today. Take a deep breath. Imagine they are all in their underwear!"

"Their underwear?!"

"Nudity is the greatest equalizer." She placed her hand on the door handle. "Now take a deep breath, follow me, and remember this will all be over soon and you can spend the rest of your days in marital bliss." She stared at me for a long while as I took in deep breaths to calm myself.

Once I was calm, she opened the door and exited the room. I followed behind her. This time, I ignored all of the strange faces that stared at me.

"We are almost there," she said as she continued to guide me, her auburn hair flowing. We entered the suite, and it was beautiful. Two white couches sat on either side of a glass coffee table. On the table were bright color flower arrangements.

Golden sconces were on the walls and provided the windowless room with light. My dress was hung on a hook on the wall. I still could not believe how perfect it was. Crystals had been added to the skirt to cause it to sparkle. Two other girls who looked nearly identical to Poppy jumped from their seats.

"Amara, these are my sisters. Lily and Rose." She gestured to each of them as she introduced them. "The three of us will be getting you ready for your big day."

"I meant to ask you about that. I did not know you had any sisters."

"There are seven of us in total," Lily said with the same sense of joy her sister had.

"Daisy, Violet, and Iris could not make it. They are busy in their realms," Rose said, a bit more sass in her voice. "No one has heard from Cassia in about a year. We want to go check on her, but the gates to Irolyth have all closed."

"Gates? I thought each realm only had one gate?" I asked.

"Elswyth only has one gate to each realm. Within the fae realms, there are multiple gates to get to where we need to go," Lily answered.

"Never mind all that. Today is Amara's special day. Rose, please get started on our blushing bride's makeup!" Poppy snapped.

"Just because you think you're the oldest, it doesn't mean you get to be bossy," Rose retorted.

"But I am the oldest!" Poppy responded.

"By three minutes," Lily giggled.

"Come with me. I will make you look flawless," Rose said as she guided me over to a seat, shaking her head at her sisters. All kinds of makeup was laid out on the table in front of me. "This is what I am best at. Just let me work my magic, and you will be even more stunning than you already are!"

I believed her. While Lily and Poppy were beautiful, Rose was flawless.

While Rose worked on my makeup, Lily came and did my hair into loose curls. She wove in a flower crown with delicate pink and white flowers. When the two of them were done, I looked absolutely divine. Once ready the three of them helped me into my dress. When I finally looked at myself in the mirror, My breath was stolen away. Never had I seen myself so beautiful.

"Amara," the three of them gasped in unison. "You are so beautiful."

I couldn't help but start to tear up at the view of myself in the mirror.

"No! None of that!" Rose rushed to me and blotted my eyes. "You will ruin your makeup!" She pulled away the handkerchief and the golden dust that was on my eyes now stained it. She sighed, "come with me." She took me back to the makeup and touched up what had been smudged.

"Why are you crying?" Lily questioned.

"I just wish my aunt and best friend were here. This feels so wrong without them!"

"I am so sorry," they all cooed in unison.

"You will see them again soon," Poppy promised, putting her hand on my shoulder in comfort. I was thankful to have Poppy here with me. She had become such a good friend, but my heart still ached for my family in Pendril.

As Rose put on the finishing touches, a servant came into the suite. "The king is ready."

Lily and Rose both hugged me. "It was so lovely to meet you. I hope to see you again soon." They spoke in unison once again.

"Likewise," I said as Poppy rushed me out of the suite.

Poppy guided me to the courtyard where the ceremony was to be held. My stomach tightened as I saw the rows of people sitting and waiting for me. To my surprise, the end of the aisle was empty. No Ezra or priestess in sight.

"There is one place I need to take you before the ceremony starts," Poppy said in a hushed tone. She guided me to a nearby study, where Ezra was pacing back and forth. There was a desk, which was covered with papers, and a shelf full of old books. Only half the sconces were lit, giving the room dim lighting. This was not where I expected to see Ezra just before our wedding. I did not think he could look any more handsome than he already did, but he proved me wrong. His long white hair was in a neat top knot. His suit matched the color of his wings, pure black with golden embellishments.

What shocked me was the human woman in purple robes. She had the seamstress's face. How was this possible? The seamstress was fae, but the woman now standing in front of me was wingless and with rounded ears. She gave me a warm smile.

"Ah, so you truly did not know who I was. Good, I was worried your answers were based on your knowledge of my intentions."

"What do you mean?" I questioned.

Ezra stopped pacing and snapped his gaze toward me. "You already spoke to Amara? How dare you!" His face contorted with rage.

"Hush boy," she snapped. "Yes, I did not want your influence on her. I wanted to see how she truly felt about you."

"And what did she say?!" He looked down at her nervously.

"Don't talk about me like I am not here! Can someone explain to me what is going on?" I shouted at them.

Ezra's gaze lowered. "I am sorry." He spoke in a quiet tone as he walked over to my side, taking my hands into his.

The woman glared at us. "My true name is Elara Mazzeo. I am the one who enacted the curse all those centuries ago."

My jaw fell slack. She looked to be in her early forties. I could not imagine her being centuries old.

"I apologize for deceiving you," she continued. "I needed to test your true feelings for the king. While Ezra is truly different from the kings who came before him, I still had to see if a woman with a stone heart who hated the fae could love a fae king."

My body tensed, and Ezra wrapped his arm around me, holding me close.

"Luckily for him, you truly do care. I will end the curse, under one condition." A dubious grin crossed her face.

"Enough of your conditions, witch! We have already met your original terms. End this, now!"

She took a step closer. Everything in my body screamed at me to run. I could sense the overwhelming power she had. Feeling it now, I do not know how I did not before.

"Seeing I am the game master and you are my pawns, you do not have a choice."

Ezra's shadows surrounded us, and my nerves eased. There was something about him that gave me an overwhelming sense of protection.

She circled us for a moment, looking at us up and down. Stopping in front of us, she placed her hand on her chin, rubbing it as she continued to stare us down. "I will end the curse if you agree to never see each other ever again." Her voice was cold.

The calmness Ezra provided was now gone. That feeling was now taken over by a stabbing feeling in my chest. He held me tighter to him. Tears welled in my eyes at her words.

"No!" We both cried out.

"No? Do you want your people to continue to turn into monsters? Would you choose a human woman you just met over your people?"

"Please," Ezra begged. His voice shook as he spoke. "Do not make me choose. I want to save my people, but I can't imagine a world without Amara. For centuries, I lived in the dark, content with lurking in the shadows. Now that I have seen the sun, and felt its warmth on my skin, I cannot return to the darkness."

Elara rolled her eyes and then her dark gaze fell on me. "How do you feel about that?"

"I don't want to leave him. Ezra has shown me a world I did not know I needed. For my entire life, I expected to be alone. Now, I could not imagine my life without him. I love him!"

Ezra smiled down at me, and gently ran the back of his fingers across my cheek. "I love you, too," he said softly.

"You have proven me wrong. I never believed humans and fae could fall in love. So, I bound the two of you together. A human who feared the fae and a fae who hated humans. But, here you are. Truly in love with one another." Elara smirked and purple energy surrounded her. She raised her arms, palms up. The ground quaked. "From this day forth, the curse is over. All fae lost to the vox shall return. May King Ezra and Queen Amara live long and prosper!"

She chanted in a language I did not recognize. The earth quaked harder. In an explosion of purple energy, she vanished, and the earth calmed.

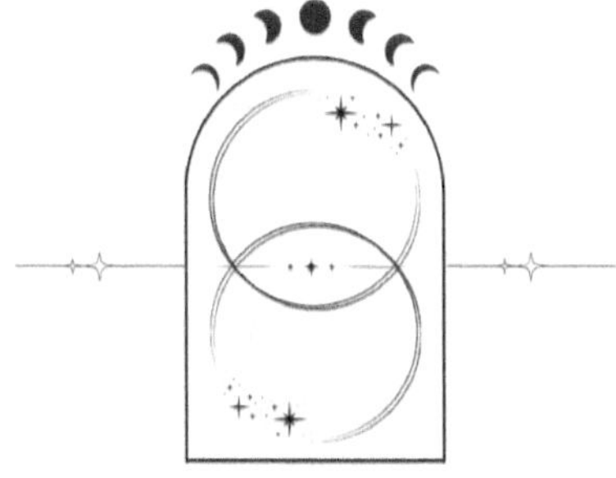

Twenty

Chaos erupted from outside the study. Ezra rushed to the door, telling Poppy and I to stay back. He yanked the door open, and the hall was full of people, running and screaming. Ezra rushed into the hallway and the crowd.

Poppy and I looked at each other. Her brow furrowed with worry. Without speaking, the two of us knew exactly what we needed to do. We both quickly rushed out of the room and into the hallway.

People were hugging and sobbing. Gil held a small woman with golden skin, hair as black as night, and wings of pure white.

"Mother above," Poppy whispered. "That is Gil's wife. She was turned into a vox many years ago. How..." she trailed off, unable to finish her question. It seemed that all fae who were transformed into vox, now somehow magically appeared in the castle.

Looking around, I saw so many reunions happening around us. Mothers who lost their children. Husbands and wives who lost each other. Fae from the other realms stood in shock as they watched the chaos unfold.

Poppy and I weaved through the crowd to try to find Ezra. I called out for him, but I was drowned out by the voices that filled the hall.

When we finally found him, a woman with white hair was sobbing into his chest. I could hear her screams and sobs over the commotion. "My baby boy! You did it!" She pulled her face away from his chest, and my heart skipped a beat as I looked at the most beautiful woman I had ever seen. She had similar angular features Ezra did, and even had the same two braids with tiny golden hoops woven in that framed her face. Her metallic silver wings were tucked neatly behind her.

A man approached them, shadows clung to him, and I swore his hair was created by those shadows. Even Ezra's shadows seemed to gravitate toward the man. His ice-blue eyes met mine, and a chill went down my spine when I saw a moon on his third eye, identical to Ezra's. The woman turned and saw the man step out of the crowd. She released Ezra and rushed to him. They held each other in a tight embrace.

His wings wrapped around them, isolating them from the chaos. His wings were as black as the void, with golden flecks throughout, they too were identical to Ezra's. I swore there were larger flecks that almost matched the tapestry from the dining room.

"Momma? Daddy?" A young girl's voice shrieked. She rushed out of the crowd. Her long dark curls flowed in the space behind her as she ran toward the man and woman. She had the same emerald eyes and metallic wings as the woman.

"Olivia," Ezra spoke in a broken tone as his gaze snapped to her, and he rushed to her, fell to his knees, and wrapped her in his arms.

"Big brother," she sobbed back, hugging him tightly.

The man and woman, who I now understood to be Ezra's parents, released each other and turned toward their children. His father's gaze fell on Poppy and me, and Poppy immediately fell to her knees and bowed her head.

"Rise," his voice was deep and smooth, just like Ezra's. "Today is a day of reconnecting and celebration. No need for formalities."

Ezra stood and walked over to me, wrapping his arm around me. "Mother, father. Let me introduce you to Amara, the human who saved us all."

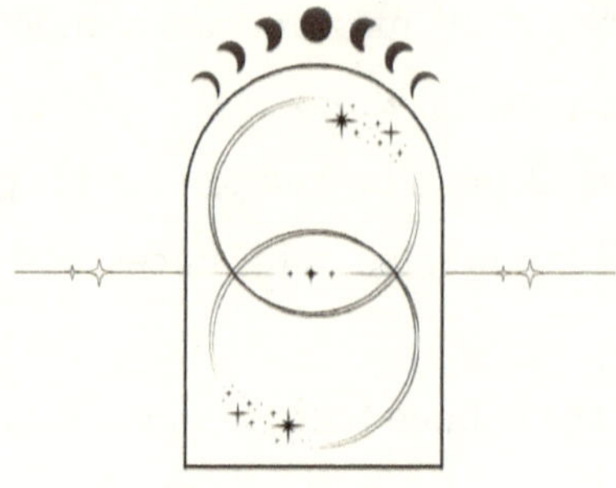

Twenty-One

"Amara!" Glenda shrieked as I stepped into the apothecary. She ran over to me and embraced me tightly. "You returned from the capital!" I held her back, trying to hold in my tears. My body quivered. I truly believed I was never going to see her again. "And who is this handsome gentleman you brought with you?" She released me and looked up at Ezra.

He had glamoured himself to look human. I was not used to his rounded ears or his lack of wings. I looked up at him and smiled, then back to Glenda. "I would like to introduce you to Ezra. I met him during my travels."

"It is great to meet you. I have heard so many good things," Ezra said softly.

Glenda rushed to the door, flipped the sign to 'closed,' and locked the door. "It is very lovely to meet you," she giggled. "Amara has never brought home a man, let alone someone so handsome. Please let's go upstairs and chat over tea! I want to hear everything about your journey!" She skipped across the room and up the stairs into the main house.

I looked up at Ezra and whispered, "I told you she would be like this."

"I think it's charming," he whispered back.

We followed her up the stairs, where she had on a kettle and taken down three mugs from the cabinet. "I hope you enjoy tea!" Glenda said as she prepared the botanicals.

"Indeed, I do." He responded as we sat down at the kitchen table. I watched him nervously and wondered what he thought of our small, modest home. "Glenda, I actually came to ask you something very important."

"Oh?" She rushed over to the table with worry in her eyes.

"Would you allow me the honor of courting Amara?" He asked in a nervous tone.

"Court? Oh my, you are truly an old-fashioned gentleman! Amara, where did you find such a catch?" She looked over to Ezra, a wide smile on her face. "I think I may like you!"

"Thank you, Glenda. I am glad to hear I made a good first impression." He chuckled nervously and shot me a grin.

"Oh, gods," I sighed. "Enough of that! Do not let his ego grow any bigger!" A laugh escaped my lips.

The kettle whistled and Glenda finished making the tea. "Amara, I already put three sugar cubes in yours. Ezra, would you like some?"

"No thank you. I enjoy the true taste of the herbs."

"Gods, you're perfect," she chuckled in response and brought us our mugs. "Jade is going to be so happy you are home! She has been here every day asking if you have returned."

"And I can't wait to see her. I have many books I need her to read. I found so many new ones during my journey!"

"Ah yes! Tell me, how was the trip? How was the capital?"

I told her the story Ezra and I practiced for the past two days. How the journey was easy, how I met Ezra in the town of Magla, and he offered to escort me to the capital and back. We informed my aunt that our client in the capital had already placed a new order with us, and would need it quickly, so I could not stay long.

Before we arrived, we talked about how we would handle telling everything to Glenda. I understood telling her I was in love with a fae king probably would not go over well.

The plan was to first make her love him just as much as I, then slowly introduce her to the truth of who he is and where I actually went while I was gone.

For now, he would glamour her into thinking I traveled to the capital often to trade herbs, salves, and other goods from our apothecary. Ezra would continue to provide me with gold to make it seem real, and to ensure my aunt would not struggle in my absence.

"I will miss you so much. Promise me you will stay safe on your travels?" Glenda's eyes misted.

"I promise. I will only be gone for a few weeks. I will be very safe."

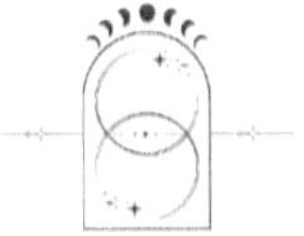

"Amara, I want to thank you officially for saving our kingdom," Julian, Ezra's father, raised his glass in a toast.

Ezra's mother, Lilianna, raised her glass as well. "Yes, and we also want to thank you for saving our son."

For the first time, the royal family all gathered for dinner after their return. Ezra still sat at the head of the table, and his father sat directly across from him, in the seat I once took. I now sat to Ezra's right. It felt so right being by his side.

"I am the King of Orilon. I do not need to be taken care of," Ezra sneered, sipping his wine.

"Big brother, you *definitely* need to be taken care of!" Princess Olivia threw her head back and laughed. She truly was such a sweet young girl. My heart broke at how young she was. When the curse claimed her, she was just a teenager.

"I am glad we were able to break the curse. I am excited to explore Orilon now that all the fae are free from their cursed forms, and it is safe again."

"It is not fully safe yet. Not until we find Elara. We won't let her get away with what she has done," Ezra snarled.

"I will be leading the hunt. You will stay here, reign over Orilon, and restore it to its former glory."

"Yes, father." Ezra nodded toward his father.

"I can't wait to get to know you better, Amara! Ezra has not stopped speaking of you since our return!" Liliana smiled at me. She had a genuine sense of kindness radiating from her.

"What is the plan now the curse is broken? Now that you don't have to be married," Olivia asked.

Ezra cleared his throat. "I am going to start from the beginning with Amara. We did not have the best start to our relationship." His gaze turned toward me. "I know I already asked your aunt, but I never asked you. Will you allow me to court you?"

Heat rose to my cheeks. "Yes!" I answered without hesitation.

"Wonderful!" He leaned in and brushed his lips against mine. Too quickly, he pulled away. "I can't wait to see where this road leads us."

"Cheers to that!" His mother raised her glass once again.

"Cheers!" The rest of us said in unison as we raised our glasses.

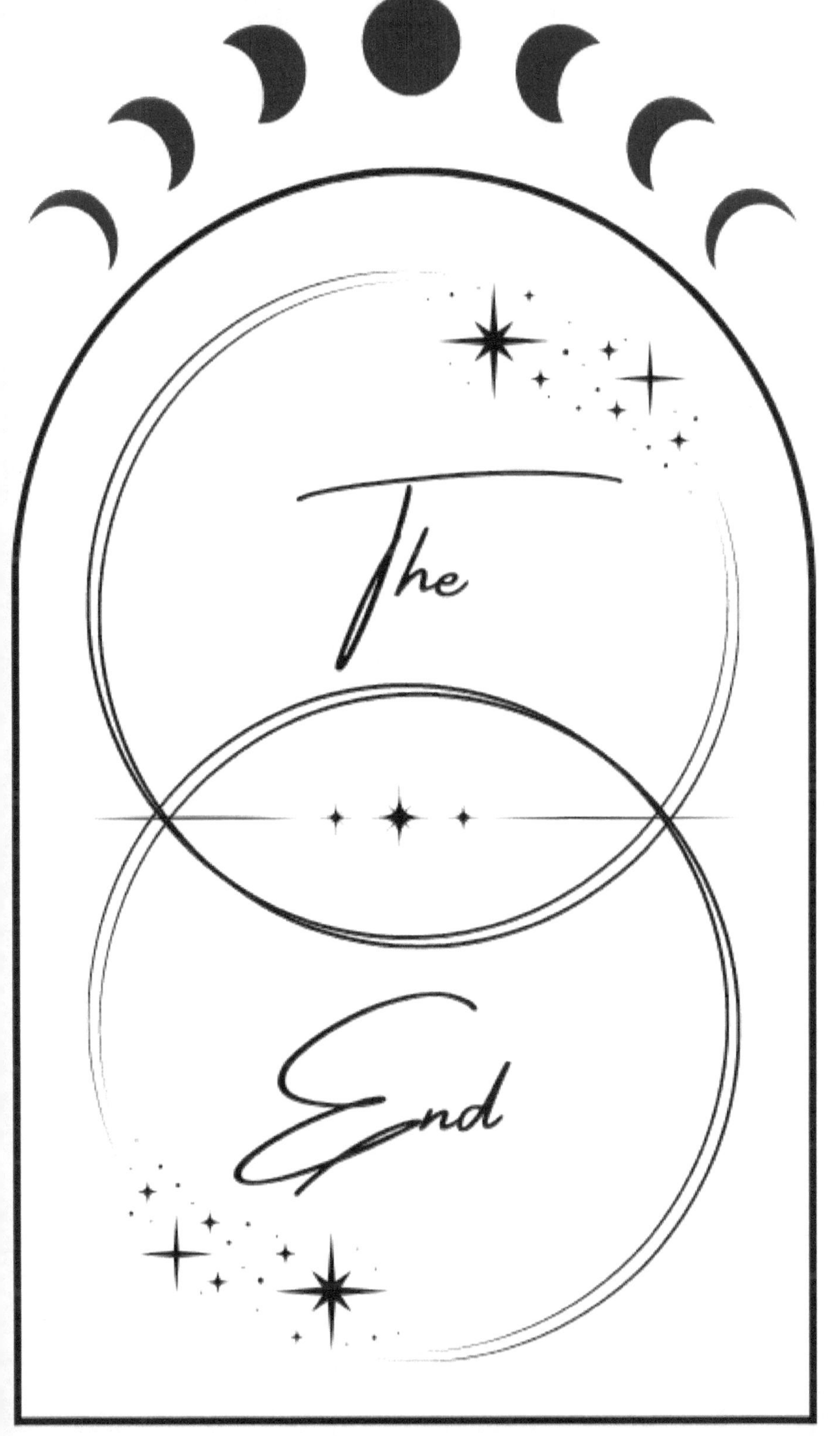
The
End

THE
ASSASSIN
OF
IROLYTH
A REALMS OF ELSWYTH STANDALONE
WILLOW ASTERIA

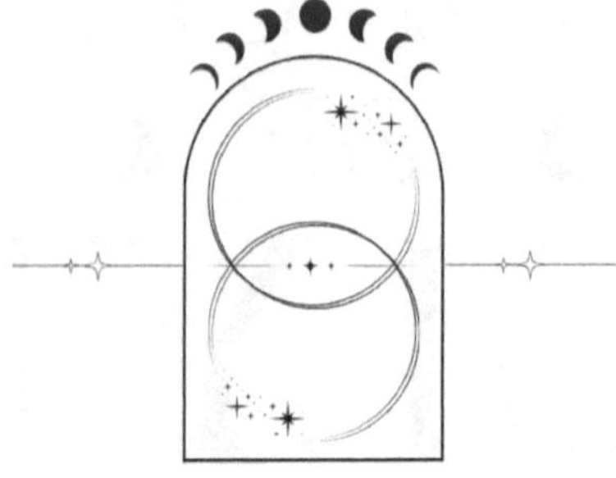

Content Warning

Please be advised that this book may not be suitable for all audiences.

This book contains sexual content, execution by hanging, death, blood, loss of a family member, graphic violence, and other topics some readers may not find suitable.

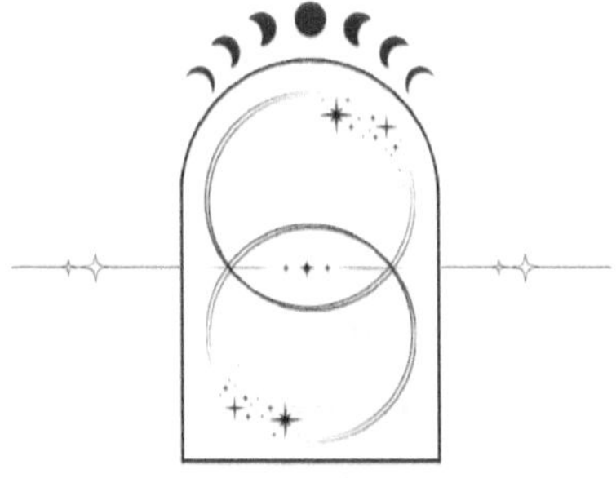

One

I pressed my back to the wall, hoping the guards in the attached corridor wouldn't see me as they rushed past. Ringing filled my ears, and my heart pounded in my chest. Lucky for me, they continued down the hall, with not a clue I was so close by. Once they were out of view, I rushed into the secret passage that left the castle.

I had to escape. If they found me, it would mean my end. There was not a single second I could afford to waste. My feet ached as I ran through the stone passageway.

After what seemed like an eternity, I found the trap door exit. Climbing the ladder, I opened the hatch and climbed out. The bright midday sun caused my eyes to squint. Now, I stood in front of the castle, just outside of the pale stone wall. Just in front of the gates, a stage had been set. The royal family hung from the gallows for the realm to see. Blood dripped from the queen's back onto the ground below her. Her orange and white wings had been ripped from her and tossed on the ground below.

I could not stop to pay my respects. I could not stop to say my goodbyes. I could not stop and let the weight of the world crush me.

Wrapping my tan cloak tighter around me, I pulled on my hood concealing my auburn locks, and disappeared into the woods just outside the wall that surrounded the castle. To my surprise, the new king already had guards searching the forest. I figured he would have focused all of his attention inside of the castle. Their angry voices echoed through the trees, but no matter where I looked, I could not tell where they were coming from.

"Any sign of the princess?" One of them called out.

"She's just a girl. There's no way she was included in this treason," another said.

My body tensed as I crouched behind a thick bush. Sending a prayer up to The Mother, I hoped they would not find me. Peeking through the leaves, I saw the two men as they argued.

"Are you saying King Joffrey is lying?" His voice was filled with venom.

"I just don't know how a sixteen-year-old girl could be a part of something so sinister."

"She has the royal flames like the rest of them. None of them can be trusted!"

They were too focused on each other to notice me. Quietly, I continued to move through the forest, hoping to get away from them.

"King Joffrey is Klaus' brother. How do we know he doesn't have the flames as well?"

I tucked behind a large redwood tree, listening to the two men argue, holding my breath when they mentioned King Klaus. He was a kind and fair king. All his people loved him, until his brother, Joffrey, claimed the royal flames were the cause of a sacred temple's destruction. Quickly, the people of Irolyth turned against Klaus and the rest of the royal family. How could the people who once loved King Klaus turn on him so quickly? Joffrey did not even give the Royal Family a chance to defend themselves against the allegations before he hunted them down to have them executed.

"Are you trying to say our new king is evil?"

"All I'm saying is we shouldn't rush to send a child to her death. It's bad enough one child was already killed."

There was silence for a moment, and I peeked around the tree to see if they were still nearby. I watched in horror as one of them quickly slit the other's throat. His body hit the ground before a sound could escape his lips.

"One less traitor to deal with," the first man said in a cold tone. He then turned away, walking in the opposite direction. The body was left on the forest floor in a puddle of blood.

Before he could find me, I ventured deeper into the woods and headed south toward the bog. I ran as fast as I could, ignoring the pain in my body as I pushed it beyond its limits. In the mire's center, I would find my refuge.

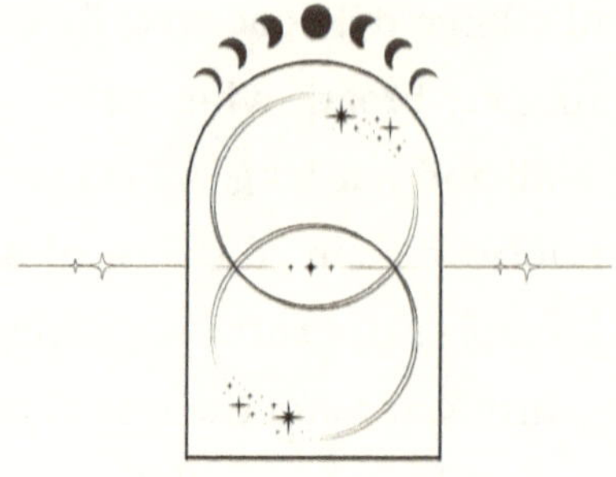

Two

"Piper! Fetch me another ale!" A patron yelled from the other side of the bar. He was an older man, about in his mid-forties. He and his friends came to The White Rabbit every Wednesday night to play a few rounds of darts, drink some ale, and enjoy the music the bards played. Other than them, the tavern was dead, compared to a Friday or Saturday night when this place was packed.

I took a deep breath. "Right away, Clarence." I put down the cleaning cloth I was using to wipe down the bar top, washed my hands, and poured him a new mug of ale. When I sat it down in front of him, I offered a soft smile. "This is your last one for tonight. Remember, you told me to cut you off at three."

"Damn, am I at three already?" He let out a joyous laugh. "Well, let me pay my tab, and once me and the boys are done with this round, we'll be out of your hair." He pulled out his wallet and removed a sizable amount of money.

Before I even counted it, I spoke. "Even if you were buying for all your friends tonight, this is way too much."

"The rest is your tip for putting up with us. Don't think we haven't noticed you stay open late on Wednesdays to accommodate us."

I counted the money, put the amount for the ales into the register, and tucked the remainder in my front pocket. "Thank you. You guys don't rush this last game. I'm betting on you to win."

He took his ale with a final laugh and returned to his friends. I continued my cleaning duties as Stephanie, the owner of The White Rabbit, approached.

"The city officials stopped by again this morning," she said as she leaned against the bar.

My eyes slowly lifted to meet hers. "And?" My heart pounded in my chest and my fist tightened around the cleaning cloth.

"Your paperwork is all filed. They believed the documents I forged. You are officially a citizen of Elswyth."

I released the breath I was holding, and tears filled my eyes. "Really?"

She nodded. "My little firecracker, you are home." A smile grew across her face.

Rushing over, I wrapped her in a hug and sobbed. After three years, I finally found somewhere I could call home. I had gone to a place where Joffrey would never find me. I now lived in the capital city of Elswyth, the human realm. For the first year I lived in Zamora, I stayed in hostels if there was room. I was lucky to meet Steph. She offered me a job, a room, and a friend. I lived on the third floor of the tavern. It was just a small one-bedroom apartment, but it meant everything to me.

"Thank you so much!"

She squeezed me tighter. "Why don't you call it a night? I'll wrap up here."

I wished her, and the guys, a good night before rushing upstairs. Once the door was shut behind me, I snapped my fingers, and the fireplace set ablaze. I went into the kitchen and found a note on the counter.

Check the ice box.

-Steph

I opened the ice chest and saw a box of my favorite cupcakes from a bakery across the city. Lemon cake filled with curd frosted with marshmallow icing with the top lightly torched. Taking the whole dozen, I sat on the couch in front of the fireplace. One by one I ate half the box while reading one of my favorite books.

For the first time in three years, I could truly relax.

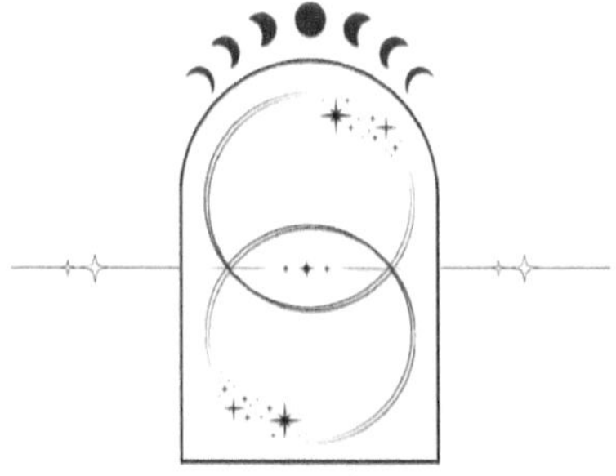

Three

That Friday, The White Rabbit was packed. I could barely catch a break as customers continued ordering drinks while Steve, my co-worker, took food orders and delivered them to the guests. If you had asked me three years ago before I ran from Irolyth, I would have laughed if you had told me I'd be working as a bartender in the human realm. This life was so different from my life back home, but this was the small life I longed for.

No longer was my day planned down to the letter. No longer was I watching my every movement. No longer was I stuck in a life that wasn't mine.

In the crowd, a tall, slender man faced away from me. Breath caught in my throat as I stared at his auburn hair. How could he be here? Did Joffrey really travel through the portal into the human realm to find me himself? He turned, and I exhaled in relief as it was a young man's brown eyes staring back at me.

I heard Steve say something, but couldn't understand the words. When I turned to face him, concern was seeded in his hazel eyes.

"I'm sorry. What did you say?" I asked.

"Are you ok? You just got paler than normal, and that's saying something for you."

"I am not really feeling good. All of a sudden I got really hot," I lied. Steve did not know the truth of where I came from. I could not tell him that I thought I saw a fae king who wanted me dead.

"Go step out back. I will take care of things for a bit. Get some fresh air."

"Are you sure?" I looked around the bar full of people. Several wanted drinks, and the chef in the back just called for a food runner.

"Go, before I change my mind." He motioned to the door that led to the back of house.

I quickly made my way through the kitchens, grabbing a glass of water before I walked outside to the alley and sat on the step. Chugging the water, I tried to gather my thoughts. No matter how much I told myself I was safe, I wasn't. I would never be as free as I wanted to be. That monster would haunt me for the rest of my life. There was nowhere I could hide from him. Nowhere was safe. Who was to say he didn't already send people through the portal to try to find me?

I allowed the cool air to calm me before returning to work. The White Rabbit now had much fewer people in it than before. I looked over at Steve as he made his way from a table in the back corner of the tavern. It was he who now looked pale as a ghost, a stark contrast to his normally tan skin.

As he poured a mug of ale, he gave me the side eye. "Whatever you do, do *not* go over to that table. I will handle it," he said in a low tone.

A shiver ran down my spine. Never had Steve spoken to me that way. "Why? Who is that?" I asked as I peered past him. A lone man sat at the table with short, spiked black hair, a five o'clock shadow gracing his chiseled jaw, and piercing gray eyes. For the first time, I found a human man to be attractive. Steve stepped in front of me and blocked my view from him.

"That is a very dangerous man, and Steph would have my ass if something happened to you. Please, just listen to me about this."

Before I could respond, I heard a voice like velvet. "I plan on being in this part of the city for a few days. Are there any rooms available?"

The man leaned against the bar. The sleeves of his dark shirt were rolled up and revealed two lean, tattooed arms.

"No vacancy," Steve spat.

"Now, I know that isn't true. I heard several people cancel their rooms after I walked into the bar. What a pity to lose out on that much money. You wouldn't want to lose out on any more, would you?" Those gray eyes darkened as he spoke. His gaze met mine, and he offered a predatory grin as he looked me over. "Well, hello there. What a pretty little thing *you* are."

Heat flushed my cheeks. There was something about him that lured me in. Steve responded to the man before I could. "Do not speak to her. You can stay here, but I don't want to catch you looking in her direction. Do you understand?"

"Oh, Steve," a dark chuckle escaped his lips. "Do you think just because you got out of the business that you are better than me? Do you *really* think you can tell me what to do? Do not make me remind you of your place, especially in front of your little friend here. Now, what is my room number?"

Steve swallowed hard and clenched his fists so tight I could see the whites of his knuckles. "204," he said through his teeth.

"See, that wasn't so hard." The man reached across the counter, grabbed the ale Steve had poured before the confrontation, and headed back to his table.

"What did he mean by you being 'out of the business'?" I questioned.

"You have your secrets, Piper, and I have mine. Go upstairs to your apartment. Do not open the door for anyone unless it's me or Steph. Understood?"

"But the bar isn't closed," I protested.

"Yes, it is. Now go. Do not argue with me on this," he said with such venom it nearly caused me to stagger back.

In the two years I had known Steve, he was always a kind soul. The man that I saw before me was not someone I recognized. But he was right, we both had our secrets, and I would not want him prying into mine.

I nodded and headed for the stairs. As I passed the mystery man's table, our eyes locked. He gave me a flirty wink before I looked away and ran upstairs.

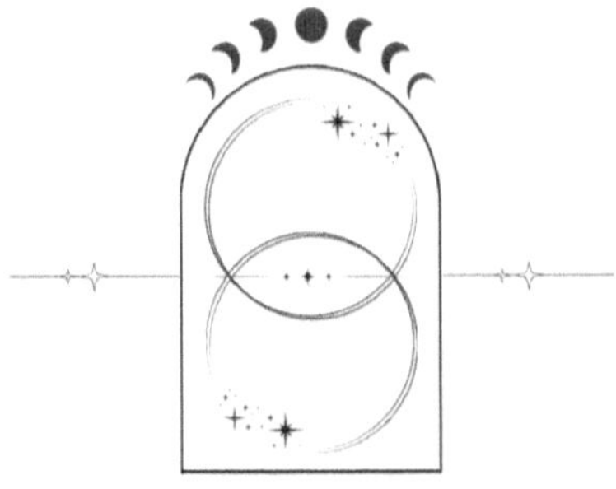

Four

The next morning, I awoke to a pounding on my door. I got out of bed, wrapped my silk robe around my body, and peered through the peephole. Steph stood on the other side, steadily pounding on the door, so I yanked it open.

"Where is the fire? What's going on?" I asked. Never had she come to me so panicked. I was worried the building was on fire.

"Oh, thank the heavens." She let out a sigh of relief and wrapped me in a tight hug. Stunned, I stood there frozen in her embrace. What was wrong with her? "Steve told me what happened last night."

"He wouldn't tell me who that man was. He just told me to stay away, and I listened." All night, I had been kept up by the thought of our new guest. Why was he so dangerous, and how did Steve know him?

She finally released me and headed for the couch, her long, blonde hair flowing behind her as she walked. "His name is Jax. A well-known assassin in the city. Extremely dangerous. I want you to take the next few days off just until he's gone. Steve is right. You shouldn't be around him."

Fear radiated through my body. His name was very well known in Zamora. Jax was credited with assassinating several high-ranking officials in Elswyth, as well as anyone else who got in his way. To decline him from staying here would have been the death of all of us.

"Understood. Just let me know when I can come back to work."

"I will, and you'll still get paid for this time."

I sat down next to her on the couch. "Do you think..." I trailed off, not daring to speak the words. Was the assassin sent by Joffrey? Could this human assassin be more than what meets the eye? If I could parade as a human, so could other fae.

"It would be impossible," she said.

Stephanie was the only one I had told my secret. When I first started working for her, she promised she would protect me from whatever I was running from. She told me a secret of her own, that she was from a line of sorceresses scattered throughout Elswyth. Magic had been forbidden by the king. Over twenty years ago, he had many of the sorceresses executed just for being born with magic. I knew she was going to keep my secret, and she knew I would keep hers.

"I have to get back downstairs and keep an eye on our guest." She walked over to the door and offered me a smile. "Stay safe, my little firecracker." With that, she walked out the door, and shut it behind her.

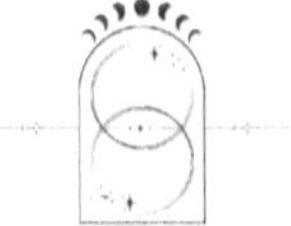

Later that night, I headed back to The White Rabbit after dining at a restaurant. I had the most delicious, spiced chicken on pita bread, with a side of dill cucumber sauce. It was the first time I tried Alivander's, and I would definitely be returning to try more of their selections. Approaching the alley where the back entrance to The White Rabbit was, I heard that familiar velvet-like voice.

"I am in between jobs right now. If you know anyone looking for work, let me know."

I took a few steps back and pressed my back against the brick wall so I could continue to eavesdrop. All day I had fought myself on approaching Jax. If he was able to kill as many officials as he had, could he kill a king?

Would he?

"I will see what's going on within the city districts and get back to you," a rough-voiced male said.

A few seconds later, a tall, muscular man exited the alley. I quickly pushed off the wall before he looked in my direction and acted as if I was just out for a stroll. He stopped for a moment and fixed his gaze on me. The scar across his eye and his angry demeanor told me that this was a man not to fuck with.

The man turned and walked away as if my presence was no concern to him.

I took a deep breath and waited until he turned the corner, then I slipped into the alley. Jax leaned against the wall with a cigarette in between his pointer and middle finger. He brought it to his lips, took a drag, and as he let out the smoke, his eyes fell on me.

"Well, well, well," he said with a grin. "I didn't expect to see you in an alley. Do you perhaps have a second job here? If so, I have an offer for you." He chuckled as he brought the cigarette back to his lips.

Disgusting. How dare he imply I was a lady of the night? I swallowed my pride and reminded myself why I was here. I leaned against the wall directly across from him. "Perhaps I have a job for you," I countered.

He kicked off the wall and strode toward me. "You do?"

"Are you as good as they say you are?"

He laughed, took another hit, and turned his head to blow the smoke away from me. Before he spoke, he threw the cigarette on the ground and snuffed it out with his boot. "Better." He winked.

"They say you are the best, but what I need you to do, I need you to be better than the best."

He lifted his arm and pressed his palm against the wall above my head. "I will be as good as you need me to be, for the right price."

"I can't pay you until after the job is done. The person I need... removed is holding all of my wealth." I looked up at him, and for the first time, noticed just how much taller he was than me.

I tried to push down how intimidated I felt. If I was human, I would be terrified, but I was thankful to have magic as my protection.

Jax laughed. "Well, I don't work for free, sweet heart. If you don't have money," he gave me an up-and-down look, "I could think of other ways for you to pay me."

My throat bobbed as he leaned in, and I took in his tobacco and citrus scent. "Over my dead body," I snarled.

"Feisty and has self-respect. I like that." He leaned in close, so our gazes met. "Tell ya what. Kiss me, and I will do it without upfront payment."

Heat rose to my cheeks. "K--kiss you?" I stumbled over my words, truly shocked.

"You do know what a kiss is? Don't you?"

"I do..." Only one other time I had kissed another. It was just after I had turned thirteen. Thinking back on it now, I could still remember her soft lips on mine. She was a noble from Khaldon, another of the fae realms. The fae of Khaldon rarely left their realm, and she and her parents only stayed with us for two short months. I always wondered if Briella had stayed, would the feelings we had blossomed into love?

I tucked away the memory and focused on the assassin whose lips were dangerously close to mine.

"Well, then I don't need to explain it to you. Do we have a bargain?" His voice darkened, and I nearly melted.

"You don't even know the details of the job." The wheels turned in my head. Bargains with the fae were life-bound contracts. If I could trick him into one, he would have to help me.

"I don't need to. Whatever you need, it's worth it. Just for a kiss."

"A bargain with me is impossible to back out of," I warned. As much as I needed his help, I had to give him the chance to walk away. This was not my first bargain, but it was indeed my most dangerous.

He lifted his other hand and tucked my hair behind my ear. "I never back away from a challenge. Kiss me, and I will be your sword."

Without another word, I leaned forward, pressed my lips into his, and saw stars.

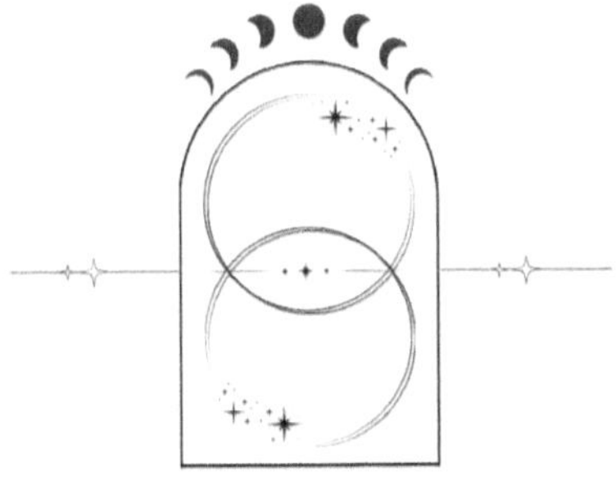

Five

The ground shook beneath our feet, and Jax staggered back.

"What was that?" His stormy eyes looked at me with a mix of confusion and fear as the tremors stopped.

"I told you. A bargain with me was serious," I said as I took a step toward him.

"What are you?" His gaze narrowed, and his back straightened as he closed the gap between us once again.

"My true name is Piper Camilla Rossi, Princess of Irolyth." Now sure he wasn't working for Joffrey, I knew it was safe to reveal myself to him. Especially since he made a deal that bound himself to my service.

"Irolyth? I have never heard of such a place." He raised his eyebrow at me.

"You wouldn't unless you were familiar with the fae." I dropped my glamour and watched his eyes widen. No longer was I a human girl with rounded ears. What now stood before the assassin was a fae princess. In my human disguise, my eyes were a dull brown, but now they were a bright emerald. My ears were now elongated and pointed. With the glamour, I was attractive to human standards. In my fae form, I was the epitome of beauty.

"I...... I thought fae only existed in the south and were horrid creatures." He stumbled over his words. His gaze darted around the alley as if he were expecting those monsters to crawl out of the shadows.

"Those are the cursed fae of Orilon. There are six fae realms that you can get to from the portals hidden throughout Elswyth." My heart broke as I thought of those cursed people. Many years ago, the fae of Orilon had angered a sorceress, and she had cursed their people to turn into horrid gray creatures with bat-like wings. Losing all their control, they now had a blood lust that could not be satisfied. Stories of their ruthless behavior had traveled through Elswyth. No one was dumb enough to travel southwest and risk being torn apart by their massive claws. The poor city of Pendril was left to its own devices to defend itself against any that found their way through the portal.

"If you are a fae princess, why do you need to work at The White Rabbit? Why hire a human assassin?" His gaze focused on me and crossed his arms in front of him.

"My uncle killed my family and stole the throne. I need you to kill him so I can reclaim my kingdom." Tears welled in my eyes as the image of my family hung for the kingdom to see flashed through my mind. I missed them every day.

"You think I can kill a fae king?" He scoffed.

"You said you were the best. You have killed several high-ranking officials. If anyone can, it's you. Besides, you made a bargain, you have to see it through."

"And if I don't? What happens if I back out now?"

"You die," I said in a cold tone. "There is no backing out until we are done."

"You can't be serious. Release me from the bargain now!"

"What's done is done. How long will you need to prepare?"

Jax turned and clenched his fists. He let out a low grumble before he spoke. "Give me three days."

"You better return."

"Not like I have a choice." He snarled as he walked out of the alley.

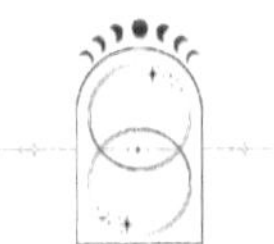

The next morning, I found Steph and Steve sitting at a table in the corner of the bar's kitchen speaking in hushed tones. Their eyes were glued to me as I joined them.

"Jax wasn't in his room this morning," Steve said, with worry in his voice.

"No. He wasn't. He will return, however," I said as I grabbed the carafe of coffee and poured myself a mug. I added three sugar cubes and a splash of cream.

"How do you know?" Steph asked with a lift of her brow.

"He and I will be leaving together when he returns. We struck a deal. He is going to help me return home." I took a sip of my coffee and it warmed my core.

Steph's eyes widened as she understood my meaning. Her mouth fell open, but no words escaped.

Anger contorted Steve's face. "How is he going to help you? Don't you remember me telling you to stay away?"

"He's the only one who can." I took a sip of my coffee, avoiding Steve's gaze. I may have the royal flames, but I swore I saw fire in his eyes.

"I don't understand. Why are you leaving with him?" He slammed his fist against the table, making the dishes clatter.

Steph reached across the table and placed her hand on top of his. "It is not for you to understand. This is a journey Piper must face." Sadness welled in her eyes. "My little firecracker, I will miss you. I understand why you must go, but, gods, I will miss you."

"I owe it to my family," I said as tears welled in my eyes. "I need to get my home back."

Steph stood and wrapped me in a hug. "Heavy is the head that wears the crown. When you are queen, don't forget about us," she whispered in my ear.

I hugged her back, just as tight. "I will never forget you. For you are the greatest friendship I have ever known."

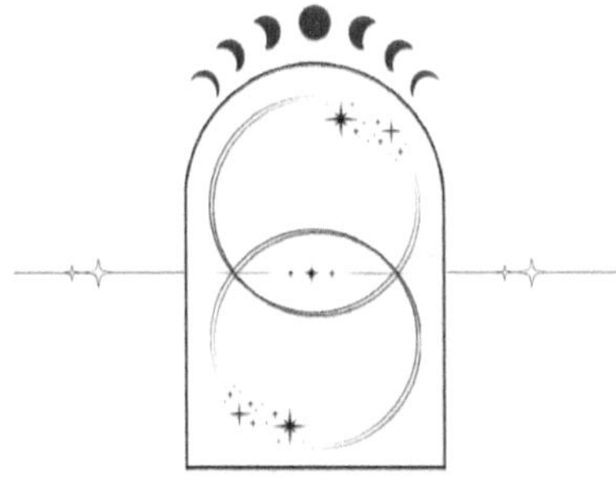

Six

As promised, Jax returned three days after his departure. Stephanie had closed The White Rabbit for the past few days so we could spend our last moments together. The two of them had truly become my family these past years, and I would miss them greatly.

But Stephanie was right. Heavy is the head that wears the crown. Once I returned to Irolyth and reclaimed the throne, I would be queen. I owed it to my family and kingdom to give them the monarch they deserved. Anyone who would slaughter their kin for power should not possess it. It was time I grew up and stopped being a coward.

I prayed to The Mother I would make my family proud. Queen was never a title I was meant to hold. The next monarch was supposed to be my twin brother, Alexander. He spent his entire life training for that moment. I was just a trophy for my parents. A pretty little doll to make sure the royal family looked perfect to the kingdom. Never was I taught anything that would be useful for ruling. I knew my fate would have been to be married off to another fae royal for political gain.

Though the six fae realms were separate, we were all tied politically for one reason or another.

Jax was leaning against the bar that evening when I had come down to wish Steph and Steve my final goodbye. He wore tight black pants and a black T-shirt. I couldn't help but to further examine the tattoos gracing his arms. They were swirls of darkness, almost like shadows.

"So where exactly are we going, *princess*?" He asked with a snarl at the last word.

I shot him a glare. "We need to head to the back alley and into the sewers."

Jax gave me an up-and-down look. "*You* are going into *the sewers*? Hard to believe it."

"Shut up." I rolled my eyes. "Let's go." I gave my friends one final hug before I headed out the back doors, with Jax following behind me.

"I don't think I much like being bossed around by a girl," he said as we made it into the alley.

I spun toward him with the royal flames in my eyes. "You don't have much of a choice. I told you a bargain with me would be serious. You made your bed, now lay in it!"

"Whoa, cool down, princess." He threw his hands up, palms facing out.

"Don't call me that! Especially in Irolyth. As a matter of fact, don't even call me Piper. No one can know who I am."

"And why is that? Wouldn't they be happy for their princess's return?"

"My family was hung before they could defend themselves against my uncle's words. I am not willing to take that chance. From here on out, call me..." I held my chin for a moment in contemplation. "Cami."

There was a long silent moment. A grave expression grew on his face. Jax took in a deep breath before he spoke. "Cami, it is. Just so you know, I am expecting a high reward for working with a future queen."

I rolled my eyes in response, then headed deeper into the alley. There were entrances to the sewers all over the city, but lucky for us, there was one in the alley near The White Rabbit. We were even luckier that there had been no rain in weeks. For that would make passage through the sewers unbearable. While they were dry, there were walkways, but if it had rained, they would be flooded.

Jax removed the grate, and I looked into the dark hole. The vile smell nearly knocked me off my feet. He motioned for me to go in first. The thin ladder felt as if it was going to collapse while I climbed down. Jax entered after me and covered the top with the grate.

As I hit the floor, I snapped my fingers, and three small fire-balls appeared in the air around me, illuminating the sewers. Concrete pathways sat on either side of dark water.

"Well? Where to?" He asked as he put both feet on the ground and looked up and down the long length of the tunnel. Finally noticing the floating balls of fire, he stared at them in awe. He reached up to try to touch one.

I smacked his hand away from it before he could. "That is real fire. Careful not to get burned."

It had been years since I had passed through the sewers. I refused to come back, but I could not deny the pull I felt in my heart. The pull had always been there, calling me home. Guiding me to Irolyth.

"This way." I motioned. We came to a wide staircase leading to a large square room after about a ten-minute walk. On the far wall sat a portal, about seven feet tall and three feet wide. Red and yellow fog swirled and mixed within it. A shiver ran down my spine and traveled through my body. I had avoided this place since I passed through it all those years ago, and seeing it now, nearly brought me to my knees. The scent of sweet smoke filled the air, the scent of home.

Like a moth drawn to a flame, I walked directly to the portal and stopped in front of it, tears welled in my eyes. A firm hand gripped my shoulder, and I turned my head and looked into Jax's gaze.

"How long has it been?" He asked softly.

"Three years." I turned my head back to the portal. I was confused about why he was showing me this softer side of him. It was very different from the Jax I knew.

"Let's get you home." He stood by my side and took my hand. Heat rushed through my body as our fingers locked. I hated how right it felt to have his hand in mine.

After taking one more deep breath, we stepped into the portal together.

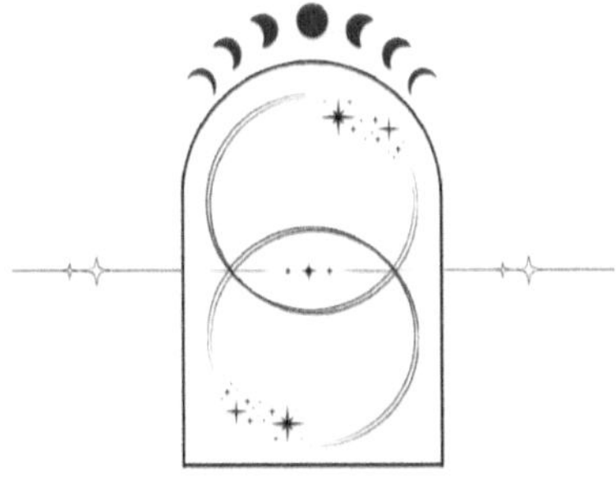

Seven

Once we were through the portal, I took a deep breath of the sweet air. Tears streamed down my face as I looked upon my homeland for the first time in three years. We stood on a small island surrounded by crimson water, and I fell to my knees and ran my hands against the scarlet grass. The sun beat down on me and warmed my skin. I'd nearly forgotten Jax was with me. It was his voice that caused me to look up.

"This place... is beautiful," he said in a hushed tone.

"This is the Sanguine Mire," I said as I stood. "Located in the southeast of Irolyth. Due to the terrain, it isn't a highly visited area."

"If I lived here, I would visit as often as I could. I've never seen anything like this."

Everything in Elswyth was dull. Color like this didn't exist there, at least not in the capital. He looked around and examined the new world around him. I had forgotten how large the redwood trees were that filled this land. The whole western and southern regions of Irolyth were taken over by the redwood forest. In the Mire, the trees grew out of the water, and they weren't as dense as other regions of the forest.

"Where to now... *Cami*?" He emphasized the name that I asked him to call me.

To be honest, I wasn't exactly sure. In my haste to trap Jax in the bargain, I failed to come up with a plan.

"You have no idea, do you?" He raised an eyebrow. "You have to be kidding me!" A deep chuckle escaped his throat.

"Sorry, I never expected to sneak back into my kingdom to reclaim my throne. I don't have some master plan!"

Jax crossed his arms and shook his head. "Well, first it would be wise to change your appearance, though you should have done that before we left Zamora."

"Change my appearance?"

"Well, you don't want people to know who you are." He ran his fingers through my hair.

Heat rose to my cheeks, and I found myself wishing he wouldn't drop his hand. For a moment, I thought I could grow to like this human. I quickly shoved those feelings down. He was right. Anyone who saw my red hair would know I was of royal blood. We were the only ones in Irolyth to have this color of hair. Inhaling deeply, my body tingled as magic ran through me.

Jax took a step back with the look of shock as I transformed. Now that I was home, I had full access to my magic. Back in Zamora, it felt as if it was only a small ember compared to the raging fire it should be. I heard rumors that across the ocean from Elswyth, there were several lands where fae roamed. I had always wanted to travel there to see if I would have a connection to my magic, but the King of Elswyth had banned travel to other continents.

While in Elswyth, I could only minimally change my appearance, just enough to make me appear human. Now, a totally different person stared back at Jax. I ran my fingers through my sleek, long black hair. My once green eyes were now a stormy gray to match his.

"Well... that's different," he said with an annoyed tone.

I smirked. "You don't like it?"

"No," he said in a cold voice, looking away. "It doesn't matter if I like it, anyway. Where is the closest town to here? We will need a place to stay. You wouldn't happen to have any money stashed nearby, would you? That would have been smart of you to do before you left."

"I was escaping death. Do you really think I had time to do that?"

"I suppose not." He rolled his eyes and walked over to the edge of the island. "Are you going to be okay walking through this, *Cami*?" Every time he called me that, venom dripped from his tongue.

"Northeast of here is a religious sanctuary called The Glade. They worship The Mother. We should travel there to seek refuge. Then we can figure out our next move."

Jax quickly picked me up and threw me over his shoulder. I squirmed in his arms, trying to get down. I was not used to being up this high. The more I struggled, the tighter Jax held onto me.

"Put me down!"

"I am not allowing you to walk in this water. I will carry you," he snapped.

I stopped fighting. "At least let me get on your back, so I'll be more comfortable."

"Fine." He put me down, and as soon as my feet hit the ground, he grabbed my chin and forced me to look up at him. My body trembled as he stepped closer, closing the gap between us. "I may be stuck in this bargain, and as soon as it is done, so are we. But I will protect you and take care of you while we are here. Do you understand me, *princess?*"

A chill ran down my spine as he said that last word. There was something about him calling me 'princess' that put me on edge. Especially since I told him not to do so. All I could do was nod in response.

"Good girl," he purred before turning around and kneeling.

Ignoring him, because I liked that way too much, I got onto his back. He looped his arms around my legs before standing. My body tensed as he held onto me tight and took his first step into the water. I wondered if I should tell him the water goes on for miles, or that it would take a whole day to get to The Glade.

He would find out on his own in good time.

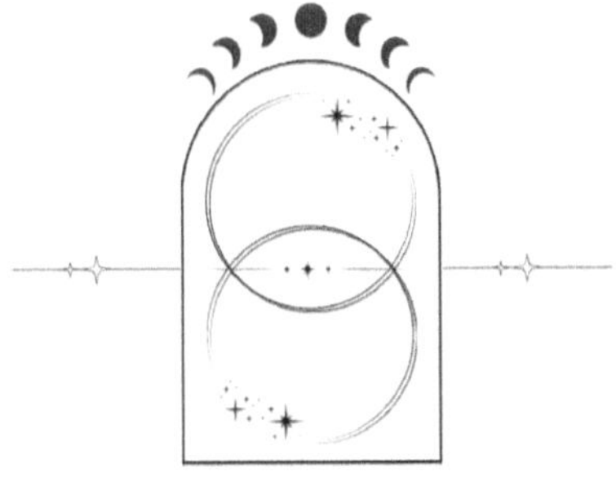

Eight

Several hours later, Jax dropped me onto the ground with a huff once we were out of the Mire and on dry land. His dark pants were soaking wet and clung to his body. We still had a long way to go before we reached The Glade. Jax began to take off his pants.

"Whoa, what are you doing?" I shouted at him as I held my hands up, motioning for him to stop.

"I am not walking around in soaking wet clothes. I need to let them dry before I put them back on," he said as his pants slid down to his knees.

"That is indecent! Put them back on!"

Jax grinned. "You know, you are the first girl to ever tell me that. Normally, girls like you beg me to remove them." He took a step closer to me.

Heat flooded my body and rose to my cheeks. I looked up to the sky, cursing myself for wanting to see more of him. Words jammed in my throat as he closed the gap between us.

"Too bad there isn't a pretty little firecracker who can dry them quickly for me."

"Don't call me that!" The words rushed out.

"Why not? I heard Steve and the owner of The White Rabbit call you that," he teased.

"Only my friends call me that." I shot him a pointed glare.

"Are we not friends, princess?" He winked, and that wicked smirk grew.

"No. We are not. Remember, you said once we are done here, then you will leave? Friends don't leave."

He chuckled. "Oh, you sweet little thing. There are many types of friendships. Ours is just situational. Now be a dear and dry my pants so we can hurry on." He shoved his pants into my hands and then looked around at the forest. "I've never seen trees like this before," he said as he raised his gaze toward the canopy. "I spent my whole life in Zamora. The only trees I've ever seen are the small ones that line the sidewalks."

Zamora was a concrete jungle. In the three years I lived there, I never saw a single park. Along some of the streets in the nicer parts of the city were small skinny trees. They bloomed little white flowers in the spring and caused the streets to be covered in petals and pollen.

"I suppose this is a huge change for you." Using my magic, heat ran through my body as I warmed the pants. The water quickly turned into steam, leaving the pants dry in little time. I tried hard not to look at his rear as he walked farther away from

me, but this man was built like a god. "Here they are all dry."
Taking a step forward, I extended them out to him.

He quickly took the pants from my hand and put them back
on as he spoke. "What exactly can your magic do? Fire magic
must come in handy often," he chuckled.

"Don't tell anyone about my fire magic," I blurted out.

"Why not?" He raised an eyebrow and cocked his head.

"Only the royal family has that power. We refer to it as the
royal flames. The Mother gifted this to the Rossi family generations ago when we first ascended to the throne."

"Understood. If it was a gift from The Mother, shouldn't the
people at this sanctuary be excited to see someone with one of
her gifts?"

"I have no idea, but it's better not to test it."

"Which way to The Glade?" he asked. "We need to get moving. Walk and talk. Tell me about The Mother."

I pointed him in the right direction, and the two of us began
our journey. "She is the creator of magic. Without her, the fae
would be nothing more than elves."

"There are elves?" As we walked, his head kept moving, on
the lookout for anything that may be coming at us.

"There were many years ago. The Mother blessed a small
group of them with magic and created the fae. Long ago, there
was a war between the elves and the fae. The fae prevailed, and
the elves are long gone."

The forest was too silent. The only sound was our voices. It
made me nervous as once this forest was crawling with life.

"That's dark."

"As is life." I shrugged. "Unfortunately, I learned the hard way, it is either kill or be killed. My father should have killed my uncle when they battled for the crown, but he spared him instead. In doing so, he caused his own death."

"They battled for the crown?"

"On their eighteenth birthday. They were twins, as are all royal siblings. When two males are born, they battle for the throne to the death. My father was the first to spare his brother. He said that ruling did not require bloodshed. Once he became king, he declared no longer brothers battle to the death. In sparing his brother, he condemned himself to the bloodshed he wanted to end." As I spoke, I increased my pace. I could not blame my father for sparing his brother. If I were male and my father did not change the laws, Alexander and I would have had to duel. I knew that I did not have the heart to kill my kin. When I lost my twin, I felt a part of me die inside. Did the other royal siblings feel this way after they murdered their twin, or was the thirst for power too great?

We continued to walk in silence. After a long moment, he spoke. "I'm sorry for your loss. I know how hard it is to lose a parent. My mother died when I was very young due to illness. I was at her bedside when she passed."

"I am so sorry. What about your father?"

"Never met him. My mother said he was a generous and kind man. But what man abandons the mother of his unborn child and leaves them to the streets?"

"No man at all," I responded.

"Exactly. Now, go back to The Mother," he said quickly, changing the subject. Jax brought his hand to his eyes, and I wondered if he thought I didn't see the silver mist in them.

I told him how The Mother granted six groups of fae different powers and provided them with their own place to reside. Long ago, all the fae realms were one, but it only caused chaos once our magics were awoken. The Mother separated the realms, to keep us from killing each other. The fae of Irolyth had fire and forest magic. Orilon had control over the shadows. Aeros had gravitational magic, and thank The Mother for it, as they needed it to escape The Great Calamity. The shifters of Khaldon lived inside a mountain. Alari was the territory of the water fae. The final fae realm was Tarak, but little was known about this realm. To my knowledge, a portal to them had not been found. They had completely isolated themselves.

Not only was The Mother the giver of magic, but she also was the mother to all of our gods. She gave away pieces of herself to create her children. Each with their own gifts. I remember sitting in church each week and staring at the stained glass that depicted all the gods, and I was always drawn to Aurora, the goddess of Flames and Light. A beautiful red-haired goddess with fire in her eyes. It was said she was the first to carry the royal flames and the Rossi line were her descendants.

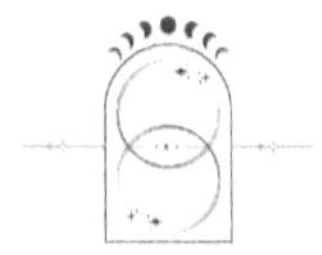

Hours into our walk, an arrow whizzed between our heads and struck the tree behind us. A woman in a white hooded robe stepped out from behind a tree with another arrow ready. Her golden hair was in two braids that ran down her front to her waist, and the silver and ruby circlet around her head told me exactly which group this woman belonged to.

"Who are you?" She asked.

Before I answered, I fell to my knees and bowed my head. Jax immediately followed my lead. "Lady of the Flame, we come seeking refuge. We have traveled far to find The Glade and rest under The Mother's protection. My name is Cami, and this is my mate, Jax." My skin crawled at calling someone like Jax my mate. He was so rude and arrogant. I hated to admit he was also extremely handsome and charming.

The Lady of the Flame lowered her bow and rushed over to us. "Are you from Mayrin? I fear the situation there has gotten worse."

My gaze shot up to meet her as fear ran through my body. Mayrin was the capital city that was just south of the castle. I spent many of my days there as a child, shopping and speaking with the locals. My father always taught me even though we were royalty, we were not better than the common man. We were all blessed by The Mother, and we should treat everyone justly.

"We are. We could not stay any longer," Jax said.

"Please rise. We will get you settled right away." She took my hand. Accepting her assistance, I stood. Jax followed suit as well, and we allowed her to guide us to The Glade. We stepped through some short and dense trees and the leaf-covered ground turned into pale stone. The Lady of the Flame waved her hand in the air, and the temple was revealed to us. It was just as beautiful as I remembered. The white marble was covered in crawling red ivy. The center structure was two stories high, the first floor was for worship, and the top housed the Ladies of the Flame. Three smaller buildings surrounded the temple. One was a library, one was housing, and the third was a well-kept secret.

"King Joffrey is ruining this land. We should have never trusted him. May The Mother forgive us for what we allowed to happen to King Klaus, Queen Cassia, and Crown Prince Alexander. Let us pray Princess Piper returns to save us."

My heart dropped.

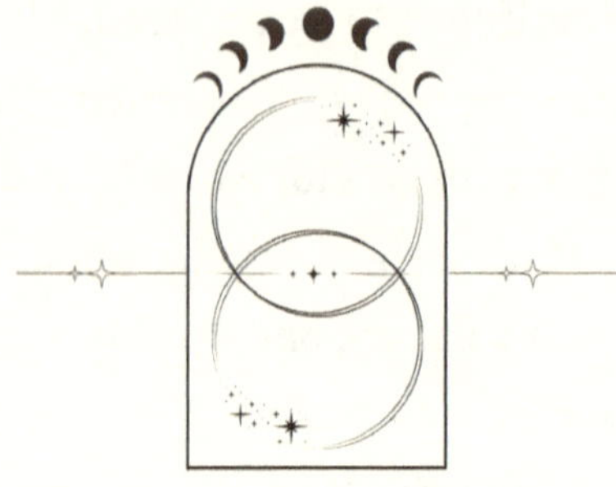

Nine

"Do you think the princess is still out there?" I asked, not wanting to reveal myself.

She offered me a soft smile. "The Mother keeps her safe. I know she is protected."

She guided us into the center building, where three other robed women stood near the entryway, all with the silver circlet in their hair. They turned toward us as we entered. I noticed the pews of the worship hall were full of people not in robes. There were several Ladies of the Flame passing out food, clothing, and other items to the congregation. My stomach turned. Were these all people from Mayrin?

"Lady Stella," one of them said to the woman guiding us. The red trim of her robe indicated she was the Head Lady. Nothing in this place happened without her approval.

"Lady Rae, I found two more refugees out in the forest. They are also from Mayrin."

The three rushed over to us. "You poor dears. We are at capacity, so I don't know if we will be able to take anyone else in," the woman with the red-trimmed robe said.

One of the Ladies stared at Jax with an intense glare. She stepped closer to him, reached up, and touched his rounded ears. In my haste to glamour myself to make sure people could not recognize me, I'd forgotten to glamour him to look fae.

"What strange ears," she whispered.

The other woman grabbed his arm and examined his tattoos. I couldn't help the anger surging through me. I hated that they were touching him.

"And strange tattoos." The second one added.

The third woman turned her attention from Lady Stella to Jax. She slowly gave him an up-and-down look, and the grin on her face grew. "Are you from Orilon? It has been a long time since we have seen a fae from there."

"He is," I said quickly. "He lost his powers due to the curse and left before he could turn into one of those horrid creatures. The Mother protects him here." It felt so wrong lying in a place like this, but I had to if we wanted to stay safe.

"How sad." The girl who was touching his ear was now running her hands through his hair.

He had the stupidest grin on his face as the Ladies fawned over him. He even was playing with one's golden locks.

With her hands still on Jax's arms, she looked over to Lady Rae with big doe eyes. "We have to let them stay. We can't abandon them."

Lady Rae took a deep breath and glanced at Lady Stella. "Prepare them for the unveiling. If they pass. They can stay."

"The unveiling?" I asked.

"Joffrey has sent in glamoured spies in the past. The unveiling will remove any glamour you may have and reveal your true form," Lady Stella said.

A lump formed in my throat. Jax pulled away from the women, came to my side, and took my hand, giving it a gentle squeeze. Calmness washed over me when he offered me a soft smile. Something about the assassin brought me comfort, even when I first gazed into his storm gray eyes and Steve had told me to stay away.

"We would expect nothing less," he chimed. "You must keep The Glade safe."

"Lady Stella," Lady Rae said, "Please take them to the inner sanctum and prepare them for the ceremony."

"Yes, my lady," she answered with a bow. Gesturing for the two of us to follow her. "Come along."

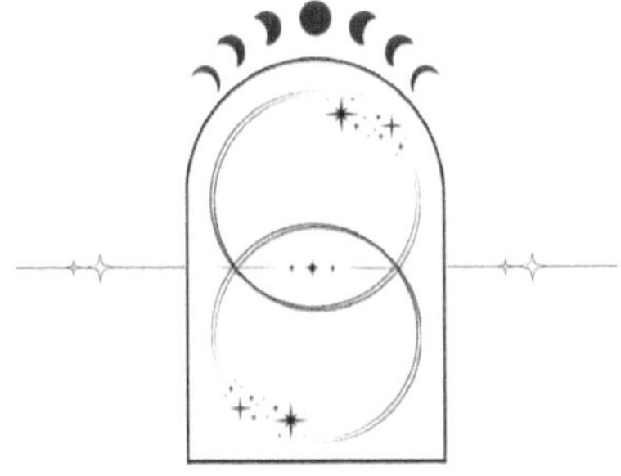

Ten

Stella guided us to the back of the temple and down a flight of stairs. As we walked, the torches lit when we neared and extinguished as we passed. My stomach twisted, and I felt I was going to fall with each step. Jax looked cool and collected, and I wish I knew what was going through his head. There was no way I could go through with this ritual. The unveiling would be disastrous.

Or would it?

They seemed to hate my uncle and saw him for the monster he truly was. If I revealed myself, would they help me? Would they be mad at for us deceiving them? Would they be what Jax and I needed to succeed in our mission? I couldn't deny I made a huge mistake in not thinking anything through before I trapped a human assassin in this deal and returned to Irolyth.

At the bottom of the stairs was a single square room made of stone. In its center was a pool of aquamarine glittering water. Steam gently rose above the water. Near the far wall, two tall, unlit red candles sat on each end of the altar. Behind it was a large golden statue of The Mother. I could feel her gaze on me, and a shiver ran down my spine.

It was then I knew I needed to tell the truth.

"Lady Stella," I whispered, my voice shaking.

She turned to me with concern on her face. "Yes?"

"Can you please bring Lady Rae down here? Just you and her. It is urgent."

Stella's eyes went wide, and she nodded. "Of course." Before anyone could say anything else, she was already ascending the stairs.

Jax grabbed me by my arm and pulled me close. "What are you doing?" He grumbled.

"We were not going to make it through the unveiling without them finding out. It's best to come clean."

"I had a plan! You do not have to tell them who you are! You stupid girl. You are going to ruin this." Anger built in his voice.

I wanted to cower as he spoke, but I held my head high and kept his gaze. "What plan? How were you going to get past the unveiling and keep my identity a secret with no magic?" My heart sank as I saw what was in his other hand. An unsheathed blade. I shouldn't have been surprised, but a part of me was. It is to be expected an assassin would resort to such things when backed into a corner. "Put that away. No one is dying today," I said in a low and serious tone.

He released me, and his lips quirked as he sheathed his blade. "You surprise me, princess. Anyone else would show fear when held tight by me with a blade."

"I escaped death once already. I am not afraid. Death excites me." I teased.

Lady Rae returned with Lady Stella and both of them held concerned looks. Rae stopped in front of me and lowered her gaze to meet mine.

"Lady Stella said you had urgent news for us?" She asked with a tone of annoyance.

"I do," I whispered, praying to The Mother I was making the right choice. "It's about the lost princess."

"What do you know?" She demanded.

Taking a deep, steadying breath, I removed my glamour and watched as Stella and Rae looked at me in shock. "I am Princess Piper Camilla Rossi."

Lady Stella fell to her knees and bowed her head. "Princess, welcome home."

Rae gave me a judgmental glare that would have burned through me if she had the royal flames. "How can we be so sure this is not a ruse?"

"I understand your worry, but it's not. I am sorry I misled you. I just returned to Irolyth, and I was afraid of what I was returning to. I did not expect a world where I would be wanted. I expected the first person to see me to call the guards and demand I be hung like my family. I will complete the unveiling and show you what I am saying to be true."

"I cannot blame you for being afraid. What King Joffrey has put you through, I could not even imagine. Please, step into the waters of truth. Unveil yourself to us," Lady Rae said.

As I stepped toward the water, Jax gently touched my hand, pulling me to him. "You're lucky this went in your favor, but next time, don't do anything without consulting me first," he whispered, then released me.

I didn't respond and walked to the pool. When I stepped into the warm water, my flames came alive within me. The two candles on the altar lit as I walked toward the center of the pool.

"Please, fully submerge yourself," Lady Rae said. All three stood at the water's edge with awaiting gazes. My eyes locked onto Rae's as I dunked myself underwater. Warmth flooded me. When I surfaced, I pushed away the hair that clung to my face.

"Princess," Lady Rae said humbly as she knelt. "I apologize. After all this time, I needed to take precautions. Stella, fetch the princess a towel."

Stella rushed and grabbed a white towel off the rock, then returned to the pool's edge. As I stepped out, she wrapped the towel around me. I took in a deep inhale. The towel smelt like roses. Tears welled my eyes, reminding me of my mother. Before she wed my father, she was a Lady of the Flame. She told me she used to tend to a rose garden here. It reminded her of her sisters, who were all named after flowers. That is where she met my father for the first time. Rae's voice pulled me from my memories.

"Well, man from Orilon, are you who you claim to be?"

He chuckled. "Not at all. I am a human from Elswyth. Trapped by duty to serve."

"Trapped by duty?" The Ladies asked in unison.

It was then I informed them all that had happened these last three years. Including how I tricked a human assassin into helping me on my journey.

"Well, human," Rae said in a stern voice, "step into the pool. Unveil yourself."

With a grumble, Jax did as she said. "I hate getting wet. This is going to mess up my hair."

When he got to the center, he turned back toward us, and his stormy gray eyes were glued to mine. He took a deep breath and dunked himself underwater. The candles on the altar went out, and the room fell into darkness. The sparkling blue water was now a black abyss.

When Jax emerged, his eyes were as dark and endless as the void he stood in.

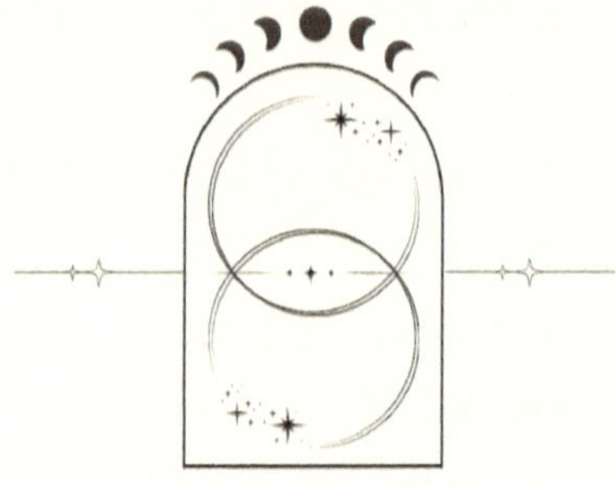

Eleven

The ladies grabbed my arms and pulled me away from the pool in a panic. I couldn't pull my gaze from Jax. His dark hair stuck to his skin, and water dripped down his body. His shirt clung to him and showed off his muscles. Looking into his darkened eyes, I knew I should be afraid. Instead, I found comfort.

"Mother save us," Stella whispered.

"Impossible," Rae said. She released my arm and stepped forward. "Begone foul beast!"

Jax turned his gaze on her. "I am no foul beast." His voice was darker and deeper compared to his normal tone.

"There are many legends of The Shadow coming to snuff out the royal flame. Begone. You are not welcome here!" Rae said in a louder tone.

My heart dropped. I had heard whispers of The Shadow. Many believed it to be the symbol of the end of times. Did Jax know who I was before I even approached him?

"Jax, when you went underwater, all the lights went out, and the water turned black. And your eyes..." I started but trailed off.

I went to take a step forward, but Rae held up her arm to block my path. "Princess, stay back!"

"No, let me go to him!" I tried to move past her, but Stella pulled me back.

"Princess, it is not safe!"

"Do not touch her!" Jax roared.

I watched as he vanished into the darkness. A feeling of unease took over me. I looked around the room frantically for any sign of Jax.

"We must go! Now!" Rae's voice shook as she grabbed my wrist and pulled me toward the exit.

I tried to yank away as I looked back at the now-empty pool. The water had returned to the shimmering aquamarine shade it had been earlier. Stella's scream startled us all. We had almost made it to the stairs, and Jax stood directly in front of us, blocking our way.

Water dripped from his body, and his shadow tattoos looked like they were moving as if they had come to life. Rae put me behind her and Stella. She looked over her shoulder, and it was terror I saw in her hazel eyes.

"I said release her," Jax said in a low growl.

"We won't let you harm the princess. She will reclaim her throne, become queen of this land, and the royal flames will rid the darkness. Irolyth will be no place for you, Shadow!"

"Hurt her? I would never hurt her." Rage filled his eyes and his nostrils flared. "I will help her claim her throne. I will rid the world of the man that hurt her." On that last word, he vanished once again.

Rae and Stella looked around in confusion. A chill shot through me, and when I went to turn my head, something inside me wouldn't allow me to. An arm wrapped around my waist and pulled me back into something firm and wet.

"Every flame casts a shadow. I fully intend on being yours, princess," Jax purred in my ear. My body finally allowed me to move, and I turned my head to see him gazing down at me with a smirk. He looked at the Ladies while holding me close. "I will protect her with my life. The only flame I plan to snuff out is Joffrey's. However, if you try to keep her away from me again, I will destroy this entire sanctuary. Do you understand?" He growled.

"How do we know you are telling the truth?" Rae asked.

"You don't. I do not blame you for the stories that have twisted my name. But, know this to be fact. If you intend on even trying to take her, you will suffer. Everyone here will suffer. She is mine. I am hers. The Mother created me for Piper. Will you go against your Mother's will?"

Something inside of me knew what he said to be the truth. When I gently pressed into him, his grip on me loosened slightly.

Rae and Stella just stared at him for a moment before they agreed. Rae took a step forward, hesitating before speaking. "We will trust you, for now. But if you do anything to harm her, you will meet your end. Come along, and let me take you to your chambers."

Jax released me and came to my side. He took my hand in his and smiled down at me. His eyes were now back to the stormy gray I was familiar with, and his tattoos were now static on his body. "I think that sounds wonderful. Our princess needs her rest after the journey we've had."

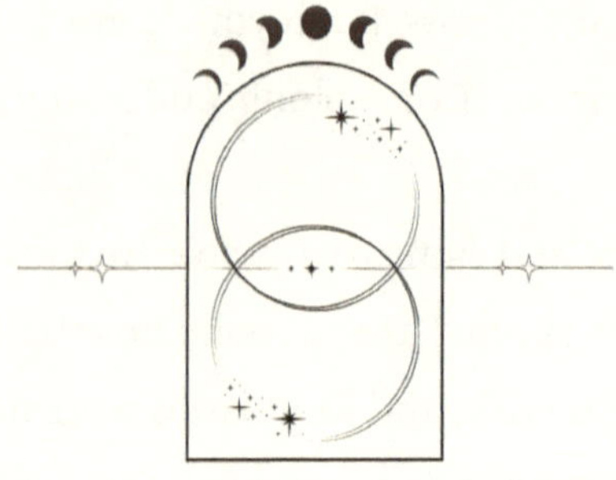

Twelve

Stella and Rae took us to the building behind the main building of the sanctuary that I had never been in before. The entry floor was a large room with beautiful white marble columns that matched the floor. The walls were painted a light tangerine. Two staircases led to a floor above and one below. A fire danced within the hearth in the center of the room.

"Up the stairs will be your living quarters while you're here," Rae said. "Downstairs is off limits for now. If you need anything, all you need to do is ask."

With that, Stella and Rae gave their goodbyes, not looking at Jax as they left. The two of us went upstairs and opened the door to our living quarters. It was truly magnificent. There was a large sitting room decorated exactly how my parents decorated their royal apartments. The furniture was upholstered with deep orange velvet with gold accents. I smiled as I admired the painting of the redwood forest in autumn hung above the fireplace. To the right was a fully stocked kitchen. My stomach growled as I thought of food. It had been way too long since I last ate. On the left side of the sitting room was a staircase that led to an open hallway. The railing was twisted golden bars.

There was a single door in the center of the hall made of stained glass in the image of flames. We entered the room and found a beautifully furnished bedroom. One large bed sat in the center against the back wall, with a dark orange covering that matched the furniture downstairs. There was a closet on the left wall full of clothes that the Ladies said we could help ourselves to. To the right were double frosted glass doors that led to a bathroom.

Jax and I hadn't spoken since leaving the unveiling. There was so much I wanted to ask, so much I needed to say. But it was he who broke the silence.

"I will wait outside while you change into dry clothes." He left and shut the stained-glass door behind him before I could respond.

I went into the bathroom and peeled off my soaking wet clothes. The towel they provided after the ritual did very little to dry me; I was still soaking wet. I quickly took a shower, dried off, and got dressed. When I returned downstairs, Jax was sitting on the floor cross-legged in front of the fireplace, intensely staring at the flames. I walked over to his side and lowered my gaze, curious if he would say anything before I did. His stormy gray eyes looked up at me.

"Did you know what you are?" Were the only words I could get to leave my lips.

"Not until the unveiling. When I was underwater, everything was revealed to me by The Mother. I swear I didn't know who you were or what I was when I walked into The White Rabbit. I only went there to bother Steve."

Taking a deep breath, I sat down on the floor next to him. "What exactly did you see?"

He let out a low chuckle. "I saw inside me lies a shadow spirit, originally from the realm of Orilon. It entered my body the moment I was born. It had been with me all along. There had been moments in my life where my powers manifested without me even knowing. The Mother showed me the truth behind those moments that I assumed were just luck. These powers have allowed me to become the best assassin in Elswyth." He turned his gaze back to the fire. "I saw it is my duty to serve you, even beyond our deal. That I am to do the hard things you cannot. That I am to be your sword and shield. That I am to help you become queen."

I leaned my head against his shoulder, and he wrapped his arm around me, pulling me in close. His touch filled me with comfort. "I'm scared," I whispered.

"Of?"

"Being queen. It was never my path. My brother was to be king, so I spent my entire life learning my place was to serve the crown. To be wed for political gain. Never to be more than a trophy."

Jax gently took my chin in his hand and forced me to look into his eyes. "You are no trophy. You are not a pawn for political gain. You will make a powerful and fair queen. It will be an honor to serve you." He leaned down and gently pressed his lips to mine.

Frozen in shock, heat rushed through my body. I saw the fire flare out of the corner of my eye. Finally, I made my move. Wrapping my arms around his neck, I pressed into him.

He pulled away and gave me a soft smile. "Gods, I have been wanting to do that since we sealed the bargain." He stood and walked toward the stairs. "As much as I'd like to stay and do that some more, I need to go take a shower. Tonight we will rest. Tomorrow we will worry about the weight of the world."

I watched him walk up the stairs until he rounded the corner out of sight. Did that really just happen? Did he really just kiss me? I sat there for a while in silence, staring into the flames just as he had been earlier.

After some time, my stomach let out a loud growl, and I entered the kitchen. We hadn't eaten since leaving Elswyth. I decided while Jax was in the shower, I would prepare our meal. Opening the fridge, I perused the ingredients. Two steaks, an onion, butter, cream, stock, a dry white wine, pasta, and seasonings were exactly what I needed.

With everything ready, the idea of the meal formed, and I got to work. I loved to cook, but it was my mother who instilled her love of cooking in me. Every Sunday, she gave the kitchen staff the day off. We would prepare the meals for the family. My love of cooking was the only thing I took to Elswyth as a reminder of my family. This meal was the first one I'd made for Steph when she took me in.

I missed her and Steve more than I could imagine, I wasn't sure if or when I would see them again. The White Rabbit had been my home, and the people there had quickly become my family when I thought I was alone in the world. When everything in Irolyth was said and done, I hoped I could return to show how much they meant to me. Part of me wondered if Steph knew Jax had a shadow spirit in him. She rarely used her magic in my presence, so I was unaware of how powerful she was.

She said her mother and aunt had used it to do terrible things. That magic in Elswyth corrupted the good within people. Power had turned them into monsters.

"It smells good in here." Jax's voice pulled me out of my thoughts.

I almost dropped the wooden spoon I was holding. He stood in the doorway with only a towel wrapped around his waist. His dark hair was slicked back, and beads of water dripped down his muscles. Heat flooded my body at the sight, and I could not help to wish he dropped the towel. I quickly returned my gaze to the onions caramelizing in the pan.

"Thank you. It's going to taste just as good." My body tensed as Jax came over and stood directly behind me. He reached around me and took the spoon out of my hand. My gaze followed the spoon as he brought it to his lips.

"You're right," he purred after he took a taste.

"Why don't you go get dressed so I can finish cooking?" I forced the words to pass my lips. To be honest, I wanted nothing more than for him to drop the towel right here.

"Is that truly what you want, princess?" Longing flashed through those gray eyes.

I turned to face him, swallowing hard as I met his gaze. "You're distracting me, and if I burn this meal, I will be very upset."

A predatory grin grew on his face. "Kiss me, and I will go get dressed."

"You already stole one kiss. Do you think you deserve another?" My entire body tingled. I couldn't believe the conversation we were having.

"Absolutely not. However, that hasn't stopped you from enjoying my kisses. I will steal another, and later, after dinner, you're going to be begging for a lot more than just kisses." Before I could respond, his lips were on mine once again. This time, they were passionate and hungry.

I leaned into his kiss and matched his fire. Wrapping my arms around his neck, I pressed my body into his. Our tongues danced with each other, and I found myself craving more. When he pulled away, I wished he hadn't.

"I-I should get back to cooking."

"I will go get dressed now, princess. I can't wait to eat. I'm starving." He slowly gave me an up-and-down glance, slowly licking his top lip. With a wink, he pulled away from me, exited the room, and walked upstairs.

I couldn't help but watch him until he vanished into the shadows, just as he did in the ritual chamber. Part of me hoped he would have sat me on the kitchen counter and taken me right here.

Quickly, I stuffed down those feelings. I turned my attention back on cooking and put all of my frustrations into making this the best dish I had ever made.

About thirty minutes later, I had the table set with two delicious plates of creamy caramelized onion pasta, topped with a sliced steak seasoned with fresh herbs. Jax returned downstairs in a loose black top and gray pants just as I had finished plating,

He inhaled deeply and a smile grew on his face. "Thank you for making this. I can't wait to eat," he said as he sat down at the table.

I sat next to him and offered a smile. "I hope you like it."

"I like you. So, I like anything you make." He picked up his fork and began eating.

Heat flooded my cheeks once again at the compliment. I didn't even know how to respond. Before Joffrey's betrayal, I did not have any men courting me. At The White Rabbit, the only men interested in me were extremely wasted. I never thought I would be in The Glade sitting at a table with a man I was smitten with.

"Eat," he said with his fork held up to my mouth. It had a swirl of pasta and a small piece of steak. I opened my mouth, and he gently slid it in. The flavors burst on my tongue, and I melted in delight.

I truly outdid myself with this meal. It was perfect.

"Now eat your own. You owe me a bite." He pulled his fork from my mouth and immediately took a swirl of pasta off of my plate and put it into his own mouth. "It's too good not to get as much as I can," he chuckled.

"Hey! You chose to give me some of yours. That's on you." I readied another bite on my fork.

"You got me there."

"I think now that we have a safe house, we need to start a plan on what to do next."

"Tomorrow, princess. We will worry about all that tomorrow. Rest."

"But—"

"Shh." He put another bite of pasta into my mouth. "Eat. Rest. I will clean up the kitchen after we are done eating."

The two of us dined together, and I found myself excited to be in his company. Once we were done eating, Jax cleaned up the kitchen just as he'd said. I went upstairs into the bedroom, and with a snap of my fingers, the fireplace ignited. I fell into bed and took a deep breath. The softness of the mattress reminded me of the luxury back at the castle. Gods, how I had missed it. For the first time in a while, I closed my eyes and allowed myself to relax.

After a few moments, Jax's voice broke the silence. "Are you ready to go to sleep, princess?"

I opened my eyes and sat up, yawning. "I think so. I'm exhausted."

He strode into the room and stopped just in front of me. "What side of the bed do you want?"

It was then it finally dawned on me there was only one bed. Did he expect to share it with me? "I plan on sleeping in the middle. You are sleeping downstairs."

He threw his head back and laughed. "No. I am sleeping in this bed. With you. I do not trust you being alone."

"What do you mean, you don't trust me?" I stood and furrowed my brow.

"I trust you. What I don't trust is this place, these people. I will give you five minutes to get into your night clothes." He winked, turned, and left the room.

All I could do was stare at the door. Never had I shared my bed with a man. My heart raced at the idea of him being so close to me. As much as I wanted to hate the arrogant assassin, I could not stop myself from falling for him. But there was no time for that now, not with everything that was on the line. I went over to the closet and picked out a red silky set. It was the only one that came with pants. The others were tiny slips that would reveal way too much. I nearly jumped out of my skin as I heard Jax's voice from behind me just as I finished changing.

"Damn, I am too late for the show. What a shame."

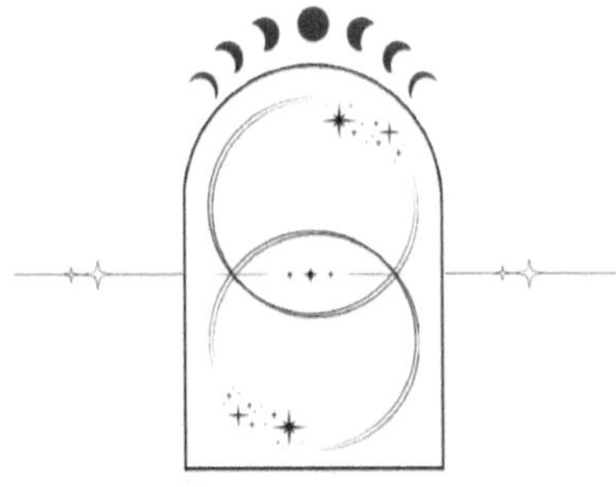

Thirteen

My heart pounded in my chest. Jax leaned against the door frame, shirtless. Heat rose to my cheeks as I met his predatory stare and he closed the space between us. Quickly, I looked away, but he placed his thumb under my chin and lifted my head, forcing me to meet his gaze.

"Do you like what you see, princess?" A delicate purr escaped his lips.

Words jammed in my throat as I tried to form a coherent response. After a moment of stuttering, I was finally able to speak. "It's time for bed. I am going to put pillows down the center. You will have your side, and I will have mine."

He let out a deep chuckle. "You think if I wanted to take you, those pillows would stop me from doing so?"

My body tensed at his words. But I couldn't help being intrigued. I hated that I couldn't get the image of his hands exploring my body out of my mind. His touch was now all I craved. Quickly, I forced down those feelings. There was no room for romance at a time like this. My main focus needed to be reclaiming my throne. I cannot allow myself to be distracted.

It was hard to tell if these feelings were real, or if they were just due to heightened emotions.

Stepping away from him, I shot him a pointed glare. "Good night, Jax."

The cocky grin on his face dropped. "Good night," he grumbled.

The two of us got into bed. Wanting to keep the most distance between us as I could, I clung to the edge. I snapped my fingers, and the fire dimmed so it could keep us warm, but the light wouldn't keep us awake. It seemed like I laid there for hours, my body refusing to give into sleep's sweet embrace. My mind kept racing and debating over matters of duty and heart.

I rolled over and saw Jax staring up at the ceiling. He looked over at me and broke the silence. "I didn't mean to upset you."

"You didn't. I just need to focus on the path ahead. The weight of saving my kingdom is too heavy to let myself worry about anything else," I said.

Jax scooted closer to me and smiled. "Well, I'm glad I didn't upset you. As for your burdens, let me help carry them. You are not alone in this. I am here by your side and will help you burn down the world if that's what it takes."

I offered him a soft smile and moved closer to the center of the bed. "The Fire Queen needs her Shadow."

"The Shadow is nothing without his Fire Queen," he responded.

On that last word, the two of us sat up and crashed our lips together. The fire across the room roared in response as I wrapped my arms around his neck and slid my fingers through his dark hair. Jax grabbed me by the waist and pulled me to sit on top of him. His kiss turned rough as he held me close. After a time that felt too short, our lips parted.

"Praise The Mother," I whispered.

"The only goddess I wish to worship is you."

His lips were back on mine, and I craved more. I cursed myself for the nightclothes I'd chosen, now wishing I'd picked something that would have given him better access to my body. I quickly pulled my top off and revealed to him my bare breasts.

"Beautiful," he groaned as he leaned down and took one of my nipples into his mouth. As he gently sucked on it, his hand found its way to my other breast, and he rolled my nipple in between his middle finger and thumb.

A moan escaped my lips. Grinding on his lap, I made small circles with my hips, and he thrusted up against me. There was nothing I wanted more than to feel him deep inside me. For the first time, I found a man who I wanted to give myself fully to. Ecstasy ran through my body as he grazed his teeth over my nipple. When he looked up at me with those stormy eyes, I nearly melted.

"Take those pants off before I rip them off of you to expose that beautiful little cunt of yours," he growled.

I quickly did as he commanded, and he did the same, unveiling his considerable length. Never did I imagine that it would be that large. It was hard to imagine that it could fit inside of me. The girth of it had my body quivering at the sight alone.

Jax pulled me on top of him once again, quickly lining himself up with my entrance. He wasted no time slowly lowering me onto him. My eyes rolled back as I felt myself stretch to be able to take him. When he was as deep as he could go, I moved my hips in circular motions.

Jax let out a groan as he started thrusting into me, in and out, with no mercy. I placed my hands on his chest for support as he pounded into me, moaning to the rhythm of him.

"You feel as if you were made for me," he moaned. A moment later, he stopped thrusting. "Bounce on my cock," he demanded.

"It was you that was made for me," I purred in response. I obliged his command and gradually increased my pace until I was slamming myself down onto him. Jax held onto my hips tightly as I rode him. Mother, he was perfect. I would give up almost anything to stay in this moment for all eternity.

Without warning, Jax flipped us over so I was on my back. He began his merciless thrusts once again. Arching my back, I screamed his name. Stars filled my vision as I found my pleasure. He slowed down but continued hitting the deepest part of me. An eruption of heat filled my core, and Jax let out a roar as he pushed deep into me and held himself there as his release filled me.

He leaned down and planted his lips on mine. Breaking up the kiss, he growled, "Mine." When he pulled out of me, his essence spilled out. An emptiness took over me, and I found myself craving him once again. Jax reached down and, with two fingers, stroked me while gathering what had fallen out. He then gently pushed it back inside.

"Don't you dare waste a single drop," he growled.

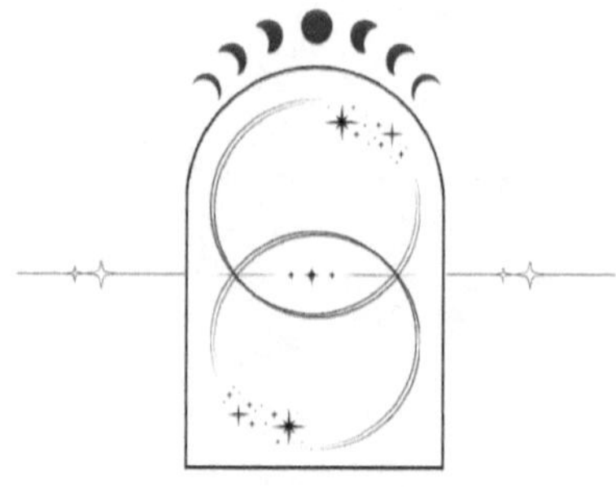

Fourteen

The next morning, I awoke in Jax's arms. The fire still blazed across the room, sending heat through my body. I snuggled my head into his chest, and my thoughts started to spiral. After everything was said and done, what would be next for us? Would he return to Elswyth, or would he stay here with me?

He gently ran his fingers through my hair. I lifted my head and saw him smiling down at me with sleep still in his eyes. He looked so calm, I wished we could stay locked in this moment for eternity. With a yawn, he held me tight against him.

"I never want to leave this bed," he purred.

"Then let's not. At least, not right now." I planted a kiss on his soft and tender lips.

A moment later, a knock sounded on the door leading out of the suite. Jax let out a growl and got out of bed, quickly put on his pants, and left the bedroom. I wrapped a robe around myself and went over to the bedroom door. I peeked out and over the balcony to see he was already downstairs and the door was open. Rae and Stella both stood just outside.

"Good morning," Rae said with venom in her words. She gave him a pointed up-and-down glare, then forced herself past him as she walked in. Stella followed in behind her.

"Why yes, please come in," Jax said, rolling his eyes.

"Where is the princess? What have you done to her?" Rae spat.

I made my way over to the railing and looked down at the three of them. "I'm here. Please give me a moment to get ready and I will be right down."

The Ladies' eyes went wide when their attention landed on me. I'm sure they knew exactly what had happened last night between Jax and me based on the way we were both dressed. Before they could say anything, I turned and walked into the bedroom. Once my clothes for the day were selected and laid on the bed, I entered the bathroom to finish getting ready.

When I was all ready for the day, I took a look in the mirror. I wore an orange and gold top with long bell sleeves and black pants. I put my wavy hair into a top bun with a few pieces left out to frame my face. When I looked into my green eyes, it took everything in me not to cry. The person I saw reflecting back wasn't me.

It was my mother.

I prayed to The Mother I would be half the queen she was. Cassia Regina Rossi was one of the most beloved queens in all of Irolyth's history. Until my uncle's lies had our people turning on us. To my mother, serving the crown meant serving the people. She wanted what was best for all, not just those who were high-born.

She came from a line of fae that had great powers gifted by nature itself. She and her sisters were all named after flowers. I never met any of them, they were all spread through the fae realms. My grandmother was one of the only fae from Tarak to leave the realm to travel to all of the realms. Unfortunately, she was never able to return to Tarak. She passed away long before I was born. My mother told me many stories about her family and how kind they were. Without my mother's magic and teachings, the farms of Irolyth would not be as successful as they are today.

As I descended the stairs, all eyes were on me. Stella and Jax both sat on the couch, and Rae was standing at the bottom landing.

"Princess Piper," she began with a deep breath, "We understand the next part of your journey is long. We understand what road you must travel down to free the people of Irolyth. However, before you can travel down that path, there is one more thing you must do."

"What is that?"

"You must speak to The Mother. You must get her approval to rule. Your father did the same before he ascended the throne, and so did all who came before him. Joffrey did not. He spat in the face of our most sacred traditions."

I raised an eyebrow. "Speak to The Mother?"

Rae hooked her arm around my elbow. "Yes, come. All will become clear in time."

Jax jumped from his seat. "Great. Where are we going?"

"You will be staying here with me," Lady Stella said.

"No. I go where she goes."

Rae shot him a glare. "Do you, too, spit in our faces? Will you also throw away our rituals and traditions, Shadow?"

Jax let out a low snarl and looked over to me. I gave him a small nod, and he sat back in his seat. "Fine. How long will this take?"

"Not long. Only an hour or so," Rae answered without a care.

"If she is not back in two hours, I will destroy this entire place to get to her."

"No need for all that. She will return shortly," Lady Stella assured him.

Rae turned her attention toward me. "Come along now, princess."

She guided me to the room where the unveiling had taken place. My heart pounded in my chest as I relived what had happened yesterday. We walked around the pool and stopped before the effigy of the Mother. On the altar in front of it was a golden bowl with some herbs and salts, surrounded by white candles.

I looked up at the golden statue and took a deep breath. Rae walked around to the other side of the altar and extended her hand.

"Please trust me. Please give me your hand, palm up," she said in a soft voice.

I gave her my hand, and she held it tightly. An athame blade magically appeared in her hand, and she quickly ran it over my palm, causing blood to pool in my hand. She turned my hand, and the blood spilled into the bowl. The candles ignited one by one, and when the last one sparked to life, everything faded to black.

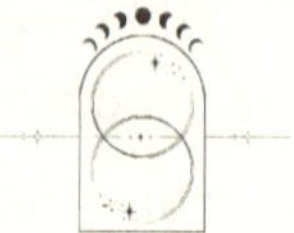

I awoke, standing in a marble room with pillars lining the walls. I spun around to see there were no doors or windows. My heart pounded in my chest, and my breathing became quick and shallow.

"Calm now, little flame," a soothing and feminine voice said.

My attention snapped to the far end of the room where The Mother sat on a marble throne in a long, white tulle gown. Her blonde hair fell in loose waves around her. Our gazes met, and calmness washed over me. She stood and stepped down from the dais.

"Where... Where am I?" I asked.

"You are in a part of my home. I closed off the rest to you. We would not wish for you to get lost in these eternal halls." In a blink, she was directly before me. She took my hands in hers and smiled. "Tell me why you are here, little flame."

"I need your blessing," I said meekly. Before The Mother, I was no one. How dare I ask her for anything? I should be grateful to bask in her ethereal glow.

"My blessing?" She raised a brow.

"I wish to become Queen of Irolyth," I said, forcing out every drop of confidence I had.

"Why now? Why not three years ago? Why not three years from now?"

"I am ready now. When I ran, I was a coward. I did not realize what I was leaving my people to." I dropped to my knees and lowered my head. "Please, allow me to save them."

She let out a soft hum. "Everything has happened just as it should have." My gaze snapped up with wide eyes. "You were not ready to reign at sixteen. You needed to find yourself. You needed to find him." She gently pulled me up to my feet.

"Jax?"

She nodded. "I spread rumors of The Shadow being a monster to destroy the kingdom, hoping they would steer your uncle's path. When he came to me for my blessing once he stole the throne, I told him it was he who set The Shadow in motion, for he would never receive my blessing. You, little flame, are of kind heart. You have the same hope and intentions as your parents, but you were not made for battle. I sent him to you so you could be free to care for your people. Free to help them. Allow The Shadow to do what needs to be done. The Shadow will always find you in your time of need."

She gently placed a kiss on my forehead, and bright light filled the room. I shut my eyes tight to shield myself from it. When the light dimmed, I opened my eyes and saw Rae smiling at me.

"Welcome back, my queen," she said with a bow.

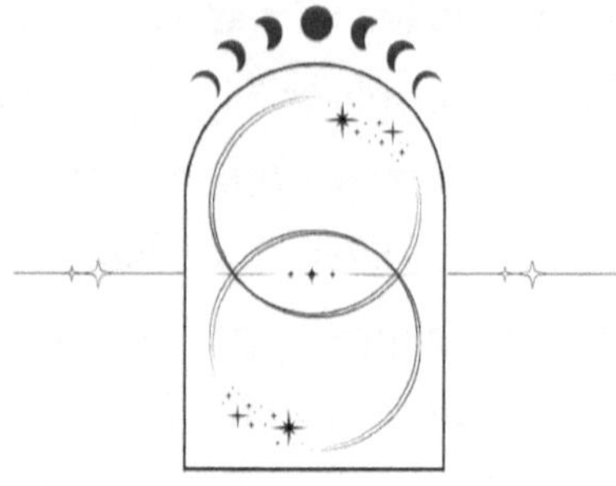

Fifteen

Lady Rae and I returned to the suite. As soon as we opened the door, Jax ran to me and wrapped me tight in his arms. Stella was sitting on the couch with a nervous expression, and as Rae went to her side, Stella stood. The two of them whispered to each other.

"I was so worried they were taking you from me," he said softly with concerned, stormy gray eyes before gently placing a kiss on my head.

"No one will ever take me from you, or you from me," I whispered back. I then told him of all that had happened in my time while I was gone. Jax stared down at me in shock as the story unfolded.

"My Queen," Lady Stella said with a bow. "Please allow me to guide you to the next part of your journey."

Jax finally released me, and we turned toward the Ladies of the Flame

"Please rise," I said, and she did. It felt so odd making such commands. I was Queen, but it still felt awkward. "I need to go to the palace. I cannot ask you to leave The Glade and travel all that way."

"The door downstairs leads to tunnels that will take you to the castle," Rae responded. "Stella will take you to them once you are ready."

"I didn't know there were tunnels," I said, confused.

"It was how your father and mother traveled back and forth to see each other during their courtship. It was originally placed as an emergency route, and is a well-kept secret," Rae said.

"Kept even from King Joffrey," Stella added. "We know that it will take you to the castle, but we are not exactly sure where. We believe there are several exits."

"Give us another day to prepare," Jax inserted himself. "I need to teach our fire queen how to blend into the shadows."

"If the queen agrees." Rae's gaze shot to me, and I gave her a nod of approval. "So it shall be. We will be here tomorrow at first light." The two Ladies exited the suite and shut the door behind them.

"We have lots of things to go over, especially if we are going to make it out alive," Jax said, turning to me. "Killing a king is no joke. I have also never done a job with someone tagging along who I had to babysit."

"You do not need to babysit me!" I crossed my arms as I looked up at him and furrowed my brow.

His eyes darkened. "Yes, I do. I cannot allow any harm to come of you. You are my number one priority. Besides, are you going to be able to defend yourself if you're attacked?"

"I can defend myself!"

In an instant, Jax grabbed both of my wrists with one hand and slammed me into the wall with his blade to my throat. "You're dead if this happens to you in the castle."

"That wasn't fair! I was not expecting that." I squirmed in his grip, trying to get away.

"That's the point, *my queen*. You need to be ready for any-thing." He held me tighter and put his face an inch from mine. The air electrified around us. "If you want to get free, fight for it."

"Jax! Let go. I don't want to hurt you."

"Hurt me, princess. I dare you," he teased.

Heat flared in my body, and I focused my royal flames on him. His hands caught fire, but he didn't react. I sent more fire, but still, he acted as if nothing had happened.

"Is that all the fire queen has?" The smirk on his face grew. "What a shame. I expected more."

I forced all of my magic out of me and set all of him ablaze. He released me and stepped back with a confused expression, but he didn't react to the heat. I quickly extinguished the flames and noticed the ground was charred where he stood. He leaned down and dragged his finger against the black floor, inspecting it closely.

"Interesting..." he whispered. "I thought it had no heat, but it seems it did, and I am not affected by your flames."

"You felt nothing?" I asked, kneeling to meet his gaze.

"Nothing at all. What an interesting discovery." Jax raised his gaze to me. "Let's work on your stealth skills."

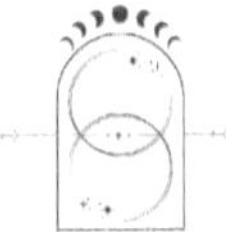

The next morning came too fast. Jax and I had stayed up halfway through the night, preparing for what was to come. When my head finally hit the pillow, I tossed and turned. My mind raced with every possible outcome, and I feared we were headed to our deaths.

Rolling onto my side, I faced Jax, who had not yet awoken. He looked so peaceful, and I found myself wondering what he was dreaming about. How could he sleep with what loomed on the horizon? I snuggled into him and inhaled his smokey, citrus scent. He wrapped his arms around me and ran his fingers through my hair.

"Good morning," he said with a yawn.

"Good morning. Lady Stella should be here any minute."

"Well then, we have another minute to do this." He gently lifted my chin and planted a kiss on my lips.

Just as we parted, there was a knock on the door. With a chuckle, Jax got out of bed, threw on his pants, and left the room. I got up to get ready for the day. After a few moments, Jax returned to the bedroom.

"Stella will wait for us downstairs."

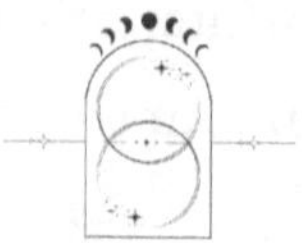

Luckily, my father had a stash of weapons for Jax to select from. Once we were geared up, the two of us met Stella in the foyer. She paced back and forth, and as soon as we came downstairs, she ran over to us.

"Good morning, my Queen." She smiled at me, then turned her attention to Jax. "Shadow," she said with a small nod of acknowledgment. "Please come this way."

She led us down the stairs and unlocked the door. Quickly, she ushered us inside and shut the door behind her. We were surrounded by total darkness. Jax took my hand and squeezed it as if he could sense my unease.

Lady Stella whispered something in the ancient fae language, and the torches lit up one by one, illuminating the long hallway before us.

"The flames will guide your way. No matter what, trust their guidance. For one wrong turn could mean your death," she said in a hushed tone as she paled.

"Our death?" Jax asked.

She nodded. "This tunnel was used for emergencies. Unwanted visitors would end up getting lost and disposed of. Please stay safe. Reclaim your throne. Save us. I beg of you."

"I promise. His reign ends here. I will restore Irolyth to the great land it once was."

Lady Stella did not say another word. She gave a quick nod, opened the door, and exited it. After it shut, the hall echoed with a locking sound, leaving Jax and I alone to finish our journey.

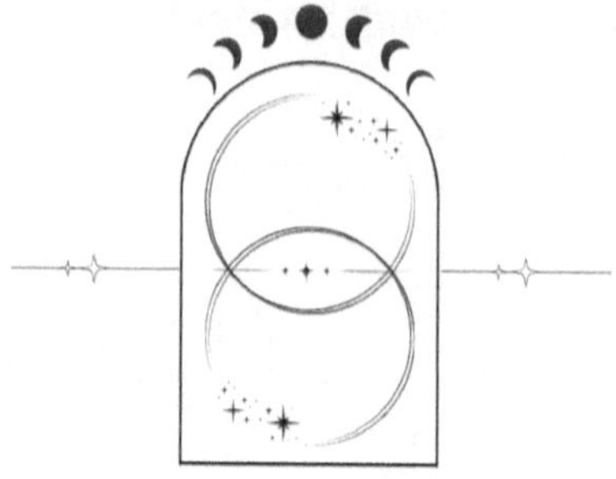

Sixteen

We had been walking for what seemed like hours down the cement hallways. The only guide is the iron torches hanging on the wall. The more we traveled, the farther apart they became. When we approached an intersection, each way had one torch. They remained unlit until we were upon them, and only one would light. When we made the turn, it would extinguish. A heavy must filled the air. The sounds of scratching, screams, and footsteps could be heard every so often, making me jump. Jax never faltered and kept his hand wrapped around mine. Fear tore through my body as a roar echoed off the walls, and I froze in place. There was no way I could do this. I can't face my uncle. I can't save Irolyth. Jax turned to me and gave me a reassuring kiss. "You're okay. Remember what Lady Stella said, just follow the flames."

I looked up at him and felt tears well in my eyes. Anxiety rattled my bones. It was all becoming too real. "Jax," I whimpered. "I don't think I can do this. I can't be queen. I can't kill my uncle. I can't find my way out of the darkness!"

He brushed away my tears with his thumb as determination filled his eyes. "You will be a wonderful queen. The Mother gave you her blessing for a reason. You will not kill that son of a bitch. I will. I will make him pay for everything he has put you through. We will get out of the darkness together." His voice rose as he spoke. "We will do this together." Then he spoke to me in a soft, calming voice. "The Fire Queen and her Shadow."

"You promise?"

He nodded. "I promise. With every fiber of my soul. We will make it out. I will kill him. You will be queen."

I wrapped him in a tight hug, and he returned the gesture. We stood there for a long moment, embracing one another. My breathing steadied, and the tears stopped flowing. The air in the tunnels changed, and a cold wind hit my back. Another loud roar filled my ears, and the ground shook. Jax's body tensed for a moment before he pulled away from me. He grabbed my wrist and pulled me into a sprint.

"Run! Don't look behind you!" He commanded.

I couldn't help but look and saw a large beast chasing after us. The bipedal monster was quickly closing the gap, but all I could focus on was the foam pouring out of its mouth and coating its long fangs. Jax yanked on my arm.

"Piper! I told you not to look!"

I turned my head back, facing forward once again, and pushed my short legs to run as fast as they could. The sound of our footsteps was swallowed by the beast's roars. Torches continued to light as we made our way through the halls. After what seemed like an eternity, the hallway suddenly split into two paths, but neither torch lit. Jax and I froze, gasping for air, and turned toward the beast barreling toward us.

"Well, Fire Queen, time to put that name to the test," Jax said as he readied his blade.

Heat filled my body as I focused on calling my magic. My eyes locked onto the beast's golden eyes with slitted pupils. I raised my hand, and fire formed in my palm. I hurled my flame at the monster, hit it in the shoulder, and caused it to stagger back.

The space darkened, and I noticed Jax was gone. When he reappeared, he was on the monster's back, plunging his dagger into its eye. It screamed and shook, raising its arm and trying to swipe its long claws over its shoulder. Jax vanished before contact could be made, leaving his dagger stuck in the monster's eye.

The beast ripped out the dagger and threw it toward me. I ducked and heard it clatter on the ground behind me. I barely had time to stand before the beast had closed the distance between us and backhanded me with its massive paw, sending me flying into the wall. I let out a scream on impact, felt as if my bones cracked, and then used what little strength I had left to cast another fireball. It hit dead center in the monster's chest, causing its fur to set ablaze.

A blade pierced through its stomach, and the beast's mouth pooled with blood. The blade was pulled out of the beast, and the monster fell to the ground, revealing Jax with a sword in hand. The fire roared and engulfed the beast entirely. After a moment, it was nothing but ash.

Jax dropped the weapon and rushed to me, fell to his knees, and cradled my face in his hands. Worry filled those stormy eyes. " Are you alright?" Panic rose in his voice.

"I... I am alright," I groaned. My body ached from being thrown into the wall, but it was nothing that wouldn't heal quickly.

A flash of bright light filled my vision. One of the directions in the forked hall had lit up, illuminating a dark wooden door up ahead. The gold Rossi family crest glittered in the firelight.

I was home.

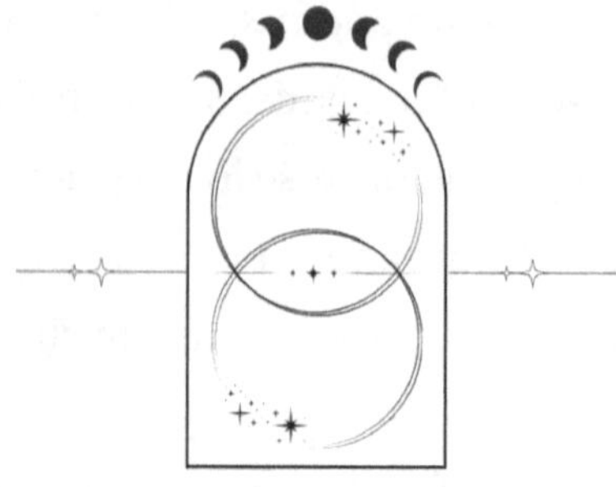

Seventeen

Before we opened the door, I threw on my glamour. Jax opened the door, and on the other side was a small, dust-filled square room with an iron ladder leading to a hatch on the ceiling. Jax put his finger to his lips, then went ahead of me. Unsheathing his blade, he put the steel between his teeth. After testing the stability of the ladder, he slowly climbed the rungs and cautiously lifted the hatch. He silently motioned for me to wait here. Then he vanished into the shadows, and the hatch shut.

Silence hung in the air and uneasiness settled in my core. Left to my own devices, my thoughts raced. I wondered where we were. If we were in the castle, where? What was beyond this room? What was Jax facing alone?

My stomach turned as I thought of what lay ahead. I thought of what The Mother had told me. I would not be a queen of violence. The Shadow would be my sword. Something in me cracked when I thought of forcing Jax to do terrible things on my behalf.

Was it forcing if he was already doing those things long before our paths crossed?

The hatch swung open, causing me to nearly jump out of my skin. Jax poked his head through the space. "Come on up. The coast is clear."

Once I was through the hatch, I knew exactly where we were. Dust gathered on the shelves of the pantry of our townhome in the city of Mayrin. I was surprised, as I thought the tunnels were to take us to the castle. My family and I would spend a week here every year in the winter for the Festival of Fire; a celebration held on the Winter Solstice.

In the center of the city, we would light a large fire to banish away the long nights and the cold weather. Once the fire was lit, the celebration would last for three days. There were so many street vendors, artists, and performances. It had been one of my favorite festivals.

"Do you know where we are?" Jax asked softly.

I gave him a nod. "This was our home in the city." The row of townhomes was against the wall that surrounded the palace grounds, and only nobility lived there.

"I searched the entire place. It's empty."

The two of us exited the pantry and entered the kitchen. I squinted from the bright sun shining through the dusty windows. When he said empty. He wasn't wrong. All furniture and decor had been removed from the entire house. A surreal feeling took over me. How could a place once filled with so much life be so dead?

"Are you ready to go into the city? Do you think you could get us into the castle from here?" Jax asked.

I turned my head to him and looked at him nervously. "I'm not sure. Maybe we should check the castle wall and see if there are any spots we can get through."

He stood there for a moment with a look of contemplation. "I think we need to see what type of guard presence is throughout the city first. We need to see exactly what's causing the people to run to The Glade. Once we know how many guards are around, we can plan our next move."

I nodded. The Mother knew exactly what she was doing when she put the two of us together. I needed someone who understood strategy. I needed someone to guide me through these hard times. I needed Jax.

We both agreed venturing out after sundown would be the best time to explore the city and begin our plan. There would be fewer people in the streets, and hopefully darkness would hide us. Until then, we would rest. We went back into the pantry and down the hatch to the empty room. The more hidden we were, the better. The two of us sat on the ground with our backs against the wall. Jax wrapped his arm around me and pulled me close. I rested my head against his shoulder, and within the comfort of his arms, I fell asleep.

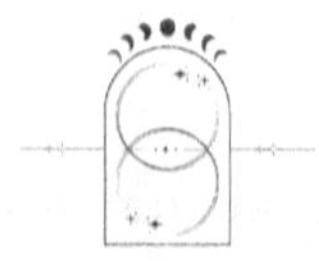

Loud voices jolted me awake, and I noticed Jax wasn't with me anymore. Climbing the ladder, I entered the pantry. The door that led to the kitchen was open. The space was filled with bright orange light. It must be sunset.

Voices chanted something I couldn't make out. Walking into the kitchen, I noticed Jax crouching by one of the windows. His eyes went wide when he saw me.

"Get down!" He commanded in a hushed tone.

I did, and he motioned for me to come over to him. Crawling across the kitchen floor, I joined him under the window.

"What's going on?" I asked.

"War." The coldness of his voice sent a shiver down my spine.

A loud boom filled my ears and rattled the house. The voices started chanting louder, and I was finally able to decipher what they were saying.

"Join the flame or be swallowed by it."

My heart sank as I peeked through the window. It was not the orange glow of sunset that had filled the room. Flames had engulfed large sections of the city. The streets were filled with guards. Some rushed toward the fires, others guided citizens into carriages.

"Don't even think about it," Jax snarled.

"What if those are our way into the castle?" I asked, pointing to the carriages.

"And what if they are to be set ablaze?"

"Fire can't hurt the Fire Queen and her Shadow," I responded with a grin as I jumped up. Before Jax could say anything, I glamoured myself into appearing as a guardswoman. In a flash,

I was outside and in the center of the chaos. Jax rushed out of the house behind me.

A rough man's male voice grated in my ears. "Oi! Grab that man! He knows the rules. Anyone out past curfew is to be sent to the dungeons!"

"Yes, sir!" I grabbed Jax and guided him to the carriages.

"This is the stupidest thing you've ever done," he whispered so softly only I could hear.

A tall female guard approached us as we neared the carriages. "Throw him into this one. You will be the lucky one to drive it in. The previous driver got stabbed by one of the prisoners." She pointed over to a carriage. A man in the guard uniform laid on the ground in a pool of his own blood. "It's full once you add that one. You are good to go." She took a step closer. "What a shame too, because this one is interesting looking. Hopefully, the king won't send him immediately to his death."

With her final word, I pushed Jax toward the carriage. Rage boiled inside me. It took everything I had not to set all of the guards aflame and liberate the city, but I needed to stick to the plan. Another guard unlocked and opened the door. Once I forced Jax inside, the guard slammed the door shut and locked it. I walked to the front of the carriage, sat in the coach box, and drove it toward the castle, following the other carriages.

Panic welled in my mind as we passed through the gates. I tried to focus on the two black horses leading the carriage to calm my nerves.

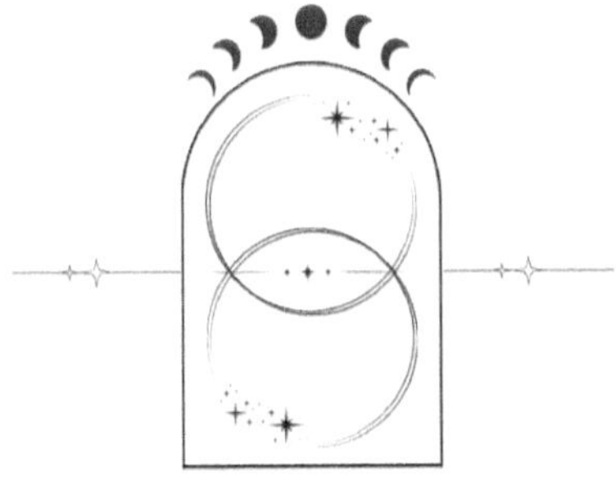

Eighteen

As soon as I stopped the horses next to the dungeon entrance, several guards rushed to the carriage. Prisoners were ushered out of the back of the carriage and led through a door leading to the dungeons. One of the guards pointed me in the direction of where to park the carriage and yelled for me to go down into the dungeons once I was done.

Doing as I was told, I parked the carriage and then made my way down to the dungeon. I was shocked no one had asked questions about a guard they had never seen before. My mind raced with all the things I had just seen. Anger continued to build in me. How could Joffrey treat the kingdom this way? How could he set the city ablaze and take his people prisoner?

Frigid air surrounded me as I descended the stairs and entered the dungeon. Both sides of the hall were cells filled with men, women, and children. My heart broke as I stared at their shivering bodies. Many had their ribs visible through their skin. I avoided their gazes. It took everything I had not to allow the tears to fall. I needed to find Jax and get us into the main section of the castle.

"You!" A deep voice shouted. I looked up and saw a large man in a captain's uniform. "Come with me."

A chill ran down my spine as he commanded me. I gave him a nod and said, "Yes, sir," trying to hide the shaking in my voice.

He guided me into a side room where a man sat tied to a chair with a burlap bag over his head. The captain walked over and ripped off the bag, revealing the man's bruised and bloody face. He looked defeated, and there was no light in his eyes. "This man was said to have been seen with a red-haired woman. He is refusing to give us any information." The captain grabbed the prisoner by the hair and yanked his head back. "My hope is that he will tell us something today."

"I told you, there was no red-haired woman!" The prisoner spat.

"You lie!" the captain spat back and punched the captive in the jaw.

My heart pounded in my chest as I watched the captain assault the man. He did not deserve this. All for being thought to be seen with me. After three years, Joffrey still sought me and punished anyone even rumored to have been seen with me. Fury burned in my heart until it morphed into hot determination. I was the key to ending all this pain.

Just as the captain's fist almost met with the man's face again, I yelled, "Stop!"

The captain quickly turned to me with anger in his eyes. "Did you just give me an order?"

"Yes, I did," I snarled. "As your queen, I command you to stop. I command all of you to stop!" My voice raised with every word. It was now or never. I needed to end this. Jax would find me later. The Shadow always followed the flame.

"Oh, you think just because the king brought you to his bed that means something? News flash, sweetheart, he brings all women who work in the castle to his bed." The captain walked toward me, and I held his rage-filled gaze.

"My name is Piper Camilla Rossi, the rightful Queen of Irolyth." I dropped my glamour, and a fireball formed in my hand. "Take me to my uncle."

His eyes widened, but his look of shock quickly turned to one of hatred. "You made a grave mistake, *princess*. You really think you're coming out of this alive?" The captain snarled at me.

"I know I will," I said with all the confidence I had left. "The Mother gave me her blessing. I will not disappoint her."

He laughed. "Turn around. There are four guards blocking your path. Do you really think you can take all five of us?"

"How about we even the score?" A familiar voice filled my ears as Jax stepped out of the shadows and ran a blade across the captain's throat. My Shadow raised his gaze to look beyond me. "Are you ready to meet the same end as your captain?"

The guards gathered at the door looked on in horror. Without hesitating, I quickly threw fire at their feet, causing them to shout in panic and disperse. I did not want to kill anyone who did not deserve it. For all I knew, they were forced to follow their king's orders under penalty of death. Learning who was truly on Joffrey's side would need to come after I reclaimed my throne.

"Come on. We have to run!" I said to Jax before rushing out of the room. The two of us raced through the halls. Finally, we neared the door leading into the main section of the castle. A large man blocked our path with a great axe in hand. Before I could even stop to face him, two daggers flew past me and hit him in his eyes. The man screamed and staggered, falling to the ground.

We ran past his prone body, up the steps, and entered the main castle. It was cold and dark. Not a single sconce on the wall was lit. Jax slammed the door shut and slid a piece of furniture in front of it so no one could follow us through.

"You stupid girl," he growled at me. "Do you have any idea how reckless all of that was? What if I hadn't been there?" He caged me against the wall. My back pressed into the cold stone.

"I knew you would be." I stood my ground.

"How? How could you have known?" He leaned in close.

"Because where there is the flame..."

Before I could finish the sentence, he continued, "there is the shadow. When I was underwater, that phrase was repeated over and over. And when I was taken into the dungeons, I knew exactly what room to wait for you in."

A smile crossed my face. "You will always find me when I need you."

"Because you are mine. Mine to protect. Mine to cherish. Mine to serve. I don't know why The Mother connected us, but I am so glad she did." He closed the gap between us and quickly kissed my lips. "But don't you ever do anything that stupid ever again."

"I cannot promise you that," I giggled.

A low orange glow filled the space, followed by a high-pitched scream. "Princess Piper?"

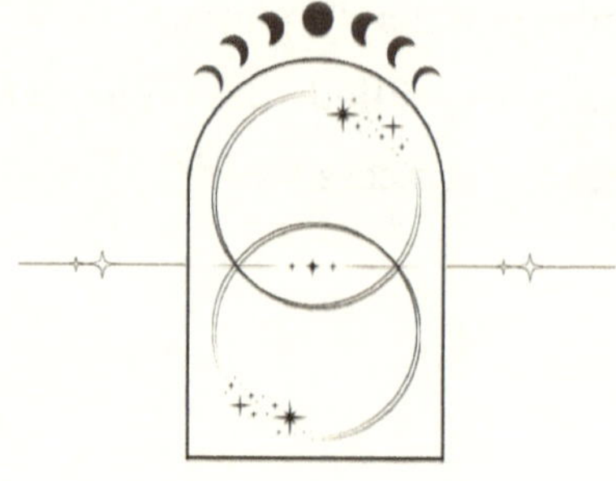

Nineteen

My head snapped in the direction of the sound as the woman dropped her torch onto the stone floor. My jaw dropped when I saw the sister of my lady's maid. Shock rattled through me. She looked so different than she did three years ago. Once plump and tan, she was now thin and sallow. The darkness under her eyes broke my heart. Her dress had tears along the hem.

"Mabel, is that really you?" My voice cracked as I spoke.

She ran to me and wrapped me in a hug. "Oh, thank The Mother. I thought you were dead."

I held her tight. "I am alive. I am well. I am here to save us all." Tears I could no longer hold back fell from my eyes.

"Who is this?" Jax questioned in a cold tone.

Mabel released me and gave Jax an up-and-down look. "A human? You brought a human here?"

"He's no human. He is The Shadow."

Mabel staggered back with a gasp and pulled me to her. "Mother, save us."

"The Mother sent him to me. Everything we learned about The Shadow was wrong," I said, hugging her back. "The only flame he is extinguishing is Joffrey's. Jax is my sword and shield. I would not be here without him." I pulled from her embrace and turned toward Jax. "Jax, this is Mabel. She was the sister to my lady's maid, Ingrid." Turning back to Mabel, I asked her, "Is Ingrid still here? I can't wait to see her!"

Mabel hung her head. "She was hung a week after you vanished. The king was convinced she knew your whereabouts."

My eyes went wide, and my body shuddered. "No," I rasped. "No!"

"Unfortunately so, my Lady. Come, let's get you out of these halls before someone else sees you."

Mabel guided us down the hallways and some stairs into the servant's quarters. Once a clean area hosting many private rooms, the space was now filled with dust, and the walls had been knocked down to create one large room. Dirty and ruined bedrolls filled the floor. As I stood there, taking in the depressing sight, Mabel told me Joffrey treated the people who worked in his castle like animals. Most of the workers were out doing their chores, as they were now done mostly at night to avoid the king. Only a few older ones remained in the quarters, curled up in their bedrolls. All of them had a horrid cough. Mabel informed us of how a deadly illness had quickly spread. Anyone who caught it was lucky to survive, as the servants were receiving no medical treatment. In the back of the room, there was a small hole in the wall. She ushered us in, ducking our heads to avoid the top of the opening, and we now stood in one of the secret passageways that were throughout the castle.

"When King Joffrey ordered the tearing down of the individual rooms, they made this hole in the wall. They did not care enough to fix it, nor did they think to check it." Mabel said with a smile.

"I am so sorry this has happened to you all. You know my father would have never stood for how you are being treated." I gave her another hug.

"Oh, my sweet princess, I know. I was always grateful for how your parents treated us all as equals, no matter our position. And I know once you are on the throne, you will restore our dignity. Now please, go. Down this way." She pointed to the left. "This will lead you to his throne room. Around this time, he sits there and has the servants worship him." A disgusted look took over her face. "Kill him and save us all."

She squeezed me tight before releasing me. We said our goodbyes, and she exited through the hole in the wall. I turned back to Jax with a fire in my eyes.

I would save them.

I would restore peace to Irolyth.

I would be the Queen they deserved.

"Are you ready?" Jax asked, with a look of determination on his face.

"Born ready." I gave him a quick nod.

The two of us quickly traveled down the dark pathway. I had summoned a fireball to light our way. After what seemed like an eternity, we came to a dead end. It would be an impasse for anyone who did not understand how the secret tunnels worked.

Ingrid and I used to play hide and seek throughout them my entire childhood. I walked over to the wall and pressed on the center stone. The wall popped outward and slid open to reveal the back of the throne.

Where once sat two thrones, now there was only one. The memory of my mother just tossed. Joffrey thought of us as disposable to his plans.

Today would be the last time he would tarnish my family's name.

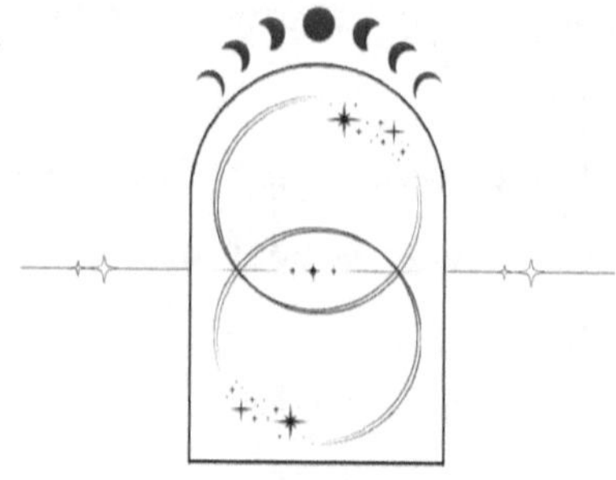

Twenty

"Hello, uncle. Remember me?" I snarled.

Joffrey jumped up from the throne and spun toward us. His eyes went wide, and his face paled. The servant woman who had been kneeling before him rushed out of the room, leaving the three of us alone.

I stepped out of the secret pathway with Jax behind me. Joffrey's eyes met mine, and we stared at each other in silence. He was nearly skin and bones, and his skin had grown so pale. His once long, red hair and beard were now white as snow, but his emerald eyes were still as piercing as I remembered them to be. I wondered how someone could deteriorate so vastly in only three years.

"I know it must hurt seeing the face of your 'favorite niece' after all this time." Anger burned through me as all the lies he told me ran through my mind. How he loved me. How he loved my brother. How he loved my parents. How everything he did was to serve the crown and the people of Irolyth.

His face soured. "Piper, after all this time. After all the searching I have done, what a surprise to have you come to me." Venom dripped off his words.

"I have come to reclaim my throne. You have brought Irolyth to ruin, and I intend to restore it to its former glory."

Jax placed his hand on my shoulder. A silent reminder he was here to support me. Behind me, every step of the way as my Shadow.

"No." He clicked his tongue. "You have come to die, and when you do, The Mother will finally bless me with the royal flames. I will burn Irolyth to the ground, and a new Irolyth will rise from the ashes."

"The Mother will never give you her blessing. Irolyth was thriving before you framed my father and had him hung!"

"Irolyth was weak! Klaus and I had a vision for Irolyth! It all went out the window when he met your mother and allowed her to make him weak. He was too worried about harmony that he didn't see the signs of contempt brewing. He didn't see the nobles were unsettled by the policies he set in place. He didn't see I was his enemy."

"Don't you dare speak ill of my father. The only mistake he ever made was sparing you when he won the crown. Do you want to know what I see? I see you are a monster. That you destroyed our once beautiful land and people. I see how you are weak and your reign is over. I see it all. What I have planned for you isn't punishment enough. You deserve to suffer the way the people of Irolyth have suffered."

Joffrey laughed. "It seems your friend has abandoned you. The man just vanished into..." he trailed off, and fear and realization grew in his eyes. "No. It can't be."

I smirked. "Vanished into *what*, dear uncle?" I asked in an innocent tone.

Joffrey spun on his heels and ran. I waved my hand in the air and brought up a wall of fire in front of him, forcing him to stagger and fall onto his bottom.

"What happened to you?" I asked. "When I last saw you, you were strong. But now you are nothing more than a frail old man. I almost feel bad I am about to destroy someone so pathetic. Allowing you to meet your end is a mercy. A mercy you don't deserve."

Joffrey quickly stood and faced me. "You! *You* are what happened to me. All because I didn't kill you. I made a pact with a demon. I promised him the royal family's souls in exchange for the royal flames and power. It was he who set the sanctuary aflame three years ago that set everything in motion. Since my bargain was incomplete, he slowly took my soul from me. You ruined everything!" He lunged at me, but before he could take a second step Jax reappeared in front of him.

Joffrey pulled a dagger from his waistband and stabbed at Jax. In one quick movement, Jax grabbed my uncle's wrist and twisted it. Joffrey let out a cry and the dagger fell to the floor. Jax kicked it away and vanished once again into the shadows.

"No." I shook my head, and Jax reappeared by my side. "You did. You ruined everything, including yourself," I said in a soft tone.

A fireball formed in my hand, and I hurled it toward Joffrey. He screamed and wailed as he burned and withered to ash. By betraying our family, he refused to join the flame, and in the end, was consumed by it.

Tears fell down my face. After all this time, it was finally over.

Jax pulled me into his chest, and I fell against him, sobbing. He held me tight and smoothed the back of my hair and kissed the top of my head. "It's over. It's over. You are safe. You freed Irolyth."

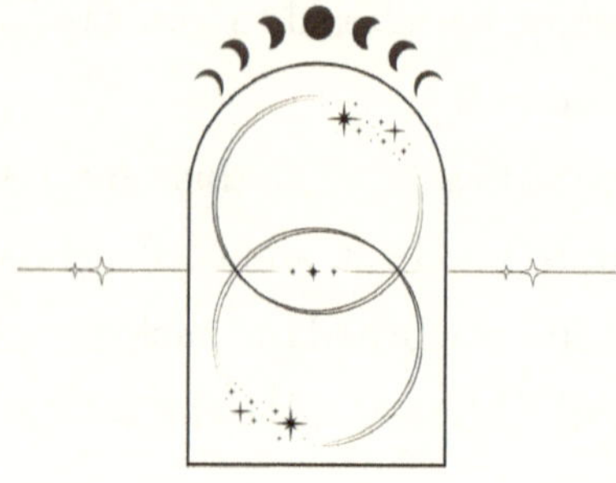

Twenty-One

Three months later, I had successfully rebuilt the capital city of Mayrin. All the refugees from The Glade had moved back, and things were finally beginning to feel normal. Jax removed any guards who had the same ideals and values as my uncle. The castle workers were given time off to rest so I could have the quarters renovated to what they once were. I also made sure that any who had fallen ill received proper treatment.

I sat in my bed and stared out the window, watching the sunrise. Never did I think I would be back in my old room. It seemed as if I had lived so many lives between that fateful day three years ago to now. Jax was staying in my brother's room. The two of us spent most of our free time together, but since becoming queen, there was little free time to be had.

Jax had left on business three days ago. He and I had an agreement I would not ask him what kind of business he had.

As my Shadow, I expected him to do some unsavory things on my behalf for the best of the kingdom. He promised me after taking out my uncle, I would never have to do anything like that ever again.

He also promised he would be back before tonight, and I hoped that to be true.

A small knock sounded on my door. "My queen, it's me. May I come in?" Mabel asked.

"Come in."

"Happy coronation day!" She said as she brought in a tray full of food. She sat it down on the bedside table, and I took note of the coffee and apple pastries. Taking a deep breath, I inhaled the aromas. Mabel sat on the edge of my bed. "Are you excited?"

"I have been queen for three months. I'm not sure a party is necessary or appropriate now."

"It most certainly is! If anyone deserves a party, it is you. The people of Irolyth also need some joy after what we have endured." She jumped up from the bed and set the table next to the window. "Now, make sure you eat up. You won't be able to eat again until the feast tonight. I made sure to grab all your favorites: apple pastries, bacon, poached eggs, grapes, and peaches!"

"Thank you, Mabel." I offered her a smile as I got out of bed and sat at the table. "Has Jax returned?"

"Not yet. I am sure he will be back before the party!"

I let out a sigh and took a sip of the coffee. "Run through the agenda for today," I said.

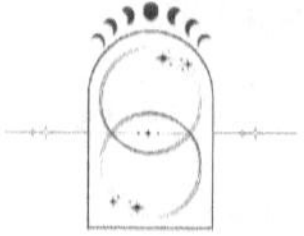

I knelt before the throne. The room looked vastly different than it had when I battled Joffrey. He had kept the room so bare. Now, there are floral arrangements, statues, and paintings. Lady Rae stood in front of me, holding a golden crown with rubies on the tips in her hand. My head was bowed as she spoke in the ancient language. A language that, for the past three months, I had been struggling to learn. Typically, only the line of succession was taught the language. Since I was never meant to be queen, I was not offered those lessons.

"Queen Piper Camilla Rossi," she said in the common tongue. "Blessed by The Mother, and savior of Irolyth. I bestow upon you the crown." She placed the crown on my head. "Long live the Queen."

"Long live the Queen!" The crowd erupted behind me.

I slowly stood and turned to them with a wide smile. "Thank you. I will spend my entire life continuing to prove I am worthy of this land, its people, and its throne. Let the festivities begin!"

On my final word, music filled the hall, and everyone began dancing. I looked around the room, trying to find Jax. Trying not to show my disappointment, I stepped down from the dais and made my way over to the table lined with drinks and food.

Before I made it to the table, a dark voice purred in my ear. "My queen, you look stunning in that dress." Jax stood in a black suit with golden trim. His tie was the same shade of red as my dress.

"I was beginning to worry you weren't going to make it!"

"I wouldn't miss this for the world. Come, I have a surprise for you." He took me by the hand and guided me through the crowd. We exited the throne room and entered the courtyard. In the center was a gazebo with two people standing in the center.

My jaw dropped as I recognized them. I lifted my dress and sprinted toward my friends, who met me halfway. The three of us entered a huge embrace.

Steph laughed. "Being queen looks good on you."

"I can't believe you never told me you are fae!" Steve added.

"I missed you guys so much. You have no idea." I turned back to Jax and smiled. "Thank you."

"Did you think I would let you experience your big day without your best friends?"

The three of us caught up on everything that had happened over the last three months. Stephanie had sold The White Rabbit to Steve. I had inspired her to return to her roots as well. She had heard of a sorceress who lived in the northern island, Varia, that may be related to her and she planned to find her.

Once we were caught up, I took Jax by his hand. He gave it a gentle squeeze and a cocky grin grew on his face.

"Would you give me the honor of dancing with me?" He asked.

I got up on my tippy toes and gave him a soft kiss. "I thought you would never ask."

The four of us walked back inside, and we joined in the celebration.

The celebration of Irolyth.

The celebration of life.

The celebration of The Fire Queen and her Shadow.

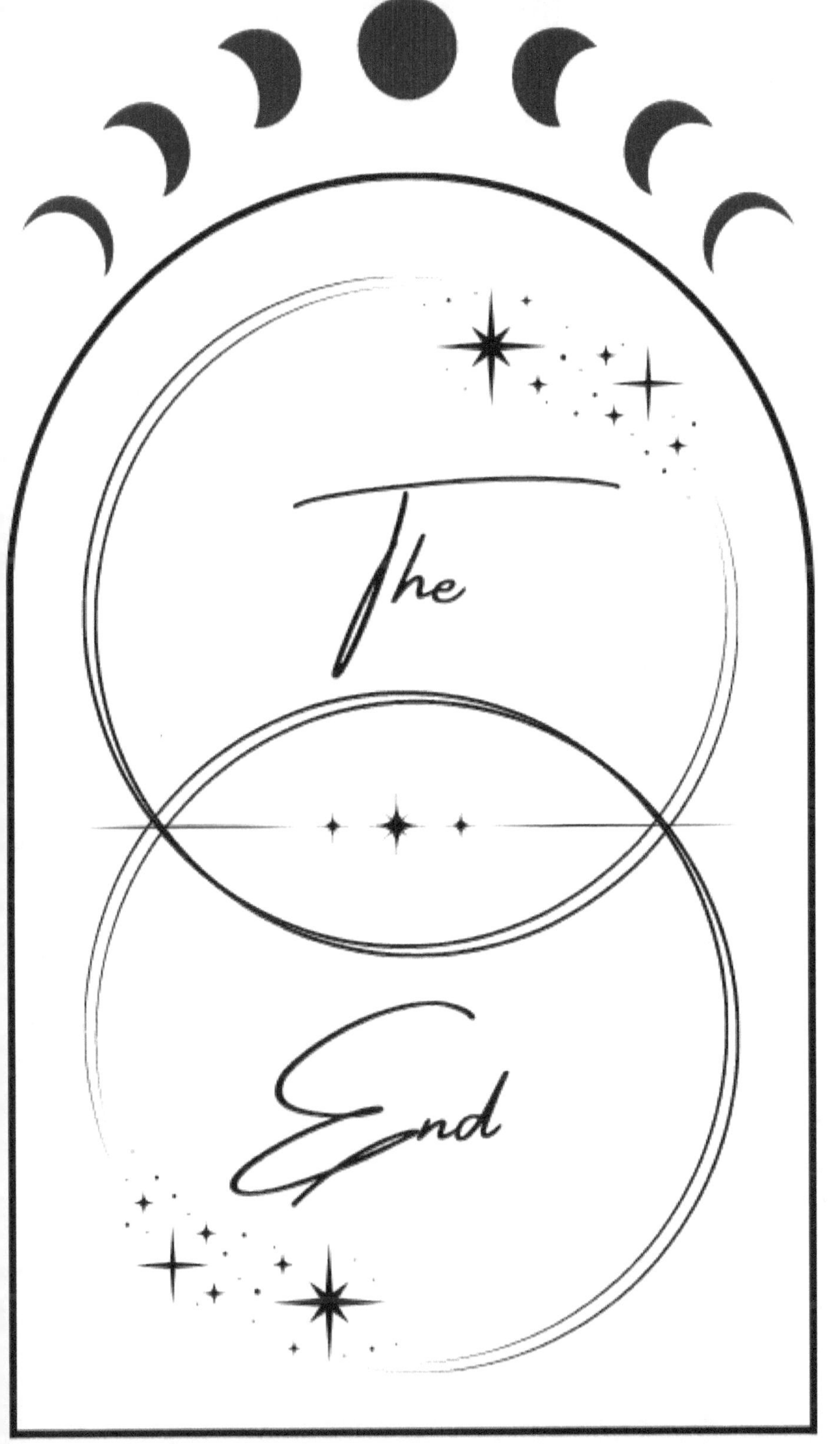

THE
VENGEANCE
OF
ALARI
A REALMS OF ELSWYTH STANDALONE
WILLOW ASTERIA

Content Warning

Please be advised that this book may not be suitable for all audiences.

This book contains sexual content, mention of past sexual assault, mention of spiked drinks, mention of physical emasculation as a form of retribution and punishment, death, blood, graphic violence, and other topics some readers may not find suitable.

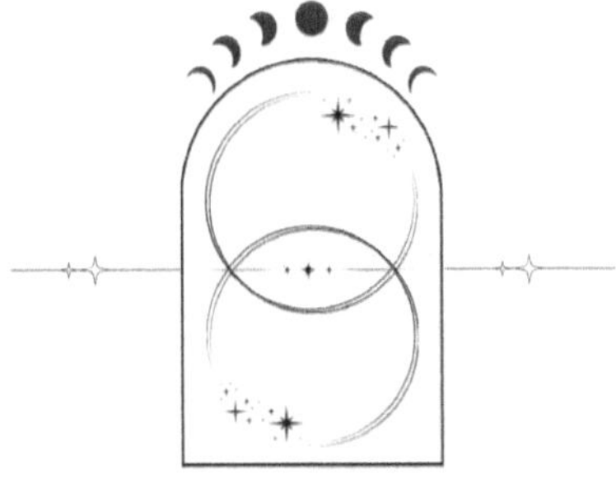

One

Today marks sixty years since the King of Alari vanished. Arik Tristian Delmari left the castle one day with the royal family's trident. To this day, no one knows where he went or why. Before he left, he gave his twin sister, Ariella, the Gem of Alari. The Gem had been embedded in the trident and the two have never been separated in all of Alari's history, until then. Stories were told that the trident was given to the first king of Alari, Triton Marrion Delmari, by The Mother and her daughter Nera when they first split the realms and created the merfolk. The trident was to keep us safe, and the Gem was what gave it its magic. It, too, vanished over the years.

No one outside the royal family speaks of the king who stole our trident. He was removed from Alari's history. Even saying his name would get you banished from our kingdom. The

Queen, Ariella Delphina Delmari, gave no one-second chances. When you were exiled, it was a death sentence.

Years later, the Princess was born, and it was discovered she had the gift of voice. With her voice, she could influence or cause pain to others. The Queen used that to her advantage. For the last twenty years, the princess's voice has been used to force the people to forget about Arik entirely.

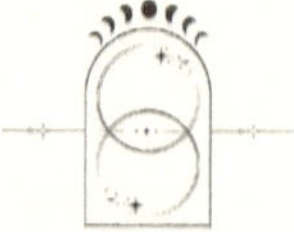

I was so tired of being my mother's puppet. A gut feeling was told my uncle did not leave of his own accord. Could my mother have something to do with his disappearance so that she could steal the crown? I was tired of her using me— using my voice to make the people of Alari forget my uncle. For the past year, I've been sneaking around the castle, trying to prove it. So far, I haven't found anything of use. Everything about him had been removed from the royal library, and not even in my mother's private writings did she mention him. Even though I had found nothing so far, I refused to give up.

Late at night, once the castle was silent and all but a few guards had gone to bed, I snuck out of my room and swam back down to the library. There was a single shelf left of books that I had not combed through. If I didn't find anything on this last shelf, I did not know where I was going to look next. I bent down to grab the first one off the shelf and noticed that some of them stuck out more than others. When I examined them closer, I saw a small journal stuffed behind the tomes. As I pulled it out, I was startled by a voice from behind.

"Princess Calliope? What are you doing here so late?"

I spun and met the eyes of our royal archivist, Varun.

Quickly, I grabbed a few more books off the shelf to hide the notebook I found. "Oh, I couldn't sleep and figured I would take some of these back to my room tonight for some late-night time reading," I said nervously.

"I did not know you were a reader. The only time I have ever seen you in the library is during your lessons when you were a child." His eyes lit up as he spoke.

"I do not have time during the day to stop by, and I don't like getting in the way. I will return these in the morning!" Not wanting to be questioned further, I started to swim past him.

"Wait!" He stuck out his bright yellow tail to block my path.

I swallowed hard. "Yes?"

"I see you have the work of Lyric Kai. Have you read anything under her other pen name, L.K. Wake?"

"I have not. I will have to check out those works tomorrow when I return." I smiled.

He moved his tail. "Let me not keep you any longer. Good night, princess."

I wished Varun a good night and raced to my chambers. As soon as I was inside, I locked the door behind me and pulled out the journal. Many pages had been ripped out, and others had barely legible scribblings. The first page that made any sense had only one sentence on it.

'My name is King Arik Delmari. I will make Alari great again.'

Flipping through the pages, I saw a drawing of a mermaid and arrows pointing to the next page. It showed the same mer but with legs instead of a tail. The following page detailed how the mer could transform into bi-pedal creatures to travel on land. There were more ripped-out pages, and then a page covered in scribbles to the point it was almost blacked out. The last two pages were a drawing of a cave that had six portals. Each was labeled, and the one marked 'Elswyth' was circled over and over. The final page was a map detailing how to get to the cave.

I smiled as I studied the map. This had to be where my uncle went. I had to find him. I had to bring him home so I could prove that my mother was up to no good. She refused to tell me why my uncle had to be forgotten by the people.

I vowed to make them remember.

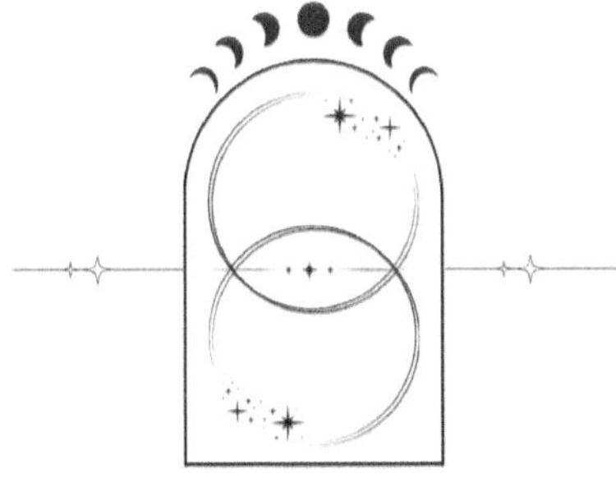

Two

The next night, I was ready to go on my adventure. Once the lights in the town below went dark, I swam off my balcony and into the open ocean. The map showed landmarks to look out for, and which direction to go. The first landmark was a large coral reef. Once the coral forked into three paths, I was to follow the third path. Continuously, I looked behind me and watched as the castle got smaller and smaller. Anxiety welled in my core. How long would it be until the queen sent guards looking for me?

Eventually, I found the second landmark, a ship. Before the fae realms were split, all the fae lived together. Now we were all in our own realms, with little contact with one another. This ship was from that time. Now nothing lived above the waters of Alari, as it was now an endless ocean. The ship was now almost all gone and was overgrown with barnacles, algae, and coral.

Fish swam in and out of the ship, over the years it had been turned into their home. A golden mermaid statue sat straight up out of the sand. Her arm was extended, and I swam in the direction of her pointed finger. I let out a yawn as I pushed myself forward. Traveling for hours without stopping was beginning to take its toll. Finally, the last landmark came into view, and a second wave of energy hit me. I looked down at the giant trench beneath me. My heart pounded in my chest as I stared into the darkness.

Was I making the right choice? Is this truly where I was to go? Or was this a trap set by whoever really left this journal?

I traveled all this way, no reason to turn tail and run now. Without a second thought, I swam down into the total darkness. The farther I swam, the more nervous I got. Stopping the descent, I looked back up and realized how far I traveled. The sun now illuminated the world above. Morning had come to Alari. It would not be long until mother had her guards searching the ocean for me.

Looking back down, I mustered all the courage I could. Could I find my way through the inky blackness before I found what I was looking for? I started my swim downward again, and the trench narrowed. It was now only wide enough to fit two merfolk.

Just as I thought I needed to travel back up to get a better view now that the sun was up, I was caught up in a strong current. I tried to fight against it, but it just caused me to flip and tumble over my tail. As I reached out to grab hold of the side wall, the rocks slipped out of my grasp. All I could do was allow the current to take me. It eventually had to stop, right? I turned to see that I was headed straight for the wall of the trench. I reached its end. The water had not slowed down a bit, and I was about to be slammed directly into the jagged rocks.

Just before I smashed into them, my body was pushed downward by another strong stream. Tumbling through the water, the trench continued straight down. I fell for what seemed like an eternity in the all-consuming darkness. The undertow slowed, and my body hit soft sand. The forceful waters vanished. I shivered from the icy temperature, above the trench the waters were warm. I was not used to the cold. Looking around, I was in a cave with red translucent crystals sticking out from the dark stone. They gave off a soft glow that illuminated the space. I reached into my bag, thankful it didn't get yanked away from me. Pulling out the journal, I looked at the red crystals drawn on the map. All I needed to do was go through the opening on the opposite side of the cave and it would take me exactly where I needed to go. I was so close to finding the portals. Rising from the ground, I brushed the sand off my scales and pushed my loose hair out of my face.

Ringing filled my ears as I swam down the path. I prayed to The Mother that at the end of this tunnel I would find what I was looking for just as the map showed.

Endless twists and turns snaked their way through the dark stone, the only light was from the red glow of the gems. Just when I thought I would never leave the tunnel, it opened up to a large circular room. Unlike where I started, white glowing crystals jutted out of the ceiling. The tunnel I came from was the only entrance into the space. Embedded in the walls were six white arches. At the top of each arch was carved the name of each realm in the ancient language of the fae. Though I do not speak it fluently, I recognized some of the words as it is still used in some of our religious texts and rituals. Each archway was filled with different colored smoke. Orilon was purple. Irolyth was red. Aeros was white. Khaldon was brown. Tarak was yellow.

When I came to Elswyth's arch, I was not met with smoke. I stared back at my own reflection. It rippled as if it was made from silver water. I stared into my blue eyes as I pushed back my dark navy hair. The white lights gave my ice-blue tail a silver sheen. Once I went through this portal, everything would change. Would I even recognize the person I transformed into? What type of world would I enter? I could not imagine a world not underwater. My mind could not even picture what such a world would look like. It was now or never.

To free Alari from my mother, I would face the unknown.

With that last thought, I swam through the portal.

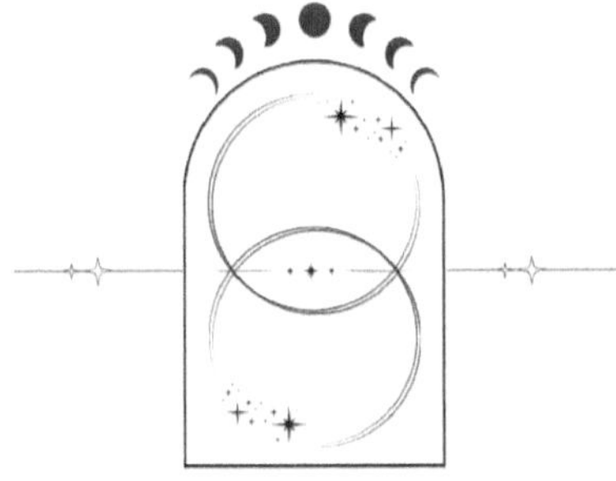

Three

On the other side of the portal I found myself surrounded by warm water. I was in a dark cylinder-shaped space, and the only way to go was up unless I wanted to go back through the portal. The water here had a strange green hue I had never seen. The ocean of Alari was all blue.

Propelling upward, I finally breached the surface, throwing my head back to get my hair out of my face. To my surprise, it was nighttime. Either I was in the cave for longer than I thought, or this realm was on a different time. Looking around, I found I was surrounded by sandy dunes and beach grass. I pulled myself out of the small pool of water and sat on the sandy shore. Closing my eyes, I tried to focus my magic. The journal did not provide any information on how to transform. Before finding the journal, I did not even know that was a thing that the merfolk could do. All I could do was force my magic to work in ways it never had before and prayed that it worked. A tingling sensation took over the base of my tail as if it was going numb. I opened my eyes and let out a huff of air when nothing had happened, and I splashed my tail in the water. Trying one more time, I did not even feel the tingle of magic.

I looked up into the night sky, focusing on the full moon overhead. Throwing my prayers to The Mother once again, I begged for her to help me. To allow me to shed my tail and gain two legs. Allow me to walk, to be a part of this unknown world. I closed my eyes once again to focus. My magic welled inside me, and my entire body tingled. The sensation of the water bubbling around my bottom half overwhelmed my senses. When the bubbling stopped, I opened my eyes and looked down, a smile grew on my face. I lifted my right leg from the pool and watched as beads of water dripped from it.

Quickly, I jumped up, and a cry of joy escaped my throat. My legs wobbled as my bare feet hit solid ground for the first time. The soft sand got in between my toes, and I wiggled them in deeper. Once steady, I walked through the sand, down a path in between the dunes. The sweet and salty air filled my nose. Just beyond the white dunes was the shoreline. The ocean beyond the sand was almost black. Large, jagged rocks jetted from the dark waters. Far across the ocean, lights from a town glittered on the horizon. Truly, I was in awe. My thoughts drifted to the people who lived there. I had never met anyone who wasn't merfolk. I had read some pieces about non-mer in books, but there were very few of those available back home. Who were these people and what were they like?

Staring off into the ocean, there was something that felt so wrong about it. I wish I could put my finger on exactly what was calling this ill feeling. As the waves crashed onto the shore, I was careful not to allow the water to touch my skin. Following the shoreline, I learned I was on a small island surrounded by large rock formations. The longer I stayed on the island, the more the feeling of dread crept over me. I did not see a way out of the cave system in Alari. The current blocked my only path. I needed to find another way home. Could there be another portal somewhere in this strange land? Even if there was, that would require me to enter the sea that filled me with terror.

Who would have thought the Princess of the Mer would be afraid of the ocean?

The white sand transitioned into a slate of rock. A large wave crashed against it, and the water settled on top of the rock. My foot slipped on the slippery stone, causing me to fall. I was able to catch myself before my face smashed into the hard ground. However, one of my new legs was not so lucky. It had scraped against the rock, and blood now dripped down. I hobbled over to a spot where a clump of seaweed lay on the sand and sat next to it. Staring at the ocean, I hesitated. Fear rattled me as I reached down to touch it, and a shiver ran down my spine from the frigid temperature. I used the salt water from the sea to clean the wound, hissing as it made contact. Using the seaweed, I wrapped my leg to keep the cut clean. The waves crashed against the shore and washed away my blood.

Maybe this was a fool's errand. Maybe I should return home. Maybe this world was not meant for someone like me.

I pushed myself up and headed back toward the portal. There had to be a way out of the tunnel I found myself in. I could return home for a while, just until I had a better plan. Just as the portal came into view, I heard a deep and dark voice from behind me.

"It has been a long time since I have seen another from Alari."

I slowly spun to see a tall man with long blond hair staring back at me with dark blue eyes. He appeared human, but I had a strange feeling he wasn't. Water dripped off his bare body. We stood in silence for a moment before I responded. "Another?" It was the only word that would escape my lips.

Everything about this man screamed for me to run, from the darkness in his eyes to the predatory smirk on his face, but all I could do was stand there as he stepped closer.

"Yes. I once called Alari my home. Long before the Queen took over and betrayed me," he growled.

"Betrayed you?" Could this man have the answers I have been looking for?

He took another step forward, and I looked down to avoid his burning gaze. He grabbed me by my chin and forced me to look up at him. A chill ran down my body as his touch was like ice. "Yes. She stole something very precious to me." He stared at me intensely for a long silent moment. "You have her eyes." He dropped my chin and took a step back, giving me an up-and-down glance. "What brings you here? The human realm of Elswyth is not a place for young mermaids."

"I came looking for my uncle. I found his journal with a map showing the way to this place. I was hoping I could find him."

"And if you did find him? What would you do?" He raised his eyebrow and slowly circled me.

I spun in place, not wanting him out of my sight. "I want to know why he left. Why would he leave our people? Was it the Queen who chased him away? Did she make him disappear so the throne would be hers?"

He stopped and burst into laughter. "Do you think him to be some kind of hero? Someone who was banished for stopping a sea witch from destroying Alari? Let me tell you something about the Queen, princess." Large red tentacles appeared from behind him, coming out of his back. "She should have done a better job at keeping you away from me. Now that I have you, there is nothing that will stop me from finishing what I started."

I spun and ran toward the portal. Fuck, I should have brought something to defend myself with. Why did I not think of that? Just as I reached the small pool of green water, a tentacle wrapped around my ankle and yanked. I fell to the ground and hit it hard. My face planted into the sand, and it filled my mouth. Lifting my head, I tried to spit it out. Grabbing at the ground to hold myself in place, the grains just fell through my fingers. My skin burned as it scraped against the ground. Another tentacle wrapped around my waist and pulled me up into the air. Three more held my wrists and legs as I hung in the air in front of the man.

"Dear niece, please don't take any of this personally. It seems that what your mother stole from me is embedded within you. This won't be a pleasant removal, and you won't be able to return to Alari after I take it. Which is good news for me. We can't let the Queen know I am one step closer to my plan."

I could not believe the words that fell from his lips. I was not aware of anything embedded in me. The thought of not being able to return home nearly broke my heart. I could not allow that to happen.

"Arik! Let me go!" I screamed as I squirmed, trying to break free. "It doesn't have to be like this! I am sure whatever happened between you and mother can be resolved!"

My uncle chuckled under his breath. "I will take the Gem of Alari from your throat, steal back the trident from those pesky pirates, and then I will drown Elswyth and take it as the new home of the mer. You see, Alari is too small for us. We deserved better than what The Mother provided. I will make the mer great again, and it will all be mine."

All this time the missing Gem was within me. One of the most sacred relics of our people was within my possession. I couldn't help but wonder if that was where my gift of voice had come from. Or, was it a gift from the gods who had once given us our tails and home?

I opened my mouth to sing, hoping I could lure him to sleep and escape. Before the first note escaped my throat, a tentacle was shoved into my mouth.

"Not so fast. You don't think I would know Ariella's one trick? You cannot charm me, brat." The tentacle pushed its way down my throat. I choked hard on it as it forced its way in deeper. Just as quickly as it entered, it was pulled out, and I heaved as it was fully removed. Strands of drool connected me to the tentacle and the red gem that it now held in its grasp. Arik took the Gem and held it up in the moon's light and it glimmered. A wicked smile grew as he dropped me onto the ground, and a cold and empty feeling took over my entire body. I could not move. I could not speak.

"Well, I would say it was great meeting you, but in all honesty, you were quite a bore. I was hoping for more of a fight from someone who held the power of the Gem. Now that I have your power, say goodbye to any idea you have of returning home. Your shifting abilities are gone. Also, good luck getting off this island. No boats dare to come this far south, lest they wish to endure my wrath. Goodbye, dear niece. I am off to find the damn pirates who have my trident."

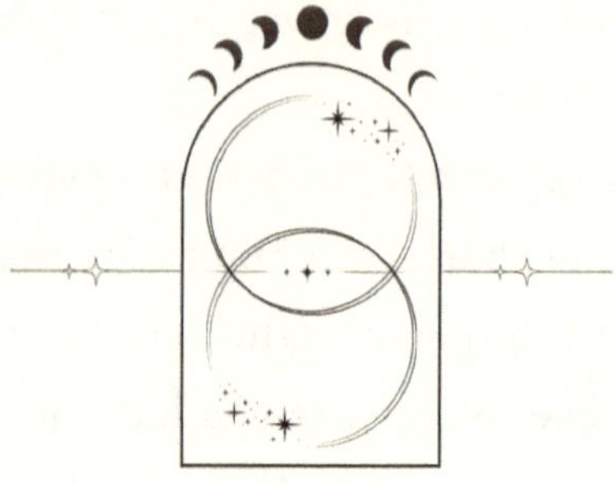

Four

I laid on the sand for hours with tears streaming down my face. Each time I tried to scream from the pain, the sounds refused to escape my throat. After my uncle left, I dragged myself back to the pool. My magic refused to come to me as I tried to shift back to my tail. Just as Arik told me, nothing happened. I no longer could feel my magic. Emptiness filled my chest. A piece of me that I had held near and dear had been ripped from me.

How did the Gem of Alari end up inside me? Did mother know about that this entire time? Why would she not have told me? Maybe I would have been more careful if she had been honest about the fact that I held something so powerful and sacred to our people. If she knew Arik was a monster, why would she not tell me, or the kingdom? If I had known the truth about him, I would not have sought him.

Since I was left here, I floated in and out of consciousness. The sun peeked over the horizon and illuminated the island. Forcing myself up, I walked over to the shore, where the waves crashed onto my bare feet. I had hoped that the water would offer me comfort, but all it did was exaggerate the hollowness in my chest. Boats now floated on the ocean's surface, both large and small. All but one were far from the island. I stared at the large black ship as it got closer to me. Mounted in the front was a golden mermaid statue. I couldn't help but wonder how they knew what we looked like. The people of Alari had not been to Elswyth since before the splitting of the fae realms. Was there another community of mer still here in this strange realm? If there was, would they be able to help me return to Alari?

The large ship threw down an anchor just behind the large rocks. My eyes traveled up the ship to a man who stood on the bow. The sunlight made his dark skin glow. He grabbed the tip of his red and gold tricorn hat and tipped it to keep the sun from his golden eyes. Even from so far away, I swear they locked on to me before a grin grew on his face. He spun away and walked out of view. The sounds of men yelling could be heard from across the sea, but I could not make out the words they were saying.

Should I try to call out for them to help me? Ever since I arrived, I wanted to know what the people of this world were like. Now that I had my chance, I wasn't sure If I did. What if they were just as vile as my uncle? I had thought the best of him, and that turned out to be a huge mistake. Walking back toward the center of the island, I looked for anything I could use as a weapon.

Even though my entire body ached with sorrow and hollowness, I would not allow myself to be a victim ever again. Walking had become much easier, almost second nature.

There was nothing in the center of the island, so I continued to the far shore. I stood on the shoreline for a moment and looked out to the endless ocean. There was no land in sight. The cold water splashed against my feet, causing me to jump. It was time I returned to my search.

After a few minutes of searching, I found a large piece of wood that had washed ashore. The tip was pointed, as if it had been once a part of something else, but was snapped apart. I returned to the front of the island to watch the large ship again and was surprised to see a smaller boat beached. Quickly, I looked around for whoever brought it here. A few feet away stood the man I had seen from the ship. His hat was gone, revealing long braids that had been pulled back. My gaze trailed up his body and I examined his many nautical-themed tattoos. He turned and looked at me with a smile that melted my soul. The sun glimmered in his golden eyes.

"Well, there you are. I was beginning to wonder if the seas were playing tricks on me. It's not every day you see a nude woman with blue hair on a deserted island. Where did you come from?" He slowly stepped closer to me.

My heart pounded in my chest. After what had happened with my uncle, I wasn't sure what to make of the mystery man that now stood in front of me. I opened my mouth to speak, but all that came out was a small squeak.

The man frowned as his eyes fell on the piece of wood in my hand. "Let me help you. Put down the wood, let me take you back to Caldor." His gaze dropped and focused on the piece of kelp wrapped around my thigh. "See over there?" He pointed to the ship. "That's my ship, Pearl of the Southern Sea. We have a medic on board who can take a look at your leg." Looking me back in the eyes, he raised his hands, palms facing me.

He took another step closer, and I stepped back, looking him up and down. He seemed nice, but was this some sort of trick? I raised the wood and pointed it at him.

Stopping his advances, he removed his coat and extended it out to me. "Please let me help you. Take this, cover-up, and I will take you to the mainland. Once there, we can get you help, and try to get you home."

Our eyes locked, and I stared him down. We stood there in silence for some time. My gaze darted from him to the ship then back to him. He seemed as if he really wanted to help me. I couldn't stay here forever, and he may be my only way off this island. Finally, I dropped the makeshift weapon, stepped closer, and took the coat from his hand. Draping it around my shoulders, the weight of it nearly crushed me. I rubbed my hands on the inside of it, taking in its silky texture. Back in Alari, we would never cover ourselves with this much fabric, if anything at all. Often tops would be made from shells and coral, but those were typically for special events or ceremonies.

The man stepped closer, grabbed each side of the jacket's opening, and pulled it closed. "There we go. My crew would have a field day if I brought a naked woman on board. Make sure to keep this closed tight. If I catch any of them looking at you the wrong way, I will throw them overboard to sacrifice them to the Delmari."

"What did you just say?" The words shot out of my mouth before I realized I had spoken. They scraped against my throat as they were forced out. Several coughs escaped my lips to try to clear my throat, but it didn't ease the burn.

The man smirked. "Ah, so you do speak. Very good. One-sided conversations are very awkward. I also have a feeling we have a lot to talk about." He spun me around and wrapped his arm around me, forcing me to walk with him toward the little boat.

Again, I forced out words, this time they came out easier. "What do you mean, *the Delmari*?" I tried to pull away from him.

He held me tighter. "You're on his island. The last time someone was on this island, my grandfather fought a monster to keep Elswyth safe. I am following in his footsteps. Now get in the boat, love. Don't make this harder than it needs to be." He pushed me toward the boat, and I stepped in and sat on the bench. "Good girl. See, that wasn't so hard."

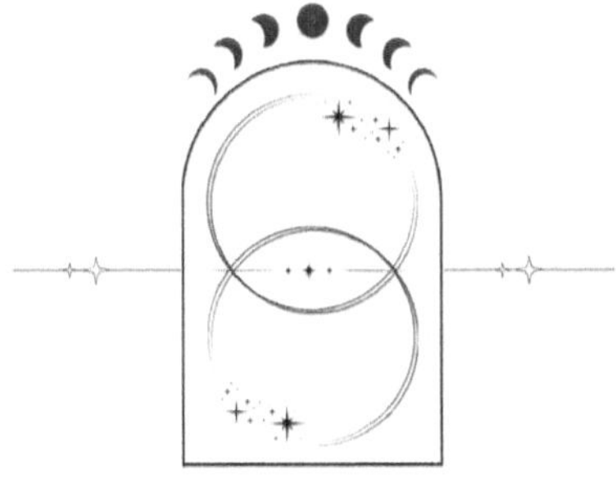

Five

We rode back to the ship in silence. I cursed myself out in my mind. I told myself I would not be another victim, yet here I was, being forced onto a ship without the one thing I found that could protect me. Once onboard, I could not escape the gaze of the crew. For the first time, I felt anxious about my body. Pulling the jacket tighter, I wished I could jump overboard and swim off into the deep blue to escape them.

"What are you looking at?" My captor boomed. "Get back to work! If I catch any one of ya looking at her again, I will feed you to the Delmari. Understood?" He pulled me in close to him once again, and I breathed in his salty citrus scent. Being close to him brought me comfort. I was happy that he was true to his word that he was going to help me.

Again, he brought up the Delmari and a shiver shot down my spine. What was the thing that he was referring to by my family's name?

"Aye, Captain!" They all responded and returned to their duties.

The captain guided me toward the back of the ship. As we walked, he eyed a tall woman and motioned for her to follow us. He opened a door and pushed me through it. Once they were in behind me, they shut and locked the door. The room was a small office with a long table with a map, a few chairs, a window looking out to the sea, and a staircase leading downward.

"Killian, what the hell is this? When you said you wanted to run ashore, this is not what I thought you meant," the woman sneered.

"After the Delmari attack last night, I thought he would return to where it all began. That is why I wanted to come here. I did not expect to find a naked woman! But, I guarantee you she knows something about the attack!" He snarled.

"She looks frightened! Do you not have any manners? Did you even introduce yourself to her, or did you just abduct her?" When the man said nothing, the woman pushed past him and walked over to me. "Hello. My name is Vari, and this is Killian. I like to call him Captain Ass Hat." She sent him a pointed glare, then looked back at me with a smile. The sun shone through the window and illuminated her dark-olive skin. "What is your name?"

"She won't answer you. After I got her off the island and into the boat, she refused to speak to me. Hell, I only got her to say one thing, and that was after I brought up the Delmari!"

"My name is Calliope!" I cut him off before he could say any-thing else. "Tell me about this Delmari. Please." Dread washed over me. I had a feeling I knew exactly who they were talking about. The name had to be no coincidence.

"Sixty years ago, a tentacled creature came from that island, attacked us, and tried to take our land. While the creature was here, it rained for months. Coastal lands flooded. That island used to be a part of a larger archipelago, but those islands are now lost to us," Killian began.

Vari continued for him. "Our grandfather defeated the mon-ster and sent him back to the fathoms below. He returned last night and destroyed many ships."

Tears filled my eyes as they spoke. "I am so sorry. I didn't mean to cause all this destruction."

"So, you did bring back the Delmari!" Killian whipped a blade out from the sheath on his thigh. He pushed forward, and I stepped back until I was up against the table. He continued and held the blade to my neck. "Tell us everything, or I will slice your throat. As Captain of the DarkSea Pirates, I am not afraid to do what is needed to get the answers I seek."

"Killian!" Vari yelled.

He shot her a glare. "That's *captain* to you!" He looked back at me. "Now tell me everything."

I whimpered as he gently pressed the cold steel to my skin. "My full name is Calliope Mariana Delmari, Princess of Alari. I came here in search of my uncle, thinking my mother had done something terrible to him to steal the throne. Unfortunately, I brought him something he needed to complete his plans. I did not mean to. I just want to go home. On that island is a portal that will return me, but my uncle, the Delmari, as you call him, stole my magic. I cannot shift back into my mer form. I am stuck here at the mercy of a pirate who hates me for just being at the wrong place at the wrong time." Sobs rattled from me as I spoke, and my vision blurred from the tears that filled them.

Killian held my stare for a long, silent moment. Slowly, he lowered the blade and took a step back. "I am not the type of man who treats women like this. I apologize." He sheathed his blade and looked toward his sister. "Vari, get her some clothes. We are gonna finish what our grandfather could not." Killian looked back at me with determination in his eyes. "I will get you home, little mermaid, if it is the last thing I do."

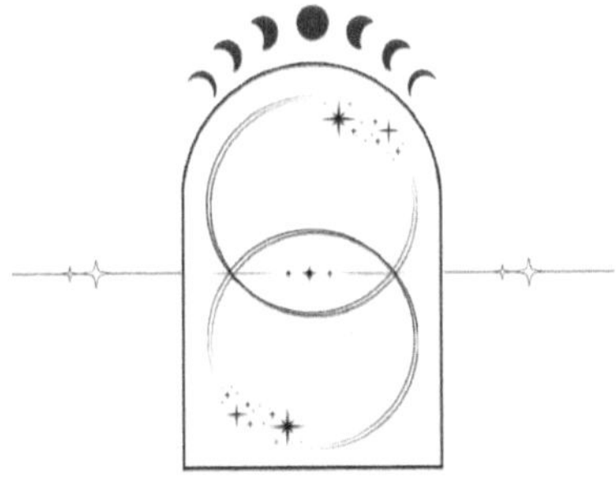

Six

Vari provided me with a pair of light blue pants that were tight around the ankles and had a long slit down the side that exposed my legs. The top she gave me wrapped around my breasts to cover them, but had no sleeves and stopped right above my belly button. Vari tied the wrap behind me in a beautiful bow. Even though I was not used to wearing clothes, these were light and flowy enough that they did not bother me.

Killian had the medic see me, a woman named Wren. When the kelp wrappings were removed from my leg, I was in shock to see a tattoo that was not there before. It was as if my skin had been cut open and pulled back to reveal the ice-blue scales underneath. A reminder of what I once was, and would never be again.

Killian informed me during the journey, I was to stay in the room below his office, which was his private chamber. Off the side of his room was a small balcony. The top of the banister was gold, and the spindles were black wood that was twisted together. I sat on the floor of it, looking out at the sea for the entire trip to the mainland. My heart ached as I stared off at the dark, sparkling water. How I wished I could jump in, and swim deep into its depth to explore. I stood and clenched the railing so tight the whites of my knuckles showed.

All of my frustrations finally forced their way out of me, and I screamed until the sound formed into words. "I will find you! I will kill you! I will reclaim what is mine!" I repeated the words over and over. Tears streamed down my face and fell into the ocean below. How I hated them for being able to return home.

A firm grip held my shoulder and pulled me back away from the railing. I spun around to Captain Ass Hat, as Vari called him, worry filling his eyes. We stood there for a moment in silence, and then Killian pulled me close to him and gently rubbed my back.

"Shh, little mermaid. He can't hurt you anymore. I made a promise to you, and I intend to keep it. We will get your magic back and return you home," he said in a hushed voice. Releasing me from his embrace, he ushered me back inside. "We will get to shore in about two hours. Why don't you lay down in bed and rest?"

I looked down at the rectangle we stood in front of. Large pieces of cloth were draped over it. Raising my eyebrow, I looked back up to him.

"Have you ever seen a bed before? Let me show you." He pulled back the cloth and laid down. He patted the spot next to him.

Laying down next to Killian, my body sank into it. "Wow, this is really soft."

"What do you sleep in back home?" he asked.

"Giant clam shells. We curl up in them." Now laying in this bed, I was not sure that I could ever return to a clam shell. This was the most comfortable I had ever been. It was so soft and warm, I never wanted to get up.

"Interesting," he said softly. Wrapping his arm around me, he pulled me into him. I took in his salty citrus scent and nuzzled into his chest. Never had I laid with a man before, but with Killian, it felt natural. "I really am sorry about earlier," he continued. "The last time someone was on that island, they brought destruction to our realm. I should not have assumed that about you." Killian tucked a piece of my hair behind my ear. Heat rose to my cheeks as I stared into his eyes.

"It is ok. If I was in your position, I would have done the same. Maybe even worse if my mother wished it."

"Does your mother often make you do 'worse things'?" Concern grew in his eyes.

Pressing my lips into a firm line, I thought about it for a moment. Everything I believed she was doing to harm the people of Alari was most likely to protect them from Arik. Could the people she had executed have been his accomplices in the nefarious plans he had? Was I so wrong about everything? Was I also wrong about my mother making me use my voice to make people forget?

"Looking back, I think everything she ever did was to protect the people of Alari. All she wanted was for them not to remember Arik. I wonder if the reason she wants them to forget was because of the way he really treated the mer." I pulled my gaze away from him and frowned.

Killian gently lifted my chin so my gaze met with his honeyed eyes. "I never want to see those beautiful blue eyes cry, or those pouty little lips frown ever again." Pulling away his hand, he slowly sat up. Gently, he petted my cheek with the back of his fingers. "I have to get back to the crew. Close your eyes and rest. I will wake you when we get to shore." Killian got out of bed and walked up the stairs.

When he was out of sight, that ache returned to my chest. This time, it wasn't due to my magic being gone.

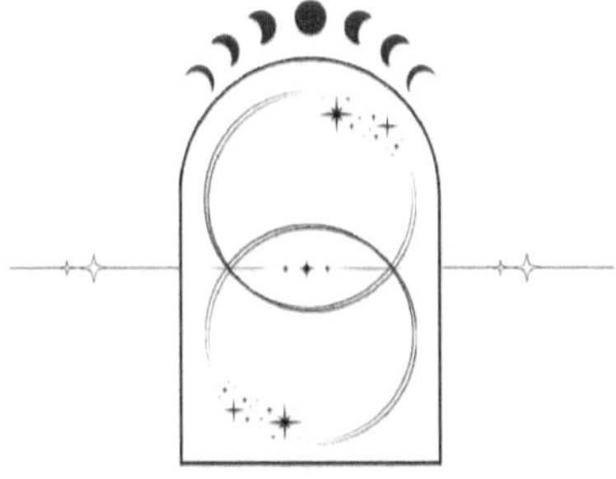

Seven

All eyes were on me as we walked the gangway to the dock. Part of me wished I had accepted the shoes Vari had offered me, the wood of the dock was rough against my bare feet. But, the shoes were too constricting. I could hear the whispers of the people, all talking about the girl with the blue hair. Apparently, that was not common for the people of Elswyth. Back home, it was not strange to see a rainbow of colors through the the mer. Here it seems that only shades of black, browns, reds, and blondes existed. Killian wrapped his arm around me and pulled me close. When he shot a glare at anyone gawking, they quickly looked away. Many left the docks entirely.

When we were halfway up the pier, a short bald man came rushing toward us. Stopping right before us, he bent down and placed his hands on his knees, breathing heavily. Killian let out a groan.

"Captain Killian, we did not expect you back so soon," the man finally spoke in between his heavy breaths.

"I do not need to report my comings and goings to you. Or have you forgotten?" Killian growled.

Vari came from behind me and stood by my side. She let out a laugh, pointing her nose in the air. "Little Milly thinks he's in charge now?"

"My name is Milton!" He finally straightened his back and caught his breath. "As mayor of Caldor, I am in charge."

Killian released me and took a step forward. "Is that so?" His voice grew so cold it sent a shiver down my spine.

Milton stepped back and stuttered on his words. "It was just that since we did not expect you, we did not have your payment prepared."

"Prepare it. You know where we will be. I expect it by sundown." Killian turned and pointed toward another large ship. The men on this boat were carrying crates of fish to shore. "If not, The Seafarer goes down."

Milton gulped. "You can't. That ship is the most important for our watermen."

Killian turned back to Milton and leaned down so they were at eye level. "Well, then you better figure it out." He straightened his back. "Girls, come along," he chimed.

Vari hooked her arm through mine, and we followed Killian as we walked past Milton. Neither Killian nor Vari spared him a glance.

What type of people did I get myself wrapped up in? I was still so unsure about Killian. He went from being kind, to forcing me on his boat, to holding a knife to my throat, to telling me he would help me return home and care for me. The man I just saw on the dock in Killian's body was not someone I wanted to provoke.

Once off the dock, we stepped onto a stone pathway and walked into town. All eyes were on us. Women and children were ushered inside. Whispers hung in the air. Doors and windows were slammed shut. None of this seemed to bother Killian or Vari, and neither of them said a word as we walked through the streets. I was in awe of the first human town I had ever been in. I wished we walked a little slower so I could take it all in. The only thing I was able to see were buildings made of dark-colored wood. Back home, everything was made from hardened sand and seashells. Some buildings had small flower gardens in front of them. I tried to pull away to reach down to pick one, but Vari tugged on my arm, pulling me away and forcing me to keep moving before I could touch it.

Killian led us up a hill and to a singular structure on the cliffside. It had to be the largest building I had seen since arriving here. It was made from rich brown wood and had a wrap-around porch. I looked out to the ocean, and that ache returned to my chest.

All I craved was to return home, to feel the salt water surround me.

We stopped just a few feet from double doors. Engraved onto the doors were a wave wrapped by a circle. The symbol was one solid line. Killian turned to face me. "Listen to me. Tell no one who you are. If anyone asks you anything, tell them you are with me. Do not say anything to anyone other than that. As a matter of fact, stay with either Vari or me at all times. Got it?"

I nodded in response.

"Good girl," he said with a nod and walked toward the door.

This was the second time he had called me that, and I could not help but blush. I could not help but crave hearing it again from his lips.

Vari leaned closer to me and whispered, "Don't worry. Everything will be just fine. They may seem a little rough, but most of them are good people." She continued walking, pulling me along with her.

Killian opened the double doors and stepped inside. The building was full of people, and I recognized it to be some kind of tavern. Back home, I actually never left the palace grounds until I snuck out to travel here. My mother always wanted to keep me close, she said it was dangerous. I found it to be enthralling, I could not wait to see more of this world above water.

The room smelt strongly of rum and smoke. I coughed several times as I inhaled the scent. There was a bar across the back wall and tables scattered throughout the room. A singular musician played a string instrument on a small stage in the far corner. On the left-hand wall in the back was a staircase leading upstairs.

All eyes turned toward the door and silence hung in the air. But not for long. When the patrons realized who had entered, all mugs rose to the air, and greetings to their captain filled the room.

"Yes, yes, I have returned," Killian teased. "No reason to get too excited." His eyes scanned the room. "Hawk! Van! Upstairs now," he called out.

Two men stood and immediately complied, heading toward the stairs as Killian guided us in the same direction. Once on the second floor, we silently traveled down a long hallway. I loved the feeling of the dark red runner, it was so soft on my bare feet. We entered the room all the way to the end. Despite the intimidating shift in Killian's behavior, I stayed close to him. Vari closed the door behind us once we were all inside. It had a large table in the center of the room with chairs around it. A large window overlooking the ocean. We could see the docks from here. Hawk and Van moved to stand next to the table.

"Take a seat," Killian said, and they did. "We went out to the island earlier, and this is who we found. She is also a victim of the Delmari. It is now the Darksea's top priority to defeat the Delmari and return something it stole from her. Understood?"

"Aye, Captain," they both said in unison.

Killian looked toward me. "Calliope, meet Hawk and Van." He pointed at each one as he said their name. "I trust these two men with my life. They also have ships under my rule."

"Were you able to find out anything else about the beast's location while you were out at sea?" Van asked.

"No," Killian answered in a somber tone. "I also went to the wreckage of The Belle. There were no survivors. Hawk, I want you to coordinate a sailing for Sadie and her crew."

"Aye Captain. I will arrange that for tonight at sundown."

The door behind us opened loudly, causing me to jump out of my skin. I turned and saw an older man walk in. His long white beard was in heavy contrast to his dark skin. He walked with a cane and marched over to Killian.

"You said you were out searching for the Delmari, and you came back with a whore?" The old man yelled. "Your father would be so disappointed! I told him leaving the crew to you would be a mistake! I hate you are proving me right!"

"Adrian!" Vari exclaimed.

Killian's eyes darkened as he looked down at Adrian. "This *whore* was actually found on the Delmari's island. She is the key to finding him and ending him. I do not care you were my father's first mate. I am the captain now. You will not speak that way to me or my crew any longer. Apologize to our guest, or else," he growled.

"How could some girl be the key to finding the monster? You are just making things up to cover your own ass!"

Killian let out a dark laugh and walked over to a bookcase against the wall. He pulled out a book and the shelf slid open to reveal a weapon's cabinet. He reached in and pulled out something that made my jaw drop. "I bet you she is the only one who can wield this thing's magic, and without paying the same price my grandfather did."

Killian walked over to me and forced me to take the silver trident that had been stolen from Alari by my uncle.

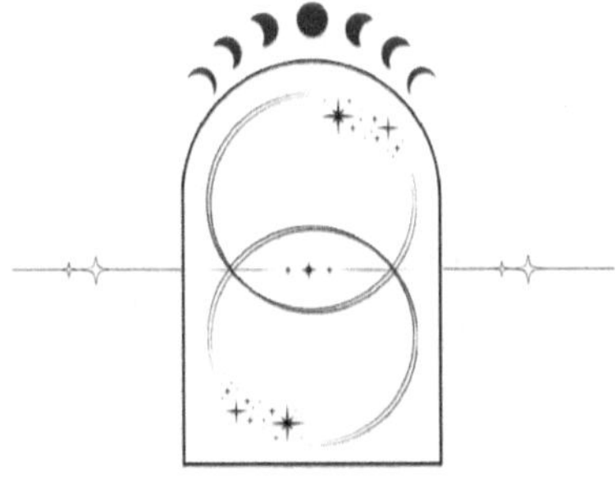

Eight

Its magic pulsed in my hand and traveled through my body. Tears welled in my eyes. Not from pain, but from the only thing in this world that reminded me of home. The ache in my soul lessened as it was refilled with the magic of Alari. I looked up at Killian and offered a smile. "He's looking for this. He said he would destroy the pirates who took it from him."

"My grandfather was able to steal it and use it against the Delmari in their final battle. Unfortunately, he learned the hard way that magic comes at a price. After he defeated the Delmari, the magic took from his essence to replace what was used during the battle," Killian said.

"Being human, grandfather could not handle what the trident took from him. He passed two days after the battle," Vari continued.

"It was then passed on to my father, and then to me once he passed," Killian added in a somber tone.

Adrian looked at me with anger still in his eyes. "And why do you think the trident will not take from her as it did Caspian?"

"Because I am from the world this comes from," I said plainly.

Adrian's face dropped to a blank expression. All he could do was stare and blink at me. Silence hung in the air for a few moments. "That means you are..." Adrian finally spoke but trailed off.

"A mermaid. Yes. I was before he stole my powers. Now I am nothing more than a human. The only reminder I have is this." I pulled the cloth away from my thigh and revealed the tattooed scales.

"I..." Adrian began, then paused. "I am sorry," he said softly.

I nodded in response, then examined the trident. Gently, I ran my fingers across the cold metal, finding the indent where the Gem once laid. We had to get it back and return it home.

Vari was next to her brother and whispered something in his ear, too quiet for me to make out.

Killian's response was loud enough for me to hear. "It belongs to her. We all have the same goals. I know we can trust her with it. You worry too much, Vari."

I stepped closer to them. "You can trust me. I promise you that. However, this is my first time seeing the trident in person. I am not even sure of the magic it wields. Arik stole it from us all those years ago."

"Who is Arik?" Van asked.

"Arik is the monster we are after. Delmari is our family name." The words slipped out of my mouth before I could stop them. My chest tightened as anxiety crept in. I prayed to The Mother that they wouldn't react poorly to that tidbit of information.

"Our?" Adrian's eyes narrowed.

"Yes. Arik is my uncle. I did not know him prior to meeting him yesterday. I wish I never did. I wish I just stayed in Alari."

Killian walked over to me, gently taking the trident from my hands. "Then you wouldn't have met me. And I promise you all of this will be worth it in the end for that alone," he laughed. "I am going to put this away for now." He walked back over to the weapon's case, put it back, and moved the bookshelf to hide it once again.

"Excuse me, Captain," someone said from the doorway. All eyes quickly turned toward the voice. A tall man stood there. "Sorry to interrupt. Baldy is here. He says he's got something for you."

A smile grew on Killian's face. "Send him up. Hawk, you have your orders. Van, I want you to make sure all ships are seaworthy." He turned his honeyed eyes to me and smiled. "Vari, will you take her up to my room and let her rest and bathe?"

"Aye!" Everyone responded.

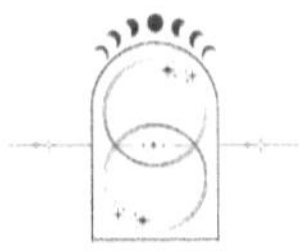

Vari led me down the hall and up another flight of stairs to a large apartment. Vari quickly gave me a tour. It had a sitting area and a kitchen in the entry room, and in the back was a bedroom with a wall of glass that overlooked the sea. Once in the bathing room, she gave me short instructions on what everything was and how plumbing worked. Humans require so many different solutions to keep themselves clean. In Alari, we used natural mud to nourish our skin, scales, and hair. Then we would allow the ocean to wash it away to keep us clean. I stared up at the running water for a long moment. Never in my entire life had I heard of anything called a shower. Before she left the bath chamber, she told me this was going to be one of the best experiences as a human I would ever experience.

Stepping in, I allowed the hot water to run down my body. Once it did, all the tension I did not realize I was holding was released. A soft moan escaped my lips. There was nothing I loved more than the sensation of water on my skin. I put two pumps of something called shampoo into my hand. The scent of mint and citrus filled my nose. Slowly, I worked the shampoo into my long hair, focusing on the scalp. Once that was thoroughly applied I rinsed it out and applied a deep conditioner. Vari told me it was best if I let it sit on my hair for a few moments before rinsing it out.

As I waited, I allowed the water to wash over my body. Vari was right. This was a magical experience. Where did this steady supply of water come from and why did it lack salt? Still, I had not fully gotten used to my legs. After all the walking and standing today, they had grown tired. The floor of the shower was slightly slippery, and I really had to be careful, or I could easily slip.

After a while, I heard a soft knock on the door.

"Just checking to make sure you are doing alright," Vari called out from behind the door.

"Everything is fine. You were right! This does feel amazing," I responded.

She chuckled before she answered. "See, being human isn't all bad. I will be just out here if you need anything."

"Thank you."

No, being human wasn't all bad so far... for someone who was used to it. But, for me, all I wanted was my fin and to dive into the depths of the ocean. There was truly a lack of a place to soak, I craved the feeling of being fully submerged in water. I wanted to return home. While the view of the sea here was beautiful, and the people were interesting, my heart belonged in Alari.

I belonged in Alari.

I ran the water through my hair to remove the conditioner, washed my human body, and exited the shower. Wrapping the large fluffy towel around me, I walked over to the mirror. Steam coated the shiny surface, and I wiped it away to be able to stare at myself. I had the same face, and the same blue hair, but I was missing the gills that were on my neck. Slowly, I ran my fingers down the smooth skin that was now there. Before I knew it, tears filled my eyes, and I let out a sob. Everything I had been holding in finally forced its way out. No longer able to hold myself up on my exhausted human legs, I fell to the floor, rolled onto my side, and pulled my knees to my chest.

The door busted open, and Vari rushed inside. Without a word, she sat me up and wrapped me in a tight hug. We sat there in silence for some time as she gently rubbed my back.

Slowly, my sobs turned to soft sniffles. I raised my gaze to meet hers, and she offered me a warm smile.

"I cannot imagine what you are going through, or how you are feeling," she said in nearly a whisper. "I promise you that my brother and I will make sure we get you home. We will take care of you until then."

"Thank you," I whimpered. "It means a lot."

Her face grew somber. "I know what it is like to have a man take away something from you. Do not let what happened define you. You are strong. You are brave. You will get your vengeance on him."

My eyes grew wide as I realized what she meant. "Did you?"

"Damn right, I did. My brother and I hunted him down all the way to the isle of Varia in the north. He won't be hurting anyone else. Can't when your weapon was removed." A smirk grew on her face. "He thought I showed him mercy when I spared his life. But it was not mercy I gave. For the rest of his days, he will live knowing what it is like to have your body violated, to have your choice taken. I hope when he is offered a drink from a bar patron, panic rattles his bones. When he wakes in the middle of the night, I hope he fears what lurks in the shadows. Since then, I have opened the crew to all women who are in search of finding a place safe from those who wish to harm us, and to teach them the true strength we all carry within our hearts."

Turning to her, I wrapped her in a hug. We sat there for some time in each other's embrace. Physical affection was not something that I was used to, but I found it extremely comforting. After a while, she stood and extended her hand out to me. "Let's get you dressed and get you something to eat."

I took her hand and stood. "That sounds wonderful. I am starving."

"What do mermaids eat, anyway?" She asked with a raised brow.

"Fish," I responded plainly.

"Oh! You are going to love this town then. Down the street, there is a restaurant that serves the best seafood you will ever have! You have to get this pasta dish with lobster, scallops, shrimp, and muscles!"

"What is pasta?"

"Oh, this is going to be so much fun!" She squealed. Vari pulled me into the bedroom where my clothes had already been laid out on the bed. "Hurry and get dressed! I am going to take you around town and show you how humans live!"

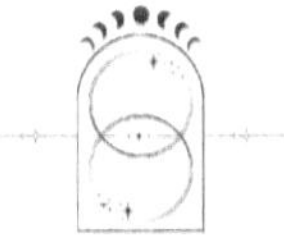

That night, we all stood on the beach. Small wooden boats lined the shore. The sky was clear, and the moon's light reflected off the ocean. The crew from the ship and patrons from the tavern were all in attendance, as well as some faces I did not recognize. Everyone wore black, and since I literally had nothing, Vari let me borrow a little black dress that hugged my curves.

This ritual had always been performed after a pirate had lost their life. According to them, sailing was a way to release souls from this world and pass on to the next.

Killian stepped forward and turned to face the crowd, clearing his throat before he spoke. "The Delmari has returned. Last night, one of our ships was just off the harbor when many of us witnessed the brutal attack by the beast. This morning, I took a crew out to the wreckage. Unfortunately, the crew of The Ocean's Belle did not survive the attack. Sadie was a wonderful second mate and will be missed, as will all the people who we lost."

He listed off every name of who perished. As he did, one of the small boats was pushed out to sea. Once all names were said, archers stepped forward and loaded their bows with arrows tipped with fire. They shot the watercrafts, and when arrows landed, each vessel went up in flames. Everyone around me stood in silence. Some of the women were on their knees, sobbing into their hands. Vari and Killian both had somber expressions, and tears streamed down their cheeks. Their eyes locked onto me, and they slowly walked over. Killian pulled me close to him and looked out toward the ocean. It took only a few minutes for each of them to be lit. The burning boats all drifted off to sea, and we all watched in silence as they traveled farther and farther. I could not help to think of the traditions of Alari when we had souls pass on. There was a sacred trench south of the castle. The bottom of which is a volcano. We would send the bodies of the deceased down the trench to return. Tears welled in my eyes, and I wiped them away. One by one, the flames extinguished as the burning vessels sank.

Before the last one could sink, dark clouds formed quickly, hiding the moon and stars. Lightning flashed across the sky and thunder boomed. I cowered from the sound. Never had I heard anything like it. Not even a second later, the sky opened up, heavy rain poured, and the final flame was finally extinguished. Killian rushed over to me with a worried expression. "Hurry back to the tavern. We need to get to high ground now. We are in our dry season. It is not due to rain for another month."

Vari took my hand and squeezed. "Hopefully this is just some freak storm, and not one brought on by the Delmari."

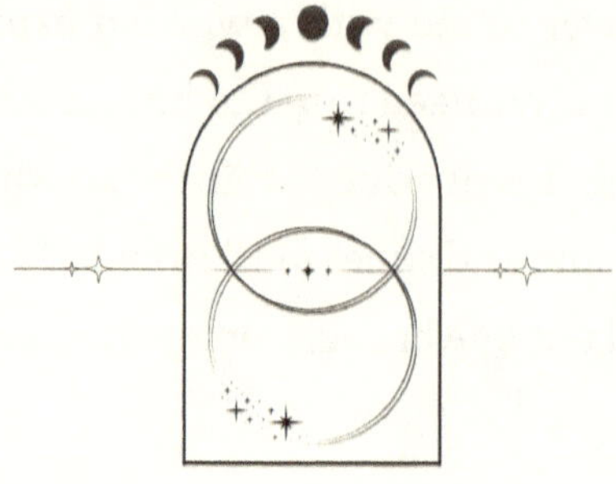

Nine

Three days had passed, and the heavy rains continued. The beaches no longer existed, and the water was nearly up to the first building of the town. Killian opened the tavern to those who lived close to the water so they could escape the flooding. Any boat that attempted to sail out was attacked by Arik. He only returned early in the morning for fresh clothes. Never had he slept in here, so I wasn't sure exactly what he was doing throughout the day and night. He claimed it was important for me to stay hidden. According to him, it was important not to let Arik know I was here.

Vari had brought me some books about the land of Elswyth. I learned of fae attacks to the west, which I had assumed to be the cursed fae of Orilon. My mother had talked about that poor realm once or twice. While we did not visit the other realms, we did often receive written communication from them, all except Tarak.

I was getting antsy. Sitting in here all day was driving me mad. We needed to do something, hiding here would not stop my uncle. I stayed up all night, waiting for Killian to return to his room. Once he had, I locked the door and blocked his path from leaving so he could not rush away again.

"Killian, I want to help. I cannot just stay locked in here all day with nothing to do but wait! It is driving me crazy!"

He turned to me and sighed, and it was then I noticed how dark bags had settled under his eyes. "I need to keep you safe until it is time to strike. You cannot leave this room until then."

"When will be the time, then? And what is the plan? I have no idea how to even wield the trident! I am not even sure I could!"

He stepped closer to me, so quickly that I staggered back. My back was now pressed against the wood of the door. He placed one hand above me to cage me in, and the other gently lifted my chin. Breath caught in my throat as he looked down at me with a placating expression. "Oh, my little mermaid. I am trying to get it all figured out for you. I promise. Please, just give me one more day."

"Give me the trident. That way I can at least begin to attune myself to its magic."

Killian smirked at me, released my chin, and booped the top of my nose. "You are so bossy. It's cute, but no."

"No?! You said you trusted me!"

"I do. But we cannot risk the chance that if it is out, your uncle may be able to find it."

"Killian, I will not ask again. Give it to me, now."

"Make me." He leaned in closer so his face was just an inch from mine.

The air electrified around us as the thunder boomed. My entire body tingled as his hand dropped from my chin and his fingertips gently grazed down my arm. Heat flooded my cheeks.

"Killian..." I breathed. "What are you doing?"

"Shh, little mermaid. I need to blow off some steam, and I am sure you want to explore your new human body. Am I right? You want to know why heat is building in between your legs right now, don't you? Let us help each other out, then I will give you the trident. Deal?"

I squirmed a bit. How did he know the feeling I had? It wasn't just heat that built. It was an ache. I gave a small nod.

A low growl escaped his throat and hunger grew in his eyes. "Oh no, love. I want to hear you say yes. I will not touch you until I have your full consent. Will you let me explore in between those sexy thighs of yours?"

"Please," I whimpered. My core ached for him. Never once had I experienced the touch of a man, but I craved Killian.

"Good girl," he breathed. His hand slipped down in between my legs and gently rubbed the apex of my thighs.

I cursed myself for the pants I was wearing. His fingers rubbed harder, and I let out a small moan.

"That is music to my ears, Calliope," he said just before he pressed his lips to mine.

The kiss was much gentler than I imagined it would be. Just looking at him, you would never expect the pirate captain to be a gentle lover. He pulled his soft lips away from mine. His citrus and salt scent filled my nose, and I kissed him back, increasing the passion between us. I could feel him harden against me. My heartbeat quickened as I slowly reached to touch it.

Quickly, he pulled away. "Such an eager one you are. Strip for me," he demanded. I did just as he asked. Killian took my hand and guided me to stand in front of the full-length mirror that was mounted on the wall and stood behind me. "Gods, you have the most beautiful body I have ever seen. Sit."

I did as he said, and he sat behind me, positioning me in between his legs. "What are you doing?" I asked.

"Don't ask questions. Spread your legs for me."

His commanding voice made my knees weak. Doing as I was told, he smirked. His hands found their way to my breasts, and he rubbed them. As he slid my nipples between two fingers and pulled, a gasp of pleasure escaped my throat. Staring at myself in the mirror, my gaze fell from where his hands were making me forget how to breathe to the little wet slit in between my legs.

Killian's gaze followed mine. "Oh, curious about that, are we?" His hands traveled down my body and gently brushed against the outside of my most intimate part. Too slowly, his fingers ran up and down it. "You are so wet for me." He pulled his fingers away and put them in front of my face. They glistened with my juices. "Lick it and tell me how you taste."

Slowly, I dragged my tongue up his fingers, tasting myself. "Sweet."

He lowered his hand and pushed two fingers inside my entrance. He quickly pulled it out and brought it to his own lips. A huge smile grew on his face as he groaned in delight. I watched him as he sucked on his fingers. "I had to taste for myself. You're right. You are delicious." He lowered his hand once again and slid his fingers inside of me. Slowly, he thrusted them in and out.

I let out a moan as he played with me. "Please, harder," I demanded.

"Beg, and maybe I will." The temptation in his voice only made me want him more.

"Killian please," I begged. "I need more."

He continued, increasing the force. My body filled with pleasure, but it ended all too quickly. He pulled his fingers away, stood, walked over to the front of me, and forced me to look up at him.

"I am sure you are curious about what a male body looks like." He removed his shirt, then slowly removed his pants. His considerable length sprung into my face. My eyes crossed as I focused on it. "Like what you see, love?"

"That is huge," I whimpered.

Killian chuckled. "Wrap those beautiful pouty lips around it."

I got onto my knees and looked up at him. Breath caught in my throat as I examined his full length. Nervously, I wrapped my lips around its tip and sucked gently on it. Killian threw back his head and let out a groan. His fingers ran through my hair and stopped as his hand reached the back of my head. Pushing just a little, he made me take more of him into my mouth. My eyes went wide as he slid deeper inside me. Once half of his length was in, he stopped pushing on my head to allow me to adjust to him. I swirled my tongue around as I continued to suck on him. After a moment, he pulled away, and a strand of spit connected me to the tip of his cock.

"Don't move," he commanded. Walking behind me, he sat on the ground once again. He grabbed my hips and pulled me back, causing me to mount him. He lined himself up with my entrance but did not enter me. One of his hands grabbed me by my cheeks and forced me to look into the mirror. "Watch how I fuck you, Calliope." Slowly, he lowered me onto him. I let out a moan as the head fully slipped in. My body opened up to take his full girth. "Gods, you are perfect."

Killian thrusted upward to make me take more of him. A moan escaped my lips as more of him entered me. Through the reflection, I watched as his length disappeared. The feeling was overwhelming as he stretched me beyond what I ever imagined. I begged him for more, and he obliged. It was not long before the full length of him was deep inside me. Looking into the mirror, I watched him slide in and out of me. My body was overcome with pleasure I never experienced.

A pleasure that I could easily become addicted to.

"Don't stop please." I could not describe the feeling building inside me. It was beyond pure euphoria. Quivering against him, I was about to explode from the pleasure.

Killian stopped thrusting and nearly pulled out all the way. "Oh no, you are not allowed to come yet, love. Fuck yourself, and maybe, just maybe, I will give you the privilege of coming on my cock."

"No, please, don't stop," I pleaded. "I need you deep inside me." Nervousness took over. If I were to be in charge of my own movements, would I be able to please the man who brought so much pleasure to me? Would I continue to feel that pleasure?

"If you want it, take it." He leaned back and rested on his elbows. Looking back at him, I slowly bounced on him. "Good girl. You take me so well. Don't stop until I say so."

I bounced harder and faster on him until I had him slamming on my innermost wall. The moans that escaped my lips got louder with each bounce. I could not believe I was doing this, I loved this, or that I craved this. Back home, I never imagined such carnal pleasures.

Killian grabbed hold of my hips and started thrusting again, harder and faster than before. The pleasure was overwhelming just before he exploded inside of me, and stars filled my vision. He continued to fuck me until I felt his cock twitch.

Quickly, he sat up and pulled out of me. He spun me around and sat me back on the ground. Getting on his knees, he stroked himself until his tip shot out his essence, and it covered my chest.

A satisfying ache filled my body and I smiled up at him in a daze. This man was a god. He had to be to provide such over-whelming pleasure.

"If I thought you were beautiful before, I cannot deny you are even more stunning with my cum all over your chest." He smirked and stood. Offering his hand to me, he assisted me up. "Let's get us cleaned up, then we can go train with the trident."

"Will you join me in the shower?" I asked with a smile.

Killian's honey-colored eyes lit up. "Absolutely."

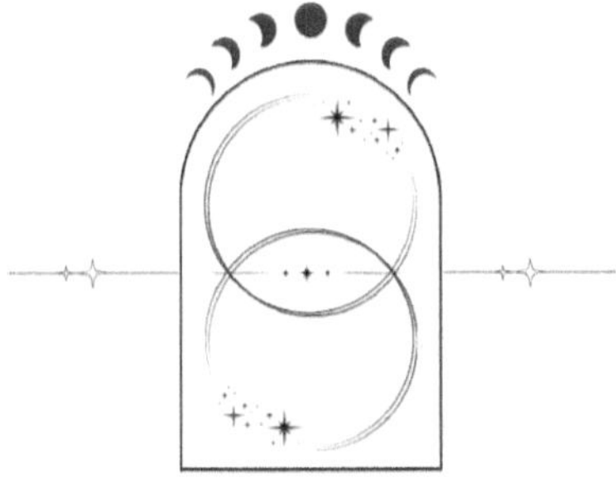

Ten

Heavy rain continued to fall, soaking both Killian and me to the bone. We were just outside of town, out of the view of the sea and away from prying eyes. Gripping the trident tight with both hands, its magic pulsed through me. For the last hour, I tried to connect myself further with it. Even though my magic was gone, I tried to call forth a kernel of it to see if it would combine with the magic of the trident. With all the stories I had been told of the trident, it was our family's most powerful weapon. It was gifted to the first mer king and my ancestor by The Mother and her daughter Nera. Was it anything without the Gem of Alari? Even without the Gem, I could still feel its power. What exactly could the trident do without it?

For over an hour, Killian watched me as I acted out using the trident in battle. Thrusting it forward, I pretended to stab my imaginary foe. Quickly, I spun and mimicked the movement as if someone was attacking me from behind. He shook his head and let out a chuckle under his breath. "Love, if that is how you fight, I don't think we have any hope of defeating your uncle."

I shot him a pointed glare. "I am doing my best!" Marching over to him, red filled my vision. "I am in a new world, dealing with a new body, and without the comfort of my magic to guide me. The trident had not been in Alari for at least thirty years before I was born! My mother never even talked about it or its capabilities. I have no idea what I am doing."

He pushed off the tree he was leaning against and took a step to close the gap between us. Rain ran down and dripped off his chiseled face. "Calliope. I am sorry. I didn't mean anything by it. It was a joke."

"The joke wasn't funny!" I shouted at him.

Killian let out a deep breath. "May I show you what my father taught me?" he asked in a soft voice.

I glared at him for a moment before nodding and handing over the trident.

Killian took it from my hands and stepped into the clearing, going over all the stances and positions he was taught. The silver glimmered in his hands, and Killian's eyes glowed as he wielded the weapon. It was then that it clicked for me. The trident was no longer just a Delmari family heirloom. Three generations of the Darksea line had guarded the trident from the monster my uncle had become. Though this land seemed to be one of no magic, could it be possible that the Darkseas created their own to protect the trident? And in doing so, change it from being responsive to a Delmari heir?

"Killian?" I spoke softly, but not weakly.

"Yes?" He stopped mid-movement and looked down at me.

"What do you feel when you wield the trident?"

He turned to face me, with his head slightly cocked and an eyebrow raised. "What do I feel?"

I nodded and walked over to him. I placed my hands on top of his. "Close your eyes. Focus on the Trident."

Killian closed his eyes and took slow and even breaths. "I am not sure how to describe what I feel."

"Try."

He stayed silent for a long while. The rain poured down on us. "Like it is flowing through me and becoming one with my soul."

A smile grew across my face. "Killian. The trident is not mine to wield. It is yours. It has attuned to you."

He opened his eyes and looked down at me with a look of shock. "Impossible. I know nothing of magic."

I shook my head as a smile spread across my face. "It doesn't matter. It chose you. When your family became the caretakers of the weapon, your soul mixed with it."

Killian stepped back, pulling away from me. "Give me some space. I want to try something."

I obliged, creating more distance between us.

Killian raised the trident into the air. "I am Killian Darksea," he boomed. "Captain of the Darksea pirates, protector of the Southern Sea. Hear me, Tempuno." He spoke directly to the god of storms. Silence fell in the air for a moment, and then three bolts of lightning flashed across the sky, followed by a loud roll of thunder. "Hear me, Calypso." He now called out the god of the seas. "Here me, Nera." When he spoke to the mother of the mer, my heart pounded in my chest. She was the goddess that I had the closest relationship with. I prayed she would help us above all others. "Grant me strength and guidance, for tomorrow, I will take a small crew back to the Delmari's island. Grant us safe passage. Allow us to end the storm that threatens the balance of this world. Allow the little mermaid to restore her magic, and return to the sea she calls home. For if you grant us this, I will dedicate my life in your honor."

Killian stared up at the sky. The only sound was the rain growing heavier. Killian did not falter. He stayed there with the trident raised to the sky. After another moment of silence, a bolt of lightning struck the trident on its head. Electricity buzzed around the prongs. Killian lowered it so it was at eye level with him.

"Thank you," he said softly. "I will not disappoint you."

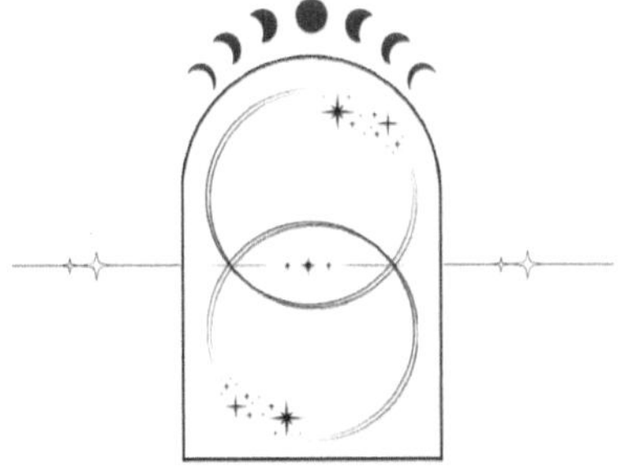

Eleven

Three more days passed, and still the rain did not let up. The sea level had now risen to the point it was flooding people's homes near the shore. Early that morning, Killian gathered a small crew, and we boarded a ship, sailing off to return to where it all began. Anxiety filled me to my core as we walked toward the dock. I was not sure if I was ready to face my uncle, but it was now or never.

When we got to the seashore, most of the boats that had been docked were missing, and some were adrift out in the harbor. Killian's ship, The Dark Seafarer, was still docked. Lucky for all of us, this was a floating dock. If it was built into the ground, we would have been out of luck.

Quickly, we all made our way down and onboard the ship. After about a half hour, we were ready to sail. Killian instructed me to stay in his office. That way, I would be out of the way of the crew until we got to our destination. The sway of the boat from the massive waves had a knot growing in my stomach. It was as if at any moment I was going to release the contents of it.

After a short amount of time, Vari entered the office. A puddle of water formed under her feet as she leaned against the door for support. "I wanted to bring you this," she said as she extended her arm and held out a small pouch.

"What is that?" I questioned as I slowly walked over to her, swaying with each step.

"Ginger candy. I know if I am feeling sick, you must be. I know you lived in the sea and all, but being aboard a ship during a storm is a whole nother beast. These help, a little," she said with a smile.

I took the pouch from her, removed a piece of candy, and popped it in my mouth. The spiced taste caused me to scrunch my face.

"I know they taste horrible, but it's totally worth it. Please keep the whole bag. You will need it."

"Vari!" I heard Killian call from beyond the door. "I need you at the helm."

"I have to go, but I will check on you again if I can."

Before I could respond, she had gone out the door. In the short amount of time I had known her, Vari had become a good friend. As much as I hated to admit it, so had Killian. Truly, I was going to miss both of them when I returned home. Hopefully, mother was not too mad at me for running away, and would allow me to visit. That was if I was ever allowed to leave the castle again.

The sound of splintering wood pulled me from my thoughts of home. The ship rocked with such force that I fell on my ass. Screams could be heard from the outside. I forced myself up and rushed over to the door, pulling it open. My mouth fell agape at what I saw. Large red tentacles arose from the surface of the sea and waved in the air. They towered over the ship.

"Abandon ship!" a man called out.

"I am not getting into the water with that beast!" another said.

"It doesn't matter if you go in the water, or stay aboard. We are all dead!" a third answered.

A tentacle smashed down on the ship again, and my body slammed into the door frame from the force. A tentacle swept across the deck, knocking several of the crew into the water. It slammed into the mast, breaking the solid wood. The loud cracking sound overwhelmed my ears. It wrapped around the pole and threw the mast into the ocean.

"Calliope!" Killian called out.

"I am here!" I responded.

He jumped down from the deck above with the trident in hand. When his eyes landed on me, they went wide with worry. Quickly, he rushed over to me and wrapped me in his arms. "Don't worry, love. I am going to get us out of this safe."

"Wh-where is Vari?" I asked, holding on to Killian for support.

"She is getting the lifeboats ready!" He looked around at the remainder of his scrambling crew. "Everyone to the lifeboats now!" On his last word, another tentacle rose and slammed down onto the ship, breaking through it. The ship rocked back from the impact. Screams filled the air. Killian threw me over his shoulder. He held me tight with one arm, the other gripped the trident. "Here goes nothing," he said under his breath. He pointed the trident toward the tentacle, and when nothing happened, Killian let out a growl.

Another tentacle arose from the water behind him and shot toward us.

"Killian, behind you!" I screamed.

Quickly, he spun us around and stabbed the trident directly into the assaulting tentacle. Bright blue electricity shot through it. The tentacle pulled back from us before it convulsed and fell into the ocean.

"That is what I am talking about!" Killian cheered.

Another tentacle came our way, and again Killian struck it with the trident, whose prongs buzzed with electric power. This time, all the tentacles wrapped around the ship retreated into the dark water. I released the breath I had been holding.

"Don't count this as over yet." Killian placed me back on my feet. Taking my hand, he rushed us to the side of the ship where three small boats floated below us. Two were already full with the remaining crew, and the last boat only carried Vari. Killian ushered me down the rope ladder to get on the small lifeboat. While working our way down, the ship was taking on too much water. Between that and the damage from Arik, the stress on the wood was too much, and it snapped in half. The front nose dived into the water. Once the bow was submerged, it slowly sank. The aft tilted, causing Killian to stagger. Once he steadied himself, he quickly descended the ladder. Before he got halfway down, he jumped onto our small lifeboat, causing it to rock so hard that Vari nearly fell overboard.

"Quickly, get to shore!" Killian called out. He pointed over to the town, which seemed so far away. How long would it take us to reach shore? Would we be able to do so safely?

Vari pulled two paddles out from under the seats. She gave one to Killian. "The two of us will row. Calliope you sit there." She pointed to the bench behind me. The two of them sat on the one across from me and rowed.

"I can help, you know!" I said.

"Oh, love, I am sure you could, but this will be a long trip," Killian responded.

"And, no offense, but with those little noodle arms, we would not make it far," Vari let out a laugh.

"Hey! I can't help my thin arms."

"How about this, love?" He extended the trident out to me. "Hold on to this like your life depends on it."

"May I remind both of you it does?" Vari retorted.

The sea grew eerily silent as we rowed our way back to shore. The only sounds were the rain hitting the surface, and the paddles pushing the water. Even the choppy waves calmed. After about an hour, we seemed no closer to shore. Both Vari and Killian struggled more and more with each row, but they continued to refuse my help. The other two boats were now a good bit ahead. Each had at least four people rowing at a time.

I looked up at the sky, and let the rain wash away the tears that had been flowing down my face. Again, lives had been lost because of me. If I never traveled to this land, Arik would have never gotten the power he needed. His tentacles had grown so much since I had last seen him, and I feared how much power he had gained from the Gem. The sound of bubbling water filled the space around me. When I looked down, it was as if the sea was boiling.

"Vari, give it all you got!" Killian called out. The two of them started to row faster.

But it was no use. A red tentacle shot from the water. Before anyone could react, it wrapped around Vari and pulled her under. She did not even have a chance to scream before she was claimed by the sea. Her paddle floated to the surface and bobbed against the waves.

"Vari!" I called out. I leaned over the side to look down, but I could not see anything in the dark ocean.

Killian let out a scream as he ripped the trident from my hands. "Give me back my sister, you beast!" On that last word, he dove into the bubbling ocean.

I reached out for him, trying to get him to stop. But he, too, vanished into the water. Now alone, in the small lifeboat, I contemplated my next move. Before I could decide, I heard a gasp from behind me. I spun to see Killian's head emerging from the sea.

"It is too dark! I can't see anything. He took her! I can't let him keep her," he sobbed. "I promised my father I would protect her. I can't fail him again." He dove under once again.

And again.

And again.

Each time it felt like an eternity before his head broke the surface. All I could do was helplessly watch. My body would not allow myself to jump into the water to help him.

After the fifth time, he climbed back into the lifeboat with his head hung. He took both paddles in hand and began to row. I sat by his side, and he leaned against me. Taking one of the paddles from him, I helped him row us back to shore.

We went the entire way in utter silence.

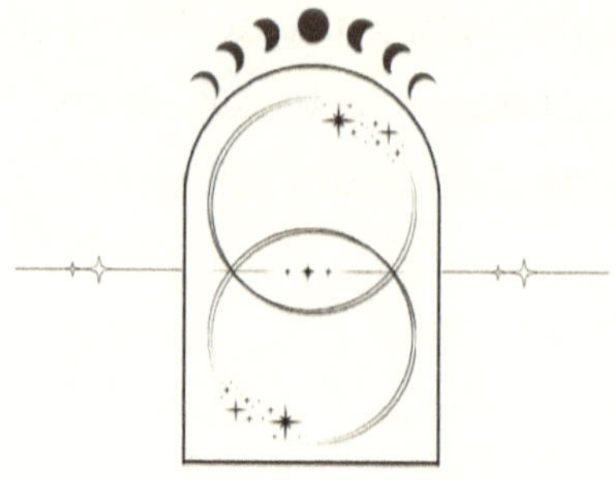

Twelve

Killian did not get out of bed for three days. I moved to a room downstairs to give him privacy. Every day Hawk, Van, and I tried to enter his room to check on him. The door would be locked, and he would not respond to us. Without Vari, the tavern felt so empty. I missed her laugh and her smile. We all did. With the rain still somehow growing harder, it was impossible to give the lost souls a sailing. Not being able to perform the rite lowered the morale of the entire Darksea crew even more.

Without completing the sailing, the Darkseas believed the souls of the lost were trapped here.

With the rain continuing to get worse, most of Caldor had flooded. The cliff kept us dry, but it would not be much longer until the tavern, too, was underwater. Many of the town's citizens have traveled north to the capital of Elswyth. Though there were mountains to the west, no one traveled that way. No one wanted to face the monstrous beasts who would tear you limb from limb and feast on your flesh beyond the mountains.

One night, I was jolted awake by a familiar sound. This had to be a trick of the mind. Jumping out of bed, I quickly dressed and marched out of the tavern. It was a dangerous game I was playing by leaving without telling a soul. If this was a trap, I was falling right into it, but I had to take the chance. The sound continued to ring in my ears. As I got closer to the waterline, it got louder. The song of the mer called to me. A sweet melody of welcoming and acceptance.

There was no denying what I heard.

These mer sang for me. They knew my name. They called for me. Tears filled my eyes. Could they be from home? Could this be the rescue I craved?

I boarded one of the small lifeboats and paddled as fast as I could toward the sound. The rough seas made it difficult to row forward, but I refused to stop. Praying Arik would not sense my presence, I hoped I would reach who called to me in time.

The wind picked up, and the waves worsened, and I could feel every ebb and flow of the ocean beneath me. With each wave. I rose and crashed hard as it passed. Still, the song continued.

Calliope.

Calliope.

Calliope.

Princess of Alari.

They called my name.

Until they didn't. The only sounds now were of the hard rain and the violent ocean. I turned to see how far I ventured offshore. The town was now on the distant horizon.

"I am here!" I screamed out into the vast ocean. "I am here. Please, take me home," I sobbed.

There was no answer. Was the song something I imagined? Something I had conjured just to make me feel close to home?

The waves continued to grow in size, and I grabbed my paddles tight and fought against them to turn back to shore. A large wave was coming directly my way. There was no way this small boat could make it over. No, this could not be it for me. I paddled harder, hoping I could make it past.

Why did I allow the phantom voices to call me so far from shore? Out of anyone, I should have known how dangerous the lure of the voice could be.

The wave finally met my boat and caused it to capsize, throwing me into the dark sea. I spun in the water from the force, and it was impossible to get my bearings. I tried to kick my feet to swim, but I made no progress getting closer to the surface. On instinct, I opened my mouth, but my human lungs were not made to take in water. The waves continued to beat against my body, and would not allow my head to break the surface. My head felt light, and my eyes fluttered.

I swore arms grabbed me just before everything faded to black.

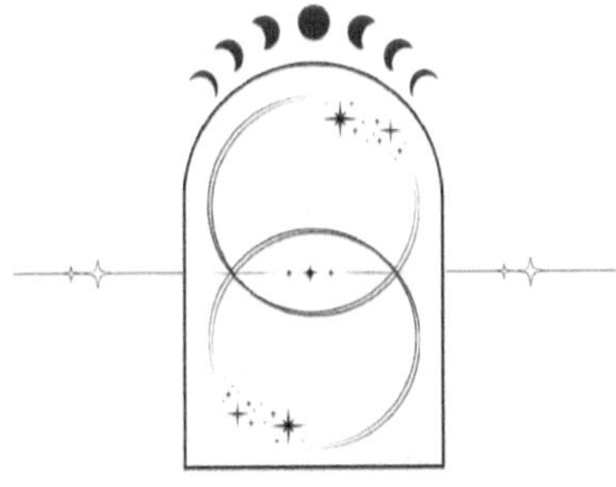

Thirteen

"Is it really her?" a gentleman's voice asked.

I tried to open my eyes, but they refused to cooperate. The voice sounded so far away... as if it was in another realm... as if this was a dream.

"She answered a call only meant for the Princess of Alari, did she not? It has to be," a woman answered.

"Do you think she will wake soon?"

Again, I tried to open my eyes. The voices started to fade as if they were getting farther and farther from reality.

"In her human body, it is hard to tell," the woman responded.

The two continued to speak, but I was unable to understand them. The harder I tried to make out what they were saying, the more the words softened until there was just silence.

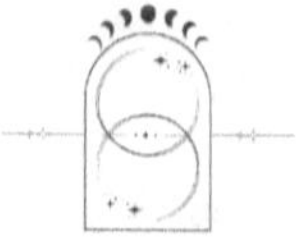

My eyes shot open, and I quickly sat up. Wooziness filled me at the sudden motion. As my vision came into focus, I saw an older woman sitting at the edge of the bed. Her white hair was pulled up into a tight bun atop her head, and her light blue eyes nearly glowed.

"Easy there. Don't hurt yourself. You are safe."

It was the woman I had heard in my dream.

"Where..." My throat was so dry and hoarse, it was hard to get words out. "Where am I?" I finally forced out.

The woman stood and walked over to the table next to the bedside, where she picked up the glass of water and extended it to me. "Please drink."

I took the cup from her hand and brought it to my lips. At first, I struggled to swallow, but the more I drank, the easier it became.

"Good, we will get you more in a moment. My name is Nera. You are in my home. My children pulled you from the ocean."

My eyes went wide in recognition. "Nera..."

She let out a chuckle. "So you have heard of me? I was wondering if the people of Alari had forgotten the old ways after all this time. Do not fret, for I have not forgotten you. I would not forget any of my children."

I could not believe my ears. Was I truly in front of the woman where all mer originated? According to legend, Nera was one of The Mother's children. It was she who created the mer and granted us our gifts. We called her the mother of the mer. "Thank you for saving me." That was all I could force myself to say.

"No need to thank me, my dear, for I would save all my children. Pulling you from the Southern Sea was not the only way you needed saving. There is another way you need to be saved, correct?"

I nodded.

"Come with me, child. for I can return to you what was stolen." She turned and walked toward the door.

I jumped out of bed and followed her. As we exited the room, we came out to a small landing in a circular room. Along the wall was a silver spiral staircase leading to more landings and doors. Walking over to the railing, I looked down and my stomach flipped. We were very high up. The entire space was only the stairs that hugged the wall and all the doors.

"Come along," Nera called out. She had already begun to descend the stairs.

I rushed to catch up to her. There were a few others on the stairs, and they bowed as we passed them. Once at the bottom, she opened the door and rushed me outside. The sun hit my face, and I embraced its warmth on my skin. Off in the distance, dark storm clouds loomed in the sky. Nera placed a gentle hand on my shoulder, and I turned to meet her gaze.

"Do not worry. He cannot reach you here. Only those I allow are welcome here. Neither he nor his storm are welcome."

I turned and offered her a warm smile, and she gave me one in response. Releasing me, she continued to walk forward. Before

I followed her, I turned to look at the building we exited. It was a very tall lighthouse. The color of it matched my tail exactly, even down to the silver sparkles.

"Come along now so you don't get lost!" she called out to me. I turned toward her and followed. The sandy shore turned into a small jungle where the canopy blocked the sun's rays. A myriad of bright-colored flowers hung from the trees. After a short walk, we entered a clearing with a shimmering pool in its center. It mirrored the pool I had traveled through when I first entered Elswyth.

"Is this..." I began to ask.

"A portal?" Nera finished for me. When I nodded, she smiled and returned the gesture. "Long ago it was before I closed it off to keep this island safe. When your uncle first gained the crown, he found this place and asked me to grant him more power. I saw him for what he truly was and refused him. To ensure he could never return, I sealed this portal. However, the magic of Alari still exists within its waters. Now please strip and enter."

I did as she instructed and removed the slip dress I had awoken in. Once nude, I stepped into the water and found that it was very deep. Kicking my feet to stay afloat, I looked up at Nera.

She tilted her head up, and the sun illuminated her face. She chanted in a language I was not familiar with. The water slowly started to bubble. A tingling sensation spread through my body. Nera dropped her gaze down to me. "Calliope Mariana Delmari, Princess of Alari. What will you do with your powers once returned to you?"

"I will return to Caldor, defeat my uncle, and stop the rains from flooding this land."

"What if stopping the rains meant you could not return home? Would you stay here to help the humans or would you flee back to Alari, as if this land never existed?"

I never expected to have to stay here. All I wanted was to return home, to see my mother again. I hesitated for a moment before I answered. "I will stay. I could not leave these good people to drown."

A smile crossed Nera's face. "For centuries, the rulers of Alari have always been born in pairs. One to rule the realm of the mer, the other to protect this world from the wrath of the storms. It was your mother who was to come to Elswyth and Arik was to rule Alari. But your uncle was selfish. He wanted to keep your mother as a political bargain. Arik came to Elswyth to allow the storms to continue. When he arrived, he realized that once the storms continued, he could keep the realm of Elswyth for himself. He made a deal with the storm's spirit and the two became one. It took three long years, but the humans defeated him and stole the trident, he was unable to maintain the magic needed to keep the storm's powers. When he stole the gem from you, it gave him the power to reconnect with the storms." She knelt, so we met eye to eye. "Once your uncle is defeated. You will need to stay, to be able to keep the storm spirit away."

"What will happen in Alari if I stay? I have no twin to rule the realm in my absence."

Nera's smile grew. "Your mother will live a long and happy life. Before her time is over, there will be a new generation of the Delmari line to continue the cycle. Or should I say, *the Darksea line*?" She offered me a wink.

Heat rose to my cheeks. "Killian and I will not only be togeth-er but also have children?"

"As the way the future is currently written? Yes. But fear not, once balance is restored you will be able to visit Alari as you please. As will your children be able to visit you here in Elswyth. Do you agree to restore balance to the realms?"

"Yes. I will restore the balance. I will save Elswyth, Alari, and their peoples."

Nera offered me a nod and stood. Looking back to the sky, she continued her chant. When she was done, the bubbles van-ished. I looked down, and instead of legs, my tail wadded in the water. "Thank you." Tears streamed down my face. I felt whole once again. Not only did I feel whole, I felt more. My magic felt stronger than it ever had. It flowed through my veins and sang in harmony with my body.

"You are so welcome, dear."

I pulled myself out of the pool, shifted into my human form, and stood. Now that my magic had been returned to me, I could easily switch between my two forms. Wrapping Nera in a hug, she nearly staggered back from the force. Once she steadied herself, she hugged me back.

"Do you need to rest another day before you return to your pirate?"

"Thank you for everything, but I must return as soon as I can. I cannot waste another moment."

"Then go, my child. Remember your promise. And, as long as it is held, you are welcome here anytime."

Without another word, I turned and sprinted toward the shore. Running into the ocean, the gentle waves splashed against my legs. Once deep enough, I transformed into my true form and swam as fast as I could to Caldor.

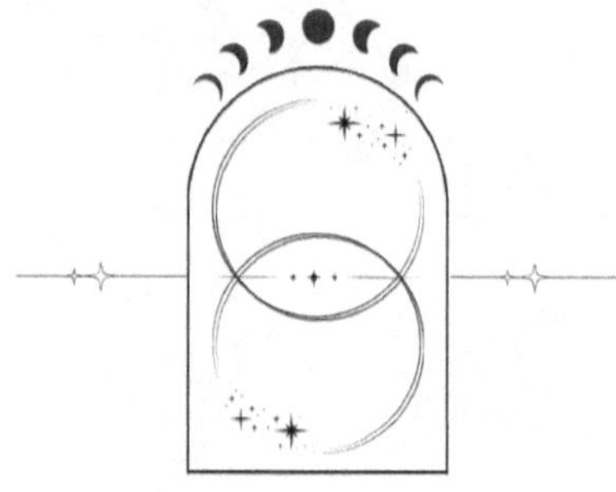

Fourteen

When I entered the tavern, all eyes were on me. Killian's voice boomed through the crowd as he pushed past people to get to me, fury raged in his eyes. "Where have you been? Why would you leave without telling anyone?"

I rushed over to him, wrapped my arms around his neck, and pulled him into a kiss. He pulled away and gave me a look of confusion.

"I have my magic back!" I cried out.

"You what?" He asked in surprise.

"I can transform. I have my magic back!"

He offered a smile that did not meet his eyes. "So, this means you are returning home?"

"No!" I released him, took a step back, and hit him in the arm. "This means we have more of an even playing field with Arik. We can defeat him this time!"

"We will not be sending any more good people to die!" Van said from the bar. Killian and I turned to face him as he continued. "That's enough. There is no way we can defeat such a monster."

Hawk, who sat next to Van, nodded in agreement. "Killian, you have to stop this madness before you get us all killed!"

Murmurs filled the tavern. Some agreed with Van, some thought it was crazy to speak against the captain.

"Van," Killian growled. "If we don't stop him, we all will die. All of us. All human life will cease to exist!"

"I have gotten letters from family who traveled north to the capital. There is no storm there!" One of the pirates said.

"Don't you understand it will expand?" Killian asked.

Van stood and walked over to Killian. "Hawk and I are leaving. We refuse to die for this. Anyone who wants to join us is welcome." Van walked out of the bar, with Hawk and half of the crew following behind him.

The room stayed silent for too long after they left. Tension hung in the air. Killian looked around the room, seeing who stayed. "I will not ask you to put your lives on the line for this."

A woman named Jaki stood and walked over to us. "You and Vari took me in when I had nowhere to go. You both taught me I had worth beyond what others thought of me, beyond how others treated me. I will always lay my life down for you. Whatever you need."

It was then I realized that most who stayed were women. Vari had told me she had organized a part of the crew of survivors. To give them a home, to remind them of their strength.

A smile grew on my face. "Another man has tried to steal something away from us." As I began, all eyes were on me. "This time, we will not allow him to take from us. We will get our vengeance upon him. We will make him feel powerless and afraid. We will show no mercy, as he and so many others have refused to show us any." As the women cheered, I took Killian's hand in mine and smiled up at him. "I hope you have another ship because we are ready for war."

"I do, but it won't hold all of us. It only holds five."

"I will go!" Jaki said.

"We will too," shouted two sisters, Maria and Belle, from the back of the tavern.

Killian looked down at me. "Well, it appears you have your crew. What will you call yourselves?"

"The Vengeance of Alari. We leave at dawn."

"Aye, captain!" The three women and Killian responded.

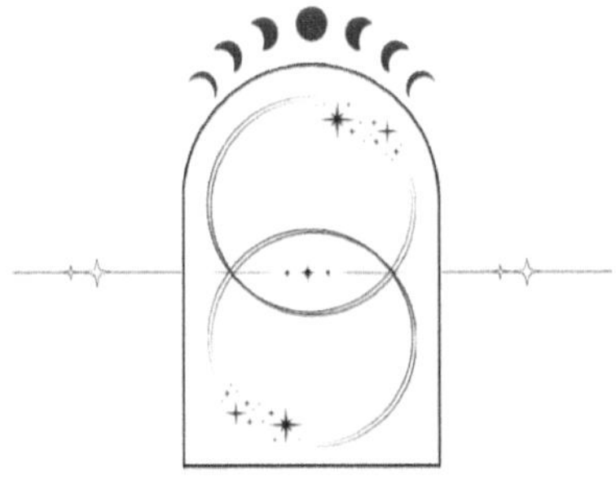

Fifteen

We spent the day in each other's company. We did not know if this would be the last day we would have together. With dawn looming over us, we did not want to waste any time. After dinner, we all retreated to our rooms to rest. Killian took me by the hand and guided me into his bedroom. Once inside, he locked the door behind us. He glared down at me with a displeased look.

"What's wrong?" I questioned.

Killian let out a heavy sigh. "You left and did not even say goodbye." He dropped his gaze to the floor.

My eyes widened, and I staggered back. "You haven't spoken to me for days. When I heard the call of my people, I couldn't resist it! I couldn't waste any time!"

"Is that all I am to you?" He walked past me, not sparing me a glance. "A waste of time?"

"No!" I spun to face him. "Not at all." Grabbing his wrist, I pulled him to face me.

Tears misted his eyes. "I know we just met, but when I thought I lost you too, it broke me."

I wrapped him in a hug. "I am not going anywhere, Killian." I couldn't imagine leaving him, even before my promise to Nera.

"Won't you be returning to Alari once we defeat your uncle?" He pulled away from my embrace. His face and tone were cold as stone.

"No. I am going to stay here. I have a very important duty to uphold once Arik is gone. The goal is to return here with you once it is over."

His face softened as he looked down at me. "You want to stay here with me?" He raised an eyebrow.

"More than anything," I whispered.

Without another word, Killian stepped toward me, lifted me in the air, and planted his lips firmly on mine. Wrapping my arms and legs around him, I increased the passion in our kiss. My tongue pushed past his lips and danced with his. He tossed me onto the bed and offered me a predatory smirk.

"Shall we explore that beautiful human body of yours again, love?" He dragged his tongue across his top lip.

I sat up on my elbows and smiled. "Please. Make me forget about what lies ahead."

"Don't say another word," he commanded.

I nodded, and he quickly situated himself between my legs. Lifting my skirt, he ducked his head under it. Slipping my underwear off my body, he tossed them onto the floor. A moan escaped my lips as I felt his tongue slowly drag up my slit.

Gripping onto the sheets, I tossed my head back from the pleasure. Killian's tongue pathed circles over my most delicate part. When he reached my clit, his tongue flicked over it, causing another moan to escape my lips.

Killian pulled his head out from under my skirt, licking my juices off his lips. "Gods, you are divine." He pulled himself to meet my lips and kissed me hungrily.

Reaching down, I gently stroked him through his pants. All I wanted was his considerable length deep inside me once again. "I need you," I moaned in between his kisses.

He pulled away, and my lips ached in his absence. "And you will have me, love." Quickly, he removed his pants and shirt and pulled up my skirt to reveal myself to him. Stepping forward, he lined himself up with my entrance. He slowly teased, leaving me craving more as he gently pushed his tip in and out of me.

"Killian, please. I need all of you," I pleaded.

"So eager." He offered me a smirk as he eased more of him inside me. Slowly, he thrust to allow me to adjust to his girth.

"Please," I continued to beg. It was all my body allowed me to do.

In one quick motion, Killian pushed himself deep inside, making me take him fully. I let out a scream of pleasure as he picked up the pace. Reaching forward, I grabbed him by the back of his head and pulled him in for another kiss. As we kissed, Killian ripped my dress off my body, leaving me bare for him.

Each time I thought I was going to reach my climax, he slowed, pulling me away from that ledge I was so desperate to cross. Over and over, he built my pleasure and brought me down just before I could explode from it. My body ached by the time he finally allowed me to find my pleasure. I let out a scream as stars filled my eyes. Clenching around his cock, I quivered around him.

Pushing deep inside me, Killian let out a groan as he found his release. Heat flooded my body. Holding himself there, it twitched inside me as all of his essence shot into me. When he pulled out I was left with an emptiness, as if my soul ached to be intertwined with his.

"I am glad you're staying here," Killian smirked down at me.

"Why is that?"

"Because, even if you wanted to, I would never let you leave." He leaned down and planted a kiss on my forehead.

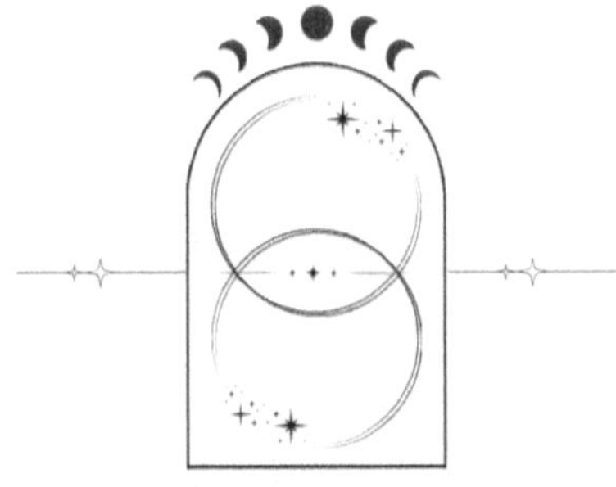

Sixteen

At dawn, the five of us were aboard the small ship and headed to the island where it all began. The sea was calm, and the air was filled with the sound of the rain falling into the ocean. Pacing back and forth on the top deck, I tapped my fingers against each other over and over. I did not know if or when my uncle would show himself, which left me and my crew feeling on edge.

This time, I would be ready for him. This time, I would get vengeance for what he had done to me, the lands of Alari and Elswyth, and my friends.

Killian stood at the helm with his gaze focused on the small deserted island off in the distance. After I walked over to him, he looked down at me and gave me a smile that did not reach his eyes. I thought back to the first time I had laid my eyes on him, and how confident he looked then. Even though he wore the same red outfit today, and had the trident strapped to his back, most of that confidence had been washed away by the never-ending rains.

"How are you feeling?" he asked.

"Nervous." I could not lie. My magic felt so much stronger than it ever had. Even when the source of my magic was the Gem I did not have this much power flowing through my veins. Still, I needed to be cautious. I could only imagine how much power the Gem gave Arik. "Nervous, but ready."

Killian turned his gaze out toward the sea. "Calliope," he said nearly in a whisper, "I am sorry. When I first found you on the island, I underestimated you. I should not have done that. Neither should your uncle. Luckily, I corrected my mistake before it was too late."

"I won't give Arik the chance to make that same mistake," I snarled. Turning away from Killian, I looked out at the ocean in the direction of Nera's island. A smile crossed my face as I saw a familiar and comforting golden flash on the horizon. Never would I forget the kindness she had shown me. In my time of need, the mother of mer was there for me. I would not disappoint her.

The winds picked up as we got closer to the island. As we anchored, I expected Arik would have attacked by now, but he had still not made an appearance. Boarding a small boat, Killian and I both rowed to the island. The three women we brought with us stayed on board, just in case.

When we reached the shore, Killian jumped out of the boat and pushed it onto the beach. Taking my hand, he helped me up and out to stand at his side.

My gaze was fixed on the rocks just down the shoreline. The tattoo on my leg stung from the memory of me slipping, scraping my skin, and bleeding into the ocean. My eyes widened, and I inhaled sharply as I realized what had happened. Was it my blood that awoke him? Is that how Arik knew I had traveled through the portal to this island? A chill ran down my spine.

"Are you alright?" Killian asked.

I offered a small nod. "Give me your dagger," I commanded.

With a raised eyebrow, he unsheathed the dagger from his waist and handed it to me, handle first. Taking the dagger, I turned to face the ocean.

"Arik Tristian Delmari," I called out. "Let us settle this in the old ways. I call upon you for a blood duel. Face me." I sliced into my palm and allowed my blood to drip into the sea. "Are you willing to lay down your life for your cause? I am willing to take you down for mine."

"Calliope, what are you doing?!" Killian grabbed me, pulled me against him, and snatched the knife from my hand. A mix of anger and confusion was on his face as he stared down at me.

The rain abruptly stopped, but the dark clouds still loomed. A rumble filled the air as the earth quaked, causing me to fall into Killian as we both staggered from the tremor. Before us, the ocean parted and created high walls of water. The sea floor was now bare, and the kelp lay limp on the sand. Arik walked toward us with a cocky grin on his face. His red tentacles lurked behind his back, poised, and ready to strike. The clouds parted, and the sun hit his face, illuminating his golden hair and blue eyes. Slowly, he clapped as he walked toward us.

This man thought himself to be a god.

"I am surprised you were able to make it all the way back here without alerting me and had to use your blood to summon me. I must say, I am delighted to learn it is still as sweet, even after I took your magic. I hope there are no hard feelings about that, dear niece. I did what had to be done." He stopped about halfway between us, a wall of ocean behind him. "I hope you do not plan on begging for your magic back. I cannot allow you to have it. I also cannot let you return home and report to my brat of a sister that I am still alive. The last time I faced her, I barely made it out alive. However, If I faced her again, the outcome would be very different. I don't want to have to kill all of my remaining family."

Killian gripped my shoulder but did not say a word. This was my fight. He promised me he would let me have my moment.

I let out a chuckle. "It is not my mother you need to fear, but you are still correct. This time, it will end differently. You won't make it out alive."

"Foolish girl," Arik snarled in response. His gaze flicked toward Killian, and his eyes widened. "It seems you brought me another gift. After I took the Gem, I never expected you to bring me the trident." He raised his hand, and the center of his forehead glowed red. The Gem of Alari had been implanted under the skin. Arik raised his hand and extended his fingers toward the trident. Anger contorted his face as nothing happened. Slowly, he clenched his hand into a fist so tight the whites of his knuckles showed.

Stepping to my side, Killian wielded the trident. "Sorry, the gods have a different idea about who should wield this." As if on command, lightning struck down, hitting the forks, and filled them with electric power.

Arik's eyes darkened and the walls of the parted sea slammed shut. Just like that, he was gone, and the rains returned. Taking a step forward, I extended my arms and waved my hands through the air to part the sea where Arik had been. Only, where I was expecting to see the corpse of a mer or man, a single fish flopped on the sand. Releasing my hold on the ocean I let out a scream. I could not let him escape. I ran out into the ocean, transformed, and swam out into the dark waters.

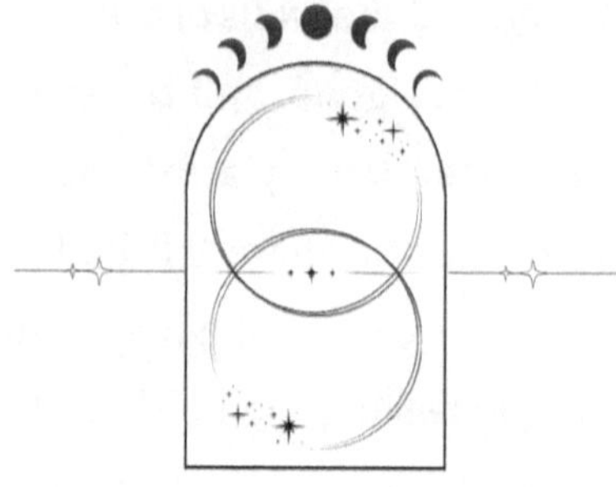

Seventeen

White coral reefs were scattered about the seafloor. Only a few fish were seen while I searched for Arik. A chill ran through me. Coral reefs were meant to be full of color and life. Whatever Arik had done to these waters, destroyed them. There was no way I would be able to search this entire ocean for him. Sitting on a rock, I allowed a sweet melody to escape my lips. I hoped the sound would lure him directly to me, but there was no response. Again, I sang the melody, this time louder than before. I continued to raise my voice until I was sure the entire ocean heard my call, but I was greeted by silence.

Rage boiled within me as I swam back to the island. How could he have gotten away? How could I *let* him get away? I knew that was not the last time I would see him, but it did not ease the anger within me. Arik Delmari needed to die.

When I got back to the island, I transformed into my human form and walked onto the beach. Looking around, I was not able to see Killian. The small wooden boat was still beached, so I knew he should still be here. I hoped he was not too mad at me for swimming off into the sea after my uncle. As I walked the shoreline, worry filled me.

"Killian?" I called out. There was no response. "Killian!" I screamed, but my voice was lost in the sound of the strong winds and rain.

It was then that I heard a grunt coming from the center of the island. Turning, I ran toward the sound. Next to the pool of water that housed the portal to Alari, Killian laid too still in the sand that was now stained red. The trident was still gripped tightly in his hand. Arik loomed in front of him with the look of victory on his face.

My stomach turned. No, was I too late? By leaving, did I allow Killian to be killed? A tentacle reached down and tried to grab onto the trident. An electric shock went through it, causing it to jolt back to its owner. The bright red tentacle was now a dull burnt color.

"You will have to let it go at some point, you worthless pirate," Arik snarled down at Killian.

Killian finally raised his head, smirking up at my uncle. Relief filled me as the sound of his voice hit my ears. Not dead. The man I loved was still alive. "Over my dead body," he said weakly, blood leaking from his lips.

Arik kicked Killian in his side, forcing him to toss onto his back. He let out a wince in response.

"That can be arranged," Arik growled.

Before Arik could do anything else, I called upon the water from the pool to rise and force him away from Killian. Taken off guard, my uncle flew back several feet. I stepped out from the dune grass. "The only dead body that will be here today is yours."

"Ah, so the little mermaid returns. Tell me, how did you get your tail back?" Arik snapped at me.

"Nera," I said coldly.

Anger flashed in Arik's eyes. "No, she hates the people of Alari. She would never help you!"

"It is *you* she hates. For you spit in the face of the gifts she has given us." Walking over to Killian, I reached down and gently took the trident from his grasp. "Go," I whispered. "Go back to the ship. Get the girls out of here." Killian did not argue with me. He struggled to stand, but once he was on his feet, he pulled me into a firm swift kiss. When he pulled away he gave me a quick nod before he limped away. All I wanted was for him to be safe. I would not let him die here. Focusing my attention back to Arik, I hardened my gaze. "It is I who will guard the oceans of Elswyth and keep the spirit of the storm at bay. I will make Nera and The Mother proud of me, proud of Alari, and proud of its people. You are nothing more than a small obstacle in my path."

"You are so naïve. How did Ariella raise such a foolish child? Don't you see? There is only one way this will end." A tentacle shot out at me.

I inhaled deeply and mimicked one of the moves Killian taught me when he was training me with the trident. The prongs jabbed into the tentacle, pierced it, and black blood spilled onto the sand. The appendage recoiled back to its master.

Over and over, tentacles lunged for me, and I fought them off with the trident. I was able to get one pinned to the ground and send a bolt of electricity through it. When I went to pull the trident out, it stuck. As I gave it a second pull, another tentacle came at me. It smacked into my side and caused me to fall into the pool of water. The force was so hard that I sank deep into the pool, and I was on the other side of the portal. The warm waters of my homeland greeted me. I secured my grip on the trident and kicked my feet to swim back up to the surface.

When I emerged, Arik was at the edge, waiting for me. "Stupid girl. That was your one chance to return home and live."

Using my magic, I forced the water to shoot me out of the pool, where I landed behind Arik. Before he could spin to face me, I thrusted the trident into the spot on his back where the tentacles emerged. Arik let out a scream. He pulled away from me and used his tentacles to rush across the sand to get some distance between us.

"You bitch!" He screamed as he looked down at the blood-covered sand.

The water of the portal bubbled, and both of our attentions focused on it. Not even a second later, my mother emerged from the water. Rage contorted her face as she glared down at me. Despite the anger, she looked perfect, as she always did. Her long hair was in a braid, wrapped around the crown of her head. Even out of water, she did not have a single hair out of place. I wondered what she thought of her daughter, who was covered in blood and sand.

"Hello, brother," she snarled at Arik before her intense glare shot at me. "Always too curious for your own good, but, I knew this day would come."

"Sister, return to your castle and take your brat with you! This world is mine."

"No, this realm is the humans. Do not disrupt the balance. Not everything is yours for the taking." Mother slowly looked back toward Arik. "Return the Gem, and allow me to take both it and the trident to its rightful home."

"You will need to rip it out of my cold, dead body."

"That can be arranged," I heard three female voices say in unison. Turning, I saw my crew, each with a weapon in hand.

"You humans think you can defeat me? I am the monster that has haunted your seas for decades."

"Enough!" Forcing the power of voice into my scream, I hoped to render my uncle helpless. Arik covered his ears and scrunched his face. The four women did not react to my high-pitched cry. My voice brought him down to his knees and blood leaked from his ears. Never would I allow him to silence me again. Arik would feel my wrath and the pain he caused me. A smile crossed my lips as I watched Killian sneaking up behind Arik. Though still with a slight limp, he seemed to be much better than before.

"What are you smiling at?" Arik snarled.

"The fact you let a worthless pirate get the upper hand," Killian said as he ran a blade through Arik's tentacles, severing them from his body.

They all dropped to the ground, squirting black blood and twitching several times before becoming motionless.

"No!" Arik screamed. He looked down frantically at the parts of him lying on the ground. I thought back to Vari and the story she told, wondering if this was what he looked like after she had cut off that man's weapon.

While Arik was distracted, I rushed toward him and thrust the trident into his stomach. Lightning shot from the trident, electrocuting my uncle. When I removed the trident, Arik fell to the ground, and I watched the light leave his eyes. Killian ran toward me, pulling me away from my uncle's lifeless body. Pushing away from him, I took the dagger off his belt, knelt, and made a small cut into Arik's forehead, where I saw that glowing red light. Once the opening was wide enough, The Gem popped right out. Taking it, I placed it in the small indent of the trident's head. Once in place, it flashed a bright red light before going dark.

Immediately, the rains stopped, the sky cleared, and I felt the warmth of the sun on my skin.

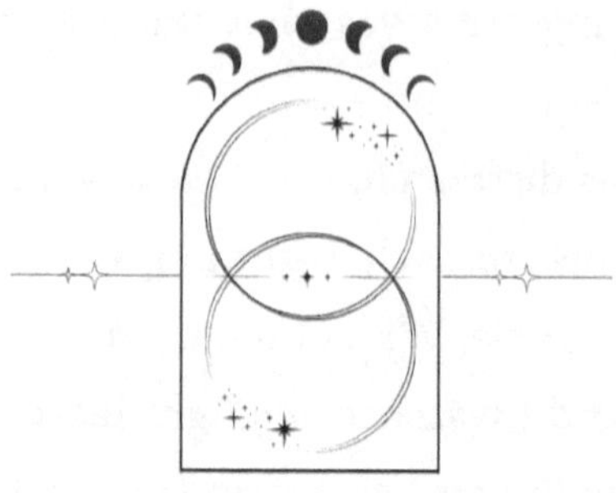

Eighteen

Two weeks later, the ocean retreated to its former levels. No longer were the homes of Caldor flooded, though they had sustained much damage. Killian and the remaining crew helped restore a lot of the damaged homes. He continued to offer the tavern to anyone who needed a place to stay during the repairs, even the mayor.

Several of the Darksea pirates had returned to Caldor and apologized to Killian for leaving. Being the kind man he was under all that armor around his heart, he understood and welcomed them back.

For the first time since defeating Arik, we were all on a ship, headed back toward the island. The entire time, I sat on the top deck, behind the helm, soaking in the sun's rays. Killian and I, once again, boarded the lifeboat and rowed to the sandy shore of the island.

There, Nera and my mother waited for us.

"Calliope, maybe now you can formally introduce me to your human companion?" My mother offered a smile toward him.

Killian bowed. "Hello, your majesty. I am glad we are meeting in better circumstances. My name is Killian Darksea."

"Darksea?" She raised her eyebrow.

Nera let out a chuckle.

"Yes," he nodded.

"Well, that is not a name I have heard in a long time. Not since before..." My mother's gaze wandered, and her voice trailed off.

"You have heard of the Darksea name? How?" I questioned.

"Because the Darkseas were once a powerful family in Alari," Nera finally spoke. "But they traveled here, with your uncle, all those years ago."

"That's impossible. My grandfather fought Arik and tried to stop him!"

"That is true. Your grandfather did not know what Arik was doing before it was too late. Arik had brought over several powerful families from Alari. Your grandfather was the only one who survived after Arik harvested their magic."

"That means..." I struggled to force the words out as I looked at Killian. "You're part mer?"

"Oh, thank The Mother," my mother sighed. "I was worried about having a human son-in-law."

Killian looked at my mother with wide eyes, then back to me.

"No need to fret," Nera continued. "Besides, today we are here to bestow Calliope with her title and gifts. We can teach the pirate about how to access his tail another time."

My mother took my hand and guided me back to the portal, and Nera and Killian followed us. An altar made of coral and seashells had been placed in front of the pool. On top, it sat a crown of shells and sea glass.

Walking over to the altar, Nera stopped just before it. "Kneel, child."

Stepping to face her, I did as she commanded.

She raised her gaze to the sky and spoke in a language I was not familiar with. Slowly, she looked down at me. "Calliope Mariana Delmari, do you agree to protect the seas of Elswyth and keep the spirit of the storm from returning?"

"I do," I said with every ounce of confidence I had. For the first time, I felt right. I felt at home. Looking over to Killian, I smiled. This was where I was meant to be.

Nera placed the crown on my head and chanted once again. Heat washed over my body, but was gone just as quickly as it arrived. "Rise my child. You have made Mother proud." She bent down and gently kissed my forehead.

I stood, and as soon as I was on my two feet, my mother wrapped me in a tight embrace. "I hate leaving you a realm away. Please promise me you will visit?"

"I promise." I hugged her back tightly. The feelings of guilt about leaving lingered in my mind. How could I ever think it was her that was the villain?

Nera slowly walked over to Killian. "Do you want to unlock your true self, boy?"

He hesitated for a moment, looked at me, then back to Nera. "Yes."

"Get in the water." She pointed to the pool.

He did as instructed, and Nera repeated the same ritual she did while I was on her island. The water bubbled around where he swam and once it was over, Killian no longer had legs but a bright red tail with golden sparkles.

With wide eyes, he smiled up at me. "It is all clear now." He got out of the pool and transformed back to his legged form.

"Return to your town. Though the war is over, there is still much work to be done," Nera said.

I gave both mother and Nera a final goodbye before walking back to our small boat. When we reached the shore, I looked up at Killian and smiled.

"Want to swim back?" I questioned.

Killian offered me the brightest smile. "Absolutely."

With that, the two of us ran into the ocean, transformed into our mer form, and swam home.

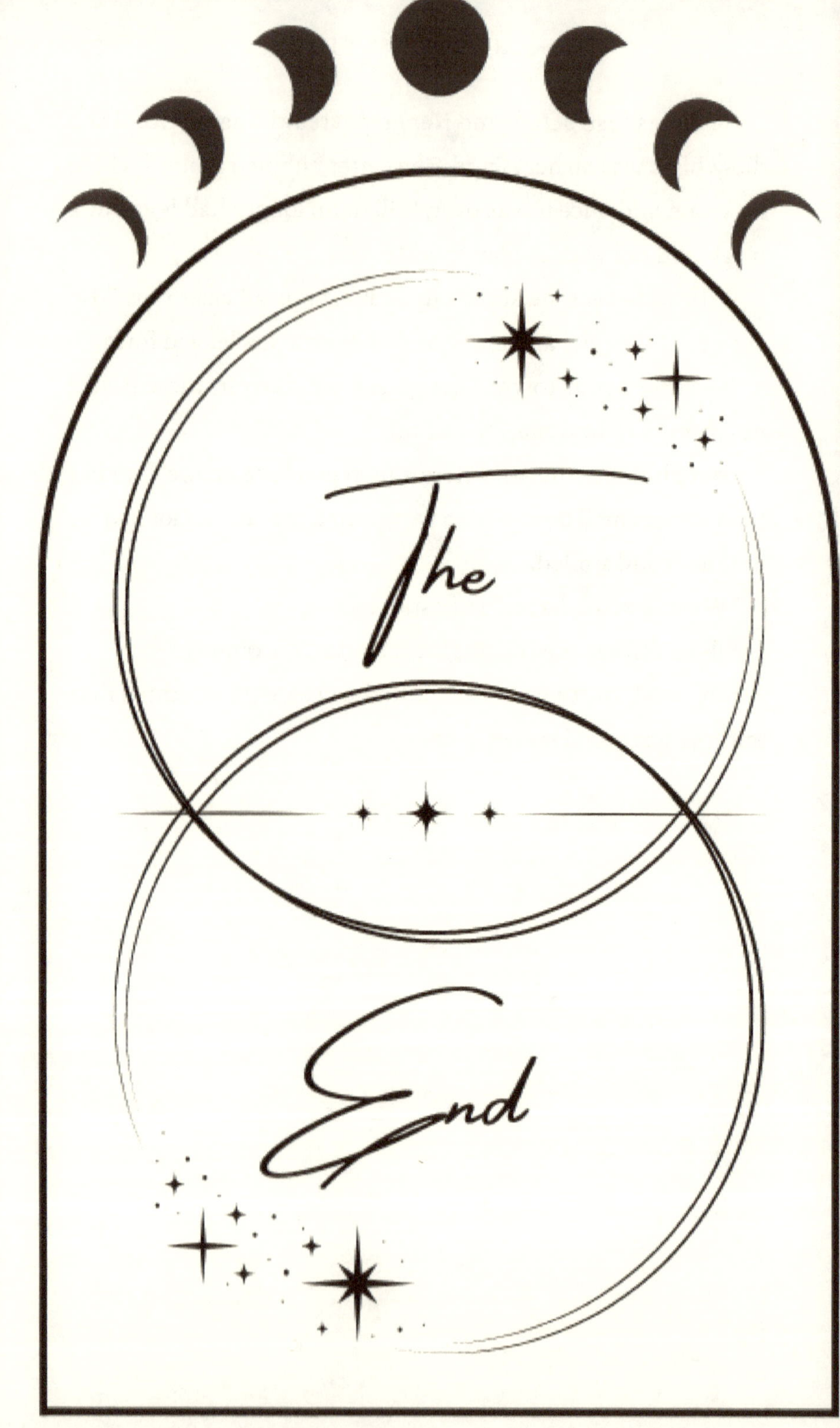

The
End

THE
SACRIFICE
OF
AEROS
A REALMS OF ELSWYTH STANDALONE
WILLOW ASTERIA

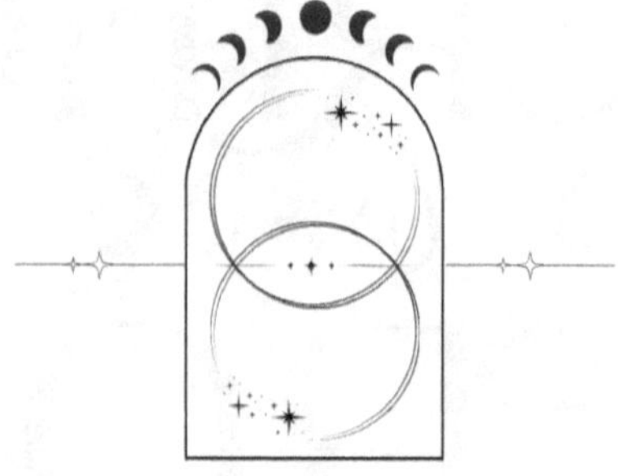

Content Warning

Please be advised that this book may not be suitable for all audiences.

This book contains sexual content, strict religious upbringing, death, blood, graphic violence, and other topics some readers may not find suitable.

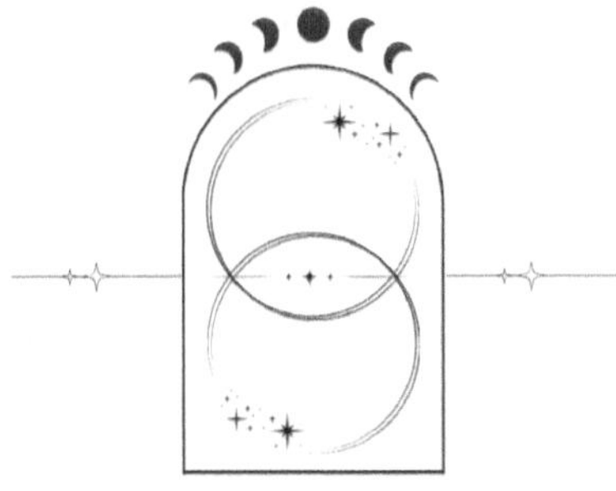

Prologue

Sage and rosemary filled my nose as I entered the sanctum. My knees buckled under me as I walked down the aisle. Looking down, I stared at my white shoes and the red runner through my thin veil. I focused on my breathing as I took one step after another. All eyes were on me, judging my every movement. Today was the most important day of my entire life.

My eighteenth birthday, and the day I would make my vows to The Mother.

She was the queen of our gods, and everyone who lived in the sanctuary on the small island of Varia pledged themselves to Her. Unlike my other sisters, I was raised within the sanctuary, and I worshiped her since I was little.

I should be happy to make these vows to Her. Instead, I felt ashamed of the apprehension I had. My entire life had been spent within the walls of the sanctuary. There had only been a few occasions I traveled into the town that was also on this small island.

What if there was a whole world waiting for me beyond the sea? What if I was meant for more than being shut away from the rest of the world?

Reaching up, I gripped my white pendant necklace as I approached the altar. It always brought me peace, and I hoped it wouldn't fail me now. I raised my gaze and looked at the Elder through my veil. She stood behind the altar, looking somehow more perfect than usual. The Elder strived for unity and excellence and would accept nothing less.

My heart pounded in my chest, and as I stopped before the altar, I found myself worrying about my appearance. Was my bun neatly tucked? Was my veil on straight? Was my robe white enough?

"Oriana. Today you enter womanhood. Today you give yourself to The Mother," the Elder said. "For it is She that gives us life and light. It is She that blesses these halls. Are you ready to give yourself to Her, sister Oriana?"

Inhaling deeply, I responded, "Yes, Elder. I am ready to give myself to The Mother. For it is She who guides my path." For months, I studied this ritual and the lines I was to say. Over and over I repeated the vows in my head. I prayed that now, in my panic, I would not forget them. Something within me told me to get up and run. Run into the ocean, toward the white light that was on the small island that housed a portal to a realm unknown.

"Kneel, sister." The Elder's voice pulled me out of my own head, and I did as she instructed.

I looked up at her and hoped that through my veil she could not see the nervousness in my eyes. I prayed I was holding my hands so tight it would stop them from shaking.

The Elder looked up at my sisters who sat to my back. "Sister Oriana has been at this sanctuary since she was a young babe. All of you should take a lesson from her. She has walked with The Mother longer than most, today will only make it official." She looked down at me. "Recite the vows, sister Oriana."

Swallowing hard and lowering my head, I made my vows to The Mother, and with each one, I felt my freedom slipping away.

Modesty, to live humbly with no attachment to goods. Chastity, to love The Mother above all others. Obedience, to follow Her will.

With these vows, I swear to live by The Mother and allow Her to guide my life as she sees fit.

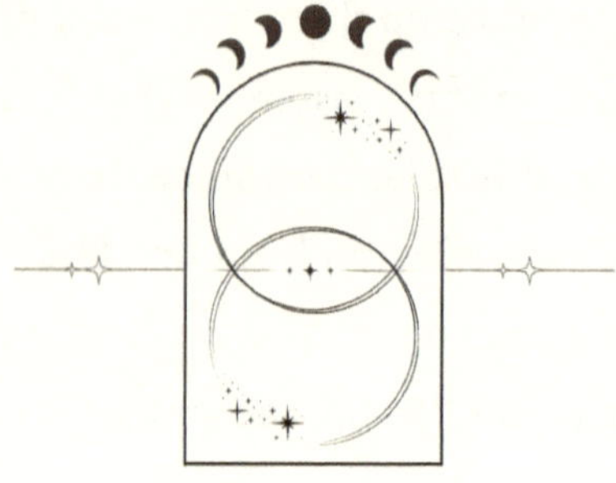

One

We had three days until the King of Elswyth arrived and forced another one of us through the portal to unknown lands. This would be the fifth year he sacrificed us to the fae realm. There were now only three sisters left in the age group he was sending, and unfortunately, I was one of those girls. Despite our pleas, the king refused to tell us why one of the sisters of this sanctuary born twenty-five years ago needed to go through the portal.

When the King first demanded us to offer ourselves as sacrifice, our Elder placed all of us in a room together. Each year, we gained more and more space as our numbers dwindled.

Cassandra and Larisa were able to find sleep. I could not. I tossed and turned in bed, begging for sleep to take me. However, the anxiety of the selection results filled my mind. What if it was me who was selected next? What if I was forced to travel through realms? What would I find beyond the portal?

I was certain it was death.

My sisters believed it was The Mother's will that sent our four sisters into the fae realm, and whoever was chosen next would be Mother blessed.

I spent my whole life devoted to The Mother at this sanctuary. Many of my sisters joined later in life, and I was the only one raised in the sanctuary from infancy. According to the elders, one day I appeared on the front steps, with no indication of who dropped me off. The only thing I was left with was a blanket with my name embroidered in the corner and a white pendant necklace, which I wear every day. Without it, anxiety filled me more than normal. Slowly, I rubbed my finger across the smooth face of the white oval stone.

Getting out of bed, I silently walked over to the balcony door and exited the room. The bright light of the full moon reflected on the sea, and the waves crashed onto the rocks down below. Closing my eyes, I took in the scent of the salty air. Trying to find my peace, I prayed to The Mother, begging Her for answers about why this was happening for the fifth year in a row.

Would there be an end before there were none of us left?

Opening my eyes, I looked to the west, to the small town of Varia. Not a single light was on, as everyone was likely settled into their beds. Our island was off the northeast coast of the continent of Elswyth. It was a crescent shape and wrapped around a smaller island. My gaze traveled over to the small island, and to the white light that shone from it. The portal to Aeros called my name. On the wind, soft voices called for me. It had for as long as I could remember, but each year it was not I who was chosen to travel through.

Reaching up, I held tight onto my pendant, and the whispers on the wind silenced. I let out a sigh of relief as the voices quieted. When I turned eighteen and took my vows, I swore that I would give up my longing for adventure. Returning to my bed, I sat up and stared at my sisters for a long moment.

Three more days until our lives changed forever.

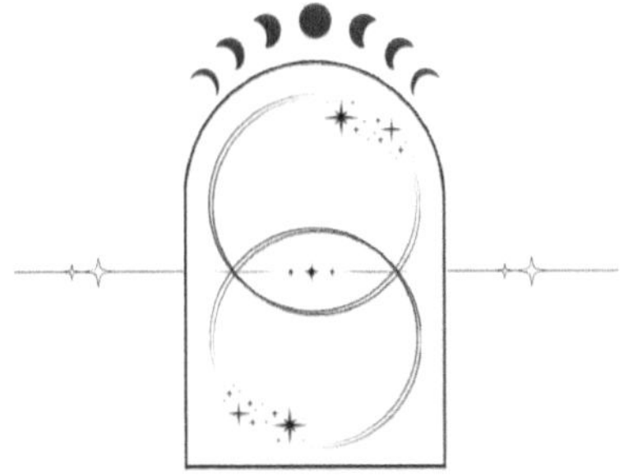

Two

Sat in a wooden pew with my head bowed, I listened to the Elder speak about the will of The Mother. How we are not to question it. How the Mother knew best. And, how everything happened for a reason. I closed my eyes as I took in her words. She gave this same sermon last year, just before the selection. During the first selection, many sisters were up in arms that the Elder allowed a man to come in and take one of us.

What was she to do? How do you say no to the King?

Little was known about the King. He isolated himself in his palace in the capital city. The only thing I knew about him was that he hated magic. He outlawed it and cut off relations to the continent to the east. It was a land full of vampires and fae, from what I understood, but there was not much literature about those lands. When the King made magic illegal, he demanded all books on magic and magical creatures destroyed.

This made the selection much more concerning. For a man who hated magic and the fae so much, why would he force us to travel to the fae realm beyond the portal? Before the selection, we all avoided the portal. Everyone in Elswyth knew of the poor village of Pendril and of the nightmarish creatures that came out of the portal just south of that small town. The people of Varia were terrified we would fall to the same fate if we approached the portal. We knew nothing about what was beyond it until the King showed up that fateful day and declared Serena would enter the portal and travel to the fae realm of Aeros. Her cries still haunted my dreams. As did my other sisters, who were lost to the portal.

"Oriana," the Elder's voice rang in my ear, and I felt a gentle hand on my shoulder.

Opening my eyes and lifting my gaze, I was surprised to see only the Elder and myself remained in the church. She offered me a smile that did not reach her eyes and sat next to me.

"The service has been over for about fifteen minutes. Want to talk about what weighs so heavy on your soul?"

I hesitated before I answered. This woman was like a mother to me. She had raised me to be the perfect acolyte of The Mother. I knew if I told her my fear about the selection, she would be disappointed in me. She, like my sisters, believed it to be The Mother's will.

"I cannot lie, Elder. I am nervous about the selection. I cannot quiet my inner fears about who we will lose next. And, if it is me, what waits for me in the realm beyond?"

"Oh, child," she sighed and shook her head. Even as she lowered her head, her perfect white bun did not move an inch. The

Elder was perfect in every way. I struggled to keep my long blonde hair in a bun. Once during a ritual, my bun had fallen loose. The look of disappointment in her eyes mirrored how she looked at that moment. "If it is The Mother's will, you will go. And she will protect you in what lies ahead. The Mother does not give more than you can handle. Out of anyone, you should understand this. You have lived under The Mother's guidance your whole life. Listen to what she tells you, and you won't make a wrong choice." She stood and walked to the aisle, turning to me and offering a nod before leaving the church.

I sat there for another half hour, in silence.

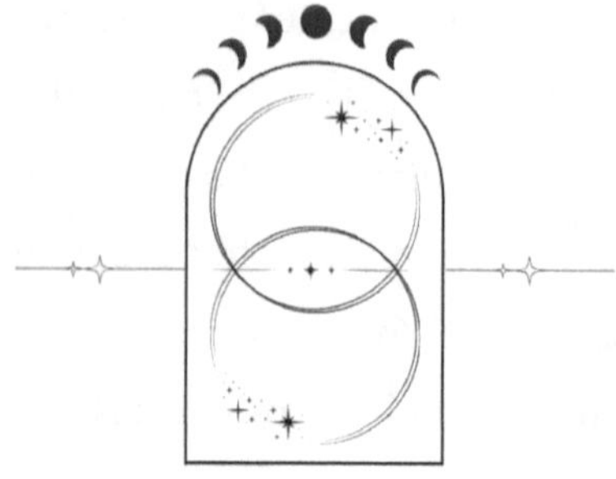

Three

Today was the day the King was going to arrive. According to the Elder, it needed to be us three that greeted him. Never in previous years had we done this. Before, the Elder met with the king in private. She would then come and tell us which of us he selected to travel to Elswyth for an undisclosed task.

This would be the first time I would lay my eyes on the king.

The Elder, Cassandra, Larisa, and I all walked down the street in a single-file line to the docks. It was very rare this many of us would travel in town together. Normally, we always traveled in pairs. I kept my eyes down on the cobblestone, avoiding the gaze of the townsfolk who always gawked at us as if we were some oddity. I suppose we were in our long white robes and veils that covered our faces. Even in the heat of summer, we wore our robes. Luckily, in the warmer months, our veils were made of a thin, breathable material.

It had been many months since I left the sanctuary. The crowds always put me at unease. However, in the back of my mind, I could not help but regret I spent so much time shut away. What if I was selected and my end was near? There was so much in life I missed out on, so many sights unseen. My entire life had been wasted hiding away on this tiny island.

The last time I had been to town was to gather supplies from the general store. I met a woman who traveled here from the capital city. She was convinced there was someone in town who had magic. Apparently, it was some long-lost cousin of hers from her mother's side. I often wondered what happened to her. I believe her name was Stephanie. I prayed no one reported her for speaking of magic. There are people in this town who would report people for discussing magic to gain a reward from it. She was a kind girl, but very confused. As no one in Varia — or in all of Elswyth — had magic. Were people from the capitol that brazen to go against their king's order that they would actively search magic users, and admit themselves to be one?

When we arrived at the dock, I was in awe of the massive ship that belonged to the king. On the sail was printed the royal crest. The symbol of the royal family never made sense to me. It was made of four squares of two different patterns. The first was a pattern of red and white diamonds that was on the first and fourth quarter, and the second was a black and yellow oddly shaped cross. According to history, these were the two coats of arms from the first families that founded Elswyth centuries ago.

A tall and skinny man in a suit far too nice to be a dock worker approached us. He offered a small bow and looked up at the

Elder. "Excuse me, you must be the Elder of the sanctuary. May we speak in private before the king disembarks?"

"Of course," she responded. Her gaze then slowly fell to us. "Girls, stay here," she said before walking off with the man.

Cassandra took my hand and squeezed it tight. I looked over to her and saw the worry in her eyes. Larisa walked closer to us, and the three of us formed a tight circle.

"What is wrong?" I asked in a whisper.

"I wasn't nervous until I saw the ship. This is really happening again, isn't it?" Cassandra's voice quivered as she spoke.

"Cas, this isn't like you," Larisa responded. "I have never seen you this nervous about anything." She leaned in closer and drew her eyebrows together.

Cas took in a deep breath before she spoke. "What if Ori is right? What if beyond the portal is nothing but a cold and lonely death?" She pulled her hands to her chest and wrung them together.

Larisa shot me a glare. "Ori doesn't know what she's talking about. I am sure the others are over there having the best time of their lives. Maybe they all got married to fae nobility."

"Fae nobility," Casandra scoffed. "No such thing. I never told anyone this, but the town where I am from, Pendril, has a portal there, too. The fae that travel through that portal are blood-thirsty beasts! Savages! Monsters!" Casandra got louder with every word.

Glancing up after catching movement in my peripheral vision, I noticed more townsfolk looking at us. Taking Casandra's hands, I held them tight. "Will you lower your voice? Everyone is starting to stare at us. We do not want to displease the Elder."

Casandra let out a deep sigh. "I'm sorry," she now spoke in a softer tone. "If I am chosen, I am not sure if I have the strength."

"The Mother only gives us what we can handle." I mimicked the words of the Elder, hoping they would bring comfort to my sister. It was nice to think that way, though I wasn't sure if I believed it.

Before anyone could say anything else, the Elder approached us. "Come along, ladies. It seems the King is a bit seasick from his travels. He will meet us tonight in the sanctuary for dinner and explain everything to you then."

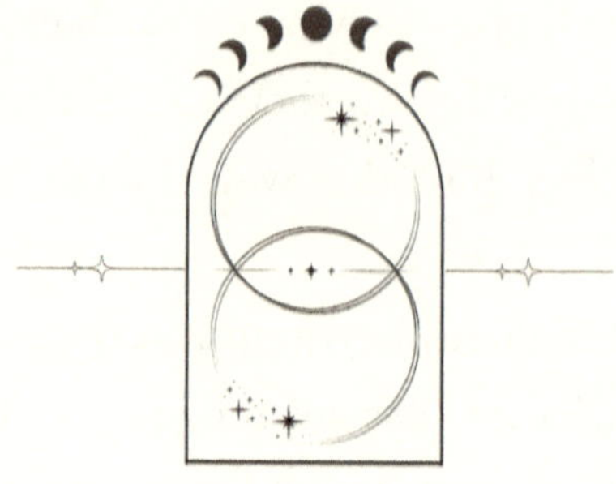

Four

My sisters and I returned to our room as soon as we got back to the sanctuary. We only had a few moments to rest before we had to complete our duties before the king's arrival. The first thing I did was remove my veil.

"Ori, your bun is a wreck," Cas laughed.

"It's this humidity! Nothing I do keeps it nice." I tried to slick down the flyaways with my hands but was without success.

"Come sit." She motioned to the vanity stool. "I will fix it."

"You're Mother sent. You know that?" I smiled up at her as I sat.

"Hey! What about me?" Larisa teased. She rushed over and sat in the chair next to the vanity against the wall.

"You both are!" I watched in the mirror as Cas let down my bun and ran her fingers through my ashy blond hair. I looked very different from the rest of my sisters. While most of them had tan skin, like most people from the island, I had very fair skin. While their eyes were brown or green, mine were a dark blue like the raging sea. I was also the only one with ashy blonde hair.

Cas fixed my hair into the most perfect bun I had ever seen. "There you go." She walked over and sat on the edge of her bed. "No matter what happens, I want you all to know I love you all." Tears misted her dark brown eyes.

Larisa and I rushed over to her, sitting on either side and wrapped her in a tight hug.

"No matter what, we will all meet again someday," Larisa said softly.

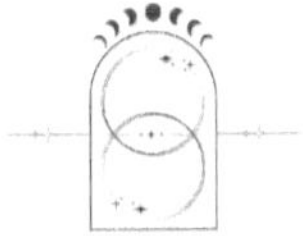

The Elder had her private dining room set up for a feast. We spent all afternoon preparing the meal for our king. This was the first time he would dine with us at the sanctuary. Never had I made a meal for someone so important. I believed I was a good cook, but tonight would put my skills to the test. It would also show if my sisters were being kind, or if I really could cook. We had just finished setting the table when one of our other sisters rushed into the room.

"The King is here! The Elder is coming up with him now. She said everything must be done within the next two minutes." Ellie said in between breaths.

"Well, luckily everything is ready for him," I said with a smile.

"Shoo. You don't want to be caught up in the mess we have found ourselves in," Cas said.

Ellie was five years younger than us. I was always so envious of the women who lived here who were not within our age range. How I wished and prayed we could live as carefree as they did. She left us, and the three of us stood at the door, awaiting the King's arrival. It was not long after that we could hear the Elder's voice and one of an older man. When the door opened, my sisters and I all fell into a curtsy.

"Please stand," the man chuckled.

We did. My heart skipped a beat as my eyes fell on the King. A top of his ash-blonde hair sat a crown of white stones that matched my pendant. When I stared into his dark blue eyes, it was almost like staring into my own. I wished we had worn our veils tonight so I could hide the shocked look on my face.

The King's eyes also went wide as he looked at me. I swore I saw a silver mist in them. "It really is you." His voice cracked as he spoke. "I did not want it to be you."

"What... What's going on?" Casandra asked.

"Why don't we all sit for this conversation?" The Elder said, walking more into the room. She pulled out the chair at the head of the table. "Please, my king, sit here. Oriana, please sit next to him." The Elder then assigned seats to my other sisters. Two royal guards stood in the doorway as we all sat. The king never once removed his eyes from me, and I was unable to look away from him, either.

Once everyone was sat, the words spilled from the King's lips. "Many years ago, when I first became king, I met a very beautiful woman. She worked in the castle as a sorceress. Her name was Ariana."

I was shocked to hear a sorceress had worked within a castle. What shocked me even more was how close her name was to my own.

The king continued. "She was the most beautiful woman I had ever laid my eyes on, but I was already sworn to another. A noble girl who would strengthen my line. That woman is now my wife and the Queen of Elswyth. But I still could not stop thinking of the sorceress who had stolen my heart."

My sisters and I all listened closely to the king as he told his tale. My heart pounded in my chest.

"I was a weak man and allowed the sorceress into my bed, time and time again, behind the queen's back. It was not long before she came to me and told me she was with child. My first child, a child I was not supposed to have." He took a deep breath. "During that time, the vampire king to the east threatened our land. He had been sending letters, telling me this land was his, and soon we would all be his chattel. I did not know where to turn, so I prayed to The Mother. I could not allow my land to be turned into a farm for vampires. Ariana worked hard, trying to find us a solution against the vampire king. She sent out a call to the fae realms. That call was answered when the fae king of Aeros wrote to me, claiming he could help keep away the vampires. In exchange, he wanted my magical child, and that on her twentieth birthday, she would be wed to his son. I agreed."

My breath quickened as I listened to the king. I focused on his fair skin, his ashy hair, and his blue eyes that mirrored mine.

No, this cannot be.

The king continued speaking. "I had no intention of letting him take my daughter. I tried to hide Ariana and my child from him, but when she gave birth, Ariana lost her life. I could not bring an illegitimate child into the palace and inform my wife of my affair. Instead, I did what needed to be done. I outlawed magic. I gave my baby a pendant that belonged to her mother and named her after her mother, so she would always have a piece of her true family. With no other choice, I sent her to the one place I thought The Mother would protect her and bound her magic to keep it hidden." He paused for a moment, looking at me. "On her twentieth year, her betrothed wrote to me, claiming it was time to pay up. I sent a random girl into the portal, but she did not make it. She could not handle the passing. I learned too late that the king placed a curse on the portal. Any who passed that did not have magic in their blood would die."

A sob ripped from Casandra and Larisa's throats, and my hand rose to cover my mouth and muffle my own reaction.

"I didn't mean to kill those poor girls. I did not know." He turned to look at me. "I simply wanted to protect you. My only daughter. But now the King of Aeros is coming to take you, and there is nothing I can do to stop him."

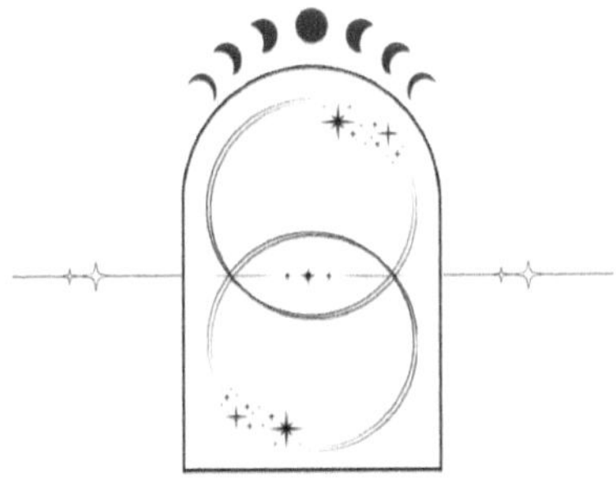

Five

No. This couldn't be true.

Ringing filled my ears, and I felt my stomach turn. This was all too much. I could not handle the reality that was being forced upon me. This all had to be a dream of some sort. The room filled with the sounds of Larisa's and Casandra's sobs. When I looked over to the Elder, her face was cold as stone and her gaze was set on the King.

I stood up from the table and rushed out of the dining room. I could not face the man I now knew to be my father. My whole life I wondered what happened to my parents, wondered why they would abandon me.

It was so hard to love yourself when the people who were supposed to love you didn't love you enough to keep you. I struggled with that my entire life. To learn my father was the king, my mother was a woman he had an affair with, and that he threw me away as if I never meant anything to him tore my soul to shreds.

I marched my way out of the sanctuary, ignoring everyone I passed on my way out. Tears streamed down my face as I made my way to the rocky cliffside. Waves crashed against it as I stood there for a while, staring at the white light off in the distance. I heard my name whispered in the wind, calling me to it. Rage boiled inside me at the sound. My sisters were dead. That white light was a reminder of everything wrong in my life.

What waited for me across the portal was a fae male who was to be my bridegroom. A man I had never met. I vowed myself to The Mother. Never once did I ever think about breaking those vows. Some of the other sisters may have blurred the line, but never me. I understood the role of a wife, and I refused to be that for this male. For *any* male.

My hand reached up to grab my pendant. Over the last twenty-five years, I had used it to find comfort, but for the first time, it made my stomach turn. I ripped it off my neck and threw it into the ocean, letting out a scream. A bright white flashed from the portal, nearly blinding me.

I screamed and screamed, long after the necklace fell into the dark water.

"Those are some lungs you have." A deep voice came from behind me.

I nearly jumped out of my own skin. There were no men who lived at the sanctuary, and this was not one of the voices I recognized from the King's men. I spun and saw a very handsome man. Never had I seen anyone so tall and muscular in the village. He must have come with the king. He had his hands tucked into the pockets of his dark jeans, and his white ink tattoos of geometric shapes popped against his dark skin. He looked down at me with a concerned expression.

"You scared me!" I said, held my hand to my chest, and took in a deep breath.

"Well, I guess we are even. When I heard your screams, I thought you were being murdered. Glad to see you're not." He took a step closer to me.

I bit my lip as I met his gaze. For the first time in my life, I found myself enthralled by a man. The bright white light of the portal reflected in his chocolate brown eyes. Something deep within me was calling for this man, and I found myself hating my chastity vow. Quickly, I pushed down those desires. "What are you doing here? I don't recognize you from the village. Are you here with the king?"

The man offered a chuckle. "You can say that. Tell me, why were you screaming out at the sea?"

I stared at him for a long moment, narrowing my eyes. I wasn't exactly sure about how I felt about this man. "Quite nosy, aren't you?"

"I'd like to think of it as inquisitive." He smirked.

"There you are!" I heard the king's voice off in the distance.

Turning toward the king, I watched as he and the Elder quickly approached us. Fear grew in the king's eyes as he got closer to and looked up at the mystery man.

"You said I could have one more day!" The king shouted.

"You promised her to me five years ago, human," the mystery man said in an aggressive tone. "I could not trust your words. Not after four women died due to your deceit. My father may have continuously allowed you to try to snake your way out of the deal, but now that I am king, you won't be so lucky." He took a step toward the king.

My eyes widened as I realized who stood before me and fear froze me in place. Even though my mind screamed for me to run, to jump into the ocean to escape, my body would not comply. My betrothed turned his head to look down at me and winked. His true form was revealed to me as he grew to seven feet, his ears became pointed, and white feathered wings unfurled from his back.

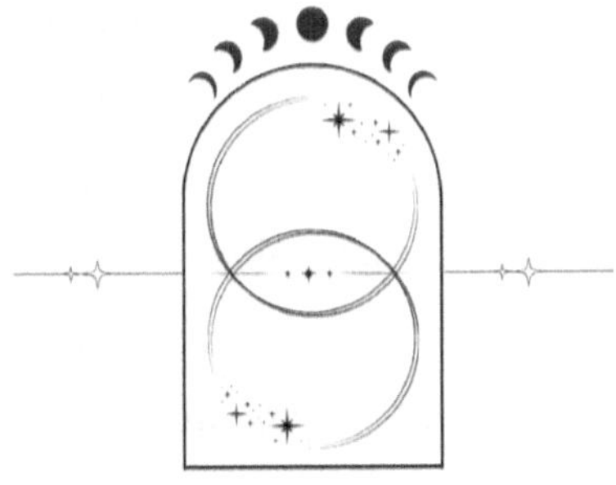

Six

My heart pounded in terror as the world around me spun. This had to be a nightmare, as I did not want to accept this as my reality. I looked over to see the Elder had fainted and collapsed. The King rushed to her side, trying to wake her. My betrothed had his hard stare set on me, and it burned into my skin.

Staggering back from the fae male to gain distance from him, I screamed, " I will not go with you! I will not marry you." The calling that I had toward this man still pulled on my heart, but I could not allow that feeling to win. I would be no one's bride.

The male let out a deep chuckle, and a heavy weight pressed down onto my body.

Falling to my knees, I looked up at him and snarled. He stepped forward, closed the gap between us, and knelt before me. Gripping my chin, he forced me to stare directly into his rich brown eyes. "You have no choice. A contract was signed.

If broken, the deal my father had with yours would be undone. Tell me, do you want your land to be conquered by vampires? Would you rather be a vampire's pet than my wife? At least I won't feed from you. Take from you what gives you life. All I ask is for your loyalty and cooperation. Magic for magic. A favor for a favor." His voice was like rich velvet.

My stomach turned as he spoke. There was no choice here. It was time I accepted the fate The Mother planned for me, no matter how much I hated it. Frustration filled me, tears misted my eyes, and I tried to hold them back. I could not let him see me falter. "If I come with you, will you still protect this land from the vampires?" I asked softly, but not weakly.

"Of course. Fae are bound by their word." He shot the King of Elswyth a pointed glare. "We do not try to trick our way out of bargains made." He lowered his gaze back to mine. "Do we have a deal, darling?"

"We have a deal," I said in defeat.

A smirk grew on his face, and the weight I felt on my body lifted. "Come along." He reached his hand down to me. I took it, and he assisted me up. The fae male looked back over to my father. "Be lucky we are not the fae of Irolyth. For if you tried to swindle your way out of the deal you made, it would have been *you* that died, and not innocent women." He picked me up, cradling me in his arms. "Hold on tight, darling. Flying can be a bit scary for first-timers."

"Let me go! I need to say goodbye to my sisters!" I squirmed in his grasp.

"We have wasted too much time already. Maybe you will see them again when the task I need you to complete is done." With that, he flapped his wings and launched us into the sky.

I wrapped my arms around his neck, clinging to him. Shutting my eyes tight, my body trembled against the solid muscle of his chest. "I'm going to fall!" I cried out.

"No, you aren't. I would never drop a pretty little thing like you."

After what seemed like an eternity, I felt the fae's feet hit solid ground. Relief washed over me. Only then did I open my eyes. White light nearly blinded me as I did. When my vision adjusted, I realized we stood directly in front of the portal. My heart pounded harder in my chest.

"No need to be scared. I've got you, darling," he said softly.

"What if I die, too?" My voice quivered as I spoke. My thoughts raced with the fear I would meet the same fate as my sisters. What if no mortal was met to pass through into the fae realm?

"You won't. You were born for this." He offered me a soft smile that did not meet his eyes. That expression offered me no comfort.

Before I could answer, the man stepped through the portal, pulling me with him, and a flash of white filled my vision.

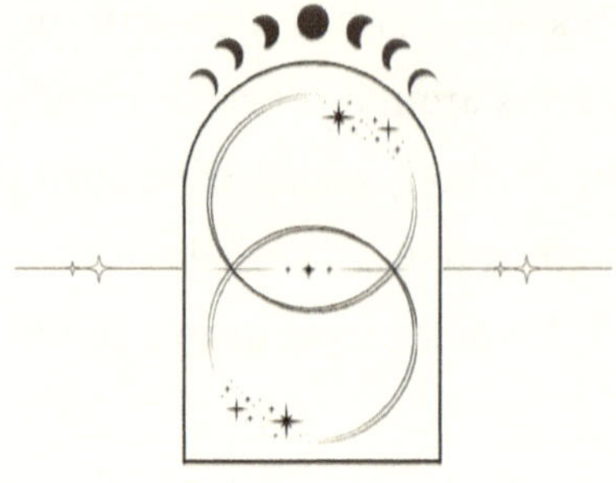

Seven

Everything came back into focus, and we were now standing in a small grassy field. The sun was shining, and it warmed my skin. The fae male gently set me down on my feet. I turned to face him, and the glow of the portal haloed him, making him look like a god.

I turned away and then realized where exactly we were. The small grassland we stood in was an island, but beyond the land was not a sea, it was clouds. I took a few steps forward and looked beyond. Three more islands floated in the sky. The underneath of the islands were rough and jagged as if they had been ripped from the ground. One had large oak trees, another a massive city, and the farthest one had a castle.

"Welcome to Aeros, darling. Be mindful not to get too close to the edge. I wouldn't want you to fall to your death before your usefulness wore out."

I spun my head and shot him a pointed glare. "I am plenty useful! I do not need a man to tell me what I am worth or not worth."

He let out a chuckle. "Feisty. Good, I like that. Keep that up. You will need it for what lies ahead."

"What exactly is that?" I raised my eyebrow at him.

"All in good time. Come along. Let's get back to the castle so I can take you to your room." Stepping toward me, he lifted me into his arms holding me close. He launched into the air once again.

This time, I forced myself to keep my eyes wide open. I wanted to take in everything I could about the new realm I found myself in. The island with the trees was the first we flew over. Half of it was a forest, the other half was farmland. Winged fae waved up at us as we flew overhead. Other than the wings and pointed ears, the ones below us almost looked normal. They looked human.

Would they act human? Or, would the fae be brutal beasts?

The next island was a large city. It resembled images of the capital city of Elswyth I had seen, with towering buildings and bustling streets. If the inhabitants were not fae, I would have thought this to be a fairly normal place. Just as we passed the city, another fae male flew up next to us. My entire body tensed as he came into view. He had similar white tattoos to my bridegroom. They stood out against his tan skin.

I wondered what they meant.

"My King, you have returned!" He cheered as he flew by our side.

"Indeed. Glad to hear your senses are still intact, Artemis," my betrothed responded in a sarcastic tone.

"You are such an ass," he laughed. "I see the human king did not try to escape his deal again. Hello, little one."

I tried to speak, but words did not escape my throat. Being in the air made me uneasy, and all I wanted was to be on the ground.

"Again, such a great observation. Maybe notice the girl is afraid, and that this may not be the best time for introductions?"

The other man flew ahead and looked back at us. Cocking his head, he shrugged. "Well, I am already here. Hello, human. I am Artemis. Captain of the Guard and King Malachi's best friend. It is a pleasure to finally meet you!"

Ah, so my betrothed's name was finally revealed. Honestly, I thought his name would be something much more.... Mystical? Something in a tongue I was not familiar with. I did not expect the fae to have names like Malachi or Artemis. Maybe they were more like the people of Elswyth than I believed.

Malachi let out a low growl. "Art, I have one nerve left, and you are getting on it. Shoo!" He flapped his wings hard, forcing us to fly faster and to pass Artemis.

"That nerve has my name seared into it. It is mine to be on as much as I see fit!" Artemis caught up to us and flashed a bright smile.

Malachi rolled his eyes but said nothing in response. A moment later, he was planting his feet onto the ground in front of the castle, and Artemis landed next to us. Gently, Malachi put me down, and I stumbled a bit as I found my footing.

Artemis rushed over to me, took my hand in his, and brought it to his lips. They gently brushed against my skin. "Welcome home, little one. Glad I'm finally meeting you after all these years. What is your name?"

My eyes widened, and a blush took over my cheeks. I stuttered as I stared into his emerald eyes. Now that I was firmly on the ground, I could speak my name. "Oriana."

Malachi forced himself in between the two of us. "Artemis. This is my soon-to-be wife. Please don't try to charm her like you do every other woman you meet."

A smirk crossed his face. "Well, don't you have your serious pants on today." He huffed. "We have shared before. I'm sure she wouldn't mind. Would you, little one?"

"Yes, I do mind! I am not a toy to be shared!" I glared at him.

"Oh, you misunderstand me. Not a toy, a treasure." He offered me a wink and a predatory smirk.

"Artemis, fuck off before I send you below. Don't you have something to do?" Malachi crossed his arms and glared down at his friend. Artemis was tall, but Malachi was a few inches taller.

"I suppose I do." He gave a nonchalant shrug. "Nice meeting you, little one. Hopefully, we will meet again soon." With a strong flap of his wings, he launched into the air, leaving dust in his wake.

Malachi watched until Artemis was a good distance away. "I am sorry about him. Ignore him. He is a thorn in my side." He turned to look at me. "Shall I give you a tour of the castle and then take you to your chambers to rest?"

"That sounds great, actually."

"Wonderful. I will allow you a few days to adjust to the time here, as we are on an opposite day-night cycle compared to Elswyth. Once adjusted, I will teach you how to use your magic." He gave me an up-and-down glance. "I understand that I pulled you away from dinner. You must be starving."

I wanted to deny him, but the growling of my stomach couldn't. I had been so busy all day preparing for the king's visit that I barely had time to feed myself. "Do you have food a human could eat?"

Malachi threw his head back and laughed. "We eat the same things. Come along. I will take you to my private dining room after the tour."

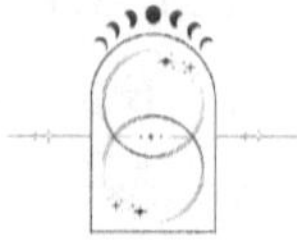

The castle was very beautiful. Never in my life had I been anywhere so opulent. It was full of gorgeous white marble floors and pillars, courtyards filled with colorful flowers in full bloom, and a massive library. Never had I seen so many books in one place. Often in the sanctuary, I would find myself in the library, but that was just a small room with about five shelves. The library here was beyond my imagination. It was seven stories tall, and not a single shelf was left unfilled.

At the end of the tour, Malachi led me to his private dining room. It was a cozy space with a fireplace on one wall. On either side of the fireplace hung two black tapestries that had similar markings to my bridegroom's tattoos. Malachi pulled out my seat, allowed me to sit, and then gently pushed me closer to the table. He then took his seat at the head of the dark mahogany table.

As soon as we sat, one of his servants brought out a roasted pheasant on a silver platter and placed it in the center of the table. Another servant had an entire cart full of sides.

"Would you like light or dark meat?" The servant asked as he carved up the bird.

"Light, please," I offered a smile. It was so odd to have someone wait on me, back at the sanctuary it was required that we were self-reliant.

"Ah yes, the breast is my favorite as well." A familiar voice teased from behind me.

Malachi's gaze shot in that direction. "Artemis, you were not invited to this lunch. Leave."

"What kind of guard captain would I be if I allowed my king to be alone with some strange human girl? Besides, I am hungry." Artemis walked to the other side of the table and leaned over it. Taking my hand in his, he gently placed a kiss on my knuckles. "Lovely to see you again, little one," he said with a wink.

Malachi let out a low growl. "Sit. Eat. Be quiet."

Releasing my hand, Artemis rolled his eyes as he took his seat. "What a benevolent king. So, tell me, Oriana, what do you think of Aeros so far?"

"It's beautiful. Never did I expect to see islands floating in the sky. The castle is wonderful as well. Back home, I lived on a small island. We had nothing like this." Everything in this castle broke my vow of modesty. It was lavish and flashy. I prayed that The Mother would not resent me for being here in such luxury.

Artemis leaned forward. "Oh, I would love to fly you around the islands and give you a tour of the city."

"Enough!" Malachi slammed his fist on the table and the dishes clattered. "Stop flirting with my betrothed. She has gone through enough today."

"Just for today?" Artemis smirked.

Malachi picked up his table knife and threw it toward Artemis, who quickly dodged out of the way. The knife stuck into the wall behind Artemis. "Hm. What a shame. Next time, I won't miss, but since you live, you can stay for lunch." Malachi offered Artemis a genuine smile and looked toward the servant who finished carving the bird. "Torin, please bring out a third plate for Art."

"Awe, see. I knew you wanted me here!" Artemis laughed.

Torin left and quickly returned with a plate. Once Artemis' place was set, Torin served us some of the carved pheasant. He placed a slice of breast meat onto my plate first before attending to the men. The other servant came to my side and offered a small bow.

"Good afternoon, my lady. I have some sides for you to choose from." She listed all the options on her cart. There were way too many to pick from. Many looked familiar to me, but some were unrecognizable and exotic. After a moment, I decided on the sweet potatoes with pecans and the garlic butter green beans. "Please enjoy," she said before moving on to the king.

I took a bite of the meat first, and it melted in my mouth. The taste of rosemary and sage exploded on my tongue. The sweet potatoes were fluffy and delightful, and the garlic butter on the beans was one of the most delicious sauces I ever had.

While I ate, Malachi and Artemis bickered back and forth about everything. The two seemed more like brothers than king and guard captain. I could not help but wonder how close they were, especially after Artemis commented on them sharing women in the past.

"I cannot tell if you guys enjoy each other's company or not," I said in a moment of silence.

"We are best friends," Artemis answered. "No matter what King Grump says."

Malachi rolled his eyes. "I am not grumpy. Will you stop? Yes, Artemis and I have been friends since we were boys. He was assigned as my personal guard when we were ten, and when I became king, I made him captain."

"It has been an honor to serve by your side and constantly piss you off for the last thirty years," Artemis said as he took a big bite of meat.

"A thorn in my side until the very end." Malachi offered a genuine smile.

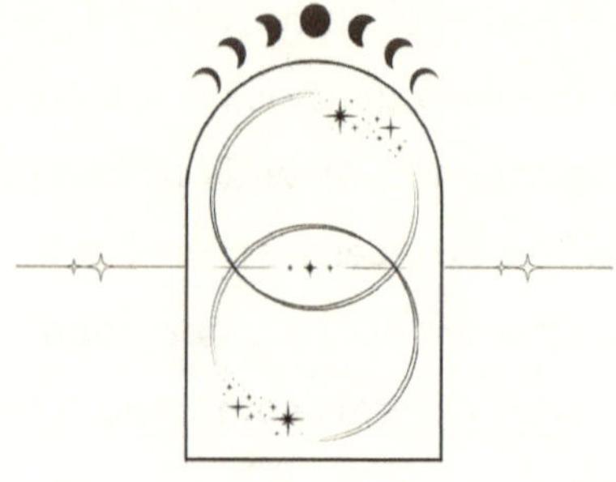

Eight

Three days passed, and I still was struggling to adjust to the day and night cycle of the fae realm. It was the complete opposite of my old schedule. Even though it was day here in Aeros, it was the middle of the night in Elswyth. My anxiety also made it hard for me to fall asleep, so I would not find rest until the early hours of their morning, and woke up just after lunchtime. It was not a sleep schedule I would recommend to anyone.

During those three days, my soon-to-be husband was nowhere to be found, and neither was his guard captain. However, I was provided with a lady's maid named Violet. She looked very different from the other fae I had seen here. While she had wings like the others, they were orange with a white border and delicate, almost like butterflies. Most of the fae of Aeros had darker hair, her fiery red hair was cut into a short, pointed bob. She was very kind and always made sure I had a meal waiting for me when I awoke. She also made sure to keep my bathing chamber stocked with luxurious soaps and perfumes.

Rolling over in bed, I stared out the window and stared out into the clouds. My room was in a tower of the castle that gave me a great view of the sky and the three other islands. There was a soft knock at the door, and it caused me to sit up.

"Who is it?" I called out.

"It's me, my lady," Violet called out from beyond the door.

"Come in," I responded.

She walked in with a small pile of folded clothes in her hands. "Good afternoon. The King has requested your audience."

"And if I refuse to see him?" I questioned.

"No one refuses King Malachi." She narrowed her eyes at me and put the clothes on the bed next to me. "This is what you will wear to meet with him."

I picked up the clothes and examined them. "I have never worn pants before. Can't I wear one of my dresses?" At the sanctuary, it was forbidden to wear pants. It was not ladylike and was not The Mother's will. Some of the sisters who joined later in life told stories of what pants felt like when wearing them. Honestly, I saw no issue in others wearing them, but too much had changed for me over the last three days. I could not stand the thought of anything else changing.

"A dress would not be suitable for what he has planned for you. Today, you will start exploring your magic! How exciting!" A smile grew across her face.

Not exciting at all. Ever since I learned I came from a line of sorceresses, the thought of my magic was at the forefront of my mind. What type of magic was I capable of, and why did the fae king need it so badly that he would make a deal for my hand in marriage to his son? "Give me about five minutes, and I will be ready to go see the king."

"Please let me know if there is anything you need. I will be waiting just outside." She curtsied and exited the room. The very first day we met, she tried to help me undress. That was terribly awkward. I informed her I had no issue dressing myself, and for her to wait outside until I was ready.

I stripped from my night dress and put on the tight leather pants. Looking across the room, I examined myself in the full-length mirror, my focus traveling down my curves. Never had I worn something so form-fitting. As I put on my top, I prayed to The Mother that Artemis would not be there as well. Based on how flirty he was, I was not sure if he could handle seeing me in these pants. Or, how I would handle his reactions.

Once I was dressed, I braided my long blonde hair and allowed it to fall down the center of my back. Taking one more look in the mirror, I did not recognize the woman who looked back at me. A few days ago, I was an orphan and a devout follower of The Mother. Now, I was an illegitimate princess betrothed to a king and a fledgling sorceress.

Pulling my gaze away from myself, I sighed deeply.

Joining Violet in the hall, she offered me another warm smile. "You look wonderful! Just as expected. Come along, we wouldn't want to keep the Kking waiting any longer." She turned and walked down the hall toward the stairs that led down the tower. I was not a prisoner of the tower, but after the initial tour, I found myself rarely leaving. Violet led me outside to a training ring behind the castle. The plush grass gave way to rocks and sand.

Malachi sat on one of the large stones across the grounds. His stare burned through me as his attention focused directly on me. "Thank you, Violet. Leave us."

"Yes, my King." She bowed and quickly flew off.

The fae king slowly rose from his rock and made his way toward me. "What a shame," he sighed.

"What?" I raised my eyebrow in response.

Malachi continued to walk in my direction as he spoke. "It is a shame what your father turned you into. That he locked away your magic and kept you from being who you truly are. I was hoping by the time we wed, you would be a powerful sorceress. No worries. I have taught many fae children how to control the magic of Aeros. I do not imagine it would be much harder teaching you." He stopped directly in front of me and offered me a comforting smile.

"The magic of Aeros?" This place was so strange. From the floating islands to the white tattoos. It was hard to accept that this wasn't some odd dream.

"Yes, we here practice gravitational magic. Thank The Mother for it. My great-grandfather would not have been able to save our people from The Great Calamity without his powerful magic." With a rise of his palm, a large rock on the outside of the training circle rose into the air about three feet. When he dropped his hand, the stone crashed back to the ground.

I stared at the rock in shock. It was the first time I had seen magic. I wondered if this was what I could do as well. I spun my head back to Malachi. "The Great Calamity?" I raised my eyebrow.

"You really know nothing of Aeros, do you?"

"Nothing at all." I hated I was in a place I knew nothing about. It made me feel helpless.

"Come sit." He turned and pointed to the smaller rock that was next to the one he went to sit on.

Walking over, I sat down on the warm stone, looking up at him. He looked down at me with a smile that did not reach his deep brown eyes, inhaling deeply before he spoke. "Many centuries ago, Aeros was below the clouds. There was a great calamity that occurred that ruined the land and destroyed the kingdom. My great-grandfather raised the capital city, the castle, and the surrounding lands into the sky to save our people. We have tried several times to go below the clouds to see what is happening down there, but all who go, never return. There is a prophecy that has been passed down by our people that a daughter of a sorceress with sapphires for eyes will save us, and return us to the land below."

"What was the calamity?" I asked.

"No one here knows. My great-grandfather did not make it into the sky. And anyone who was around before the rising never spoke of it. I was hoping you would be able to shed some light on what had happened. But, seeing you never even knew your mother, I doubt you will be much help."

I wanted to be angry at that statement, but he was right. How was I going to be able to help? I knew nothing of this world. I barely knew about my world. How was I supposed to save them from this calamity? "I am sorry, but you know I cannot help you. Why not return me home?"

"Because I have not given up on you. Your father may have cut your worth into a nobody human destined to live a life hidden away, but I know you can be so much more." He stood. "First, we will see how much of your magic you can feel. We will start there and then progress to see what you can do with it. Stand." He turned toward me, offering me a hand up.

I took it and stood. How could someone who just met me have so much confidence in me?

"Close your eyes, darling." I did as he instructed. "Breathe slowly. In. Out. In. Out. Find your inner peace deep within yourself." I felt him release my hand.

For a moment, there was silence as I took in my deep breaths. I searched for that inner peace he wanted me to find. It seemed as if nothing was working. I was just standing there, breathing, and feeling the sun beat down on me.

"Darling, you got this. Focus harder. Search for the light inside yourself. For your core. Your essence." His voice was calm and soothing. It sounded as if he was directly behind me.

Focusing harder, I was finally able to see a soft, glowing light in the distance. It flickered and struggled to stay lit, but it was there, and fighting.

No, it was me that was fighting. I was fighting to keep the light on. Fighting to pull power forward and to claim it as my own.

Before I could focus enough to gain control, the ground trembled, causing me to lose my balance and fall. Malachi caught me in his arms before I hit the ground. I looked up at him with worry as the quake stopped.

"Never in my forty years has there been an earthquake on the islands." His voice shook as he spoke. He helped me stand. I held tight to his muscular arms as I regained my balance.

A short moment later, Artemis landed beside us.

"Sir, half of island three has fallen."

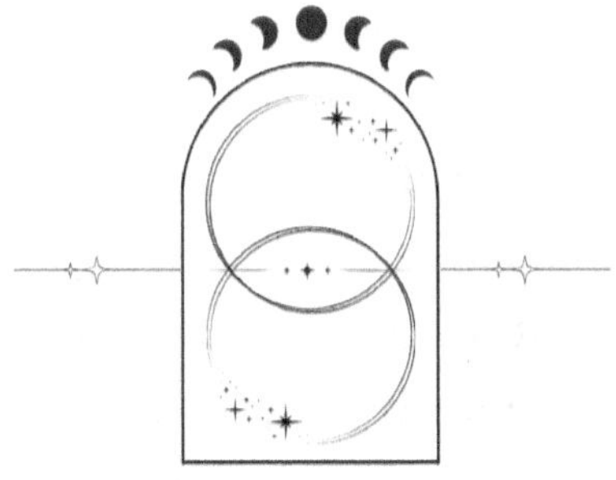

Nine

Two days had passed since the falling. Malachi sent me back into the castle after Artemis had shown up in the training yard, and I had not seen him since. According to Violet, never had any of the islands fallen below the clouds. Some part of me couldn't help but wonder if it was my fault. Did my magic cause the quake? Maybe the prophecy was about me causing the collapse of Aeros, instead of bringing it safely to the ground.

Even with everything that had happened, I was able to get more adjusted to my new sleep cycle. For the first time, I was able to get restful sleep and was awoken by the rising sun. Looking out the window, I could not help but admire the golden hue that was cascaded across the clouds. Quick knocks rattled off the door, and it opened before I could say anything.

"The king wishes to have breakfast with you!" Violet squealed with excitement as she skipped toward me with a teal dress in hand. "Quickly get dressed! We do not want to keep him waiting." She handed the dress to me, exited the room, then closed the door behind her.

I could not decide if I was excited to see him again or not. There was something within me that gravitated toward him, but there was something else that longed to return home and forget any of this had ever happened. I was relieved that today I was given a dress to wear. While the pants were nice, they were not something I really wanted to wear daily.

Once dressed and ready for the day, I met with Violet outside in the hall. She guided me down the tower steps, and to the King's private dining room. He was standing right outside of the entrance waiting for us.

"Thank you, Violet. You are dismissed."

She bowed to him and rushed away.

My eyes met with Malachi's, and he offered me a soft smile.

"I am sorry I have not had much time to see you these past few days. We are still working on figuring out what caused the collapse. That is no excuse. As your soon-to-be husband, I should be making time to see you. Please come in, sit, eat. I had the chefs prepare us a lovely breakfast!" He turned and entered the dining room.

"You don't think it has anything to do with me trying to connect with my magic do you?" I asked as I followed him into the dining room.

Malachi stopped. He stood there for a moment, then turned to me. "Of course not. Who said that to you? I will send them below the clouds right now." Anger flared in his deep brown eyes.

"No one! No one said that to me. I was just worried it was." I looked down and fiddled with my thumbs.

He took a step forward, closing the gap between us. Gently, he lifted my chin to force my gaze to meet his. "Darling, do not ever doubt yourself. Do not ever speak poorly about yourself. You are new to magic, yes, but in no way are you the cause of what happened. You could never be responsible for something so terrible," he said in a soft tone. "Now sit, eat." He pulled away and walked over to the table, pulling out a chair, and motioned for me to sit.

I did and my eyes went wide at the food that was laid out for us. Malachi sat next to me. "This looks wonderful!" My eyes scanned across the table at the fruit, meats, and pastries available.

"It tastes amazing. I have the best chefs in all of Aeros." He said as he piled meat onto his plate.

I made myself a small yogurt parfait with berries and almond granola and took a few pieces of extra crispy bacon.

"I hope this is all to your liking. If there is something you want that is not here, please let me know. I can have the chefs make it." He said as he took a bite of sausage.

"This is more than enough. Thank you!" Looking over the table again, I wondered what anyone could want more. Never had I seen such a wide selection of foods.

"Wonderful. Now we can discuss why I really wanted to see you this morning." His eyes narrowed as his tone got more serious.

"What is it?" I raised an eyebrow at him.

"Our wedding. It will be tonight at sundown." He said as he stuck a piece of ham into his mouth.

"I'm sorry. Our wedding?"

"Yes. You were promised to me. We will be wed, per our deal. Trust me, I am not thrilled, either, by the pace of things. I would love for us to be able to get to know each other more before we make everything official. However, it may be another key to unlocking your magic and returning us to below the clouds."

"I—I am not ready to be a wife," I stumbled on my words. Even though I knew he was my betrothed and knew I was to marry him, I was shocked it was so soon. I thought I would have time to adjust to my new life. Have time to get out of this arrangement.

"Darling, Ori." The way he purred my name pulled me from my own thoughts. Made me crave to hear it again. "I understand the lifestyle you used to live before coming here did not prepare you to be a wife. Other than in ceremony, we will go at your pace. You shall keep your private room. I will never force myself or anything upon you. I want you to feel safe and comfortable. I also do not want to rush into anything before I get to know you, your wants, your passions, and your desires. I know this is not how you imagined your life, but you have had my heart ever since our fathers made their deal. Please give me the chance to win yours."

My jaw dropped slightly as I took in his words. He bared his entire heart for me. What kind of woman would I be to not give someone a chance who showed such venerability?

To be honest, I liked this side of him. The side that was honest about his feelings. The side that was not afraid to say what was on his mind.

"I understand. We will wed tonight, and I will give you the chance you desire."

"Really?" His eyes lit up with excitement.

I nodded in response. Offering him a smile.

"I will spend every day trying to make you the happiest woman alive. You will not regret this." The smile on his face dropped, and his eyes widened. "Oh, I almost forgot!" He jumped up from his seat and dug into the pocket of his jacket. He pulled out his hand in a balled fist. "I went back and got this for you. I know you threw it away, but I could sense the immense power coming from it. I think it is something you may want to hang onto." He extended his arm toward me and opened his palm.

Inhaling deeply, I took in the sight of something that I never expected to see ever again. The white pendant necklace I'd thrown into the ocean in anger lay flat in his palm. "How did you find it?" Taking the beloved piece of jewelry from his hand, I examined it closely. It was hard to believe this was the same necklace I had my whole life. I threw it never expecting to see it again.

"To my surprise, when I returned to look for it, it washed up on the shore of the small island the portal is on back in Elswyth. It seemed it was making its way to you, whether I had gone to retrieve it or not," he let out a deep chuckle.

I thought if my necklace was gone, my problems would be as well. It was the one thing my father left me with when he abandoned me at the sanctuary. This pendant was the thing that linked me to my mother, to my magic.

At that moment, I hated it. But now, with it back in my possession, I was glad to have it.

"Will you allow me to put it on you?" Malachi asked nervously.

I gave him a nod in response. He took the necklace from my hand, walked around so he stood behind me, and placed the chain around my neck. Once the clasp locked, I felt as if, once again, I was whole. I did not realize the piece of me that was missing while it was not with me. It was then it hit me, the entire time I was here, I was not hit with the anxiety I would have felt if I was back in Elswyth without the necklace.

Was there something about this place that made me feel at ease, or was it the man who was now in my company?

"Thank you. You don't know how much this means to me," I whispered.

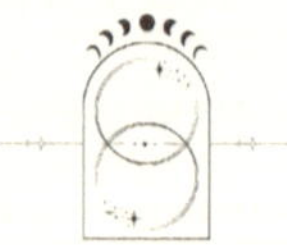

The rest of the day I spent with Violet. She was well aware of the King's plans, and during breakfast she had the royal seamstress fill my room with wedding dresses to choose from. The three of us spent hours trying them on and deciding which I looked best in. After too many dresses to count, I chose an ivory A-line gown with long lace sleeves.

After that, I spent hours getting my hair and make-up done. My ash blonde hair was styled in a low bun, with a few strands hanging loose to frame my face. If the Elder saw my hair like this, she would freak out from the amount of loose strands. However, I felt more beautiful than I ever had. Just as the make-up artist applied the finishing touches on my face, Violet came rushing into the room.

"It's time! It's time!" She squealed.

My heart pounded in my chest. Yes, Malachi and I agreed the marriage would be in ceremony only, but butterflies still filled my stomach at the thought of being his wife. Our conversation from this morning kept replaying in my mind all day. His heart was mine. He opened up to me in such an intimate way, and I could not deny it made my heart flutter. It would take time, but I could see myself giving my heart to him as well.

Violet took my hands in hers and offered me a warm smile. "You are gorgeous. If the King doesn't cry when he sees you, that man has a heart of stone."

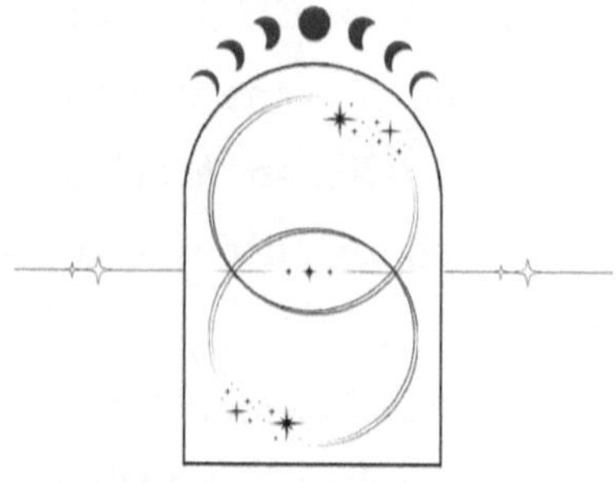

Ten

Outside the castle, facing the city, there was an archway made of white flowers. Under it stood a priest, Artemis, and my soon-to-be husband. My heart skipped a beat as my eyes locked onto his. That familiar pull toward my bridegroom returned, and a warmth washed over me. He had frozen mid-sentence as I came into view, and his jaw fell slack. Artemis used his hand to shut Malachi's mouth for him. Violet's arm was linked with mine as we walked closer to the arch. With each step, my heart pounded in my chest. I reached up and held my pendant, hoping it would bring me some peace.

As we got closer, I saw silver mist in Malachi's eyes. When I first met the king, he seemed so cold. He was to the point with my father, snarky to his guard captain, and gave me the cold shoulder for the first few days I arrived. Something about our conversation from this morning changed the way I looked at him. This man was not cold. He did not have a heart of stone, but a wall he put around it. He only allowed himself to be vulnerable with those he held close.

It was not my necklace that brought me peace in this moment, it was knowing that I was about to wed a good man.

Once we arrived at the arch, it was then I noticed all the fae were in flight, right off the edge of the island. They were all here to watch the wedding between their king and me. It was in that moment it hit me, really hit me. I was marrying a king. Even though I was just brought into this realm, I was about to marry the most important person in theirs. Violet released my arm, bowed gently, and stepped back.

"Wonderful. Let us begin." The priest opened a book and moved, so he now stood on the other side of us, giving the crowd a better view of the bride and groom.

I moved so I was next to Malachi. He looked down at me and smiled. A single tear fell from his eyes, and he quickly wiped it away. "You look beautiful, Ori," he whispered loud enough for only me to hear.

Artemis stood a few steps behind him, and Violet just a few steps behind me.

The priest finally lifted his head from the book and spoke in a language I did not recognize, projecting his voice loud enough for the crowd to hear. After several minutes, he turned his head to Malachi. "Would you like to say a few words, my king?"

"Oriana, I know we have not known each other very long, and this was not how you expected your life to turn out. I made a promise to you this morning. A promise I will now make to you before my entire kingdom. I will do everything in my power to make you happy. Do everything I can to make sure every need and want you have is met." He took in a deep breath and then looked out toward the crowd. "And on this day, I crown you Queen of Aeros. Not consort as many kings before have taken, but queen. My equal in every way. You will always be treated with the same respect I am given. You are free to do as you wish, as any queen does." He looked back at me and smiled.

The crowd cheered, and the priest turned his attention to me. "Oriana, do you have anything you wish to say?"

I swallowed hard. "Malachi, you are right. This is not how I expected my life to go. However, ever since you flew into my life, something felt more right than it ever had. Being in Aeros, I can sense this is where I belong. That these people, your people, are my people. Our people. I promise as Queen, I will do everything I can to do right by them. And I promise to do everything I can to do right by you as your wife." I smiled up at him and stared into his eyes. "My heart belongs to you."

His eyes widened. "Really?" Malachi's voice shook as he spoke.

I nodded in response.

"How beautiful," the priest said. He then continued in the unknown language. After his speech, he looked down at me and smiled. Raising his gaze to Malachi, he spoke again. "You may kiss your bride."

Malachi looked down at me. "Is this ok?" he whispered as he closed the gap between us.

"Kiss me," I whispered back.

A grin crossed his face as he pulled me toward him, leaned down, and gently pressed his lips to mine. Fireworks flashed in my mind. His lips were so soft and warm. I wrapped my arms around his neck and got on my tiptoes to deepen the kiss. His hands slid down to my lower back and held me closer. Too quickly, he pulled his lips away and gave me a longing expression.

"Oriana," he breathed.

Before anyone could say anything else, the ground beneath us rumbled.

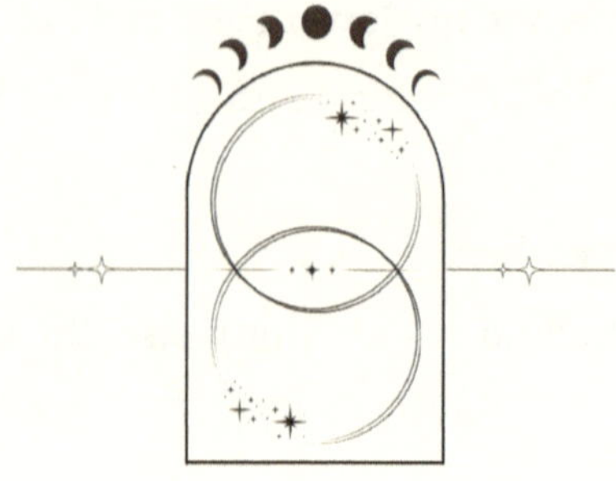

Eleven

My husband released me and staggered forward a few steps to look out toward his people. "Return to the city! Make sure everyone is safe!"

It was then I realized not all in the crowd were civilians. There were several dressed in royal guard uniforms, similar to what Artemis was wearing. The guards from the crowd took off quickly. However, many of our other guests panicked. I could hear them scream about their children and other loved ones as they all flew toward the city.

After a long moment, the quake finally stopped. Violet rushed over to me and wrapped me in a tight embrace. Malachi turned to me with a worried expression and then looked to Artemis.

"Art, I need you to make sure there were no more fallings," he commanded.

"Yes, Sir!"

Before he could take off, the tremors started again, this time much worse than before. Pulling away from Violet, I wobbled and fell to the ground. Malachi called out to me with panic in his voice. He took a step in my direction, and as his foot planted into the ground, it crumbled beneath him. The edge of the island plummeted, and in waves, more land followed. My husband quickly flew upward to avoid following the crumbling land.

Looking up, I noticed that Violet had also fallen to the ground. She was a few feet behind me. The quake abruptly stopped, and before I could stand, the land between the two of us cracked.

My stomach dropped and fear ran through me as I watched the ground split. Firm hands grabbed me, pulling me up. Glancing up in panic, I was relieved to see Malachi. Too quickly, the land disappeared beneath our feet, and the two of us were falling. He held me close to him. The section of the island we were on was breaking into pieces. As Malachi flapped his wings to launch upward, a large hunk of rock slammed into him. I could hear the crunch of bone as Malachi wailed into my ear.

"My King!" Artemis called.

I turned my attention to his voice, and he was diving right for us. Violet was flying just above the island, avoiding the crumbling land. Her eyes were filled with agony and desperation.

Another rock hurled toward us, and Malachi held me tighter and turned his body to protect me from the falling debris.

"Hold on tight, I won't let you fall," he yelled to me.

I clung to him for dear life. My arms were wrapped so tight around his neck that I was worried if I held on any tighter,

I would choke him. He grunted as another piece of debris crashed into him. His undamaged wing flapped, trying to fly, but the two of us continued to fall.

Artemis finally made it to our side. Malachi gave him an intense stare. "Take her and get her to safety!"

"My king, I cannot leave you like this." Artemis choked on his words.

"Take her!" Malachi commanded, in the strong voice of a king to his most trusted guard captain. "She is your queen!"

Artemis nodded and extended his arms to take me. As they were transferring me over, another large piece of the island slammed into Malachi's good wing, knocked him off balance, and sent him tumbling. He was forced away, and both of them lost their grip on me, and I began to free fall. I looked up and felt tears flow as I gazed upon the only two men who could save me. A king with two broken wings, and his most trusted friend. A friend who, with the choice of his king or a human woman he just met, would choose his king every time. I could not blame him as I watched Artemis dive for Malachi. Air wooshed around me, and I was too afraid to turn to see how much space was between me and the ground below. So, I looked up and watched as the castle that was to be my home crumbled and fell. No part of the island made it. In a detached thought, I was thankful Violet had gotten away. She was smart enough to fly up before the island started to collapse.

"Are you insane? Go get my queen!" Malachi's screaming pulled me out of my own head. "My wings can heal themselves!"

Artemis dove toward me, dodging the debris. Within a moment, he scooped me up into his arms. "You know, this was not how I pictured the first time I was going to hold you."

Malachi wobbled as he tried to steer himself to us. Somehow, even with his damaged wings, he was able to keep himself from falling to his death.

For the first time, I gained the courage to look down. The ground below was finally visible, and all I could see was the top of a dense forest. The trees were dark green and gray. In the center of the forest, there was a large dead zone, where everything was black. What struck me was seeing the small village in a clearing to the west. To the east, there were four large craters.

"Impossible," Artemis breathed as he hovered in the air, staring at the village.

"Art! Watch out!" Malachi called out from the distance.

Too late.

We turned to see a large piece of debris as it slammed into us. Artemis held me tight, but the two of us tumbled. Unable to catch his balance, we fell below the treetops. His warmth enveloped me as he tried to shield me. We slammed into branches, and after smacking into three of them, Artemis released me. Tears flooded my eyes, as I accepted that I would not survive this fall. My human body would not make it.

My body screamed in pain as another tree branch slammed into my mid-section, but instead of falling to the next one, this branch stopped my decline. I exhaled deeply as the impact stole my breath away.

Artemis continued to tumble until he finally hit the ground and landed on his back about fifty feet below me. He offered me a weak smile as blood leaked from his mouth and nose. The ground around him was littered with chucks of rocks. Finally, he stood, shaking off the daze. He turned away, took a few steps, and looked around. His wings were slumped, and I watched as he writhed in pain as he tried to spread them.

"Are you alright, little one?" He called out to me. "I can barely move my wings, but I will find a way to get you down."

"I..." It was painful to speak, but I forced out the words in a soft voice hoping he could hear me. "I'm in so much pain, but I am alive."

Artemis took a few more steps away from me as he surveyed the scene. He then turned and looked up at me with his head cocked. "Are you able to move at all?"

His eyes went wide and full of fear as the terrifying sound of hundreds of branches snapping filled the air. A guttural scream left my throat as a large piece of land crashed directly on top of Artemis.

Only the tip of his wing was left uncovered. Its white feathers were now red with blood.

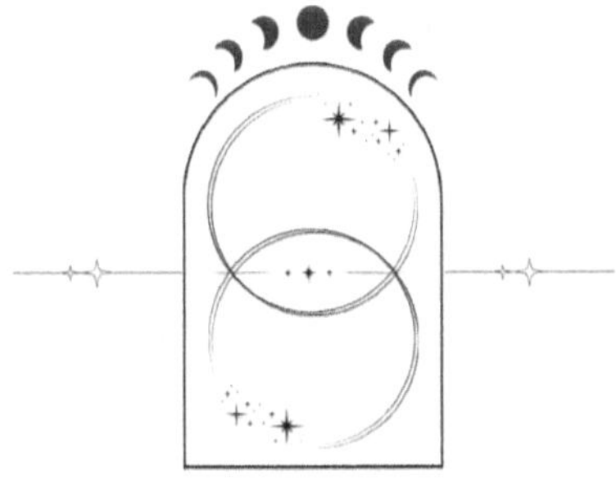

Twelve

I hung from the tree, staring down at the blood that leaked from under the boulder. Tears streamed down my face, and I screamed until my throat was raw. Pain still overwhelmed my body, and I was not able to even attempt to climb down. After Mother knew how long, Malachi came flying through the trees. He was not as fast or stable as he had been in the past but was able to avoid running into any branches. When he said he would heal, he meant it, and I was glad for it.

His eyes locked onto me, and his speed increased. Hovering in the air, he lifted me off the tree limb and held me close to his chest. I buried my head into it and sobbed. His fingers gently went through my hair.

"Darling," he whispered. "It's ok. We made it. You're safe now." His voice trembled. "Where is Artemis?"

Another sob escaped my throat in response.

I felt a gentle thud as Malachi landed. He asked again. "Oriana, where is Artemis?" Fear rattled his voice.

Finally, I was able to lift my head to meet his gaze. Words still refused to leave my throat. Instead, I looked over to the large hunk of land that was to the right. It hit me how little of a chance Artemis had to survive the impact. The boulder was nearly twice as tall as Malachi, and as wide as I was tall.

A cracked whimper escaped Malachi's throat. "No." He pulled me tighter to him and rushed over to the rock. Using one arm, he tried to push the boulder away. It did not budge. "Hold on to me tight. I need to use both hands, and there is no way I am letting you go. I can't lose you, too." Tears flooded his eyes and streamed down his face. I held onto him as tight as I could, and he used both hands to try to push the boulder away. Again, it did not budge. An angered scream escaped his lips.

He tried over and over. Eventually slamming his whole body into it. Nothing he tried worked. After hours passed, he finally gave up. He sat on the ground, held me tight in his lap, and looked down at the wing tip sticking out from the rock. "Artemis, I am so sorry. I am so sorry I could not save you," he sobbed.

Reaching up, I wiped the tears from his eyes. Guilt ran through me. If only my father kept his deal with the fae. Would we have been able to prevent this from happening, or was it my coming here that set off this chain of events?

Malachi's wings sat limp on his back. Normally, he kept them neatly tucked in. Red stained some of the feathers. He grabbed my wrist and pulled it away from his face. "My magic is gone," he said coldly. "With my wings broken, I am not able to fly us back up to Aeros. They healed enough so I could barely fly down here, but they stopped healing. There is something wrong about this place, but I swear to The Mother, I will find a way to get you home safely."

"I saw a town when we were falling," I finally spoke. My throat felt so sore as I forced out the words. "Maybe we could travel there and see if we can find someone who can help us? It's north of here."

Malachi gently took me off his lap and sat me on the ground next to him. Standing, he looked down at me nervously, then to Artemis' wing tip that was peeking from under the rock. He walked over to it and picked off one blood-stained feather and placed it in his breast pocket. Whispering something in the language the priest used during our wedding, he knelt and hung his head, continuing to whisper for a few moments. He then quickly stood and turned to me. Without a word, he scooped me up in his arms and headed north.

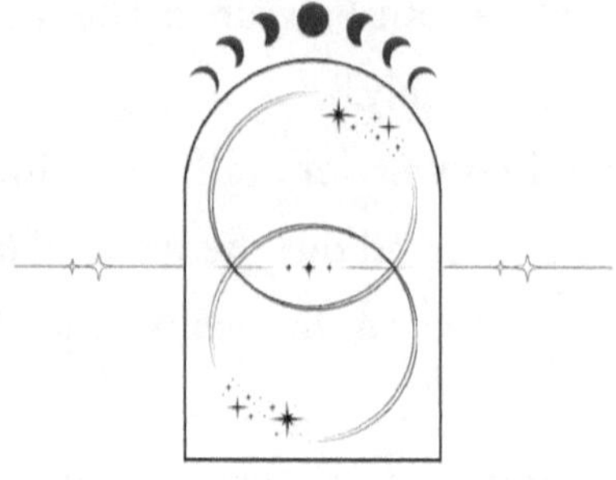

Thirteen

Malachi traveled through the ever-darkening night and kept walking until long after the sun came up. For several hours, I could feel him slowing down, but even as exhaustion crept into him, he never once loosened his grip on me. Neither one of us had spoken a single word during the trek to the unknown village. I found myself slipping in and out of consciousness during the journey. My body and mind had been pushed past their limits. While I was awake, I took in the sights of the evergreen forest. The fresh scent of pine filled my nose.

Finally, the sun began to rise and Malachi allowed himself some rest. He sat under a tree, sat me by his side, and wrapped his wing around me to keep me close. Leaning against him, I closed my eyes and allowed the sun to warm my face. After a while, I opened them to see Malachi looking down at me.

"I am sorry," he said softly.

"You're sorry?" I gave him a confused look.

He nodded. "If I did not keep the terms of the deal, you would not have been put through this. I should have let you stay in the life you knew. The dealings of our fathers had nothing to do with us." He turned his gaze away and looked up at the treetops, which were blocking the view of the sky. Before I could say anything, Malachi jumped up, a growl escaped his throat. "Who's there?"

Five warriors stepped out from behind trees. Each of them wore half masks that resembled birds, and all but one had black masks. The warrior in the center wore a golden mask. They were battle-ready with weapons in hand. Two of them had bows that were loaded and pointed directly at Malachi, and one of the smaller members had their spear pointed at me.

My body tensed as I watched them carefully. Malachi was not in any shape to fight, nor was I. Never had I been in any physical altercation or had weapons pointed at me. The closest thing I had experienced was a small tiff between my sisters and me. Those were bound to happen with close living quarters with multiple women. The one with the golden mask stepped closer, holding his hand up to signal to the others to wait. "It has been a long time since we have seen a winged one. Why have you returned?" he growled.

Malachi stepped closer to him, blocking the path between me and the strangers. "We live above the clouds. The island I called my home collapsed, bringing me and my wife down with it."

Heat rose to my cheeks as I heard him call me his wife. The ceremony was completed moments before the island fell. How could I have forgotten that earth-shattering kiss? I stuffed down those feelings, as now was not the time to wish to feel my husband's lips on mine once again. There was too much at stake.

"We saw a village as we fell. I broke my wings, and we are looking for refuge while I heal. As soon as I am, we will be gone," Malachi continued.

The golden-masked man stared Malachi down for a moment before sidestepping to get a look at me. He chuckled under his breath and shook his head. "A human. You expect me to believe that a fae wed a human? Didn't anyone tell you after you are married you don't need to keep the outfits on?"

It was then I stood, and I inhaled sharply, suppressing a groan as pain shot through my body. It was the first time I moved on my own since before the fall. I did not realize how badly I had been injured from it. Staggering forward to Malachi's side, I snarled at the masked man. "We had just fin-ished the wedding ceremony before the collapse." Rage boiled inside of me. It was one thing after another, and I have had enough. Finally, I allowed myself to feel the pain, the anger, the sadness from everything that had happened since I met the King of Elswyth, and he told me the truth of who I was.

It was then something deep within me clicked. That same powerful sensation I felt during my first training session was now one with me. As if it had been there my entire life, my magic flowed through my veins. "We mean you no harm. Look at us! We clearly pose no threat. So lower your weapons and help my husband!" I commanded. If I needed to, I would use my magic to destroy anyone who opposed us.

I was a threat, and I prayed they could not feel the power I now sensed within myself. I would not hesitate to explore the extent of it if I was pushed to do so.

The golden-masked man pulled it from his face and cocked his head as he examined me. His eyes went wide as they trailed down my body and stopped at my neckline. "Stand down!" He called to his warriors.

Malachi once again moved to protect me from these warriors, this time, pulling me close to his side. "Why are you looking at her like that?"

"That necklace. Where did you get it?" he asked quickly.

One of the bow-wielders stepped forward to their leader's side and removed her mask. "Necklace? Since when do you care about jewelry from above? Let's bring them into the Elder and allow him to decide their fate."

"Silence, Katerina!" He turned and snarled at her. "I care when the necklace looks exactly like the Calamita."

The other warriors let out a gasp, and the second bowman pointed his weapon at me.

The Calamita? What the hell was that, and why did it cause a reaction from these people?

"I advise you to remove your aim from my wife. If not, I will tear you limb from limb." A deep and guttural growl escaped his throat.

I could not help but swoon over how protective this man was over me. Mother, help me. The vows I made to her were going to be nearly impossible to keep. The more time I spent with my husband, the less I wanted to keep the vows with The Mother. I just prayed she would forgive me when the time came.

"The necklace. Where did you get it? I won't ask again," the gold-masked warrior snarled.

"It's a family heirloom. It belonged to my mother before she died. What is Calamita? And why do you think I have it?"

The leader turned to the bowman and ordered him to lower his weapon before looking at me again. "We will take you to the village where The Elder can tell you all about it. My name is Karjo. I am the Elder's son." He turned his attention towards my husband. "No one in our village has wings, as they are all cut off at birth. However, our healer comes from a long line of healers. She may have some journals from before that will guide her on how to heal your wings."

"Why would you cut off your wings?" Hurt radiated from Malachi's voice.

"No need to have them if we cannot fly. We have not flown since the last king rose the capitol into the sky and left us to deal with what he created."

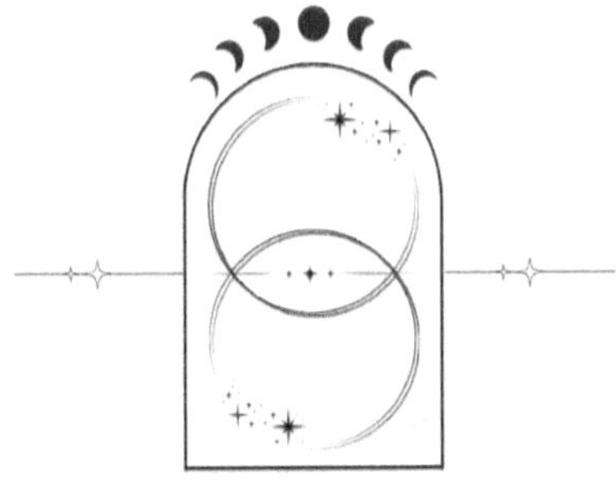

Fourteen

We walked in silence as we made our way to the village. Other than Karjo, the other four warriors refused to even speak to us as if we were beneath them, and Katerina kept her hand on her blade at all times. They did not trust us, but could I blame them? Based on the last thing Karjo said about what we know as the Great Calamity, they did not have a good last impression of Malachi's ancestors.

His last words kept repeating in my mind. What did he mean when he said it was the king who created it? Did Malachi's family have something to do with whatever had happened, and did he know more than he led on? Surely, the history of the royal family would be passed down from generation to generation.

Though, out of anyone, I should understand how easy it is for royals to keep secrets. I was the King of Elswyth's best-kept secret for twenty-five years. Was I still a secret to everyone but my two sisters and the Elder? Thinking about them hurt my heart. How I missed them so, for they were my family, not the king. He may be my blood, but blood was not what made family.

Family was formed by bonds of trials. It was the Elder who raised me. It was my sisters who made me feel loved and cherished. It was my father who made me feel like I was nothing. That all I was, was a dark secret that soiled the royal family name. Only good to be sold to the fae as a pawn in a war that had not yet come to our shores.

The forest did not get any less dense as we continued our walk. It was a few hours before we reached the village. The buildings were all made of pale logs. If it was snowing, it would remind me of a winter solstice greeting card. All eyes were on us as we walked through the village. The fae here looked like the fae from Aeros, minus the wings. Some of the elders even had white tattoos that mimicked my husbands. Karjo dismissed the warriors, but Katerina stayed with us. Taking us to the center of town, Karjo led us to a large building that overlooked the square.

"Father," he called out, "I brought guests that you will be very interested in meeting."

"I am in my office," a deep voice called out from the back of the building.

Karjo guided us through the halls and into the Elder's office. Katerina stood guard in the doorway, her hand still on her blade, blocking our exit.

The Elder looked up from his desk, and eyes went wide as he met Malachi's gaze. "It has been a long time since someone with wings has been to this village alive." He stood from his seat, walked around to the front of his desk, and leaned against it. "How did you make it down here without dying?"

"Why would you kill the fae we sent here?" Malachi snarled. "We just wanted to know the state of the land after The Calami-ty!"

The Elder shook his head. "You misunderstand me. They did not touch the ground with life in their veins. Magic has been gone from this land for years. Once they flew too far from the raised lands, they lost their ability to fly, and that was a long fall. So, I will ask again, how were you able to fly all the way down, and can you still?"

The room fell silent. Nervously, I looked around at everyone as tension built. Malachi tightened his jaw before he spoke. "I do not know how we were able to make it, but the others didn't. As for me flying now, no. My wings are broken. Debris hit them as I fell, and they partially healed, but not enough for me to fly myself and my wife back to the sky."

"Father, I believe I know how they made it. Ever since I have been near the human, I could feel a tingle in my core, just as the olden ones said. Just being close to her calls for my magic to return. Look upon her neck, is that the Calamita?" Karjo interjected.

The Elder then looked at me. His eyes widened. "That neck-lace. Let me see it, please."

"Do not give it to him," Malachi snapped. He extended his arm out in front of me to create a barrier between the Elder and myself.

Holding on tight to the pendant, I looked at my husband nervously. These people were not exactly hostile, but I was not sure if I could trust them. But, they could be the only chance we have to find a way back above the clouds.

"I will give it back on my honor. I simply want to examine it for a moment. We can make a deal if that will make you feel better."

Fae deals could not be backed out of. I knew that better than anyone. The fact he even offered calmed my nerves slightly. I looked up at Malachi and he offered one nod, lowering his arm. Knowing he thought it was okay gave me comfort in my decision. Removing the necklace, I extended it out to the Elder. When his hands touched it, he recoiled with a hissing sound, as if it burned him.

"Father! Are you ok?" Karjo rushed over to him.

The Elder raised his hand. "I am fine, Son. That definitely is the Calamita. Human, where did you get that?"

"It was my mother's, according to my father. She died in childbirth. I never met her."

"Was she a sorceress, by any chance?" The Elder raised an eyebrow.

I hesitated for a moment. Scared of what this all meant, I wasn't sure if I should be honest. But if I wasn't, would we ever get the answers we needed? They also have not given us any reason to distrust them. Best not to give them a reason to distrust us. "She was. I am as well."

The Elder shot his gaze to Malachi. "I assume you want to reunite the sky and land?"

"I do more than anything," he responded.

"Do you think the sky king is fair? Would he try to conquer us?" The Elder asked in a firm tone.

"I am the sky king if that is what you wish to call me. However, I call myself the King of Aeros." Malachi hardened his gaze on the Elder. "Is this Aeros?"

"This land has not been called that for many years. We call our land Teros. Teros has no king. This village is the only one remaining in all the land. We govern through the people. Yes, while I am the Elder, we have a council, and our citizens vote on issues." The Elder narrowed his gaze.

I had never heard of a land with no king, or one that allows for its people to vote on how things should be run. I found the idea fascinating.

"I see no reason to change that. I am no conqueror. I wish the best for my people," Malachi said with a smile. "Perhaps Aeros may adopt the Teros ways once we are reunited."

If I did not think that I was falling for the fae king, I knew now. He truly wanted what was best for the people, and not just his people, but the people here as well. Many would see a king relinquishing his power as a weakness. However, I saw it as one of his many strengths.

"Perhaps you can sit upon the council. But that is all in good time. We can talk about that after the task you need to complete is done."

"We are in no condition to go on any quests!" I motioned over to Malachi. "His wings need to be healed. I feel like I am going to collapse at any moment!" However, to be honest, ever since I felt myself become one with my magic, the pain throughout my body lessened. Exhaustion had still seeded itself in my core.

"And rest you shall. For where I am about to send you, you will need to be in top shape. Come with me, for this is a story that needs to be told, and would be much better if you were sitting." The Elder walked out of his office, and Katerina and Karjo followed him out of the room. Malachi and I then left as well. Taking us to a sitting room, the Elder motioned for us to sit on an orange loveseat. We sat, and Malachi immediately pulled me close to him. As like in the Elder's office. Katerina still stood in the doorway, blocking our exit. Karjo and the Elder sat on the couch across from us.

"Long ago, before Aeros was raised to the sky, we all lived in harmony. Until a sorceress from Elswyth traveled here, looking for help. She had spent all of her power trying to save her sister from Orilon. At least that's what she told the King. However, she turned out to be a liar. She did not want to save her sister, she wanted to control her. She used much of her magic to curse Orilon and needed her magical well replenished. Being just a man, the King was powerless to the damsel in distress she presented herself as. In the center of the forest, stood an obelisk that was the core of our magic. Our king took her there, as he had fallen for her ruse. Before the king knew it, she stole from the obelisk and ripped the magic from our realm."

I could not believe what I was hearing. It was my ancestors who caused all of this. Not only this, but they cursed another realm as well. Maybe my father was right. Could sorceresses not be trusted? Would the magic corrupt me? Would I end up doing horrible things as well?

As if Malachi could sense my anxiety, he pulled me in tighter, gently rubbing my shoulder. "You would never be capable of such horrible deeds," he whispered so softly that I could barely hear him.

"To escape the spread of magic loss, the king rose the capital into the sky, leaving us here, empty. Many of the remaining fae did not survive without our magic. The ones who did survive were left feeling like husks as if we were not whole beings. I am sure you understand the feeling since I am sure you also cannot feel your magic as you once did above."

"I feel as if half of my soul has withered. Without my magic, I feel less than fae," Malachi said somberly.

"That is how my people have felt since birth. Now the two of you have the chance to correct your ancestors' wrongs. Once you are healed, you will travel to the center of the forest, restore the magic into the obelisk, and set our people free."

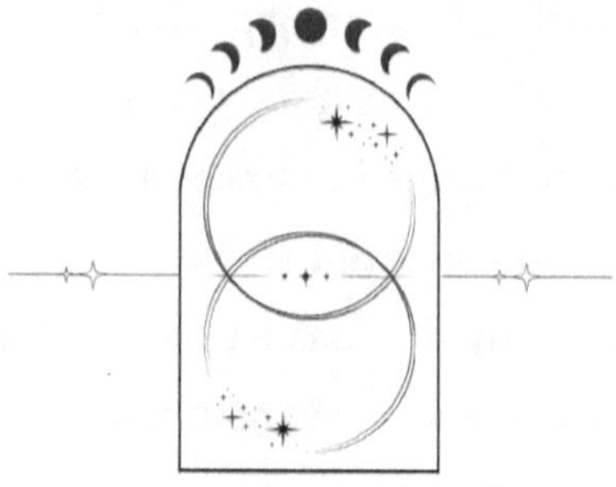

Fifteen

We had been in Teros for three days. As soon as we were finished with the Elder, Karjo took us to a small empty cottage at the edge of the village. Even after we went inside to settle in and rest, Katerina was never too far away. I constantly saw her keeping an eye on us.

On our first night, the healer had come by and set Malachi's wings so they would heal properly. In doing so, she had to break them again and move them into the correct position. I hated hearing his screams. Once his wings were set, I sat at his bedside, watching him. Gently, I ran my fingers up and down his back in between his wings. I pledged to myself that never again would he scream in pain.

My wounds, however, had mostly healed. My skin was left bruised, but most of the internal damage fixed itself. I could not help but wonder if it was me that was doing this, or if it was the magic of the Calamita.

The two of us stayed in separate rooms, but part of me wished he would knock on my door just once to ask if he could stay with me. I was not sure how much I would be ready for romantically, but I wanted to sleep in the arms of the one man who made me feel safe. I could not understand how in such a short amount of time, I had fallen for a man who I dreaded marrying. It made my heart flutter knowing he had fallen for me, too.

The Mother answered my prayers when I heard a soft knock on the door to my bedroom. I jolted up, the covers fell into my lap.

"Ori, are you up?" Malachi asked through the door.

"Come in!" I called out in response.

The door slowly opened, revealing Malachi shirtless, and in long sleep trousers. I focused on the white geometric patterns that were inked on his skin. My eyes trailed down his body and I bit my lower lip. A playful smirk grew across his face.

"Oh, like what you see, do you?" he asked in a teasing tone.

Heat flooded my cheeks, and I looked down into my lap. How bold have I gotten since meeting the fae man who turned my entire life upside down? Before I could say anything, he continued to speak.

"I wanted to tell you that my wings are all better. Whenever you are ready, we can start our journey to the center of the forest." He came over and sat on the edge of my bed. Gently, he lifted my chin to make our eyes meet. "I didn't mean to embarrass you. I apologize for that."

"It's ok. This whole thing is not something that I am used to," I said softly. In such a short time my life had completely changed. If you asked me just a few weeks ago, I would have told you that I would never marry. I would have told you I would never be in a room with a shirtless man.

But yet, here I was. It would be a lie to say I wasn't enjoying it.

"Well, at least you aren't alone in that. Neither am I."

I cocked my head and raised my brow. "What do you mean?"

He took my hands in his. "I have waited my whole life to meet you. Never once did I stray."

"Never?" When I first arrived, Artemis made it seem like the exact opposite had been going on, so I was very confused.

Malachi chuckled nervously and looked away. "Never."

"But Art—" I began, but Malachi quickly cut me off.

"He was just trying to ruffle my feathers. He liked to do that."

My heart ached at the use of past tense. In the little time I had known Artemis, he had become a good friend. Even though he tried to save his friend and king first, it was *my* life he saved.

And in doing so, lost his own.

Malachi gently wiped his thumb under my eyes, removing the tears that had fallen. "He would not want us to be sad. He would want us to continue on this quest and save our people. We will have time to give him the ceremony he deserves. For now, we need to save our energy on what is ahead," he whispered as he leaned forward and pressed his forehead to mine.

We sat there for a long moment in silence, staring into each other's eyes. The air electrified around us. I was not sure who made the first move, as it all happened too quickly. Our lips collided in fiery passion. Malachi moved forward, causing me to lie on my back as he got on top of me, our kiss never breaking. This was even more magical than the kiss that sealed our vows. Fireworks exploded inside me as our tongues danced.

My body yearned for more as he pulled away, but he only did so to remove the blanket from me. He tossed it to the floor, and a smirk grew on his face as he drank in the sight of me.

"Who knew you would go to bed in something so sexy?" he purred.

I wore a simple white silk slip. It was something very similar that I had worn back at the sanctuary. Never had I considered it sexy. Looking back, I was the only one who chose to wear something like this. My sisters all had worn longer nightgowns with sleeves.

Reaching up, I toyed with the thin strap. "I'm glad you like it," I purred back.

"Darling, I don't want you to do anything that you are not ready for. Let me know if you want me to stop at any point."

I thought about it for a moment. How far did I want to take this with my husband? Somehow, knowing he waited for me for all these years made me want him even more. Again, I struggled with the vows I made to The Mother. However, I broke many of those vows. Sisters were not to take a husband. The promise of my hand had been made long before I made my vows to The Mother. I had also made vows to this man during our wedding.

For once, I needed to stop worrying about what others expected of me and do what felt right in my heart. I loved The Mother, but when I made my vows to her, everything seemed so wrong, as if I was trapped within the walls of the sanctuary.

When I stood in front of Malachi and vowed to be his wife and give him a chance to win my heart, I felt free.

"Go slow, but don't stop," I finally said softly.

"Are you sure?" he asked again.

I nodded in response and his lips were on mine once more. His hands slid down and found their way to my side as he pushed up my nightgown, exposing my underwear. His fingers trailed down to my core and gently rubbed against the small piece of cloth that I was now so angry at for existing. I didn't want anything between us. Wetness pooled in my center, and I craved more of his touch. A moan escaped my lips. I reached down and tried to remove Malachi's pants, but he grabbed my arms and pinned them to the bed.

Pulling away from my lips, he growled, "Not yet, my queen." Slowly, he removed my underwear, exposing my bare sex to him. His fingers slowly teased my slit, just barely entering me. When he pulled away his fingers, they glistened with my wetness, and when he dragged his tongue across his fingers, he let out a groan. "Delicious."

Lowering his head, his tongue grazed across the most intimate part of me. I arched my back and let out a soft moan in response. Never had I experienced anything like this, but I trusted Malachi fully and I knew I was in good hands. Flicking against my sensitive clit, his tongue found ways to drive me wild. Never did I expect to feel so much pleasure. He removed his tongue from me, and I pleaded for more. I never wanted him to stop.

"Oh, darling. That was a warm-up. The fun has just begun," he teased.

I thanked the gods when he finally removed his own pants. My eyes went wide as his considerable length sprang free.

"Are you still ok? You're sure you want me to continue?" He asked nervously.

My core melted. He was so considerate of me and my feelings, and it only made me want him more. "Please," I pleaded.

"As you wish." He spread my legs and situated himself in between them. His tip was so close to my aching core, but yet so far away at the same time. I thanked The Mother when it prodded my entrance. Slowly, he pushed it in, and as I stretched to accommodate him, another moan escaped my lips.

Slowly, he eased in and out of me, and each time, he went a little deeper. Pleasure coursed through my body, and I cried out wordlessly. He leaned forward and kissed me hard as he thrust in as deep as he could. As I kissed him back, I truly thought I was in paradise. His pace increased, and I felt him hit the deepest part of me over and over.

My body teetered on an edge I didn't know existed. I was so close to exploding, but Malachi fully removed himself.

"Not yet," he growled. His cock slapped against my opening firmly before he pushed it back inside. Holding onto my hips, he slammed into me, this time not holding back, and I screamed in pleasure. I was so glad we had this cottage to ourselves. Hopefully, no one outside could hear us. Malachi groaned as he pushed himself in and held it there.

"Please, don't stop," I begged.

"Oh, darling. The next time I go, I won't stop until you have exploded, and I have filled you with my essence. Do you understand? Is that what you want?"

"Please!"

Malachi flipped me over, so I was on my hands and knees. With his hands firmly holding my hips, he plowed himself back into me. I did not think it was possible to have him deeper, but he was proving me wrong. My eyes rolled into the back of my head as I fell to my elbows.

"Grip the headboard," he commanded.

Reaching up, I obeyed. My hands held onto the wood as he fucked me from behind. I felt myself tighten around him and my body quivered. Pleasure continued to build within me, and I felt as if I could explode.

"Cum for me, darling," he purred.

At that moment, worlds collided, were destroyed and rebuilt. Never in my life had I had such an experience.

"Good girl." He leaned down and nibbled my ear, slowing down his thrust, making sure I felt everything as he pounded into me. Holding himself deep inside of me, my husband let out a deep groan. He twitched, and I felt something hot deep in my core. He did not stop thrusting, even as he filled me. "Mine," he growled. "Oriana, you are mine. Forever."

"Forever," I moaned back. "And you are mine."

"Darling, I have been yours since I first laid eyes on you." He slowly removed himself, and his essence dripped from me. He got out of the bed and lifted me into his arms. "Let's get cleaned up, then we can sleep in my bed tonight."

"Sounds perfect." I smiled up at him.

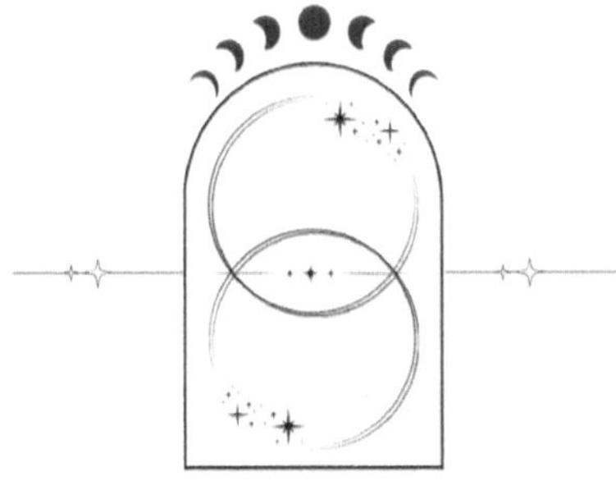

Sixteen

Two days later, Malachi and I were on our journey to the center of the forest. Karjo provided us with vague directions but insisted it should only take us about a full day's walk to get there. Apparently, no one had traveled too far from the village in decades, and little was known about what awaited us. His last words to us were a word of warning.

The last people who traveled to the center of the forest had not returned. Though fear had settled into my core, Malachi promised that we would be different from the others. We would do what needed to be done and save our people.

We traveled for hours, and I was thankful Malachi allowed me to walk. He stayed a couple of paces behind me, ready to strike if need be. To our surprise, the forest was still and silent. Not even bird song ran through these woods. The eerie silence gave me no solace. Over time, the green pines shifted into petrified wood. Many of the trees were shriveled as if the life had been sucked from them. All of them were barren of leaves, nor was there any evidence that leaves had ever been here. This cold place was truly desolate.

"We can take a break if you need to," Malachi said as he caught up to me and walked by my side.

Looking up at him, I let out a huff. "Just because I am human does not mean I am weak."

"I did not say that. I am concerned about you. We have traveled for miles, and you have yet to slow down." He took my hand and stopped walking.

This caused me to stop, so I turned to face him. "Mal, I promise you I am fine."

"Mal?" He smirked down at me. "I like that I'm getting nicknames."

"Want to hear another one I have for you?" I smirked back and pressed my body against his. "Pain in my ass."

He threw his head back and laughed. "Mother, you are feisty."

Before I could respond, a blood-curdling scream rang through the forest. Malachi pulled me close to him and lifted me off the ground. Thankfully, now that the healer fixed his wings, Malachi could fly once again. With a flap of his wings, he launched us into the sky, above the treetops. Clinging to him, I looked below to see what could have made the sound. It was not long before my eyes landed on one of the most horrifying things I had ever seen. This humanoid creature had skin as white as snow, red eyes, long claws and fangs, and large bat-like wings.

"W—what is that?" I whimpered.

"That, my dear, is one of the cursed fae of Orilon. I saw them firsthand when I attended their king's wedding. The fact one of them is here proves the Elder right. The witch who cursed Orilon is also the one who stole magic from our land."

The creature looked up and screamed again once its sights were on us. It launched itself into the air with breakneck speed. Long, blood-stained claws swiped at us. Malachi dodged its attack.

"I still can't feel my magic. This one is all on you!" Mal called to me.

Panic filled my veins. Even though I could sense my magic, I still never used it, or really even knew how to use it. I still had no idea what I could do. The Calamita grew warm around my neck as if an answer to my prayers. This necklace held the magic of the land. From what I knew, the fae of Aeros all had gravitational magic. I would use the magic from this land to my advantage. Focusing on pulling magic from the stone, heat filled my body, and built up within me, and begged for release.

I was not sure how I did it, but I felt my magic set free. As it was released, comforting heat flooded my body. The cursed fae slammed into the ground, letting out another scream on impact. Malachi flew lower, getting us a better view of the creature. It refused to die from the fall, and staggered up off the ground, letting out a hiss. Before it could take a step, I focused on my magic again. It released from me, and in one swift motion, the cursed fae's neck snapped, and its body fell to the ground. This time, it did not get back up.

Malachi landed next to the fae, still holding me in his arms. We stayed silent for a moment until he chuckled softly. "My wife is so badass."

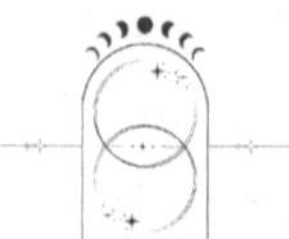

After the attack, we decided to take a short rest. After the huge burst of power, I had gained a headache from the amount of magic I had expelled. Mal informed me that there was a delicate balance when it came to using magic. If too much was used, one could easily burn out and be powerless for some time until the magical well refilled. Once we were well rested, we started the journey once again and did not stop until we reached the obelisk. Malachi flew us most of the way to make the journey go by faster. Everything looked the same as we traveled through the petrified wood. I was beginning to think we were going in circles until out of seemingly nowhere what we were searching for appeared. It was as if some form of magic camouflaged it until we got closer. The pure white obelisk sat in the center of a small clearing. My gaze followed its full length above the trees. The Calamita stone in my necklace throbbed against my skin. It got more intense with each step I took, closer to the obelisk.

Malachi stayed close behind me as I approached the obelisk. There was a small hole that matched the shape of my piece of the Calamita. I removed it from my neck and looked up toward the opening. Tightening my grip on the stone, worry filled my head. What if once I restored the magic to the obelisk, I lost all of mine? Even though this was a new part of me, my heart ached at the thought of losing it. The magic was mine; it was given to me by my family. Why should I give it back to the land who threw it away?

It was then I realized the voice in my head was not one I recognized. Still feminine, but it was cold and raspy. I shook my head hard to try to clear those thoughts. As I extended my arm to place the Calamita in its spot, it felt as if my body was fighting against me. Like there was another force preventing me from completing my task. Falling to my knees, I let out a scream as the excruciating pain of burning fire replaced the magic in my veins.

Malachi rushed to my side and knelt. "Oriana! What is wrong?"

I looked up at him and opened my mouth to speak, but no words came out. Instead, I forced myself to hand him the Calamita and pointed to the indent in the obelisk.

With a nod, he took it and held it tight. How he was able to hold it, but the other fae couldn't, I would never understand. It was just another sign from The Mother proving that we were meant to be.

Another wave of pain crashed into me, I curled in on myself, and I let out another wail. My gaze never left Malachi, even as the fire within got worse. With determination all over his face, he slammed the Calamita into the obelisk, and bright light filled my vision.

The pain instantly vanished, leaving no trace of it. When the flash cleared and my vision returned to normal, the surrounding trees were now green and full of life. Malachi ran back over to me and helped me stand. The clouds in the sky vanished, and the sun warmed our skin. Joy surged through me until Malachi looked up, and horror washed over his face.

Matching his gaze, I saw the three remaining islands of Aeros falling toward the ground.

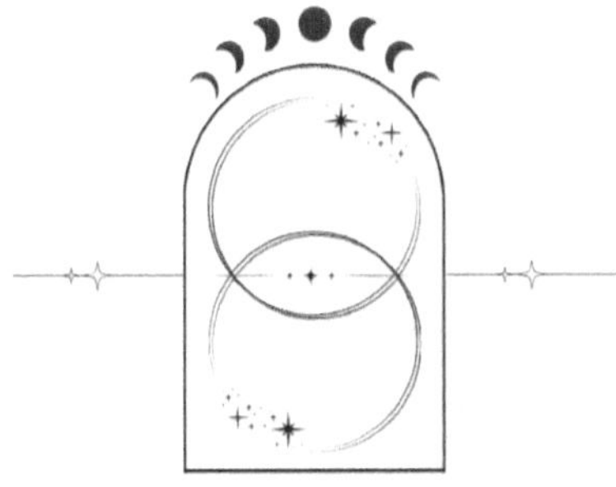

Seventeen

Malachi launched himself into the air, flying as fast as he could toward the islands. Too quickly were they approaching the land. Unlike when the castle fell, these were not crumbling or falling apart. No, three massive pieces of earth were careening toward the ground. The force would be enough to ruin the land below, and I could not help but wonder what other effects it would have on the entire land of Teros. Not only that, but the city would not survive the impact. Where would any survivors go? Would there even be any survivors?

The King of Aeros began to undo what his great-grandfather did long ago. I could sense his magic in the air. It was a large force that weighed down on me. Forcing myself to stand, I watched as he used his magic to try to stop the islands from crashing. The tattoos on his skin glowed and I swore that I could see the streams of magic wrapping around the base of the island and pulling upwards. They slowed, but not enough to make a difference. Horror continued to fill me. If the most powerful fae of Aeros could not stop them, who could? I wondered if I kept my magic, instead of giving it back to the land, would I have been able to help him?

Power radiated from the obelisk. The spot where Malachi slammed the Calamita in place was now fully fused. It was impossible to tell if a piece was ever missing. The heaviness I was feeling from Malachi's magic seemed to lift off me. It was replaced with something else.

A calling to the obelisk.

An overwhelming sensation washed over me, demanding I touch it. Unable to ignore its call, I rushed over to it and placed my palm against the warm white stone.

Like when Malachi touched the obelisk, a bright flash of light flooded my vision. When it cleared, I was no longer standing in the middle of a forest. I was now in a throne room with the most beautiful white marble columns.

"It has been a long time since a sorceress has been in my halls," an unfamiliar feminine voice rang from behind me. It was the most beautiful sound I had ever heard.

When I spun to see who was there, I immediately fell to my knees and bowed. Pressing my forehead to the cold marble floor, embarrassment washed over me. My entire life was spent worshiping the goddess that stood before me. Here I was, in dirty travel clothes and my vows for her forsaken.

"My Goddess," I finally managed to say, "it is an honor to be in your presence." My entire body trembled.

She let out a soft laugh. "Please rise, child."

I did as she said, wiping off the front of me as I got off the ground. I refused to meet her gaze, for I did not deserve to look into her eyes.

"You have spent your entire life trying to live in a way that would please me." Her tone was soft, yet commanding. "You have done well by your sisters, your family, and your husband. Yet, you believe yourself to be a disappointment? Why is this? Look me in the eye as you tell me, child."

Slowly, I raised my gaze. Her soft green eyes were filled with an emotion I could not determine. "I made a vow to save myself. I made promises that I did not keep."

She laughed again. "Child, you think I care about that? You think I care who you lie with, or how often? Tell me, how many children do I have?"

"Twelve."

She stepped closer to me. Grabbing my chin, she forced me to stay my gaze. "You do not get twelve children by remaining pure. Your teachers tell you they are all sired by the same man. That is a lie. Some have no father, and some share the same. Hell, I have even been with a woman since the realms split. Please do not feel ashamed to show love and passion however you see fit, especially not with a man who I chose for you."

"You chose him for me?" I raised an eyebrow.

She finally released me and took a step back. "Yes. Everything has been laid out as it should be. I am also offended you would believe I would send you on a quest to sacrifice yourself in the end. Women are not to be used and disposed of. Yes, the magic needed to be restored to the land. But the power in that necklace was never yours. It was a tool to help you unlock yours that was sealed away. Now, return to Aeros, call upon your power, and help the man you love."

On her last word, another flash of light filled my vision, and when it cleared, I was back in the clearing. Looking up to Malachi, I saw little change since the first flash. It was as if no time passed at all. Finally, I felt the magic flowing through my veins.

The Mother was right. It was never gone, it had just become one with me. So natural I could now feel its presence in everything I did.

Focusing hard on my magic, the air electrified around me. I followed the motions my husband was performing. Pretty soon, the islands slowed and were in our control. Malachi flew down to meet back up with me.

"Whatever you are doing, keep it up. The islands are now stable." He pulled me into his arms and launched us back into the sky. Now that the islands were no longer plummeting, fae filled the air around us. They, too, lent their magic to help us guide the islands back into the craters they were ripped from centuries ago.

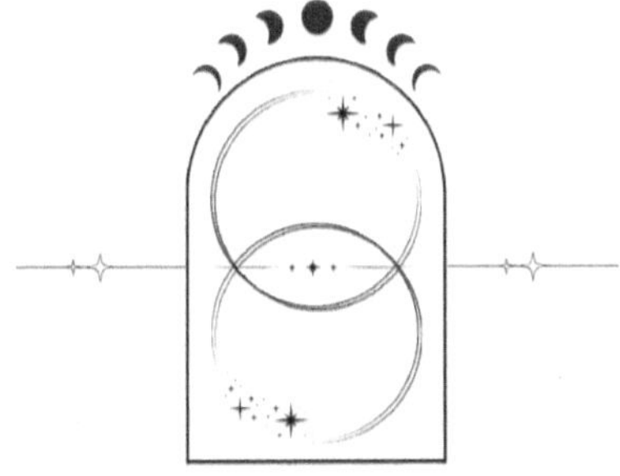

Eighteen

Two months passed since Aeros returned to the land. With the castle gone, Malachi and I moved into a penthouse in the city. He had been busy coordinating with the village elder to reunite Aeros and Teros. The first part in that plan was Malachi stepping down as king, and he joined the council that now ruled both people. The people of Aeros did not really understand the new ways, but they seemed to accept them. They still referred to Malachi as king, to many of them he would always be the king in their hearts. For he had earned it by saving them all.

Violet was so happy both Malachi and I were alright. She and I had been spending every day with each other, and the two of us created a group that met once a week to discuss the teachings of The Mother. Both citizens of Teros and Aeros attended. It was a great way to reconnect the people.

I still could not believe I had the honor of meeting The Mother. Her words would play through my mind for the rest of my days.

I was not a one-time use creature to save the realm, and then to be disposed of.

I continued my work with Malachi to help keep our people happy. Even though my title as Queen did not last long, the people of Aeros still saw me as theirs, and I would do everything in my power not to disappoint them.

Ever since returning, we had not gotten a chance to give Artemis the ceremony he deserved. Tonight, that would change. His loved ones, members of the guard, and citizens of Aeros all gathered in a field just outside the city where a pyre had been lit in his honor.

One by one, people told stories of Artemis, stories of his time in the guard, and what he was like as a young fae. He would be missed dearly.

Malachi was the last to speak. He walked toward the flame, then turned toward the crowd. "Artemis served by my side since we were young boys. He did not want to be my bodyguard, but his father was guard captain under my father's rule. They thought it would be best for both of us if he was assigned that role. One night, we snuck out of the castle, went to the portal island, and glamoured ourselves into humans. We found ourselves on a small island, and we stayed there for three days. We got into so much trouble when we returned." He let out a little chuckle and wiped the silver mist from his eyes. "The first night I brought Oriana into this realm, he invited himself to our lunch. When she returned to her room, he told me that if

I did not marry her, he would. Gods, how I wish he could see what change she has brought to our lands. He would be over the moon."

Malachi dug into his pocket and pulled out the single feather. It was now dark brown from the aged blood that stained it. He turned to the fire and released it. As he spoke words in an unknown language, the feather danced on the wind until it joined the flames. The fire roared and embers floated on the breeze.

We all stayed until the fire died out. Malachi made his way through the crowd of people, continuing the conversations about how Artemis would be missed. When he made it to my side, he wrapped his arm around my shoulders. "Well, dear wife, are you ready for me to fly us home? Sorry, we stayed so late. I know you must be exhausted."

I gave a small yawn before answering. "I understand. Please do not feel like you have to rush on my account."

He leaned in and placed a gentle kiss on my lips. "There is nothing more I want than to return home and crawl into my bed with my wife."

Pressing my body into his, I smiled up at him. "Well, by all means, don't let me stop you."

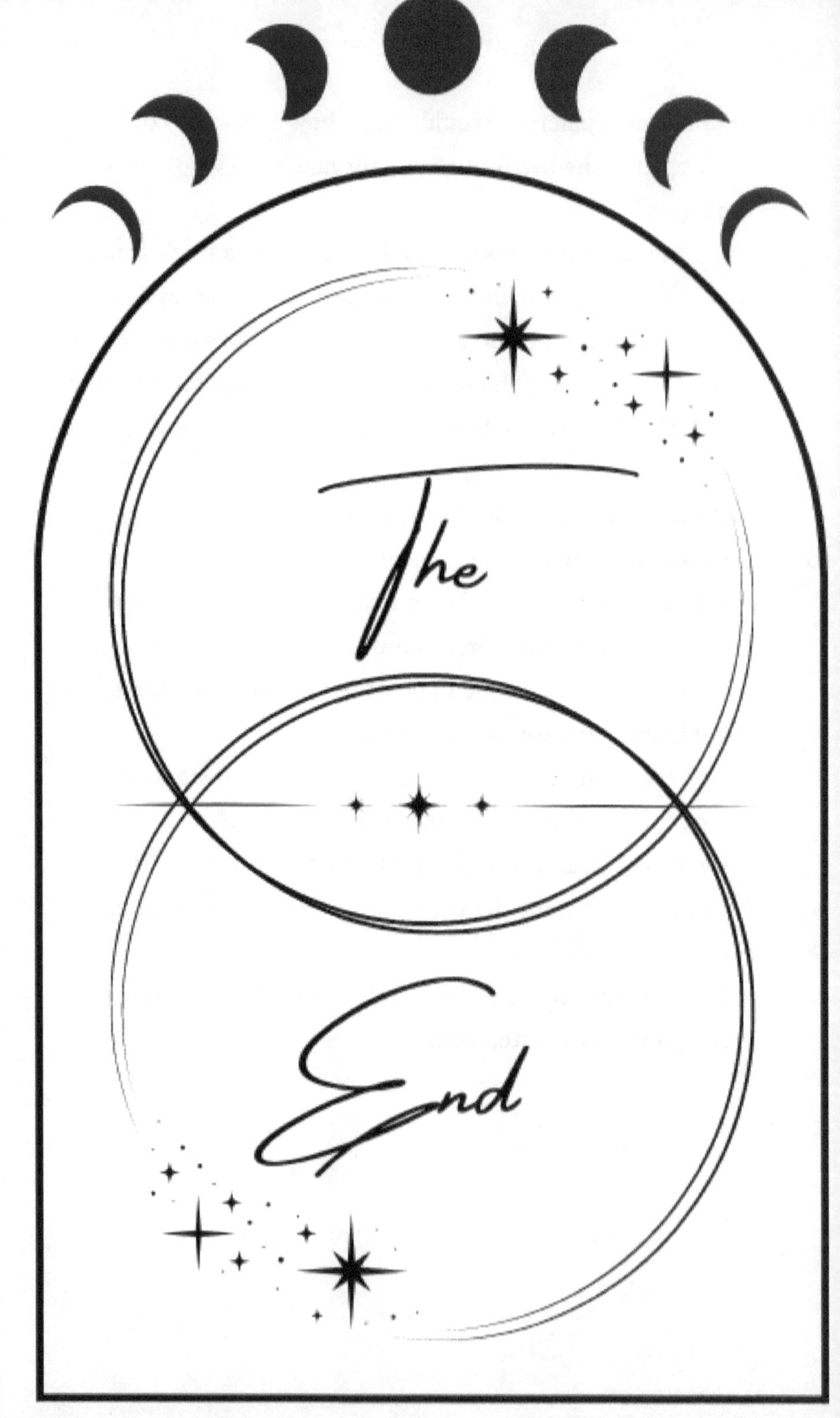
The
End

The Trials of Khaldon

A Realms of Elswyth Standalone

Willow Asteria

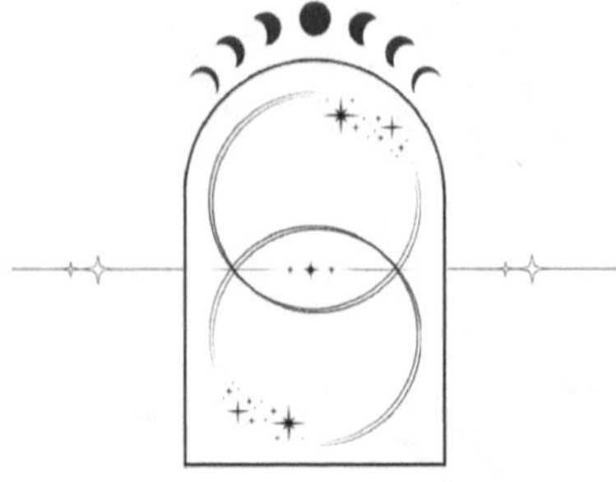

One

Music drifted on the warm summer breeze. I closed my eyes as I leaned against the old oak tree at the edge of my favorite secluded meadow. It was hard to believe that in one week, I would be married to the love of my life, Evander. Opening my eyes, I gazed over at him. As he played the lyre, the sun sparkled in his honey-blond hair. He flashed me a warm smile, and my heart melted at the sight of it.

The golden lyre in his hands glimmered as he played. I was so lucky when I came across it in the capital city. As soon as I laid eyes on it, I knew it would be the best thing I could give Evander. Two years ago, his lyre was broken when he was playing in the local pub, and a brawl broke out. The man who sold me the lyre was so happy to give it to me, and that it was going to one who loved music just as much as he did.

It was right in this spot where we first met all those years ago. My family stopped in Magla along the trade route, and when he came to see our wares, it was love at first sight. We stayed in town for a week that first time, and Evander came to see me every day.

It pained me when we had to travel to the next city. Elswyth was a large kingdom, with few cities, all too far away from my true love. Father always said we needed to stay on the move, or else we could not make the money we needed. But now that I was twenty, I could make my own life. I did not need to live the life of traveling merchants.

During our last visit to Magla, Evander begged me to stay with him and to be his bride. How could I say no to those ocean-blue eyes? So, when my parents moved on to the next town, I stayed here.

Evander stopped playing and made his way over to me. Sitting by my side, he wrapped his arm around me and pulled me in close. Gently, he grabbed my chin and lifted it, so our gazes met.

"Such a beautiful song," I said softly.

A chuckle escaped his lips. "I wrote it for the most beautiful woman I know. But it will only ever be just a fraction of how breathtakingly beautiful you are."

His soft lips pressed against mine, and once again, my heart pounded. Shivers ran down my spine as my love's fingertips gently grazed my arm. He pulled his lips away from mine and gave me a warm smile.

"I thank The Mother every day for blessing me with you. I don't know how I got so lucky," he breathed.

The kiss slowly intensified as passion grew between us. Evander reached down and unbuttoned his pants.

Pulling away from the kiss, I let out a nervous giggle. "What are you doing? What if someone sees us?"

He pulled out his fully erect cock and smirked. "Don't worry, my muse. No one is around. I will keep an eye out just in case. Go ahead and wrap those pouty little lips around me."

Quickly, I looked around to see if there was anyone nearby. To my relief, there wasn't. The two of us could not keep our hands off each other, but this was the first time we tried anything so publicly. Lowering my head to his lap, I dragged my tongue from the base of his cock all the way to the tip.

A groan escaped his throat, and he laced his fingers through my raven hair. Teasing his tip, I slowly and gently lapped it with my tongue.

"Little muse," he moaned. "Open that pretty little mouth and look up at me with those gorgeous green eyes."

Looking up at him, I smirked. "Ah, ah, ah. Not yet, my love." Ever so slowly, I swirled my tongue around the head.

"You're a fucking brat," Evander growled as he gripped my hair tighter.

A gasp escaped my throat and as soon as my lips parted, he forced my head down onto his cock. My eyes went wide as he hit the back of my throat, causing me to gag. Heat and need grew in my core as my love took control of me.

He tilted his head back, groaning once again in pleasure as he held my head down on his cock. It twitched in my mouth. I choked on it more, but did not once try to pull away.

"That's it, little muse. That's what brats like you deserve." By my hair, he forced my head to bob up and down. My eyes rolled into the back of my head as I swallowed him over and over. I loved it when he took control, and the rougher he was, the more I craved him.

He pulled me off him, and a strand of saliva connected my lips to the tip of his cock. "Have I ever told you how cute you look with my cock down your throat?"

"I don't think so," I teased.

He pressed my head back down, and I opened my mouth, then took him once again.

"Well, let me tell you, little muse. You are so fucking cute as you choke on my cock."

Looking up at him, I savored him, taking his full length into my mouth over and over. My tongue danced around in my mouth to add to his pleasure.

"Such a good girl. I am so close. You're going to swallow, aren't you?" His free hand gently rubbed down my body until firmly planted on my ass.

I responded by taking his full length down my throat and holding it there. Holding my head in place, he released his pleasure.

I made sure to swallow every last drop, unwilling to pull away until he was spent.

"Well, well. This is not what I expected to find when I followed the sound of that beautiful music," a dark and seductive female voice said.

Quickly, I pulled away from Evander, jumping up. He too rushed to put himself in his pants and stand. The most gorgeous woman I had ever seen stood before us. She was in a tight red shimmering dress that hugged her curves. But what had me frozen in fear were the blood-red eyes that matched her gown, and her pointed ears.

Evander forced me to get behind him, and I held on tightly to his arm. "Who are you?" he snapped at the woman.

She shook her head. "Oh no. I will be the one asking the questions. Which one of you played from that lyre?" Her long finger pointed toward the golden lyre that now lay on the ground.

Panic filled me. I hated the idea that it was my gift that brought this woman upon us. Throwing a prayer up to The Mother, I hoped she would leave us without harm.

He looked back at me, and then at the mystery woman. "I did."

A twisted grin grew upon her lips, and the world darkened around us. "Ah, I was hoping the one who played my lyre would be as pretty as you. Come along, pet. You now belong to me." She extended her hand toward us.

"I am going nowhere with you, witch!" Evander spat at her.

"Witch?" She faked an offended tone. "No. I am the Queen of Khaldon. I am fae, and you are mine."

Before either of us could say a word, the queen started to sing. The tune was more beautiful than anything I had ever heard. A yawn escaped my throat, and I collapsed to the ground.

Evander turned toward me. "Ophelia!" he cried out.

I looked up at him, and everything grew fuzzy. The queen came into my vision as she stepped to Evander's side.

"I had to get the human girl out of the way. Come along, pet. It's time I show you to your new home."

They walked off hand in hand, and everything went black.

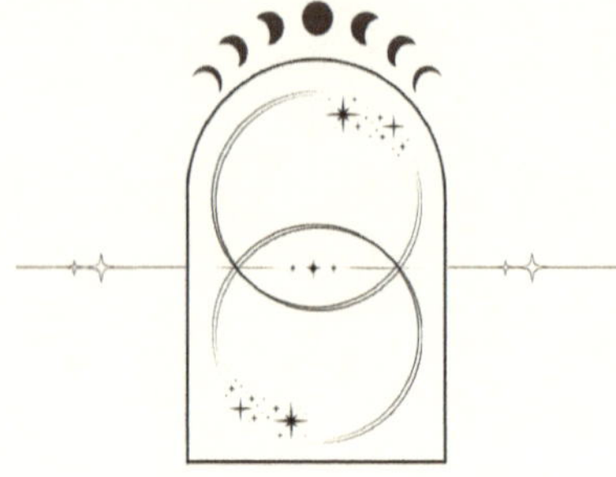

Two

"Ophelia?!" The sound of Evander's mother, Rhea, calling my name roused me from my slumber. My head pounded, and my vision was out of focus as I forced my eyes open. Everything was so dark, but the figure kneeling before me helped me sit up. It took a few moments before I recognized the features of my soon-to-be mother-in-law.

"Take it easy," Rhea whispered. "What happened? Where is my son? We have been looking everywhere for you two."

How long was I asleep? The stars twinkled in the night sky, and the evening breeze had me shivering. My stomach twisted, and I could not ignore the dull ache in my chest.

My vision gained focus, and I looked at Rhea's face. The panic in her eyes and all her questions had me running through everything that had happened before I passed out.

"She took him," I said in a sob.

In the distance, others called out for me and Evander. Rhea quickly turned her head, yelling that she had found me and asking them to come quickly.

"Who?" She turned her head back toward me. "Who took Evander?"

My heart shattered into a million pieces as I spoke her title. "The Queen of Khaldon."

Rhea let out a shocked gasp. Her husband and Evander's stepfather, Neo, joined us. His skin paled, and hands trembled as he heard me speak of the queen.

Rhea jumped up and rushed to her husband, and he wrapped her in a tight embrace. Gently, he stroked her hair as he whispered something to her.

"No! I can't go through this again. How did she find him?" She sobbed into his chest.

Neo looked down at me with a concerned expression. "Are you alright?"

I nodded and finally gained the strength to stand.

"Rhea," I said softly, "what do you mean, again?"

Her head snapped toward me, and tears flowed down her face. "That fae bitch took Evander's father, too. I begged Evander not to get into music. That is why she stole Dimitrios. She wanted him to play for her for all eternity. I tried to get him back, but I lost her game. When Dimitrios tried to run away with me after I lost, she killed him. I barely escaped from Khaldon with my life."

My heart dropped. I could not abandon Evander, but going after him would be dangerous. Fear rattled my bones as I thought of everything that could go wrong. When I traveled to Khaldon, what dangers would the fae realm greet me with? Would the fae there be like the beasts that terrorized Pendril? When I reached the queen, would she strike me dead for even trying?

Rage filled my core. I stepped toward Rhea and Neo. "How do I find him?" I said in a low growl.

"Ophelia! No, you cannot go, it's too dangerous." Rhea pulled away from her husband and closed the gap between us. Taking my hands in hers, she looked me in my eyes. "The games Helena plays are twisted. As much as I hate to admit it, my son is gone. Dimitrios may still be alive if I did not try to save him. She could kill Evander just for you trying to rescue him!"

Squeezing her hands tightly, I hardened my stare. "I will go to Khaldon and I will get Evander back. Nothing will stop me. Tell me how to get there."

She looked at me for a moment with a downturned expression and tears in her eyes. Neo stepped behind her and placed a supportive hand on her shoulder. She looked up at him, and he gave her a small nod.

She turned her attention back to me. "Ophelia, deep in the mountains, is a portal to her realm. Once you enter Khaldon, you will enter a cavernous world full of twists and turns. Follow the blue crystals. They will lead you to her palace. You are a cunning young lady. If anyone can outsmart the fae queen, it is you. Go, get my boy, and return. But please be safe."

Wrapping her in a tight embrace, I whispered in her ear. "I will not disappoint you."

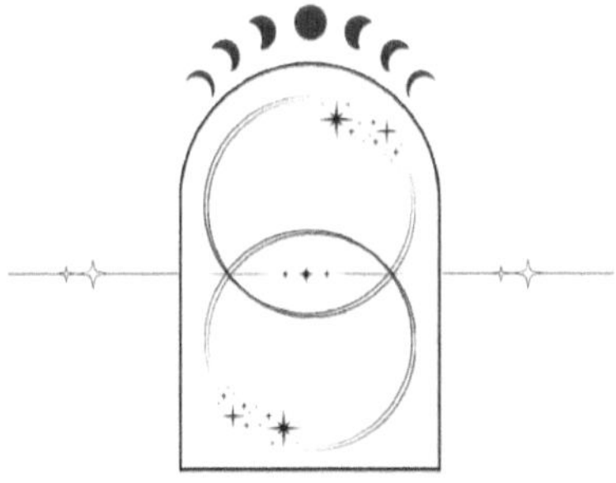

Three

I gave myself that night to rest and recover, but as soon as the sun was peeking over the horizon, I was traveling west through the mountains. It was always so strange to me that the mining town of Magla never expanded into the mountains of the west, even as some of the mines to the north closed due to a lack of minerals.

As a traveler, I did not know of the ancient legend of the fae queen. For centuries, she stole humans from Magla as her pets. All knew to stay away from the west.

The whole town tried to convince me not to go. That no one had gone to the fae realm and returned with their loved one, if they returned at all.

I would be the first, I had to be. There was no way that I would allow anyone to take the man I loved away from me. However, I could not deny the anxiety that built in my chest as

I stared down the portal to the realm of Khaldon. Dark red mist swirled within an archway carved into the obsidian stone of the mountain.

It had taken me nearly a full day to arrive at it. During the entire journey, never once did I feel apprehension. But now that I was here, there was a small voice in my head asking what a small and weak human could do against the fae queen. She had already bested me once.

But I learned from that trick. I soaked cotton balls in beeswax and used that to plug my ears. I would not allow her song to lure me asleep ever again. They did a decent job at blocking out the sound of the world around me, so I prayed to the Mother that it would be enough.

With a deep breath, I forced myself to enter the red mist of the portal. Heat flooded my body, and bright light filled my vision. But just as soon as it came, it was gone. I now stood in a large, dark cave.

Multi-colored crystal clusters poked out from the black stone and gave off a faint glow that illuminated the space enough for me to barely see. Along the wall of the cave, five tunnels led to places unknown. Only one of them had blue crystals around it.

Remembering Rhea's words, I followed the blue crystals. Every time the path deviated, those cerulean gems guided me. Even as my body grew tired, I would not allow myself to rest, not until I arrived at the queen's palace.

It seemed like an eternity until the small tunnel opened up to a massive open cavern, and in the center was a grand palace carved from stone.

About ten feet in front of me, I noticed the ground I walked on dropped off. Stepping toward the ledge, I looked down and to my horror saw nothing but endless darkness. The castle was surrounded by this canyon, with what seemed to be only one way to reach it.

The path was a natural bridge that connected my side of this massive canyon to the center platform. It was narrower than I expected. It was only wide enough for maybe two people to walk side by side and about fifty feet long. Walking over to the bridge, I felt my heart pound harder in my chest. I was so close to the castle, so close to the queen, so close to saving the man I loved. When I took my first step onto the bridge, I made the mistake of looking down. My stomach turned as I stared into the dark nothingness. It nearly paralyzed me with fear. I forced myself to look straight ahead and push forward to the castle.

Once I was halfway across the bridge, a large group of people exited the palace gates. I studied them as they approached. They all wore a uniform of deep red that matched the color of the portal, with the emblem of a wolf's head embroidered on the front, and carried halberds. Guards. Squeezing my hands tight, I tried to stop them from shaking as I held in a whimpering breath. I could not allow myself to crumble now.

The horde stopped at the end of the bridge, and only one stepped forward.

"Who are you?" His voice boomed through the cavern, so loud that even my beeswax and cotton did not muffle the sound.

"My name is Ophelia. I have come to reclaim what is mine!" I shouted back with all the courage I could muster.

Laughter filled the space and echoed off the wall. The guard in front took off his matte black helmet and pushed his dark hair from his face.

"What does a human think she can lay claim to in Khaldon?" he called back to me, still laughing.

Furrowing my brow, I stared him down and stepped forward. How dare they mock me. They would regret underestimating me.

"I am here to get my fiancé and return home. Now take me to him!"

Again, he laughed, and the rage within me boiled under my skin. He did not respond as he slowly marched down the bridge toward me. I could not allow fear to take control. As much as I wanted to turn and run, I didn't. When Evander was safe, I would allow myself to feel every emotion I was currently stuffing down.

One thing my parents made sure I knew how to do was to protect myself. Being a traveling merchant, you meet all sorts. About once a year, we were attacked by bandits, and it was always we who walked away from those encounters. If it came down to it, I could hold my own against this man.

When he was only about five feet away, his silver eyes glimmered as he smirked down at me.

"If the queen has him, he won't return with you, deary." He extended his hand out to me. "But if you are looking for a replacement, I would be happy to offer my services. I would never turn down fucking human pussy. I would love to hear your cries."

A light chuckle escaped my lips. "Oh, is that so?" I teased as I stepped forward and took his hand in mine. "I would not mind a little excitement."

His eyes lit up like a predator about to catch its prey. "I will make sure you never forget this moment."

"Oh, I'm sure neither of us will." Before he could respond, I pushed him off the ledge.

At the last moment, he gripped the ledge of the natural bridge. "You bitch!" he snarled. "Men, get her!"

I shot my gaze to the rest of the guards, and not a single one of them stepped forward.

"Cowards," I whispered as I looked back down at the dangling guard. "Too afraid to fight a little human girl? Seems to be a sign of poor training. Or maybe they know well enough not to piss off a woman."

Reminding myself of the monster I needed to become to save my lover, I did what I had to. I twisted my foot into his fingertips, applying as much pressure as I could. He let out a scream, and when I removed my foot, a smile grew on my face as I watched the fae fall into darkness.

Standing straight, I spun toward the group of guards.

"Anyone else? Or are you going to take me to Evander?" I asked in a low growl.

A smaller fae male stepped forward with nervousness in his eyes. "The queen knew of your arrival since you entered her realm. She wanted us to bring you straight to her. Percy acted of his own accord. Please come this way."

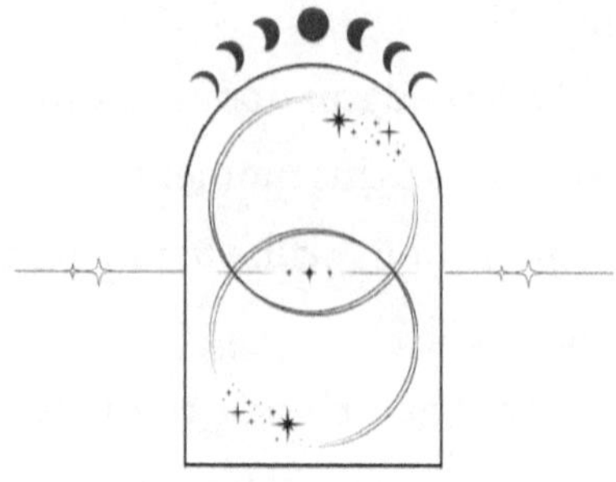

Four

The throne room was the most beautiful place I had ever seen. While the outside of the castle was plain black stone, the inside had those beautiful glowing crystals throughout it. Some were in their natural state, and some were arranged into portraits and landscapes. The throne was made entirely of dark red crystal. I could not deny the beauty of the woman who sat in it. Even if I did hate her.

The guards led me directly in front of the throne, and the queen stood once the guards knelt before her. I did not bend a knee. I would never to such a witch.

"It has been a long time since a human has come into my realm uninvited. Tell me why I should not cast you into the darkness as you did my guard." Venom dripped from her tongue.

"You took someone who belongs to me. I want him back!" I demanded.

"Oh? The lyrist? You came all this way for him?" She rolled her eyes. "Silly little mortal love." With a snap of her fingers, a golden cage appeared before us. Within the cage sat Evander, golden lyre in hand.

"I told you I will not play for you!" He stood, faced the queen, and gripped the bars of his prison.

She waved her hand dismissively. "So you have said. But look,"—she pointed to me—"you have a guest."

Evander slowly turned, and his eyes lit up as they locked onto me. Rushing to the other side of his gilded prison, he reached out to me through the bars. Stepping to the cage, I wrapped my arms tightly around him.

My love was alive and well. That was the best thing I could have hoped for. I breathed in his oak and honey scent, and a calmness washed over me. When Evander was with me, nothing could go wrong. I would do anything with him by my side, and I would get us home.

"Disgusting," the queen spat, then switched to a mocking tone. "Young love. It will wither away and die, just like your pathetic mortal lives."

Pulling away from Evander, I hardened my stare at the queen. A snarl escaped my lips, so deep and feral that it surprised even me.

"Release him. He does not belong here."

Slowly, she prowled over to me. She circled me over and over, looking me up and down in silence. My skin crawled and burned under her gaze. I wanted to cower, to flee, but I would not give her the satisfaction.

"I heard you killed one of my guards. You have some fight in you, girl. Let's see what you're really made of. I will allow you to take him home if and only if you earn him."

"Ophelia, do not play her games. It is not worth it. Please return home. Live a full and healthy life. I am not worth the risk," Evander pleaded with me.

My heart nearly broke from the desperation in his voice. Taking a deep breath, I turned my head toward him. "You are worth everything and more. You are the sun that lightens my world. The clouds and rain that shield me from the heat and give me something to drink. The moon that eases me to sleep. The stars that glimmer in the night sky to give me hope. I will do anything to bring you home."

"Anything?" The queen came to my side and gently lifted my chin so that our gazes met. A serpentine smirk looked down at me. She thought she was a cobra that caught a mouse.

How unfortunate for her.

"Anything," I replied in a steady tone.

She giggled in delight as she released my chin and sauntered back to her throne. She sat upon it and smiled down at me. "The human girl has agreed to play my game. How delightful. It has been some time since we have gotten some entertainment." She leaned back into her throne. "Guards, take the mortal girl to the arena!"

Two guards appeared by my side and grabbed me by my arms. Roughly, they dragged me out of the throne room. Evander pleaded for them to release me and return me to Elswyth. But his begging was left unanswered.

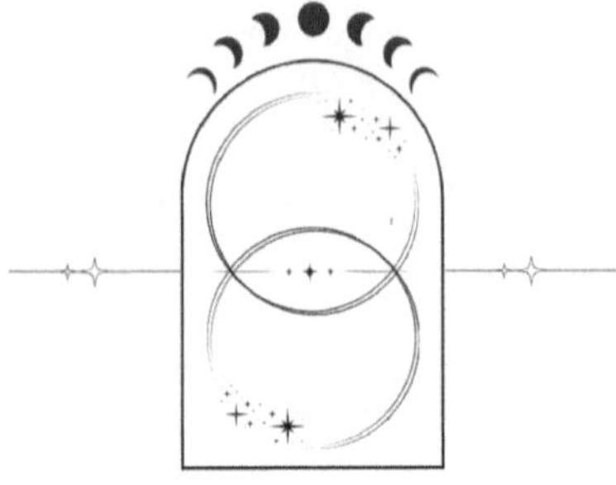

Five

The arena was a large circular pit with two entrances across from each other. The guards pushed me through one of them and then left me in the pit all alone. Statues of warriors in various poses were positioned throughout the arena, and a large variety of weapons were scattered about the dirt floor. Just like the rest of Khaldon, crystal clusters jetted from the walls of the arena in different colors. The staggered seats were filled with fae, and their roars of excitement filled my ears.

"Hush," the queen's voice boomed from her own private viewing section, and the crowd silenced. She sat in a throne-like seat with two guards by her side. Evander's gilded cage sat behind her. Even from so far away, I could not avoid the worry in his eyes. "This mortal believes that she can play my games and win. For her first challenge, it is one that few have won. Though it will be a quick death for the mortal, it's been some time since my pet has come out to play. Lift the gate and release Sarpa!"

The crowd again erupted into cheers. Slowly, the far gate lifted, and a hissing sound escaped the darkness beyond it.

"Have fun trying to return to Elswyth once you are stone," the queen snarled down to me.

My heart sank to my stomach as I realized what she intended for me to fight. In my travels, I heard of snake-like beasts that could turn their prey into stone until it was time to devour them. I could not look it in the eyes, or I too would meet the fate of every person who fought it before. Horror dawned on me—these statues around the arena were others who fought this beast and lost.

My entire body tensed, and a chill ran down my spine. I could not allow this beast to defeat me. Even though I was nearly frozen in fear, I pushed myself to run toward one of the swords left by previous challengers. Gripping it tight in my trembling hands, I hid behind a statue. The hissing grew louder, and so did the pounding of my heart. The fae queen laughed at my cowardice.

The sound of smashing stone rang through the area, and the ground rumbled. As I removed my gaze from the queen, I noticed a reflection of the arena within the crystals. My first sight of the beast had me nearly dropping the sword.

Its serpentine body was massive, nearly as tall as the statues. Its black-as-night scales seemed to absorb all light, and its eyes were glowing red. My gaze fell to my blade, and another shiver ran through me as it had to be smaller than the fangs in the beast's mouth.

"You cannot hide forever, mortal," the queen yelled down to me. "Why don't we give her some encouragement to face her demise!"

The crowd fell into an uproar, demanding me to fight, demanding my death. Something within me clicked, and the flame of courage ignited. I would not allow them to make a mockery out of me.

Gripping the sword tighter, I raised it. Never had I wielded a sword, and it was heavier than I expected. Years of carrying heavy shipments for my parents caused the weight not to be an issue. Quickly, I gave it a few test swings until I was somewhat used to it.

"Look at her! Fighting the air," the queen scoffed.

I glared up at her, but she was no longer in her seat. Her back was now toward me, and her attention was on Evander.

Just like the guard from the bridge, she would regret underestimating me.

Using the reflections to guide my way, I darted from statue to statue, making my way closer to the snake. Watching from a crystal, the serpent's gaze snapped in my direction, and it raced toward me. As it slithered in the sand and grew closer, its putrid scent hit me, causing me to gag.

My grip hardened on the hilt of my blade once again. I waited until the perfect moment to jump from behind the statue, and I forced the blade up into the beast's head. I refused to look up at it, even as it thrashed against me. Using more force, I slashed through the body of the monster. Green blood dripped down the blade and coated my hands. The serpent collapsed onto the ground, and a cloud of dust plumed into the air.

Staggering back, I finally looked at the beast. Its blood pooled under it, and the eyes no longer glowed. Around me, one by one, the statues turned back into the humans and fae they once were.

"Sarpa!" the queen cried out.

Slowly, I turned toward her, raised the sword into the air, and pointed it at her. I hardened my gaze onto her tear-filled face.

"If you don't allow me to return to Elswyth with Evander, that is your fate," I snarled.

Sadness morphed into rage as she snapped her attention toward me. "The games have just begun, mortal. You may have won this battle, but I will win the war."

In a blink, she was directly in front of me, Evander's gilded cage at her side. Stepping forward, she grabbed the sword from my hand and tossed it to the ground.

"What I will never understand is why these women from Elswyth come to claim these mortal men. Men from all realms are the same. Yes, some are better at fucking than others, but deep down in their core, they are all swine. Unloyal dirty swine." A serpentine smirk grew across her face, and she purred, "Oh yes."

Shadows enveloped me. The only thing I could see was endless darkness. Just as soon as it happened, my vision returned to normal. The first thing I noticed was Evander's prison was now open, and he was missing.

"Where is he?" I demanded.

High-pitched squealing filled the air. I faced the noise, and my eyes widened in shock. All the people who were once statues were gone. In their place, pigs ran around the arena. There had to be at least twenty of them.

"Let's see if you can find your pig within the sounder," the queen sneered.

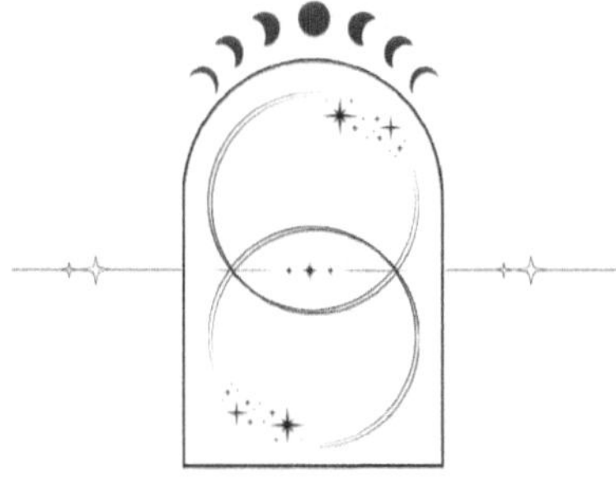

Six

The sounds of the pigs' grunts rang through my ears. They ran wild through the arena, fighting each other and rolling through the dirt. Dust flew into the air as one slammed into the ground in front of me. I coughed hard as I tried to clear it from my lungs.

"If you are so in love," the queen's voice chimed from behind me, "it should be no problem to find him."

I spun to face her, but she was now back up in her box above the arena. She reclined in her seat, the cold expression returned to her face, and her eyes locked on me.

I examined each of the pigs for anything that stuck out. To my disappointment, they looked like normal pigs of all different colors. Most were black or pink, but there were a few that were light tan or brown.

"Evander?" I called, hoping that one of them would respond to me in some way.

But again, to my disappointment, none of them did.

With all of them running around, there was no way that I could really get a good look at a single one of them. I would have to chase down these massive animals and grab hold of them.

That would be a challenge in itself. I set my sights on a smaller one lying in the sun. It seemed lazy enough to be an easy catch. Trying not to startle it, I crept toward it.

It paid me no mind as I stood next to it, as if I weren't even there. Quickly, I grabbed it with both hands. The screams that rang from it were as if I were slaughtering it. Forcefully, it squirmed in my arms and tried to escape. Holding it tight to my chest, I gently pet its head, trying to calm it.

But that did not stop its cries or attempts at escape.

Every other pig in the arena stopped what it was doing and turned toward me. Swallowing hard, I realized I made a huge mistake. All at once, the pigs charged me. Dropping the small pig in my arms, I ran.

"Look at her run!" The queen laughed. "You know, sixteen pigs can eat a two-hundred-pound person in just a few minutes! Soon, this human will no longer be a problem."

I shot her a glare as the crowd roared with laughter and demanded my death.

That moment of distraction proved to be my downfall when a large pig rammed into the back of my legs and pushed me into the dirt. Before I could get up, it bit into my calf, and I let out a scream. I used my other leg to kick it away, and it cried out in pain. Another pig rammed its head into mine, causing my vision to go blurry. Forcing myself to lift my head from the ground, I saw a third pig just a few feet away. But this one was not running toward me. No, it slammed its body into the one who headbutted me. The pig who attacked me slid across the dirt.

The third pig turned toward me, and I gazed into ocean-blue eyes full of sadness. My heart melted as I realized he had saved me. Even in his animal form, he knew to protect me.

"That one." I pointed at the pig that now sat by my side. "He's Evander."

Looking up at the queen, I smiled as rage contorted her features. One by one, the pigs turned back into men. Last, but not least, the pig at my side turned into my beloved Evander.

As soon as he was human again, he wrapped me in his arms and ran his fingers through my hair.

"I've got you, little muse," he whispered so softly. He then turned his gaze up to the queen. "She has played your games and won." More venom dripped from his tongue than I ever heard from him. "Release us!"

"Fine," she said coldly, and the crowd raged. She raised her hand, and the fae of Khaldon silenced. "You won fair and square, mortal. You may have back your male. No human is worth this trouble. Even one who is so skilled with his fingers as yours is. Please stay the night in my realm as my guest, for the journey home is long. In your condition, you may not make it out alive."

Evander gave me a small nod. "You look a wreck, Ophelia. I know you want to go home and trust me, so do I, but I don't think one night could do us any harm," he whispered.

I did not want to admit he was right. My entire body ached, and after that bite to my leg, I wasn't sure how much walking

I could handle. The queen was untrustworthy, at best, but I needed to believe in her words. This one night, we would be her guests. I raised my gaze to meet hers.

"Thank you for your offer," I called up to her. "We would be honored to stay for just one night."

That serpent-like grin returned to her face. "Wonderful." She snapped her fingers, and in a blink, Evander, the queen, and I were now in a large and luxurious bedroom.

Along two of the walls, the crystals that formed here were arranged as if they were windows looking into gorgeous landscapes. There was a glorious stone castle, redwood trees, a beautiful view of the ocean, and islands floating in the sky.

"This is the only room I had free. Ignore the horrible decor. The realm's magic has a funny way of making me suffer," the queen scoffed.

"They are beautiful," I replied, in awe that she could hate such art.

She rolled her eyes. "Just a reminder of the realms that have abandoned me and my people. But anyway, rest up." She pointed over to a door on the far side of the room. "There is the restroom. Please use it. You are disgustingly dirty, and those are sheets made from Tarakian silk, the rarest fabric in all the realms. The servants will bring you a meal shortly."

"Thank you for allowing us to go home and treating us as guests, Queen Helena," Evander answered.

She smirked in response and turned toward the door. "Good night, mortals. Hopefully, in the morning, you will play that lyre for me before your departure."

Before either of us could say another word, she vanished.

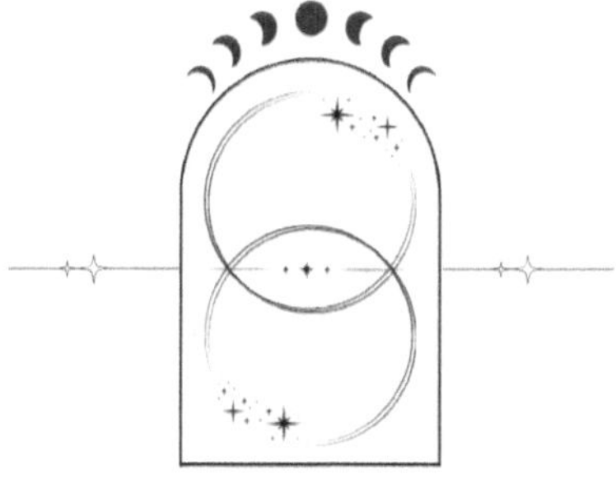

Seven

It wasn't much longer until there was a soft knock on the door, and a servant wheeled in a cart of food. Never had I seen such overindulgence. A full roasted goose, large racks of lamb, a dozen varieties of vegetables, multiple bottles of wine of different varieties, a three-tier cake, seven kinds of ice cream, and an entire serving tray full of cookies and pastries. Each of them had a strong aroma, food never smelled like this back home. The overwhelming scent caused my stomach to growl and my mouth to water. For the first time, I craved food more than air.

Just as the servant appeared, she was gone, leaving the cart behind.

Evander walked over and examined the contents. Grabbing a bottle of white wine, he poured two glasses to the brim. The liquid was like nothing I had ever seen, there was a shimmer to it that shifted from gold to pink. He handed one to me and offered a large grin.

"To the love of my life, for not giving up on me when it seemed all was lost." He took a sip and let out a hum. "This is the most delicious wine I have ever had. You are going to love it!"

The honied effervescence washed over my tongue. The sweet taste left me craving more, and before I realized it, the glass was empty. Evander was already pouring himself a second glass. I didn't even notice him finishing the first.

"Wow." A soft giggle escaped my throat. "That is amazing." Wrapping my arms around Evander's neck, I got onto my tip-toes and gave him a gentle kiss on his lips. "But nothing is more amazing than you."

He pulled me close and smiled down at me. "No, little muse. No one is more amazing than you. You are so brave and strong."

A blush crossed my face. "I would have gone to hell to get you back."

"As I would for you." He pulled away and took my glass from my hand. "Want some more? I'm about to dive into this food. What do you want? I will make you a plate."

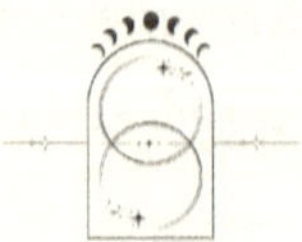

The next thing I knew, we had downed three bottles and eaten halfway through the cart. With my head on his chest, Evander and I lay in the most comfortable bed I had ever been in. I would truly hate to leave it when we returned to Elswyth.

Everything felt perfect, just as it was meant to be. I was in the arms of the man I loved most, surrounded by luxury. What more could I want?

Well, I could think of *one* other thing.

Sitting up, I smirked down at my betrothed. The world wobbled as I found my balance. "You owe me, by the way."

He mirrored my playful expression and sat up on his elbows. "For saving my life? Of course. Whatever you desire, my muse, I will make sure you have it."

"Oh no," I giggled. "You owe me for that damn blowjob I gave you back home."

In one swift movement that had my head spinning, Evander pinned me on my back. Slowly, he dragged his tongue across his top lip.

"Oh, my little muse"—a deep chuckle escaped his throat—"I am going to devour you."

In one quick movement, he pulled off my pants and threw them to the ground, leaving me bare before him. Throwing my legs over his shoulders, he drove right in and feasted upon my most delicate parts. His tongue forcefully lapped against my clit. As I arched my back, a moan escaped my lips.

"That's it, little muse. Sing that song I so love to hear," he purred. As soon as the final word left his lips, his tongue was dancing against my tender flesh once again.

I teetered on the edge of pure euphoria. Running my fingers through Evander's hair, I held his head in place. Those ocean-blue eyes looked up at me, and the hint of mischief in them had me spiraling.

My eyes widened as his fingers prodded my entrance. Slowly, they teased my slit. Just the tip of two fingers slid in, and the breath I was holding escaped my throat.

"Evander, please," I whimpered.

His tongue flicked across my clit before he responded. "Please, what?"

"Don't tease me!" I demanded.

He chuckled, slowly curling his fingertips while they were still inside of me. "You mean like this?"

"Please! I need more!"

He fully removed his fingers from me and crawled up the bed till our faces were inches apart. The air around us electrified, and it took everything I had to stop myself from slamming my lips onto his.

"And more you shall have. I will give you everything, my muse. All that I am and ever will be is yours. I will pluck every star from the sky just to give you a taste of what you deserve."

He crashed forward, and our lips collided. Evander took my hands and pinned them above my head. The passion of the kiss was beyond anything I had ever experienced back home. He was pure love and flame.

When he finally pulled away, I craved more. It was an ache deep within my soul that only his affection could heal. Just as quickly as he removed my pants, he removed his own, spread my legs, and lined himself up at my slick entrance.

Before I could beg him for it, he pushed himself in as deep as he could go.

In perfect rhythm, he drove into me over and over. The bliss of it had me undone. Even after finding my pleasure, he did not slow down. No, he continued to pound against the deepest part of me until I exploded from the pleasure over and over again.

It wasn't until I was thoroughly sated and fulfilled that Evander found his own pleasure. His essence filled me fully, warming my core.

When he pulled out, I felt as if a part of me had been taken. Lying by my side, he pulled me in close and kissed my forehead gently.

"Ophelia, what did I do to deserve you?" he whispered.

I smiled softly. He thought he'd won some grand prize, but in reality, it was me who had won. I loved Evander more than I could put into words. Instead of responding, I gently kissed his lips.

"Mother," he breathed, "you are perfect."

He kissed my forehead and got out of bed. Walking over to the bathroom doors, he opened them. He turned back toward me and gave me a wide grin.

"There is the biggest tub I have ever seen in this room. Allow me to run you a bath and treat you like the queen you are?"

"That sounds wonderful."

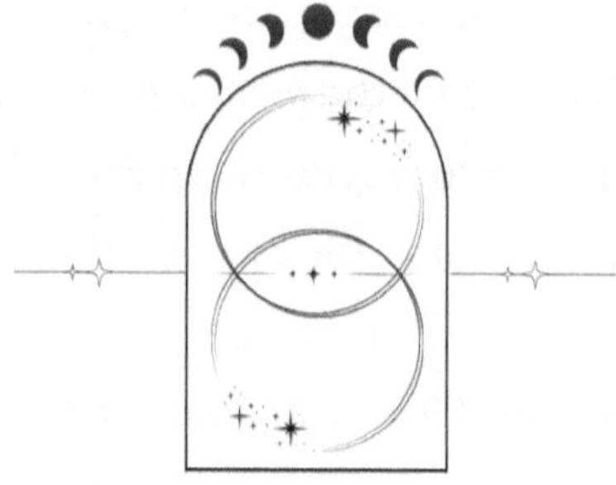

Eight

The sound of lapping waves roused me awake. Sitting up in bed, I stretched my arms above my head and gave a loud yawn. The curtains had already been pulled open to allow the morning sun to lighten the room. Waking up to the view of the glittering aquamarine ocean and white sand beach would never get old. A soft knock on the door had me turning my attention toward it as it opened.

"Good morning, sleepyhead," my husband said with a smile on his face. He walked over and sat on the side of the bed, offering me a mug of coffee.

As I sipped on the warm, sweet liquid, a deep calm washed over me. I watched glimmering gold swirl in my cup.

He gently lifted my chin so that our gazes met. I was surprised when I was met with eyes of emerald green and not ocean blue.

I must still be so tired, why would I think my husband had blue eyes?

"Deary, is everything alright?" He raised his eyebrow and tilted his head.

"Yes, my love. I am just tired is all," I said as I took another sip of coffee.

"Rest all you like. All your worries no longer matter. For it is just you and I in this paradise. Maybe today we can take a trip inland to the waterfall?"

We were the only inhabitants on this small island, my husband and I called home, other than the local wildlife. I loved walking the white sand beaches looking for shells, traveling to the waterfall for an afternoon swim, and foraging the island for the native fruits.

As these memories played back in my mind, something about them was off, as if a piece of them were missing. An instinct deep within me told me something about them wasn't right.

"I know of another way to help you relax," my husband purred, taking the coffee from my hand to set it on the nightstand.

My gaze rose to meet his once again. Instead of honey-blond hair, my husband's was black as night. He leaned in for a kiss, but I quickly pulled away.

"Ah, playing hard to get, I see," he growled. "Don't be like that, deary."

His voice was deep and rough. Nothing like the sweet tone of the one I truly loved.

"Who are you?" I growled back at him in response.

"Your husband," he answered in an annoyed tone and tried to grab my wrist.

I jumped from the bed and pushed him away. "You are no husband of mine! Where is my Evander?"

As his name left my lips, the scene around me faded. I now stood in the center of the arena. Helena sat on the edge of her seat, gripping the armrests so tight her knuckles were pure white. Her face was as red as blood as she snarled at me.

My Evander was standing at her side, and as soon as our eyes met, his face lit up.

"I told you she would never stray! Ophelia's love is eternal and true!" he shouted at the queen.

She snapped her fingers, and in a blink, she and Evander were before me. Just as quickly, he wrapped me up in a tight hug.

"You have passed the test," she sneered. "For I provided you a paradise, and you refused it." The rage melted off her face, and cool indifference replaced it. "You may think you have won, mortal, but I have one last test for you. Leave this place, and never look back. Evander will be behind you every step of the way. You will not hear him, you will not sense him, but I promise you he will be there, and no harm will come to him. If you turn back to look for him, he will be mine forever, and you will never find this place ever again."

I stepped toward her, staring her right in the eyes. "Goodbye, Helena. We will leave. We will return to Elswyth, and you will stay here alone and miserable."

A twisted smirk grew on her face. "We shall see about that, mortal."

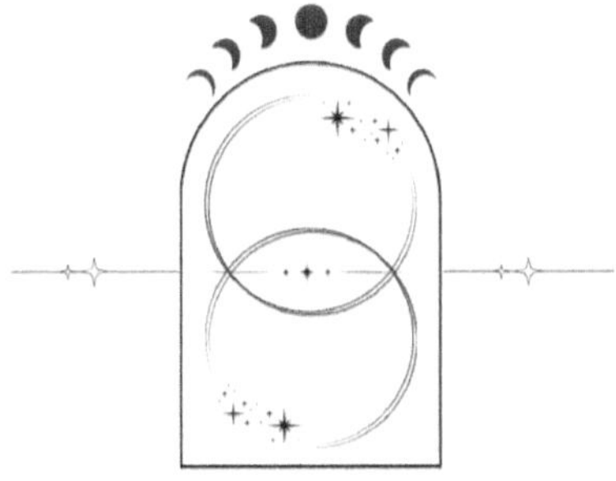

Nine

In silence, we exited the palace. I had to trust he was behind me. To be honest, after everything the queen pulled, I did not trust her. But I had to try. I had to get us home.

As I walked across the land bridge, I looked down into the endless darkness. I could not help but wonder if the man I threw over was still falling, or if he lay dead at the bottom.

Just as I stepped away from the land bridge and was back on solid ground, Evander's scream had me stopping in my tracks.

Tears welled in my eyes as I forced myself not to turn around. She promised he would be safe, this had to be one of her tricks.

"Ophelia! Help, I'm slipping!" His pleas nearly tore my heart in two.

I kept walking. Never once did I stop as my mind continued to play tricks on me. Monsters tore my love to pieces, the cavern behind me collapsed, and Evander told me he wished I would have never come to save him.

All lies. The more I ignored them, the worse and the louder they got.

The only thing keeping my mind steady was following the blue crystals back to the portal to Elswyth. Each one I passed gave me hope that it would all be over soon. When the archway full of red mist appeared, I released the breath I was holding. Part of me believed it was too good to be true. Working myself to a full sprint, I rushed toward the portal. I could not wait to be home. I did not stop even as my mind tried to play one final trick on me.

"Silly mortal," the queen purred. "The boy is mine. You really thought you could have him? When you return home, I will close this portal for three hundred years! Your children's children won't even be able to recover his bones." Her cackle echoed off the cold stone.

Bright red flashed in my vision, and when it was gone, I stood in Elswyth once again. Falling to my knees, I unleashed a sob that could have shaken the earth.

"Little muse," Evander said softly. He lifted my chin, causing me to look him in the eyes. Behind him, the sun rose to greet the world, casting him in a halo of light that made him look like a god. "You did it. We are home." He wrapped me in a tight hug.

Embracing him back, I sobbed harder. The Queen of Khaldon kept her word and allowed me to bring home the man I loved most in this world.

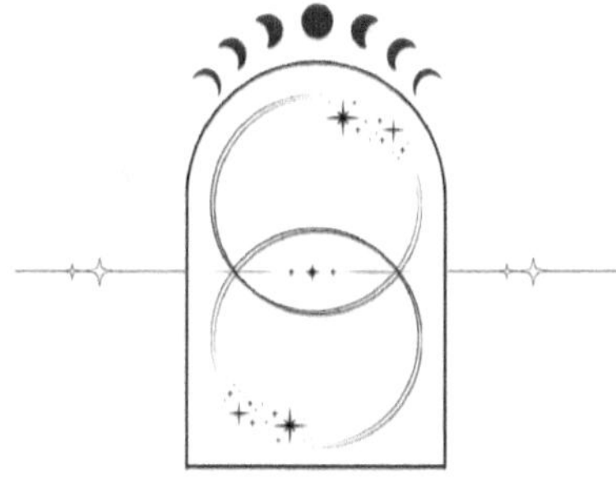

Epilogue

A month has passed since returning to Elswyth. Every day, I fear I will wake up and this too is just an illusion. I hate that Helena has seeded fear into my life, and I'm not sure if it will ever go away.

Even on what is supposed to be the happiest day of my life, I worry it will all fade and I will be back in the arena, or that she will come and take Evander away from me once again.

Even as my mother zips up my wedding gown and hands me my bouquet, that fear envelopes my brain. A knock on the door pulls me from my own thoughts.

"Is everyone decent?" my father calls from behind the door.

"Come on in!" my mother chimed. "Our beautiful daughter is the most gorgeous bride I have ever seen."

My father enters the room, and as soon as his gaze lands on me, his eyes fill with tears. Quickly, he wipes them away.

"My dear, Ophelia. Your mother is right. You are gorgeous. I hope that boy of yours realizes how lucky he is. Are you all ready to go see him? He's waiting at the altar."

Wrapping my father in a tight embrace, I thank him for the compliments. We link our arms and exit the room with my mom following close behind.

"Let me go ahead. I will tell them that you are ready." She rushes past and enters the sanctuary.

My father holds me tighter. "You are shaking like a leaf! Are you alright?"

I look up at him and offer a smile. We never told my parents what happened to us. I do not think they would believe the story. I know I would not if I hadn't lived it.

"Just wedding day nerves," I giggle.

He plants a gentle kiss on my forehead. "You know, the day your mother and I wed was the scariest day of my life. She was two hours late, and I almost gave up hope that she would marry me. But when our eyes locked, all those worries melted away. Evander is a good man, and I know you two will have the best life together."

Tears threatened my eyes. Tilting my head back, I wiped them away. I did not want them falling and ruining my make-up.

The sound of the organ filled the church to announce my walk down the aisle. Taking a deep breath, I tried to calm myself. Part of me was still so scared that he would not be there, that this was an illusion, or that Helena would come mid-ceremony to take him from me once again.

Forcing those thoughts from my head, I tried to relax. I won every trial she threw my way. Evander and I were safe. Today was the day I waited my whole life for. I should be filled with joy. Why was I letting a nasty witch ruin the most important day of my life?

Looking up at my father, I offered another smile. "I'm ready."

"Lead the way, pumpkin."

We walked to the large double doors of the sanctuary. As soon as we stepped into the room, all eyes turned and locked on me. At the end of the aisle, Evander waited for me at the altar. The sun illuminated the large stained glass window depicting The Mother and cast the room in a rainbow of colors.

Our gazes never broke as I approached him. There was more joy on his face than I had ever seen, even as he wiped the tears from his eyes.

My father and I parted ways at the end of the aisle, and he sat next to my mother. Evander took me by the hand and helped me step onto the dais.

"You look so beautiful," he whispered.

I could not stop focusing on him. His perfect honey-blond hair, blue eyes I wanted to dive into, and the sweet scent of oak and honey that I craved.

I was so focused on him that the sound of the priestess completing the ceremony was just a buzz in my ears. I could not believe this was real. This was my true paradise.

"You may kiss your bride." The words of the priestess pulled me from my thoughts.

Evander wrapped me in his arms and wasted no time planting his lips on mine, but too soon he pulled away. He looked down at me with so much adoration. My heart pounded in my chest.

"I can't believe this is my happily ever after. I love you, Ophelia."

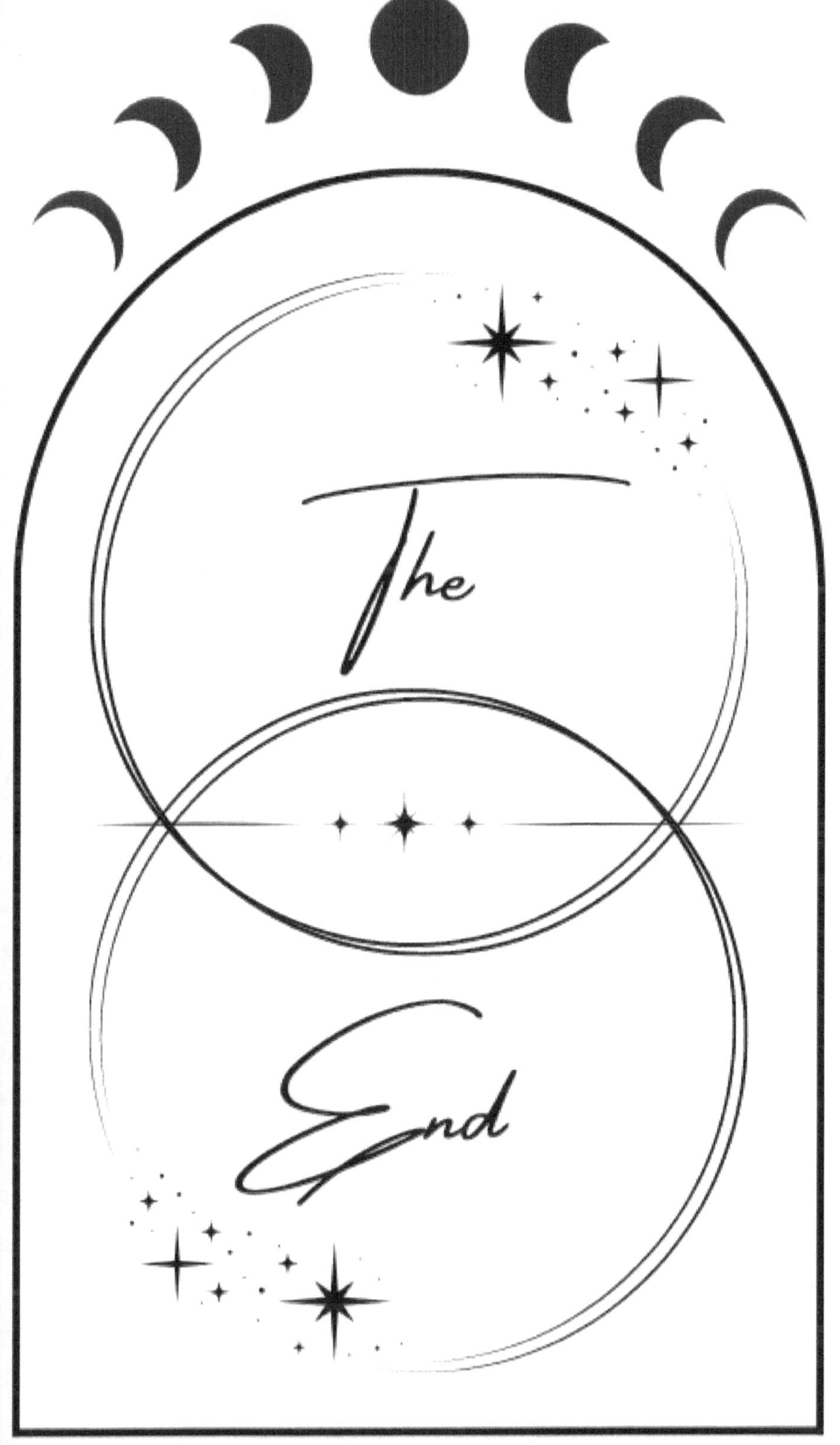
The
End

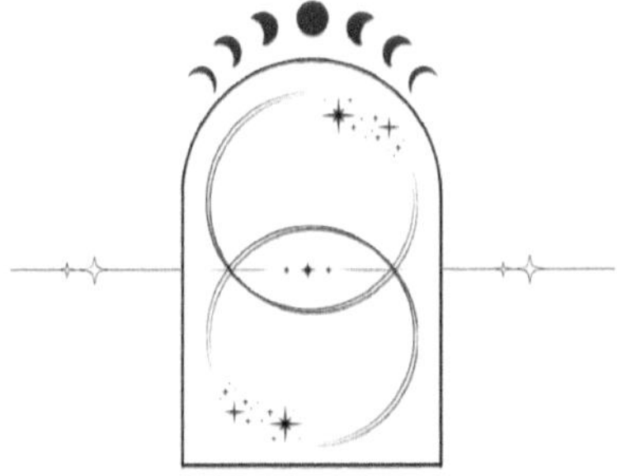

Also by Willow Asteria

The Blood Singer Trilogy
https://amzn.to/3KO4erc

The Realms of Elswyth
https://amzn.to/3xsvM2r

Learn More Here!